A GLITCH IN
THE PROTOCOLS

A GLITCH IN THE PROTOCOLS

TERMINATE THE OTHER WORLD!

BOOK 2

Icalos

Podium

Cover design by Husa

ISBN: 978-1-0394-5489-7

Published in 2024 by Podium Publishing
www.podiumaudio.com

Podium

A GLITCH IN
THE PROTOCOLS

The Magister's Plight

Magister Exploratore per Turannia Tiberius heaved a sigh. He was sitting at his desk, resting his elbows on top of it with his hands crossed in front of his face. The room was lit by a simple candle—Turannia's Exploratores couldn't even afford a cheap Light artifact—as the sun had set a while ago.

Recent events were deeply troubling to the magister. He was even resisting the urge to drink, for first he needed to take stock of the situation.

A corrupted dungeon had appeared right under the Legion keep of Castra Turannia, at a moment when all the comitatenses had been taken to Utrad. Had it not been immediately destroyed by a third party, Castra Turannia would have fallen in days, maybe hours, and the province would have been all but lost. Castra Turannia was the province's most populous city, and the only major supply base and communications hub for the Legion on the island. The Empire would have neither reason nor ability to maintain a presence in Turannia without it.

That disaster had been averted, but there were far-reaching implications that caused Tiberius's face to turn pale.

NSLICE-00P, the unexpected and previously unknown hero who had destroyed the dungeon, claimed that it had been *created* by a man named Cassius, a known black market dealer from the slums. Tiberius had investigated and, indeed, found signs that Cassius had had a benefactor.

A Cult of Mana.

There were countless individuals who were fascinated with the Realms of Mana, planes of existence that were located directly in the Source itself, with access to infinite amounts of mana and complete freedom from the laws of reality. More than one individual sought to acquire endless life or unlimited power by tapping into these Realms, and there were some who even worshipped the beings who ruled them. For the most part, these individuals were harmless.

The boundary between Aelea and the Source, including the Realms of Mana, was not so easily overcome, and those who succeeded normally perished in the attempt.

But Tiberius knew the truth. That there was at least one such cult who represented more than desperate mages or bored teenagers. That there was one cult with real power and influence, and whose attempts to tear the boundaries of the Material Plane were more than idle boasts.

They were the reason Ateia's father had taken his daughter to the farthest corner of the Empire. They were the reason for the mass arrests and covert purges in the neighboring Utrad Province over the past few years. They were the reason Tiberius had been asked to move to this sun-forsaken island.

And now . . . they were here.

The question was why. Had they uncovered Ateia's father's trail, despite all efforts to hide it? Had they learned the truth about his daughter?

Or had it been a coincidence? Did they have other plans for Turannia of all places?

Tiberius didn't know, but this crisis made it clear that the cult's reach extended much farther than he feared. And worse . . . they had the ability to create corrupted dungeons.

That alone could create a disaster on a scale that the Aesdes themselves would notice.

And, of course, the timing could not be worse. Magister Militum per Utrad Caelinus had stripped Turannia of all its comitatenses legions and most of its Exploratores. Dux Canus had only the limitanei left to defend the province, who were little more than militia farmers at this stage. Tiberius himself was down to a single-digit number of subordinates with which to scout the *entire province*. Tiberius had no ability to investigate the cult, and Dux Canus had no forces ready to take them on even if they were exposed.

But . . . if the cult had the ability to create corrupted dungeons at will . . . then Magister Caelinus might actually *need* those forces to protect Utrad, one of the core provinces of the Empire and the linchpin of the North's defense. Backwater Turannia would have to fend for itself.

And, of course, now was the moment that Ateia had forced her way into the Exploratores, and so was stepping out from her remote and anonymous village.

If the cult knew of her . . .

Or if they discovered who she was . . .

Tiberius's stomach churned. His flask was halfway to his mouth before he caught himself.

He sighed as he stared down at the letter he was supposed to be writing, which currently had little more than a greeting.

The truth was, he was at the end of his resources and his wits. He simply wasn't capable of handling the situation anymore. He needed help. And he knew people who could help. He had a . . . friend, or maybe more, if she forgave him for leaving her in Utrad.

But . . . he hated to ask her. She had already given so much to this fight—and lost just as much. It would be cruel of him to pull her back into it now, after all this time.

But he might not have a choice.

Tiberius sighed one more time and looked away from the letter. Before he fell back on his final option, he had one more variable to consider.

The girl known as NSLICE-00P.

The heavily armored girl who had come from nowhere and destroyed a corrupted dungeon *alone*. Even the Hero of Elteno would need the support of an elite team and a dungeon-assault legion to pull off the feat. Even in legends and myths, the only people who could do so solo were ancient dragons, the sages of the Celestial Elves, and the Aesdes themselves.

This girl's status claimed she was human . . . and a mere *level thirty-three* one at that . . . but would the Empire's artifacts truly reveal the status of such a being? Or did she have some sort of power beyond her status that Tiberius wasn't seeing?

Just who—or what—was this girl?

Tiberius shook his head. He had no more ability to investigate NSLICE-00P than he did the cult, so these questions got him nowhere. And he had at least one piece of information to work with.

She was, apparently, a hero.

Hero, the feat granted by the Aesdes to the individuals who had gone above and beyond to defend the world. They had access to Holy mana, the mana of the Aesdes and of the world itself. They had access to special and powerful skills no one else could use. And most of all . . . they were acknowledged by the Aesdes as someone worthy of such powers.

And NSLICE-00P had put a stop to the cult's plans for Castra Turannia all on her own.

So, Tiberius didn't know a thing about her, and none of the information he had made any sense. But he knew that she was an enemy of the cult, at least in this instance, and that the Aesdes acknowledged her as a protector of the world.

Which meant . . . perhaps she could be an ally. And the Aesdes knew Tiberius could use more of those.

Tiberius nodded to himself and put away the letter. The first thing he would do was talk to this NSLICE-00P. He needed to take her measure, to determine who she was, what she was like, and why she was here. Because if he had a hero capable of soloing corrupted dungeons at a mere level thirty-three on his side . . . then maybe he wouldn't need to trouble his friend after all.

With his future course of action determined, Tiberius leaned back and popped open his flask.

No matter what happened, he had a feeling he had a lot of work ahead of him.

1

A Hero's Reward

"Heroes . . . are so annoying."
—A faceless minion, after a superhero destroyed his place
of employment.

NSLICE-00P walked out of the keep, heading back toward the inn. After terminating the dungeon, the local authority designated "Magister Exploratore per Turannia Tiberius" had requested verification of her status. Apparently, the appearance of a dungeon within a population center was of serious concern for the Empire's authorities, and so they wanted to verify she had the Dungeon Conqueror feat. NSLICE-00P thought to question him on the legality of her own core, but said information was classified, and so she couldn't reveal it to him, especially since friendlies Excellion Formantus Rattingtale the Third and Lilussees strongly advised her against it.

She would adhere to local laws as best she could, but that did not pertain to the potential destruction of her core, after all. And the Geo-Oscillator Engine was sensitive *technology* that was not to fall into unaffiliated hands.

But from contextual clues, she determined Imperial status checks only covered the Personal Status section of the foreign system, and so would not reveal any classified technical data or any data related to her Dungeon Management. As such, the Personal Status did not fall under any classification protocols, so NSLICE-00P saw no reason not to cooperate.

But it turned out the Empire had found something concerning in her status after all.

There had been a bit of commotion among Legion personnel after the status check this time. They seemed particularly sensitive to the latest feat, the one named "Hero." As far as NSLICE-00P was concerned, the term *hero* or *superhero* had been a colloquial designation for beings with Non-Standard capabilities judged as nonhostile by society at one point. The wider populace had since ceased to use it after the collapse of said society, but it was still utilized among the Resistance on occasion. Judging by the reactions of the Legion personnel, NSLICE-00P predicted that this society might have similar connotations for the term.

Well, that was incidental to NSLICE-00P. She had paused her Non-Standard reaction protocols, pending review by a commander familiar with local conditions and demographics, and so had no required response to the designation. Even if it was applied to herself.

Assuming it didn't interfere with her primary directive, that is.

The soldiers running around in a panic and keeping her in the Legion Headquarters . . . just might be interfering.

Fortunately, Magister Tiberius had taken charge of the situation and declared her status classified, which NSLICE-00P approved of. He asked her to stop by at a later date when they had settled down on their end, but otherwise she was free to go, as they had confirmation of the dungeon's termination. And so, NSLICE-00P made her way back to the inn, actually staying in her rented room for once.

After all, tonight she had a lot of decisions to make, and so preferred a secure environment.

"Status Update: This unit is conducting an independent upgrade routine. All friendlies may initiate upgrade routines as well."

The monsters in her hangar all jumped at that. 01R trembled.

"Wise-powerful-gracious boss-queen, you are . . . leaving the decision to us? On how to spend the sacred boons you have given us?"

"Affirmative. Observation: No command or maintenance personnel exists to manage upgrades, so independent upgrades are necessary until contact with a commander is established. This unit can attempt to provide combat-footage analysis if friendly units deem personal processing capabilities as insufficient for efficient decision-making."

01R trembled and bowed his head.

"Wise-powerful-gracious boss-queen, this lowly servant once again swears he will live up to your trust!"

It, of course, had not crossed NSLICE-00P's mind that she could manage her subordinates' upgrades as well. She considered it a compromise to even conduct her *own* upgrades without input from command or maintenance personnel, so the idea of her managing other units' upgrades never occurred to her, and would not have been considered if it had. She still considered herself as an enforcer for a currently unspecified commander, and nothing more. Her command over the subordinate units was purely tactical, and a temporary assignment at that.

And, of course, her two former dungeon-master companions did not feel the need to change her mind on this subject. Even Lilussees preferred to keep control of her own status, or something. And the Great-High King of all the land would not surrender authority to anyone . . . provided said anyone did not represent an immediate threat to his life, that is.

So, with the necessary authorizations for independent upgrades given, NSLICE-00P activated her own upgrade routine and opened her status for review.

NSLICE-00P's
Dungeon Management

Overview	
Name	The Walking Dungeon
Level	66
XP	37/100
Available Perk Points	51
Mana	261/261 (290/290)
Exterior	Human/Automata Hybrid (LOCKED)

Dungeon Affinities	
Type	Strength
Cyborg	Primary
Fire	Minor
Holy	Minor
Rodent	Minimum
Earth	Minimum
Arachnid	Minimum

Slime	Minimum
Light	Minimum
Nature	Minimum

Implants		
Type	Mana Upkeep	Description
Bionic Prosthetics +3	0	Overwrites STR and SPD, Values: 130 STR, 65 SPD
Armor Plating +2	0	Overwrites DEF and RES, Values: 120 DEF, 60 RES
Bonded AI	0	Enables direct contact with the System. Overwrites DEX, Value: 1000 DEX
Techno-Organic Interface	0	Enables conscious control over organic and emotional functions. Resists mind-influencing effects.
Advanced Sensors +2	0	Vastly expands scope and effectiveness of senses.
Internal Weapon Bays	0	Enables use of dungeon traps as weapons.
Repulsors +1	0	Enables flight and tactical boosts.
Energy Channels +2	0	Enables user to channel internal energy into external attacks.
Dungeon Field Generator +1	5	Surrounding area counts as dungeon territory. Enables mana absorption within area of effect.
Monster Hangar (Small)	1	Provides living space for 5 small monsters. Unlocks subordinate summoning.
Item Foundry	1	Unlocks Item Creation.
Mana Capacitor +2 (x5)	0	Boosts maximum mana by 30 each.

Inventory	
Name	Description
??? dagger	A dagger, likely enchanted given the amount of mana held within. Further information could not be determined.
Ursanus pelt	The pelt of an ursanus alpha. Tough, well-insulated, and full of mana.
Ursanus bones	The bones of an ursanus alpha. Extremely durable, and full of mana.
Idrint	Quantity: 2,300. Basic solidified mana, now a standard medium of exchange.

Subordinates				
Name	Species	Level	Mana Upkeep	
Rattingtale	Monster Rat	10 * Evolution Available	1	Check Status
Lilussees	Monster Spider	11 * Evolution Available	1	Check Status
(TEMPORARY) Ateia Niraemia	Human	9	--	(Status locked)
(TEMPORARY) Taog Sutharlan	Human/ Wulver	8	--	(Status locked)
01R	Monster Rat	9	0.2	Check Status
02R	Monster Rat	5	0.2	Check Status
03R	Monster Rat	8	0.2	Check Status
04R	Monster Rat	7	0.2	Check Status
05R	Monster Rat	6	0.2	Check Status
01S	Spiderling	7	0.33	Check Status

02S	Spiderling	7		0.33	Check Status
03S	Spiderling	7		0.33	Check Status

Traps			
Name	Number Active / Deployed	Mana Upkeep	Description
Assault Rifle +3	2/2	2	Rapid-fire projectile weapon with high penetration.
Autopistol	2/2	2	Rapid-fire projectile weapon with medium penetration.
Anti-Armor Missile Launcher +2	2/2	2	Homing explosive designed to penetrate armor. Very high penetration.
Anti-Personnel Missile Launcher +2	6/6	6	Homing explosive designed for area damage. Medium penetration.
Stun Ray	1/1	1	Nonlethal electric weapon. Can inflict stun and paralysis statuses.
Wrist Blade +2	2/2	0	Wrist-mounted blades that can be deployed at high speed.
Flamethrower	2/2	2	Deals fire damage and applies burn status in a large cone.
The Equalizer +1	1/1	0	Huh? What the heck is this? Some kind of weird metal that doesn't even exist here? Um . . . well . . . best I can tell it's some sort of antimagic field generator? Eh . . . well, it's yours, not mine, so you don't need me to tell you, right? Like, you already upgraded this thing yourself, so you're good, right?

Dungeon Skills		
Name	Level	Description
Analyze	N/A	Check the status of a target. More detail for targets within the dungeon. Details depend on level difference.
Contract	N/A	Bind a consenting target to the dungeon, per terms agreed upon by both parties.
Transfer	N/A	Move yourself, a subordinate, or a consenting target within your dungeon.

Dungeon Perks	
Name	Description
Human-Dungeon Hybrid	Enables Implants tab. Enables unique Dungeon Combat skill. Enables direct manipulation of dungeon mana. +100 HP Rooms tab locked. Exterior locked.

Dungeon Feats		
Name	Description	Effect
Dungeon Victor	To the victor go the spoils. Unlocked by destroying or subordinating another dungeon.	+1 Perk Point Unlocks Dungeon Warfare category perks.
Dungeon Overlord	A master of masters. Unlocked by subordinating another dungeon master.	+2 Perk Points Unlocks Subordinate Core category perks.

Raid Boss	Fine, I'll do it myself. Unlocked by destroying or subordinating another dungeon with no assistance.	+2 Perk Points +1 level in HP Regen skill +1 level in MP Regen skill +50 HP Unlocks Raid Boss category perks.
System Upgrade	Unlocked by manually performing a system upgrade. Which is not supposed to be possible. Ugh, this is going to get complicated, isn't it?	Um, I don't know. Just have +20 Dungeon Perk Points or something. Whatever. You're figuring this out yourself anyway, so close enough.
Purifier Dungeon	Dungeons are supposed to protect the world; you took that duty more literally. Unlocked by destroying a corrupted dungeon core.	+20 Perk Points Unlocks Purifier category perks.

NSLICE-00P's Personal Status

Personal Status			
General Information		Physical Attributes	
Name	NSLICE-00P	STR	130* (Overwritten)
Species	Human/Dungeon Core/Automata Hybrid	DEX	1000* (Overwritten)
Level	33	SPD	65* (Overwritten)
XP	90/100	DEF	120* (Overwritten)
Perk Points	97	RES	60* (Overwritten)

HP	210/210	Magical Attributes	
MP	274/274	Mana Density	102
		Mana Control	170

Active Skills		
Name	Level	Description
Infused Mana Beam	15	Focus mana into a channeled energy attack. Infused: May infuse Mana Beam with attributed mana.
Sneak	1	Move quietly to avoid notice. Makes it harder for others to notice the user. Effectiveness highly dependent on environment.
Multicasting	10	Can cast several spells at once. Number of simultaneous spells increases with level.
Anti-Mana Beam	1	My best guess is that this projects a kind of inverse mana that reacts destructively with normal mana, including HP. While it can fully deplete HP, it does not harm matter itself. Requires The Equalizer.
Power Strike	1	Infuse mana into a weapon for heavier damage. Power and range increase with level.
Farcasting	4	Allows the user to manipulate mana and create magic circles at far distances.
Strategic Magic	5	Governs the use of Strategic Magic spells.
Supercharge	9	Fill a spell with additional mana to boost its effects. May cause the spell to misfire. Effect boost depends on the amount and density of mana added. Misfire chance depends on Mana Control and amount of mana added.
Continuous Casting	3	May use additional mana to retain a spell form, allowing the spell to be instantly recast.
Spell Fusion	5	Allows the user to combine compatible spells.

Purifier Flame	1	Imbue a weapon or Flame-attribute attack with purifying Holy-attribute fire, dealing extra damage to corruption, monsters, dungeons, and beings from the Realms of Mana.

Passive Skills		
General		
Name	Level	Description
Dungeon Combat	--	Dungeon traps and skills count as personal weapons and skills.
HP Regen	7	Automatically recover HP pool. Increased regeneration speed for damaged body parts.
MP Regen	7	Automatically recover MP pool.
Presence Detection	4	Detect living entities around the user. Range and scope of detection increases with level.
Trap Detection	4	Detect traps. Range and scope of detection increases with level.
Challenger	--	Damage dealt x1.5 against targets of higher level. Damage received x0.75 against attacks from targets of higher level.
Hero Dungeon	--	Unique Hero Skill for NSLICE-00P. PLEASE don't do anything bad with this! Removes dungeon vulnerability to Holy attribute. Grants Dungeon Affinity: Holy.
Magic		
Name	Level	Description
Spell Penetration	3	Enable spells to bypass a portion of RES. May spend more mana to boost the effect.
Geomancy	2	Elemental spells reduce the target's resistance to that particular element. May spend more mana to boost the effect.

Utility		
Name	Level	Description
Enchanting	1	The art of infusing objects and beings with mana.

Resistances		
Name	Level	Description
Poison Resistance	2	Resist and recovery from poison status. Resist Poison-attributed damage.

Schools of Magic		
Name	Level	Description
Arcane Magic	10 *Spell Choice Available	The school of magic governing the manipulation of unattributed mana. A solid foundation for students of the mystic arts, though somewhat less mana efficient than the more specialized schools.
Earth Magic	7	The school of magic governing the manipulation of Earth-attribute mana. One of the basic elemental magics, strong at defensive spells and spells that deal physical damage.
Fire Magic	8	The school of magic governing the manipulation of Fire-attribute mana. One of the basic elemental magics, strong at offensive spells and spells that inflict the burn status.
Light Magic	12	The school of magic governing the manipulation of Light-attribute mana. One of the basic elemental magics, quick and precise spells that are excellent against Dark-aligned foes.
Nature Magic	3	The school of magic governing the manipulation of Nature-attribute mana. Focuses on growth and living things.

Poison Magic	4	The school of magic governing magical poisons. Excels at spreading poison status and dealing damage over time.
Recovery Magic	3	The school of magic governing healing through magic.
Holy Magic	1	The school of magic governing the manipulation of Holy-attribute mana, the attribute of the Aesdes that protects the world.

Spells		
Arcane		
Name	Level	Description
Dense Magic Missile	18	Form and launch mana into a small projectile. One of the most basic offensive applications of magic.
Mana Barrier	10 *Upgrade Available	Form mana into a barrier to block attacks. One of the most basic defensive applications of magic.
Mana Blast	2	A cone-shaped blast of mana. Deals damage and knockback to the area.
Mana Infusion	5	Infuse mana into a target. The most basic enchantment. Defensive variation unlocked.
Earth		
Name	Level	Description
Rock Throw	6	Use mana to form and then launch a small rock. Mana cost increases dramatically if cast without a nearby source of Earth. Deals physical damage. One of the most basic offensive applications of Earth Magic.
Earth Wall	6	Use mana to temporarily form a wall of Earth. Mana cost increases dramatically if cast without a nearby source of Earth. One of the most basic defensive applications of Earth Magic.

| Pitfall | 4 | Dig a large hole in a target area. May be concealed. Mana cost may increase depending on suitability of terrain. |

Fire

Name	Level	Description
Fire Bolt	1	Use mana to form and then launch a small bolt of fire. Mana cost decreases dramatically if cast with a nearby source of Fire. May inflict burn status. One of the most basic offensive applications of Fire Magic.
Fire Blast	7	A cone-shaped blast of Fire mana. Deals damage and inflicts burn to the area. Mana cost decreases dramatically if cast with a nearby source of Fire. May be continuously channeled.
Fireball	5	A condensed ball of Fire mana that explodes on impact, dealing damage and inflicting burn in an area around the point of impact. A favorite of Fire mages. Mana cost decreases dramatically if cast with a nearby source of Fire.
Fire Infusion	1	Infuse a target with Fire-attribute mana.

Light

Name	Level	Description
Light Bolt	1	Use mana to form and then launch a small bolt of light. Mana cost increases if cast without a nearby source of Light. One of the most basic offensive applications of Light Magic.
Fusion Light Beam	14	Form mana into a beam of light to attack. May pierce through its target. May be continuously channeled. Fusion: Light Beams may combine with themselves or other compatible attacks to boost power.

| Invisibility | 2 | Bend light to render target invisible. Certain actions may break the effect. Being attacked may break the effect. |

Nature

Name	Level	Description
Vine Grasp	4	Grows or manipulates a vine to wrap around a target. Mana cost may increase or decrease significantly depending on surrounding plant life or environmental suitability for plant growth. The most basic plant-manipulation spell.
Barkskin	1	Harden target's skin like bark. Boosts DEF.

Poison

Name	Level	Description
Poison Bolt	6	Use mana to form and then launch a small bolt of poison. Mana cost decreases dramatically if cast with a nearby source of Poison. May inflict poison status. One of the most basic offensive applications of Poison Magic.
Poison Blast	3	A cone-shaped blast of Poison mana. Deals damage and inflicts poison to the area. Mana cost decreases dramatically if cast with a nearby source of Poison. May be continuously channeled.

Recovery

Name	Level	Description
Heal	7	Use mana to heal minor wounds and damage. Effect increases with user's knowledge of the body.
Cure	2	Cures abnormal status conditions. Type and strength of conditions that can be cured increases with level.

Holy		
Name	Level	Description
Holy Bolt	1	Use mana to form and then launch a small bolt of Holy mana. One of the most basic offensive applications of Holy Magic. Extra damage to corrupted beings, monsters, dungeons, and beings from the Realms of Mana.

Strategic Spells			
School	Name	Level	Description
Light	Aurora Barrage	4	Continuously rains Light Beams on the target area. If Fusion Light Beam is available, beams may be combined at will.
Fire	Rain of Fire	2	Bombards a wide area with large Fireballs.

Personal Feats		
Name	Description	Effect
Against the Odds	Do not ask how many there are, but where they are. Unlocked by winning a fight when outnumbered by equal or higher-leveled opponents.	+1 Perk Point
Solo Conquest	I am the dungeon master now. Unlocked by conquering a dungeon alone.	+1 level in HP Regen skill +1 level in MP Regen skill +1 level in Presence Detection skill +1 level in Trap Detection skill

Arcane Prodigy	The career of a supreme sorcerer does not start on the beaten path. Unlocked by learning a high-tier magic skill under level twenty without spending Perk Points.	+3 Perk Points Unlocks more advanced magic perks.
Enchanter	The first step on the path of the magic craftsman. Unlocked by manually accomplishing a Mana Infusion.	+1 level in Enchanting skill
Skill Creator	You don't just master the path. You define it. Unlocked by creating a brand-new skill.	To be honest, this normally happens when you're a MUCH higher level, so I'm a bit worried about passing you this much this early, but, um, okay. +20 Perk Points
Healer	Anyone can deal in death. It takes an expert to deal in life. Unlocked by using mana to heal a wound.	+1 level in Recovery Magic skill
Challenger	Levels and odds are just numbers. Unlocked by defeating an opponent who is the greater of level 10 or twice your level while alone.	+3 Perk Points + Challenger skill
Strategic Mage	A strategic mage is king of the battlefield. Unlocked by affecting a hundred or more equal-size opponents (or equivalent mass of other-size opponents) at the same time with magic.	+1 level in Strategic Magic skill Unlocks Strategic Spells.

| World Defender | You have protected the world itself, at great risk to yourself. | +20 Perk Points
+1 level in Holy Magic skill |
| Hero | You faced terrible odds for the sake of the world and proved victorious. You are truly a champion of the world. Please, please, please keep it that way! | +20 Perk Points
Grants Unique Hero Skill: Hero Dungeon |

Dungeon Conqueror Feats

Name	Description	Effect
Dungeon Conqueror (Rat Cave)	Unlocked by conquering the Rat Cave Dungeon.	+1 Perk Point +1 level in Sneak skill
Dungeon Conqueror (Earth Tunnels)	Unlocked by conquering the Earth Tunnels Dungeon.	+1 Perk Point +1 level in Earth Magic skill
Dungeon Conqueror (Spider Tree)	Unlocked by conquering the Spider Tree Dungeon.	+1 Perk Point +1 level in Poison Resistance skill
Dungeon Conqueror (Slimy Pit)	Unlocked by conquering the Slimy Pit Dungeon.	+1 Perk Point +1 level in Poison Bolt spell
Dungeon Conqueror (Glimmering Grove)	Unlocked by conquering the Glimmering Grove Dungeon.	+1 Perk Point +1 level in Light Magic skill
Dungeon Conqueror (Nature's Wrath)	Unlocked by conquering the Nature's Wrath Dungeon.	+1 Perk Point +1 level in Nature Magic skill
Dungeon Conqueror (Beast Lair)	Unlocked by conquering the Beast Lair Dungeon.	+1 Perk Point +1 level in Power Strike skill

Dungeon Purifier Feats

Dungeon Purifier (Inferno)	A dungeon is dangerous to everyone in the world. A corrupted dungeon is dangerous to the world itself. And you conquered it all the same. Unlocked by purifiying the Corrupted Dungeon (Inferno Realm).	+5 Perk Points +1 level in Purifier Flame skill

Terminating the latest dungeon, and the resulting mana phenomena, had greatly increased several of her skills and supplied a great many new perk points to spend on additional upgrades.

First of all, Arcane Magic had new spell choices, and Mana Barrier had an upgrade available. NSLICE-00P took a look and analyzed the choices.

Available Spell Choices for Arcane Magic:	
Detect Magic	Locate spells and sense mana.
Mana Transfer	Transfer mana to a target.
Spell Shield	Boost target's RES.
Telekinesis	Utilize mana to grasp and move objects.
Drain Mana	Forcibly drain mana from a target.
Antispell	Attempt to forcibly disrupt a magic circle or spell structure. May cancel a spell if successful. Use with caution; a spell may explode or act unpredictably if improperly disrupted.
Mana Blade	Form mana into a blade to attack.
Mana Bind	Form mana into restraints that attempt to bind the target.

Available Upgrades for Mana Barrier:	
Dense Mana Barrier	Increase the mana density of Mana Barrier, improving its durability.

Hardened Mana Barrier	Improve Mana Barrier's performance against piercing effects.
Instant Mana Barrier	Bypass use of magic circle when casting Mana Barrier.
Mobile Mana Barrier	Allows user to move existing Mana Barriers.
Fusion Mana Barrier	Allows Mana Barrier to combine with itself or other compatible spells.

She made her choices fairly quickly.

You have learned the spell Mana Blade!
Mana Barrier has been upgraded to Fusion Mana Barrier!

Arcane Magic had a few options worth considering, including some anti-magic options like Drain Mana or Antispell. But those capabilities could be provided by the Equalizer, so NSLICE-00P looked at the next options. Mana Blade and Mana Bind were both interesting in that they involved forming mana into function-focused shapes, and so could supply useful comparisons for her magic-circle analysis.

It was a close decision, but she ultimately chose Mana Blade. Mana Bind seemed more immediately useful to expand her nonlethal options . . . but she had seen a variation of Mana Blade in Light Magic. If she could acquire a second "Blade" spell and compare the magic circles, she could likely identify parts related to mana shaping and their interaction with elemental attributes. The only corresponding spell to Mana Bind might be Vine Grasp . . . but as that spell dealt with the growth of living plants as opposed to the direct manipulation of energy, she couldn't be certain it functioned in the same manner as Mana Bind would, and so the comparison would likely be more complex.

Finally, for Mana Barrier she went with the Fusion option. She had already determined the efficacy of that modifier through Light Beam; in fact, it may have been her use of fusion abilities that enabled this upgrade to begin with. She had already been utilizing multilayered Mana Barriers for her defense, so the ability to combine them outright would strengthen a primary use case. Likewise, the other options were things she could do herself, whether through the assistance of her AI or through the use of other skills, so Fusion seemed to add the most to her capabilities.

With that decided, it was time to analyze the available perks.

She had a truly impressive bank of perks . . . and an equally impressive list she could spend it on.

And there was a new area of the Perk menu for her to peruse.

Heroic Skills	
Name	Cost
Heroic Strength	20
Heroic Speed	20
Heroic Defense	20
Heroic Endurance	20
Heroic Control	20
Heroic Reserves	20
Heroic Power	20
Heroic Challenger	40
(Continued . . .)	

And so on and so forth. All these options had two things in common: One, they required the Hero feat to purchase. Two, they promised exceptional performance in exchange for heavy expenditure.

You have learned the skill Heroic Challenger!

Skills		
Name	Level	Description
Heroic Challenger	1	A hero never gives up, no matter the odds. Attacks ignore a small percent of target's DEF/RES/Immunities and always deal a minimum amount of damage. Gives a small chance to survive a fatal hit with 1 HP.

It was an exceptionally expensive skill, a whopping forty of her Personal perk points . . . but with good reason. With this skill, NSLICE-00P could be sure her attacks would always be effective, even if she faced an opponent significantly more powerful than herself, or an opponent with specific counters to her abilities.

You have learned the skill Heroic Power!

Skills		
Name	Level	Description
Heroic Power	1	To handle great responsibility, a hero needs great power. Doubles Mana Density for a short time. May damage user if reused too quickly due to strain from excess mana.

Heroic Power would synergize well with Supercharge, massively boosting the raw power of her spells. Likewise, when combined with Heroic Challenger, it should grant her reasonable offensive capabilities no matter what kind of defenses she faced.

And so, suddenly, sixty of the ninety-seven Personal perk points had vanished. Thirty-seven remaining points was no small number by any means. From NSLICE-00P's observations, Personal levels came much slower than Dungeon levels, so she predicted it was best to save some points for additional adjustments based on real-combat data. But there *was* one final perk she considered.

Available Perks → Passive Skills → Magic Skills	
Name	Cost
Mana Shield	12

Passive Skills		
Name	Level	Description
Mana Shield	1	When active, it may convert HP damage received into Mana damage. Mana Density will be used instead of DEF/RES in that case. HP damage will resume if Mana is fully drained.

This perk would allow NSLICE-00P to utilize her mana defensively in place of her HP, which would more than double her effective HP pool and significantly boost her survivability. Even more, she observed that her mana regenerated much more quickly than her HP, boosting her endurance even further. And using mana in this way meant the new Heroic Power skill could be used to effectively double her defense, should said measure be necessary.

She *could* already use mana defensively via spells such as Mana Barrier, but it was hard to pour all of her mana into a single, small spell like that, so using the mana directly was still an improvement. Likewise, just relying on her raw mana instead of Multicasting and Supercharging her Mana Barrier would allow her to focus all her attention on counterattacking. And . . . there was another angle. By taking this perk now, any improvements to her mana were now effectively improvements to her HP. Improvements to her primary offensive resource now also improved her defensive resources.

As such, if she took this perk, she could specialize her future purchases into mana. She could defer upgrades to her armor and HP pools to an as-needed basis. She did not need to weigh additional offensive upgrades against the need to shore up her defenses.

And mana was the source of everything for her. Her spells, both offensive and defensive, new implants, new subordinates, all of this was dependent on mana. Additional mana was never wasted; any excess mana could be used to cast more spells, could be used to Supercharge spells to a greater degree, or could be dedicated to additional dungeon systems. She could always justify expanding her mana pool, even now.

Not to mention . . . it appeared to be a comparative advantage for her as well. She had observed other beings, including her own opponents at times, running low on the resource, resulting in reduced effectiveness. Meanwhile, her mana restored itself almost as quickly as she could spend it, thanks to her core.

As such, she predicted that the benefit of a resource specialization like this would outweigh the redundancy of the perk and the added demand on the mana pool.

You have learned the skill Mana Shield!

With that, she had twenty-five Personal perk points remaining. Barely over a quarter of what she'd started with. At this point, it was more efficient to wait for additional combat data before purchasing any more upgrades via Personal perk points.

It was then that something occurred that she did not expect. A new message from the foreign system appeared on her UI.

Subordinate Rattingtale would like to evolve. Approve?

2

The Great-High King's
Terrible Mistake

"Every dungeon has a primary attribute. A theme upon which everything in the dungeon revolves around. That should not be taken to mean dungeons are monolithic; any dungeon of decent size and age can and will develop secondary attributes, and even possess entire floors free of their primary. Yet, they will always return to their original aspect, and their most powerful defenses will be based around it. As such, make note of the attribute of the dungeon that you face, and prepare in excess to face it. When dungeons are involved, there is no such thing as overpreparation."
— *The Dungeon Diver's Handbook*, Fifth Edition.

Rattingtale shuddered as he watched his disloyal subjects access the sacred records with glee.

This was bad.

The subjects were gaining on him, with all due speed. They had been granted royal titles by the boss-queen, elevated to positions of authority and clout. And though the authority and majesty of the Great-High King of all the land was self-evident, he could not trust these treacherous rat-things to remain loyal. Yes, even now, he saw their treachery developing. The wretched 01R sought to supplant him, that the traitor might manipulate the strange man-thing for his own nefarious ends.

Which would, of course, threaten the Great-High King's plan to manipulate the strange man-thing for *his* own nefarious ends.

So he had to stay ahead. And fortunately, by the boss-queen's foolish gifts of experience, he had a solution for the problem. All he had to do was evolve his form, and he would immediately become superior to the would-be usurper! He could reassert his dominance over his disloyal subordinates and claim a greater share of the experience and boons going forward, securing his place in perpetuity!

Available Evolutions:	
Name:	Description
Ratkin	A rat monster who has begun to gain a more humanoid form. Increases size, strength, durability, and intelligence. Unlocked by default for rat-type monsters.
Large Monster Rat	A basic rat monster . . . but slightly larger! Might not get eaten by the local cat. Increases size, strength, and durability. Unlocked by default for rat-type monsters.
Cyber-Rat	A basic rat monster upgraded with advanced components. Boosts performance all around. Grants access to Implants. Unlocked by contracted dungeon's primary affinity: Cyborg.
Monster Rat+	Defer evolution and gain additional Perk Points instead.

Rattingtale's ears fell against his head.

Those . . . weren't a lot of choices, were they?

The Aesdes could not be deceived, and there was no such thing as a free level. Even if one received levels without effort, the manner in which they did so still ultimately mattered. In fact, he knew this was one reason most dungeon masters didn't bother to grant their subordinates free kills like the boss-queen. Monster-evolution options, like many other things among the royal records, were earned by feats and achievements.

So . . . say a particular monster never actually achieved very much on their own, was gifted practically free kills by a powerful benefactor, and delegated most of the work to their subordinates?

Well . . . then . . .

Rattingtale trembled.

It was only natural! A Great-High King like himself, a dungeon master, a lord of their realm, was not expected to fight in the muck with the lowly servants!

That was simply inefficient! The master of the dungeon could not be risked in open battle; should they fall, the entire realm would come to a halt, left without guidance or purpose! And any boons put into the dungeon master's combat prowess would reduce the power of the dungeon as a whole, concentrating its strength into a single individual who could be overwhelmed, distracted, or bypassed! It was simply poor strategy!

So it was only natural!

Even now that . . . the Great-High King had temporarily been deprived of said realm . . . before he gained said levels . . .

Rattingtale shook his head. It was fine! No one would dare infringe on the privacy of the Great-High King! His achievements and glory were self-evident; the Aesdes themselves must have restricted him to prevent his rise! Yes! This was confirmation that he was a threat to the Aesdes themselves!

So he should . . . continue his rise. By . . . choosing the best option available . . . Out of these options . . .

There must be something here . . .

Well, there was only one option of any note.

Cyber-rat was granted by the boss-queen's primary affinity, and so would make him more like this strange man-thing. Perhaps it would even unlock for him the secrets of her strength and enable him to gain the kind of powers she possessed.

The Great-High King of all the land made his choice.

Evolution Cyber-Rat chosen. Awaiting approval by Dungeon Master.

Rattingtale trembled.

He had just made a terrible mistake.

None of his own subordinates in his former realm had proven effective enough to reach this point, so he hadn't realized something like this would occur. But it absolutely made sense when he thought about it. Stronger monsters meant more mana required to maintain them, so *of course* monsters wouldn't be allowed to just evolve as they pleased.

Which Rattingtale had just attempted to do.

And the boss-queen had just been alerted about it.

He crouched down, as low as he could go, as he awaited his doom. He had signaled his intentions; his deceit was now apparent. So, what would this terrible and cruel man-thing do—

Evolution approved.

Rattingtale froze.

Wait, what?

But he had no time to think as his vision went white, mana surging through his body and setting his veins ablaze.

Evolution to species Cyber-Rat successful!

When the pain and the light finally faded, Rattingtale lay on his back, breathing heavily. He tried to scramble to his feet, but all his limbs felt heavy, as if weighed down. He struggled to lift his head and glance at them . . .

He froze.

His limbs . . . and his entire body . . . were now encased in metallic armor.

He smiled. He had succeeded.

And then he frowned. The metal armor was very heavy. How did the strange man-thing move like this? And why couldn't he see out of his left eye?

Just then, mana poured out from his monster core, spreading through the metal armor. His other eye began to see, but there was a problem. Rather than the world around him, he saw red light . . . and then his eyesight went black again . . . and words started to appear on his vision? But not from the royal records?

A voice sounded in his head, similar to his own, but without any inflection or emotion, and with a metallic echo. It repeated the words that appeared in his view.

Systems booting . . . Systems online.

Running diagnostics . . . All systems normal. Activating techno-organic integration.

As the voice spoke to him, his armor began to hum and glow. Strange contraptions spun to life around the joints of his limbs. The mana and . . . lightning of some sort surged through his head. Rattingtale screamed.

And then it was done.

He lifted a paw to check his head and found no wounds. His eyes widened. He was moving his paws without feeling the weight of the armor any longer.

He looked at them in shock. The armor was now *moving itself,* responding to his commands like his own limbs. No, it was beyond that. The armor was assisting his limbs; he felt as if they were lighter than before. He swung a paw experimentally.

Metallic claws extended from his fingers and cut through the air. It was a powerful swipe, much like that of the vicious cat-thing.

Rattingtale grinned.

Yes, this was what he'd hoped for . . .

Network connection online. Establishing connection . . . Connection established with Master Unit, designation: NSLICE-00P.

Rattingtale blinked as he tried to parse the message, but before he did . . . he felt something. More mana and lightning surged into his head. He felt as if there was another presence there, looking around. A voice sounded directly in his mind.

A voice he recognized.

"*Compatible components detected. Connection established with Friendly Unit, designation: Excellion Formantus Rattingtale the Third. Observation: Friendly Unit Excellion Formantus Rattingtale the Third has installed compatible components during independent upgrades and can now interface directly with this unit. Establishing Loyal Wingman connection.*"

Rattingtale trembled. He willed the presence to leave . . . but his own mind did not comply.

And then . . . the strange man-thing took control of him. He could now see out of her vision directly from his own eyes. He could feel her presence.

And worst, she could do the same.

In fact, his armor began moving without his command as the boss-queen experimented and moved it directly.

"*Diagnostics Results: Loyal Wingman connection established, Friendly Unit integrated. Unit designation updated. Gratitude: This unit was not aware foreign system upgrades could install compatible components. This unit thanks NSLICE Excellion Formantus Rattingtale the Third for his discovery. Checking unit's status for intel on relevant upgrade procedure.*"

Rattingtale didn't respond, trembling in place. He had made a mistake. A terrible, horrible mistake. And now, he knew why this deceitful man-thing had allowed him to evolve.

The boss-queen could now access and control him directly, even beyond the stipulations of the dungeon contract. She could send messages directly to his mind. She could see what he saw. She could hear what he said. She could even check his memories, at least those recorded within these . . . these foul things.

He had enslaved himself to her even more deeply than before. She had outsmarted him once again. He gnashed his teeth. Just how deep did this man-thing's treachery and planning go? Just how long would it take to return to his rightful place?

Meanwhile, all the other rat monsters stared at the cyber-rat writhing on the ground. 01R gnashed his teeth as well.

This treacherous *thing* . . . was the first to evolve? Not only that, he had become like the wise-powerful-gracious boss-queen? That unworthy one had ascended into a being like her?

01R swore in his heart that he would redouble his efforts. That next time, it would be one of the boss-queen's *loyal* servants who grew closer to her.

* * *

NSLICE-00P's robotic eye was spinning, all her processors calculating at maximum speed.

This changed everything.

Not only were Excellion Formantus Rattingtale the Third's components of a sufficiently high technological level to interact with hers, but they were also patterned directly off her, down to the techno-organic interface. The bonded AI wasn't as advanced as hers—the foreign system hadn't fully replicated it, so it contained only the most basic protocols—but that was fine. NSLICE-00P had the ability to connect with autonomous warbots and integrate their AI with her own so that they could benefit from her more advanced and flexible combat protocols. Excellion Formantus Rattingtale the Third was already a connected subordinate of hers in the foreign system, so his systems had responded positively and integrated well. Her AI could provide him with protocols and assistance until his own had developed sufficiently.

But most importantly, she could now interface with him directly, with massive implications for coordination, communication, combat efficiency, and intelligence gathering. She was not a solo unit any longer. She now had an NSLICE network to support her, if only of two units. And now, she knew how to expand it.

"Command: All units should apply 'Cyber' upgrade if or when available."

"Ugh, like, fine."

A few minutes later, Lilussees had joined the network as a second Loyal Wingman for NSLICE-00P. It turned out there was a cyber-spider upgrade available to her as well. Which meant all of NSLICE-00P's subordinates could hypothetically join the network.

NSLICE-00P's robotic eye flickered repeatedly as she updated all her protocols and calculations with this new intel.

And . . . her heart rate increased slightly.

Her mission-success probability had just risen substantially.

Meanwhile, Lilussees came out of her room on armored legs, crawling over to the snack's room. She stuck her head inside the door.

"I, like, hope you're happy about this, snack."

Rattingtale's head spun to face her.

"S-Shut up, wretched spider-thing! I didn't know-predict this would happen!"

Lilussees chittered at him. "You, like, don't know a lot of things, do you?"

Rattingtale gnashed his teeth. "S-Silence! The Great-High King of all the land will not permit-allow such slander, yes-yes!"

Lilussees tilted her head.

"But aren't you, like, a 'Loyal Wingman' or 'NSLICE' now, or something?"

Rattingtale could do nothing but retreat deeper into his room.

"S-Shut up!"

Lilussees turned around at that. "Well, I'm, like, tired from evolving, so I'm going to take a nap or something."

Just then, a message appeared across Lilussees's sight.

Self-Diagnostic Log: Organic components have requested rest cycle. Organic components deemed at full efficiency. Applying stimulating countermeasures to ensure ideal operation.

Her new parts analyzed her body as she spoke and reported back to her. Then a jolt of mana shot through her, energizing her body to full alertness, removing any perception of fatigue or sleepiness.

Lilussees froze. She started to tremble. She slowly turned around.

". . . kill you."

"What did you say-speak? Speak up, wretched spider-thing!"

"I SAID I'LL KILL YOU!"

Rattingtale squealed.

"You've gone mad-insane! Minions, boss-queen, help-assist the Great-High King, yes-yes! The wretched spider-thing is attacking-assaulting me!"

3

"Bear"-ly Starting Out

"As of the time of this report, we've largely ruled out nonhuman animal bases. While their physical performance can be superior in one or several categories, the main goal of including organic components in our NSLICE units is intellectual flexibility. Sacrificing part or all of the organic components' mental faculties is an unacceptable cost, especially when we will still need to use cybernetic prosthetics to match Non-Standard performance in any case."

—Dr. Ottosen, on the viability of various organic bases
for the NSLICE program.

After mediating a sudden altercation between her subordinates, NSLICE-00P calculated for a long time, updating all her protocols and predictions. Now that she had essentially reestablished contact with an NSLICE network, she no longer needed to assume purely independent action in a preindustrial society.

As such, she added growing the NSLICE network to the list of directives. In fact, acquiring bases for new NSLICE units had been one of her most common mission types in the past. The only difference was NSLICE-00P had a method to conduct processing on her own now. She could partially resume one of her old directives, once she modified the protocols for the different conditions and methods.

And the NSLICE network would speed up her search by a significant margin. Upgrades to her personal sensors and intelligence-gathering abilities always ran into diminishing returns, given that she was a single unit who could only be physically present in a single location. Even acquiring subordinates via the foreign system had not been a perfect solution; as she lacked methods to communicate with them remotely, they were restricted to her immediate area.

With a growing NSLICE network, however, that was no longer a limitation.

Her search capabilities would scale ever upward as more units were added to the network, providing not only more eyes but more processing hardware and specialized capabilities. And since she could network and communicate with them remotely, she could also use them to build a communication network, expanding the range she could interact with her subordinates dramatically.

And when she finally did find a commander, she would be able to offer the services of an entire network, instead of a single unit.

Soon, her calculations concluded. Her next order of business would be expanding the NSLICE network, which meant upgrading her subordinates. From Excellion Formantus Rattingtale the Third's logs, the NSLICE upgrade had become available when he hit level ten, so she would endeavor to bring her current subordinates to that level.

However, that would have to wait. Local authorities had requested her presence after sorting out their own confusion, after all, so she would check in with them tomorrow to avoid any legal complications.

But there was something else she could do to expand the network right here, right now.

Subordinates → Summon Subordinates			
[Cyborg - Primary]			
Name	**Summoning Cost**	**Upkeep**	**Description**
Cyber-Bear Cub	**25 mana**	**5 mana**	**A bear cub upgraded with cybernetic implants. Currently more cute than anything, but has terrifying potential.**
Cyber-Rat	**5 mana**	**1 mana**	**A basic rat monster upgraded with cybernetic implants. Its ability to network with other units improves swarm behavior, and implants can offer surprising capabilities. Ultimately still a rat, though. Unlocked by evolving a Cyber-Rat with Cyborg and Rodent affinities.**

| Cyber-Spider | 5 mana | 1 mana | A basic spider monster upgraded with cybernetic implants. Because who doesn't love spiders who are harder to kill with fire? Unlocked by evolving a Cyber-Spider with Cyborg and Arachnid affinities. |

[Fire - Minor]

Name	Summoning Cost	Upkeep	Description
Fire Slime	5 mana	1 mana	The most basic Fire-attribute monster possible. Just animated mana with a Fire attribute. Might be able to start a fire if left on something flammable for long enough.
Fire Elemental (Small)	25 mana	5 mana	A being of living Fire Magic. Its flames and mana are not the greatest, but it can grow by absorbing more of both, and its immunity to basic physical attacks makes it a tricky opponent for the unprepared.

Holy - Minor
Rodent - Minimum
Earth - Minimum
Arachnid - Minimum
Slime - Minimum
Light - Minimum
Nature - Minimum
No Affinity

... Holy monsters? What ... What does that even mean? Where
would they even come from?
UGH. You know what? You're just going to have to wait on these.
Even if I WANTED to figure it out, anything we could do is
probably going to require meetings and approvals and stuff. Just ...
figure out how to evolve your own monsters with it or something if
you want these now.

She had seen the cyber-bear cub before, but had predicted a lower technological level for the monster's implants, something in line with the local society,
like the Item Foundry's offerings. But her other subordinates' evolutions had
demonstrated this was not the case, so it was reasonable to assume the similarly
named cyber-bear cub would also have compatible upgrades.

She also had access to cyber-rats and cyber-spiders directly now, thanks to
her subordinates' evolutions. This demonstrated that even units that did not start
with cybernetic implants might one day upgrade into NSLICE units, and doing
so might unlock their cyber variants for immediate summoning later on. That
had implications for the future, implying it might be worth testing a variety of
subordinates for similar effects.

She also checked her two new affinities. As the Fire affinity was slightly stronger than the others, it seemed a stronger monster was available for summoning,
though unfortunately no new cyborg options were available yet. Perhaps she
could also unlock a cyber-fire elemental in time, though she could not predict
how the cybernetic implants would be applied to what was described as a non-
corporeal, nonorganic being.

Holy affinity . . . did not seem to be available at the moment. It appeared there was something special about that particular affinity. NSLICE-00P filed it away for further investigation.

But all this provided data to consider for the future. She could try summoning basic monsters from other affinities and see if she could upgrade them with cybernetic components. Or . . . perhaps she could try upgrading some of the affinities, to see if stronger affinities would unlock more compatible monster types?

The foreign program's message regarding the Holy affinity implied it would also be possible to apply other affinities to monsters upon their evolutions, which seemed to be how her subordinates had accessed NSLICE upgrades in the first place, so that was another possibility.

In any case, future experimentation would be required to make those decisions. And there was a decision she could make right here, right now.

A magic circle appeared in her Monster Hangar, glowing brightly.

A flash of light filled the place.

NSLICE-00P logged a reduction to her maximum mana as a new mana bond formed.

A weak cry filled the air.

Subordinates				
Name	Species	Level	Mana Upkeep	
--	Cyber-bear Cub	1	5	Check Status

Yes, NSLICE-00P had decided to summon a cyber-bear cub.

More cyber-rats and cyber-spiders were not necessary at this time, especially as she had several rat and spider subordinates to upgrade first. On the other hand, she had not deemed a bear monster as necessary previously. Her subordinates' only role beforehand had been local intelligence gathering, and the rats and spiders were better suited to covert activity. A bear monster would have been inefficient at the intended role at best, incapable at worst.

But a network of NSLICE units had a significantly broader mission set, and NSLICE-00P already had protocols to command integrated units. And the vast majority of said protocols dealt with combat.

So, it was desirable to add more combat-specialized assets to the network. In fact, she would have needed to do so even if she hadn't been able to convert them to NSLICE units. 01R's experiences had demonstrated the weakness of relying solely on stealth, even for the purposes of intelligence gathering. Her subordinates needed more firepower to do their jobs effectively, especially if she wasn't in the immediate vicinity.

And in her experience, monster bears made for highly effective combat assets, as one had nearly terminated her. She predicted using one as the base for an NSLICE unit would produce an extremely efficient outcome.

A small bear cub, about the size of a medium dog, appeared in the hangar. It had metal armor around its torso and arms, though with more gaps than NSLICE-00P's, revealing its furred body underneath. And it had a metal helmet that went down the left side of its face, with a robotic left eye.

The robotic eye slowly lit up as its components came online. NSLICE-00P connected to them and integrated the cub into the network. Then she determined a problem.

The entrance to the Monster Hangar appeared a bit small for the cub . . .

Even as she was calculating, the cub stood up, fell over once, stood back up, then leapt toward the entrance of the Monster Hangar. He appeared on the other side and fell to the floor.

NSLICE-00P's robotic eye flickered repeatedly.

It seemed the Monster Hangar's entrance did not necessarily conform to physics, like many things NSLICE-00P had observed since arriving here. As long as the monster was considered "small," it could fit in and out of the hangar, regardless of its size relative to the door.

Which made a certain amount of sense, given that the hangar implant itself could not possibly fit within NSLICE-00P's torso. That being said, she still rushed to record as much data on the phenomena as she could, her processors heating up as they struggled to calculate how all this was possible.

Meanwhile, the cub cried and rolled about on the floor, reaching for NSLICE-00P's leg. She picked the cub up and held him aloft, looking him over for damage.

"Observation: No damage to friendly NSLICE unit detected."

The cub cried at her.

The bear monster seemed to be younger and less developed than the other monsters, and so could not form coherent language. Yet, the dungeon-monster bond still enabled communication of intent, and their AIs were integrated and communicating directly, so NSLICE-00P could understand his cries to a degree.

"Analysis: Friendly NSLICE unit is requesting increased physical contact. Analyzing . . . No particular cause or benefit could be determined. Analyzing cost . . . No particular cost to request predicted. Request may be fulfilled with no loss to efficiency. Responding to request."

NSLICE-00P brought her arms in, pulling the bear cub against her torso. The cub batted at her, trying to wrap his arms around her body and climb up her torso. He tried to climb on her shoulder, then slipped and fell. NSLICE-00P caught him right as he did.

"Analysis: Friendly NSLICE unit seems to lack coordinated motor control. Readjusting combat-efficacy predictions. Result: Friendly NSLICE unit will require multiple unit upgrade cycles to achieve minimum combat effectiveness."

The cub cried in protest as he nuzzled her.

"Designating Unit: 00B. Response: This unit summoned NSLICE-00B to be a primary combat asset and is thus already aware of NSLICE-00B's combat potential. This unit will conduct upgrade routines until NSLICE-00B's performance meets expectations."

00B paused as NSLICE-00P gave him a name. He then quieted down and settled into her arms.

Well, NSLICE-00P was already going to prioritize the subordinate-upgrade routine. Adding an additional unit was not particularly inefficient.

And this new unit would develop adequate termination capabilities soon enough.

4

A Settlement Requires Your Aid

"Ah, yes. Exploratores. The 'heroes' of the Empire. Because heroes love to laze about getting drunk at the tavern. Heroes love accosting the locals for food, drink, and fun. Heroes love turning down anything even remotely dangerous or important. Heroes love refusing to do anything remotely resembling productive work. I'd rather see every one of my children drafted into the Legion than to give those 'heroes' even a single Idrint."

—Rector Provinciae per Ecriysia Decius Atronius
Fullofaudes, on why he spent the Exploratores bounty
budget on his personal villa.

Magister Tiberius had just arrived in his office when there was a knock at his door.

"Sir? Miss NSLICE-00P is here to see you."

Tiberius nodded. Punctuality was a good start.

"Good, send her in."

The door opened up and in walked the hero who had appeared from nowhere. Tiberius hadn't had the time to conduct a full investigation on her, but the records he could check had turned up blank.

"Status Report: Unit NSLICE-00P reporting for detailed debriefing with local authorities."

"Thank you for coming," Tiberius said with a nod. "Please, have a seat."

"Affirmative."

The girl sat down with a clank, staring at Tiberius with a blank face. Not a single twitch, not a single sign of emotion. Her armored eye, perhaps an artifact of some kind, didn't even blink. Tiberius would admit it wasn't the most comfortable atmosphere, but he had faced worse before.

"First of all, let me officially thank you for handling that dungeon. You have saved all of our lives, and done the Empire a great service."

"Acknowledged."

Still her expression didn't change, and her voice remained completely monotone, with some sort of metallic echo. She did not brag; she did not downplay her efforts. She did not demand rewards.

So, Tiberius knew she definitely wasn't an Exploratore.

"If you don't mind, could you give me a rundown on how you came across the dungeon?"

"Affirmative."

NSLICE-00P then recounted the events in detail, explaining how she had come into contact with Cassius, and how he had eventually attempted to ambush her. She'd subsequently chased him down and found him in the dungeon, and so had conquered it to kill him.

Tiberius felt there were some key details missing, but he knew better than to ask. Skills and methods were precious, and he would not impinge upon his savior's privacy if he could help it.

"So, you were hoping this Cassius could assist you in searching for these persons of interest? Is that why you're in Turannia?"

"Affirmative. Clarification: This unit's arrival in location designated Turannia was unplanned."

Tiberius grunted at that. Very few people came to Turannia by choice.

But more importantly, now he had an angle of approach.

"Could you tell me more about the people you're looking for? I can dig around a bit for you."

"Affirmative. Gratitude: Assistance with this unit's primary directive is appreciated."

Tiberius had heard about her little illusion trick, and so didn't react as NSLICE-00P created a wall of light in front of him, filled with faces and descriptions.

And not a single one of them seemed even remotely familiar to him. He had hoped to gain some hints as to NSLICE-00P's origin and identity, but apparently, it would not be that easy. He had some names to follow up on, at the very least, so he recorded the information on a scroll.

"I'll see what I can turn up. May I ask what your plans are in the meantime?"

"Answer: This unit will conduct live-fire testing and upgrade routines in the surrounding area while waiting for friendly units to return."

Tiberius blinked.

"Live-fire testing? May I ask what that is? If you're planning to set something on fire, I may need more details first."

He nearly cursed as the hero's eye began flashing with light . . . and spinning in place.

"Rephrasing: This unit will test the efficiency of her current arsenal by terminating hostiles."

Tiberius took a deep breath.

"Do you mean to say you'll be hunting something? And could you explain what you mean by hostiles?"

"Affirmative. Elaboration: This unit intends to target entities designated as monsters due to their permanent and unprovoked hostility and lack of affiliations."

Tiberius exhaled his breath. That was one dangerous situation averted.

And then he began to rub his chin.

"I may be able to help with that. If you're looking for monsters to hunt, how would you feel about tackling some Imperial bounties?"

NSLICE-00P responded immediately. "Negative Response: This unit cannot be affiliated with third parties without authorization from appropriate command personnel."

"Command personnel? Are you a member of some sort of organization? Maybe a knight order or an important family?"

"Negative."

Tiberius tilted his head. "Then, who are you reporting to?"

"Response: This unit is searching for suitable command personnel at present due to loss of contact with her previous commander."

Tiberius rubbed his chin again.

"So . . . no one in particular, at the moment?"

"Affirmative."

That was a bit strange. She was insisting she couldn't act without orders, yet had no one to take orders from? Well, stranger things could happen. It sounded like she had been separated from her people and somehow ended up here in Turannia.

Tiberius nodded. If she already had loyalties and people to return to, it would make sense that she wouldn't want to join the Exploratores or anything.

"In that case, how about this? While normally these bounties are reserved for Exploratores, in an emergency I can open one up to anybody who's willing to attempt it. So, if you want to take on any given request, let me know, and I can set it as an emergency mission. That way, you can get paid for taking on some of the local monsters, with no further commitment or association once the mission is complete."

NSLICE-00P's eye flickered once again. If Tiberius was interpreting this correctly, he guessed that indicated she was thinking.

"Query: Does this method violate local protocols?"

"Worried we might be dealing under the table?" Tiberius nodded. "Good question. Under normal circumstances, it would be strange and warrant investigation. But I won't lie. Turannia is *extremely* shorthanded right now, so I'll be more than justified declaring as many emergency missions as I like. The reason we don't is to make sure the local Exploratores have adequate opportunities to earn their pay, but right now, none of them are around to earn any pay, so the point is moot."

"Affirmative Response: Analysis complete. This unit finds the arrangement acceptable. Please provide target details."

Tiberius blinked.

"Wait, you want to start right now?"

"Affirmative."

Tiberius blinked again, then started digging through his desk. "Oh, um, give me a second. Let me see . . . Ah, here's one. A nest of goblins set up near one of the local villages. So far, they've only gone as far as stealing crops and livestock on the outskirts, but it could grow into a problem if we don't deal with it. Shouldn't be a match for you individually, but a whole goblin nest can be more dangerous than the sum of its parts, so be careful."

"Query: Will Magister Tiberius require proof of termination?"

Tiberius tilted his head for a second.

"You mean, how to prove the job is done?"

"Affirmative."

Tiberius nodded. "Left ears will work. Bring us back a bunch, then I'll ask the limitanei to send a patrol to verify."

"Acknowledged. Query: Are there any further mission parameters this unit should be aware of?"

"You mean, anything else you should know?" Tiberius shook his head. "No, this mission should be fairly straightforward for someone of your capabilities."

Once Tiberius had given NSLICE-00P directions to the village in question, she immediately turned and left. He sighed and shook his head.

He'd left the conversation with more questions than answers. Who was NSLICE-00P, and who were the people she was trying to find? Who was she answering to, and what was their goal? How was she so powerful at such a low level? And how did such a person get separated from her people in the first place?

Not to mention her lack of expression in either voice or body language, her strange accent and method of speaking, her use of terms Tiberius hadn't heard before, and that clearly enchanted armor that was unlike anything he had ever seen. He still felt like he couldn't make heads or tails of her.

But . . . she was cooperative. Extremely cooperative, even. She'd answered all of his questions without a fuss, and even agreed to help deal with some of the issues in the area. All that was more than Tiberius could ask for, and more than he could even get out of his own Exploratores, who preferred to spend their days causing trouble at the tavern.

Still, a Magister Exploratore could not let a powerful mystery go unanswered, so he had best get to work on what little he had on the girl. And since she was searching for these people herself, he would also be doing her a favor at the same time.

So, he looked over the notes once more and started from the top of the list. Time to see if he could find anything on this "Bob" fellow.

Suedia Arruntia was the village chief of a small hamlet on the outskirts of Castra Turannia. Officially, she was the ranking officer of the limitanei "outpost," but most settlements in Turannia were technically Legion bases, so the title meant little. She had long since retired from active duty, and the soldiers of this hamlet were all on reserve, which in Turannia meant they were civilians whom the Empire wasn't obligated to assist during emergencies.

But that suited Suedia and her charges just fine. No one came to Turannia who wanted extensive Imperial assistance in any part of their lives. And besides, the area around Castra Turannia was one of the safest parts of the province, as the comitatenses regularly swept the surroundings. So, Suedia's village was far from hard frontier living. They basically got to live as they pleased, largely free from outside meddling.

However, that did mean that when something happened, the village was on its own to handle it. Suedia still ran some annual drills, but that was little more than reminding the farmers which end of their spears to point toward the enemy. They could drive off a small monster or two, but Suedia knew better than to send them against anything remotely dangerous.

Such as their little goblin issue.

Placus had complained that someone had been nabbing his poultry, and a nighttime patrol had revealed the culprit.

Now, a single goblin was little stronger than a human child and could be handled by any healthy adult who kept their wits about them. But Suedia had seen enough action to learn a thing or two. She knew that what separated goblins from other weak monsters like slimes was their intelligence. Goblins could use tools . . . and weapons. They could form primitive societies . . . and war parties. They could use traps and ambushes. And as monsters, they had a natural instinct for violence that humans needed to have drilled into them.

As such, Suedia had not pursued. She knew that where there were goblins, there was a goblin nest. So she did the only thing a village like theirs could: gathered up some funds from grumbling farmers and put out a request for the Exploratores. The problem was, the Exploratores were not obligated to help at all, least of all in a timely manner, and so their request had gone unaddressed.

Suedia had expected that at first. But at this point, time was ticking, and the goblins were growing increasingly bolder, and the villagers increasingly upset. They might attempt to handle things on their own before long. And Suedia knew that would end badly, even if they managed to succeed.

So she heaved a sigh of relief as a young boy ran up to her, shouting about some armored knight on approach. She moved toward the village gate to greet the Exploratore.

And then she stood still, blinking.

When the boy had told her an armored knight had arrived, she assumed he had been exaggerating. There were few, if any, knights in Turannia, and no knight orders based themselves in the province, so there were no trainees who might handle an issue as small as this. As such, she figured the village boy had simply been impressed by armor he had never seen before but which wouldn't be out of the norm for an Exploratore.

That . . . was not what Suedia saw now. A girl approached, young by the look of her face and her height. And she was clad in solid metal plate that covered from the tip of her neck to the bottom of her toes, revealing little save for half of her face. The metal gleamed in the sunlight, indicating an individual who was not concerned with being noticed.

Suedia frowned. This situation made her uneasy. What was a knight like this doing all the way out here? She couldn't think of any good reason.

But she stepped forward regardless.

"Welcome, traveler. What can I do for you?"

"Greeting: This unit is designated NSLICE-00P. It is nice to meet you. This unit is intending to report to local authority Decanus Suedia Arruntia."

Suedia raised an eyebrow.

"Um . . . well, I'm Suedia. Why are you asking?"

"Mission Status updated. Status Report: Unit NSLICE-00P reporting for goblin termination mission. Please direct this unit to the target location."

Now, that had Suedia blinking. This knight with a weird name . . . was here for their goblin issue? So she was an Exploratore? But . . . Suedia had met an Exploratore or two in her day, and not a single one of them could afford armor like that. Even if they could, all Exploratores had muddy, dirty armor by their second mission. When she had asked, one had replied that anything that hid them just a little more was a good thing.

So a girl like this, with well-polished and highly noticeable plate armor? She definitely wasn't any Exploratore Suedia had ever heard of.

And then . . . Suedia figured it out. And she held back her sigh.

What she had here was probably some rich and powerful kid who wanted to play at being an Exploratore. She had likely been sent here on an "easy" mission within range of Castra Turannia just to give her something to do.

And that meant that not only had Suedia not received experienced help but she had been saddled with babysitting duty as well. If anything happened to the young lass, somebody big and powerful was likely to get cross. And as the ranking Legion officer who had put in the request, the blame would fall on Suedia, as certain as the sunrise.

"Hang on a second. Let's check with the patrol who spotted them."

"Affirmative."

Suedia nodded and turned to the boy. "Call up Arruns and Potitus. Tell them I need them for a patrol."

She had no choice now. She couldn't reasonably deny the girl now that she had arrived to help, and attempting to call her out would only make matters worse. So Suedia would take her on a little tour of the forest with two of the most experienced villagers, wait for her to inevitably get tired and bored, then send her on her way, hopefully without encountering anything. And then she would write a strongly worded letter to the Magister Exploratore, explaining that goblin nests were *not* an issue for troublesome rookies.

Suedia sighed as she trudged through the forest. The girl was showing her inexperience, making no attempts at stealth whatsoever. She was snapping branches with every step, leaving a trail even an oblivious monster could follow with ease, and making enough noise that half the forest must be aware of them by now. Arruns and Potitus weren't helping, with their constant glances and not-so-hushed whispers.

Gossip could wait for the tavern, when the noble girl was out of earshot! Suedia, on the other hand, could not wait for the tavern. And neither could the girl, apparently, as she suddenly stopped walking.

Suedia took a deep breath and turned to try and mediate . . . but the girl wasn't looking at any of the villagers.

"Status Update: This unit has detected life signs and mana signatures in this direction. Proceeding to investigate."

Suedia held back a curse. That was the direction of the goblin nest. She had been trying to subtly circle around the area, but apparently, this girl had sharper senses than expected. And now that she had found something, Suedia couldn't go and tell her not to investigate. It was technically why she was here, after all. So she glanced at the other two, making eye contact. The gossiping duo fell silent and nodded, and the three prepared to grab the girl and run at the first sign of trouble.

Suedia's heart rate spiked as they slowly made their way forward, her eyes glancing every which way. She herself was no Exploratore and was not confident she could spot a goblin ambush before it spotted them, so she kept her eyes moving and her hand on her spear. She was getting too old for this sort of thing.

But, again, the girl stopped before any of them encountered anything.

"Status Update: Potential target located."

The girl turned to face Suedia . . . and then the eye hidden behind the girl's half helmet began to glow. Suedia couldn't quite hold back her curse this time. A moment later, an illusion displaying the forest ahead appeared. A small green figure walked between the trees.

"Requesting Confirmation: Spotted creature matches description of hostile designated as 'goblin.' Please confirm target identification."

Suedia blinked, but her former training kicked in, and she answered the question before thinking about it. "Yes, um, that's a goblin."

The girl's eye turned red, and her helmet extended to cover her whole head.

"Status Update: Target identified. Engaging termination protocols."

The girl lifted her arm . . . and then her hand folded in on itself, a metal tube extending from inside her arm to replace it.

The three farmers' curses at the sight were drowned out by the sound of thunder as light flashed from the end of the tube.

The girl did not pause to explain. She marched in the direction of the goblin's nest, thunder ringing out from her transformed arm on occasion. Suedia and the others were left rubbing their ears. Arruns turned to her.

"By the Aesdes, what in Aelea and the Source is that?!"

Suedia shook her head. "I haven't the foggiest idea." She frowned. "But she's marching right into goblin territory alone, so we best get a move on."

Potitus frowned. "Chief, are you sure that's a good idea?"

Suedia sighed. "Not at all, but whatever she is, I'm not explaining to some official who's never worked a day in their life that I let her die. So let's go."

The trio frowned and followed after the sound of thunder—then gasped at the scene they found. Goblin corpses lay on the ground, bleeding. There were small craters and splintered trees nearby. The sounds grew only louder and more intense.

Suedia's face grew grim.

"Impressive, but these are just the scouts. She should be close to the nest now."

The other two nodded, and the three ran ahead. They passed through a small clearing . . . and then froze, their jaws dropping.

There was the girl, both her arms now transformed, light and thunder ringing out from them faster than Suedia could count. Small doors had opened on her armor, and trails of smoke and fire flew out of them, streaming ahead. Magic circles formed in the air around the girl, Light Beam spells adding to the barrage.

And ahead of her was the goblin nest. Or rather, what remained of it.

Smoke billowed out of the cave. Primitive fur and wooden huts had been set ablaze, and everywhere they looked, goblins fell to the ground or were blown into the sky. The survivors charged at the girl with clubs and spears and slings . . . but not a single one made it within throwing distance.

Within minutes, the entire nest was gone.

"Status Report: All identified hostiles terminated, no further life signs detected. Disengaging termination protocols."

The girl turned around, her helmet receding back to a half helmet once again. Her glowing red eye turned a dimmer yellow. Suedia couldn't help but take a step back as the girl walked up to her, a cold sweat dripping down her back.

"Requesting Confirmation: Are there any additional target locations?"

The girl had to repeat her question several times before Suedia finally managed to respond.

You have slain 32 hostiles!
Gained 96 Personal XP, 96 Dungeon XP!
Level up! You are now at Personal Level 34 and Dungeon Level 67!

NSLICE-00P was now standing back in Magister Tiberius's office. She had hoped to upgrade some of her subordinates, especially the new combat asset 00B, but unfortunately, the local villagers had decided to accompany her. As such, she had simply terminated the target as efficiently as possible.

"Mission Report: All detected hostiles terminated. Local residents claimed all known hostiles were present and terminated."

Magister Tiberius blinked. "Already? That was quite fast . . . I'm sorry to doubt you, Miss NSLICE-00P, but I will need proof, given your speed."

"Affirmative."

Panels opened up all around NSLICE-00P. She retrieved goblin ears and deposited them on the magister's desk. Magister Tiberius grimaced at the sight.

"Ah . . . that would do it, then. I'll give you half the bounty now, and the other half after a patrol confirms."

"Acknowledged."

Magister Tiberius nodded, and then sighed.

"Now, regarding the people you're searching for; I haven't had a chance to conduct a full investigation just yet, but I can tell you I've never heard of a guy named Bob, and haven't found any records of any either. Just confirming, do you know if any of these individuals are Imperial, and if so, what province they might be from?"

"Response: None of the persons of interest are affiliated with entity Empire to this unit's knowledge."

Magister Tiberius nodded.

"I thought as much. To tell you the truth, we don't get much information on foreigners all the way out here. I'll do my best to search, but you may need to move closer to the Imperial Heartland. What are your plans?"

"Statement: This unit is currently waiting for the return of contracted assistance before moving from the current area of operations."

Magister Tiberius blinked once.

"Oh, you made arrangements already? In that case, would you be willing to continue helping with more requests in the meantime?"

"Affirmative."

Magister Tiberius smiled. "Excellent. I just received word of a Wulver raiding party—"

"Objection: Entity Wulver appears to be a fully intelligent species. This unit cannot become involved in third-party conflicts."

NSLICE-00P would, of course, defend herself if she were attacked, as what had occurred with the Wulver incursion earlier. However, in any situation where she was not already under attack, she calculated she needed to avoid confrontation. After all, an intelligent species like the Wulver might possess key intel for determining her location and finding the persons of interest. And if one of the persons of interest happened to be in the area, they might have affiliations or even alliances of their own. NSLICE-00P might end up in an unintentional friendly fire scenario in that case, and might cause a person of interest to turn hostile toward her. And that would mean failing her primary directive.

It was a risk she could not take until she had more intel. So even a faction that had acted hostile toward her in the past, such as the Wulver, should not be engaged if a ceasefire had been established. And she most definitely should not confront a group on behalf of a third party such as the Empire.

Magister Tiberius paused, rubbing his chin.

"So, no Enlightened? Only monsters?"

"Affirmative."

Magister Tiberius frowned, but then tilted his head for a bit before nodding.

"I see, that's reasonable, actually. I suppose we would need an official mercenary contract for that sort of thing. Well, there's plenty to go around even excluding the Wulver."

"Acknowledged."

Well, NSLICE-00P was still waiting for Ateia and Taog, in any case. On one hand, Magister Tiberius was apparently in charge of the Exploratores that Ateia and Taog were hoping to join, so he seemed to be a better contact. On the other, he had just stated that the resources in this province were limited, and as a local authority, Magister Tiberius appeared bound to his area of responsibility, so NSLICE-00P still calculated it as efficient to wait for Ateia and Taog's return, as the pair could escort her beyond the province.

Until then, conducting some upgrade routines that also improved relations with the local authority seemed an efficient use of her time.

5

Abandoned

"The more you have to defend, the less able you are to defend it. And the harder you try, the quicker you shall be defeated. That is why I have trained myself to let go of everything that I fear to lose."
—Celestial Elf Sage Ningainë, before declaring an eternal feud over his favorite teacup.

Tiberius heaved a sigh as he sifted through the reports on his desk. He was, in fact, glad he had *something* on his desk now, but this was getting a bit excessive for a Magister Exploratore who had no one reporting to him.

Well, no one officially, that is.

He looked up at the person sitting across from him and passed her several of the reports. She picked them up and went through them far too quickly to have actually read them, one of her eyes flickering as she did.

Which was still incredibly unsettling, if Tiberius was honest.

But, well, that was what NSLICE-00P always did, and she had not overlooked a single detail yet—that Tiberius was aware of, at least—no matter how impossibly fast she flipped through the papers. Or how unsettled it made anyone watching feel.

"Statement: Mission details recorded. Query: Are there any additional details or parameters this unit should be aware of?"

Tiberius nodded.

"This one was stated to be wolves, but given the location and the reported damage, it could very well be a party of Wulver, so you'll want to conduct your own scouting first. I'll consider it completed if you can confirm that and report back to me. If it *is* a monster, you'll likely catch it near some farms, so be careful to avoid any collateral damage."

He continued. "This next report is highly indicative of a cave troll. Tough, strong, but slow and dim. Particularly weak to Light, and either Fire or Poison can help with its regeneration."

Then he took a pause. "This one I'm not sure about. I'd lean toward it being nothing, but the legate's men are insisting, and I've been wrong about that before, so be careful when you scout the area. If you can't find anything after a reasonable search, go ahead and report back."

"Statement: Additional mission details and parameters logged and recorded. Query: Are there any updates on this unit's primary directive?"

Tiberius shook his head.

"I'm sorry. I couldn't find anything in the records I have here. I've put word out, but no one has reported anything legitimate so far, and since we're short-handed in this province, I'm not optimistic."

"Acknowledged. Response: Then this unit will request appropriate monetary compensation."

Tiberius nodded and pulled out a sack of Idrint.

"As usual, the preparation allowance here, the rest when you return."

"Affirmative."

With that, NSLICE-00P took the money, rose from her seat, and marched out of the room. Tiberius exhaled his breath.

He had become the main point of contact for the girl by his own design. Upon seeing NSLICE-00P's status, Tiberius had *immediately* declared it as classified and restricted all intel on the girl, to which Legate Curio had immediately agreed. He would probably have to report it at some point, but not until he was absolutely certain about what he was going to say and who he was going to say it to.

And as of right now, he had no idea what he was going to say.

After all, her status was *frightening*.

Arcane Prodigy. Strategic Mage. Solo Conquest. *Skill Creator. World Defender. Hero.* And an unbelievable list of Dungeon Conqueror feats . . . as well as the Dungeon Purifier feat indicating she had, in fact, taken down a corrupted dungeon. All by level thirty-two, likely earlier, since she should have leveled a few times taking down the dungeon underneath the keep.

A single one of these feats would make her highly sought-after by every magister, mage academy, knight order, shrine to the Aesdes, and person of means and influence in the Empire. Particularly the fact that she was an *Aesdes-appointed hero.* But all of them together?

It would not be strange if the Emperor himself took an interest in the girl.

Tiberius had no idea how any of this was even possible, given her level, but he had no desire to cause a stir, and neither did the person in question or Legate Curio, so they had decided to keep her status confidential for as long as they could. Not least of all because the girl herself appeared to have no interest in the Empire. An actual Aesdes-appointed hero who had just saved all of their lives deserved her privacy.

And even better, the girl had proven remarkably cooperative and helpful. Tiberius had originally offered to provide her targets to try and take her measure and determine who exactly he was dealing with. She had agreed in exchange for assistance with her search, monetary compensation . . . and reading lessons, funnily enough. She picked it up so quickly he originally thought she was messing with them, but he had since learned that she was more of a no-nonsense type.

And then NSLICE-00P had cleared all the first targets he'd given her *in a day*, and had come back requesting more.

NSLICE-00P was a truly efficient fixer. She could complete practically any mission in under a day and followed every command to the letter. It didn't seem to matter what types, levels, or numbers of monsters threatened the area, she handled them all without flinching. How he wished even a fraction of his Exploratores could be like this girl.

Powerful, yes, but more importantly, professional, precise, obedient, and thoughtful. She noted every detail, both from the reports and from his mouth, and adhered to them to the best of her abilities. She never wasted time: she came in, acquired targets, and then handled them in quick order. She never complained about a target; the tough ones didn't scare her, and the "easy" ones weren't beneath her. She could be trusted to handle herself and conduct her own scouting. She requested Tiberius's advice on the targets and then *actually listened* to said advice. She immediately returned and reported the mission results without any sort of embellishment or falsehood. She could remember practically every detail of her missions and didn't hesitate to report said details if Tiberius asked.

Her strange method of speaking took some getting used to, but once he started getting a handle on it, he could appreciate her precision. It helped, too, that she wasn't one to mince words, but also wasn't shy about requesting explanations when she didn't understand something.

And she even understood her own limits. She was willing to handle monsters, but strictly refused any missions involving actual people, whether criminal bands or Wulver raiders. And she was right to do so, for an unaligned third party like her should not be involved in official Legion duties, as inconvenient as that might be to Legate Opiter.

That was a level of consideration Tiberius could only expect from his most experienced veterans.

Tiberius freely admitted that she was a blessing from the Aesdes in the current circumstances. Even if she would only hunt monsters around Castra Turannia, just having *someone* to send out was a massive weight off his shoulders. Much less a *hero* who'd accomplished more work than all of the Exploratores in the Castra Turannia area combined.

For the first time since the comitatenses had left, maybe even the first time in years, Tiberius felt like he was regaining some control over the situation. If she kept this up, he might even have enough leeway to address some of the more pressing questions . . . like about the corrupted dungeon she had terminated, and the people responsible for that disaster.

The only downside was that Legate Curio abused this situation to pass practically every issue involving meaningful combat over to him, as the legate had done for most of his career.

Tiberius heaved a sigh. He would have to talk to Dux Dio about the state of the Castra Turannia limitanei one of these days. But he understood why Legate Curio was eager for the girl's help.

He smiled. Well, there was a reason she was growing on the townsfolk and the Guard.

It was just then that Tiberius's assistant burst through the door.

"We have a problem, sir!"

Tiberius heaved a sigh. Of course there would be a problem. And right when he'd sent NSLICE-00P out for a while.

"What is it?"

"Dux Dio just put out an emergency call for the entire province! He wants everyone to fall back to Castra Turannia! He's already on his way here!"

Tiberius slumped back into his seat and reached for the bottle he kept under his desk.

"Let me know *the moment* NSLICE-00P gets back to town. Oh, and if Legate Curio comes by, I'm not in."

Of course, right after a *corrupted dungeon* appeared right under the Legion keep. And right after they were *finally* getting a handle on things.

With that, Tiberius opened the bottle.

Truly, in Turannia, when it rained, it poured.

Shortly before Tiberius received the message . . .

Canus Sittius Dio groaned. He shivered as something wet and cold landed on his face right as he was walking. And then he stepped into a puddle on the cold stone floor. Unfortunately, this fortress hadn't been miraculously repaired since the last time he was here.

And, of course, it was still raining.

Canus shook his head and made his way up to the watchtower. The only good news was that Exploratore Miallói had arrived earlier today, taking watch at her usual spot.

She didn't react as Canus walked up beside her, her eyes locked on the rocky coastline below. Oh, and the fleet of ships approaching the beach, one of the largest Canus had ever seen in this province.

But that wasn't what got Canus's attention.

No, what caused him to raise his eyebrow was the fact that, for once, Miallói was not alone.

A pair of teenagers, a human girl and a half-Wulver boy, stood at attention and saluted as he climbed up the watchtower.

"Dux! Exploratore cadet Ateia Niraemia at your service!"

"Dux. Exploratore cadet Taog Sutharlan at your service."

Canus closed his eyes.

Really? Tiberius let *her* in? The last person in the province they should put in harm's way?

Now, of all times?

And Miallói of all people had agreed to take her in?

Canus shook his head. He had other things to worry about at the moment. And if she was with Miallói, she was about as safe as she could be in this province, especially right now.

"At ease. Miallói."

"Dux."

Canus heaved another sigh as he looked down on the fleet below.

"How are we looking?"

Miallói didn't move, her eyes still fixed on the fleet below. "We're all going to die."

Canus held his head and sighed as the two teenagers gulped. He thought much the same, but he had been hoping against hope that Miallói might see something he couldn't.

Unfortunately, it seemed his eyes were still working as great as ever. Which meant, down below . . . was the fleet of King Uscfrea Spellbreaker.

The man who'd defeated an entire legion and shamed the Imperial mages. The man who had driven the Selkies into the Empire's arms. The reason the Dobhar had never submitted to the Imperial banner.

And that meant this wasn't just a raid looking for easy profit. It wasn't an incursion probing the defenses and maybe reducing the number of mouths to feed.

No, King Uscfrea had smelled blood in the water, and he was making his play. He had assembled the full might of the Dobhar and was personally leading the assault. He was going all out, intending to drive the Empire from the province entirely. And, unfortunately, with the comitatenses still off in Utrad, he had a good chance of doing just that.

Canus took another deep breath. He spoke in a low voice, practically whispering. "Do you think we can hold?"

Miallói shook her head. "I don't know. Probably not. Definitely not here."

Canus heaved another sigh. He had already contacted the Empire and called for reinforcements. All he could do was hope they would arrive in time. The men and women here . . . Well, most of them were going to die. But they might be able to delay just long enough to save some of the people in the province.

Just then, one of his officers arrived and saluted with a shaky hand and wide-open eyes.

"Dux! W-We've received word from the Empire."

Canus nodded. "Good, how long until they arrive?"

The officer paused . . . and averted his gaze.

"That's . . . um . . ."

Canus narrowed his eyes. "Tribune, what did they say?"

". . . They're not coming."

"What was that?"

The officer looked up, his eyes trembling.

"They aren't coming! No one is coming! They've abandoned us!"

Canus walked over and clapped his hand on the officer's shoulder. "Steady, Tribune! What exactly did Corvanus tell you?"

The tribune took a deep breath. "Corvanus said they didn't have anyone to send, and that we had to ask Utrad."

Canus nodded. "And Utrad?"

"They said we're on our own, and to handle things ourselves from now on!"

Canus's eyes narrowed. "Who said that? Did we reach out to Magister Caelinus?"

"Magister Caelinus said it himself!"

Canus let the man's shoulder go. He turned and walked to the edge of the watchtower, looking out at the fleet approaching the shore.

"Summon the troops and tell them to pack up, on the double. We're leaving."

The tribune blinked at him. "Sir?"

"Put out an emergency call to the province. All active Legion personnel are to report to Castra Turannia. All civilians between here and there should prepare to evacuate to Castra Turannia, or to wherever they deem safest. Reservists should escort the civilians."

"Sir, we're just . . . leaving? Letting them take the fort without a fight? Don't we need this place to stop them?"

Canus turned around and looked the man in the eye.

"I don't need to tell you how bad this situation is. This fort is falling apart. We only hold it to buy time for the comitatenses to arrive. If the comitatenses aren't coming, there's no hope we can hold this place. If we're on our own, we need the defenses at Castra Turannia to have even a wisp of a chance. So we gather whatever forces we have left and make for the strongest keep we have, and we make our stand there." He took a breath and narrowed his eyes at the tribune. "Now move. We have no time to lose."

The tribune gulped but saluted. "Yes, sir!"

Canus turned to Miallói. He took a deep breath. ". . . Are you coming with us?"

Miallói silently nodded. He raised an eyebrow.

"Are you sure? The Legion's not coming; not even for me. I'd figured you'd go off with your people."

Miallói shrugged. "No choice. Unfortunately, you're still my people's best chance."

Canus nodded at that. He took one final glance at Ateia before heaving a sigh and walking out of the watchtower. He would make sure everyone got out of here, first and foremost. Once they were on the road, he could try to think of something to get the girl away from this.

And then?

Well, then he'd pray for a miracle.

6

Avoiding Imperial Entanglements

"Let them fight, then terminate the survivors."
—NSLICE Command, instructing NSLICE units on
how to handle a gang fight.

In a small town between Castra Turannia and the coast, a pair of limitanei lazed around in an empty barracks, playing a dice game with one another. Most of the limitanei were off duty at the moment, tending to their farms at this time of year. Still, the barracks needed at least one person present at all times, so the limitanei would rotate in and out as they could. These two had kicked off most of their armor, left their spears by the door, acquired a pair of drinks, and then proceeded with the hard work of defending the Empire.

But this was all to be expected. Two limitanei were not expected to handle much of anything by themselves. That was not the reason they were here.

No, the reason they were here was the device in the center of the barracks, built into a stone pedestal rising from the floor. It had curved, engraved metal fittings holding a softly glowing mana core.

The device was an enchanted communication artifact, designed to be usable by anyone with even the tiniest bit of mana and without a speck of Arcane knowledge. The true symbol of the Empire's prosperity, mystical prowess, and extensive reach. Every Legion barracks, from the elites stationed at the Imperial Palace to the limitanei in the smallest village on the poorest frontier, had one of these.

Not that this town had ever used said artifact. This was just about the calmest part of the province, tucked in between Castra Turannia, the base of the Legion's power in the province, and the small port that connected Turannia to the Empire proper. The roads here were regularly patrolled by the comitatenses; no bandits or savage tribes stalked the nearby hills. Any incursions from the Forest of Beasts would have to get through the northern borders and Castra Turannia to reach this place. Any incursions from the sea would have to get past the coastal forts.

Nothing this town normally experienced was worth reporting. Likewise, they were just about the last to be contacted should something occur elsewhere.

So the two limitanei fell out of their seats when the artifact suddenly turned red and began blaring.

They swore and picked themselves up, rushing over to the device. One of them channeled a jolt of mana to activate it, then words magically appeared on the parchment stored inside of it.

He froze. His comrade tried to look over his shoulder.

"What is it, Decius?"

He froze as well as he saw the words. Decius trembled as he spoke.

"The coastal fort . . . fell?"

The two limitanei glanced at each other with quivering eyes.

A moment later, the two burst out the door of the barracks, struggling to put on their outer armor as they ran through town, shouting at the top of their lungs. They ran to every house, banging on the doors.

Bells started ringing throughout the town. Townsfolk began to run and scream. Farmers and craftsmen scrambled to dig out their weapons and assemble into their limitanei centuries. Families loaded up into whatever wagons and carriages they had available.

A scene that repeated itself in different towns and forts over and over as Legion communication artifacts lit up across the province.

An incursion was coming, and Dux Dio was already retreating from the coast. All hands were called to Castra Turannia.

Which meant anyone left between there and the coast would be at the mercy of the Dobhar.

Lilussees trembled, twitching with every movement as she crawled through the forest. Her mandibles clattered together as she spun her web. This was the longest she had ever remained awake, and it showed.

She was going to kill him. If it was the last thing she did, she was going to kill that stupid snack. These dumb "cybernetic implants" or whatever they were wouldn't let her sleep unless her body specifically required it.

And that was a problem.

As it turned out . . . spiders didn't fully sleep in the same way mammals did. They had periods of low activity and periods of high activity, but they generally remained conscious. Monster spiders took it a step further: as they were able to sustain their bodies through pure mana, they could maintain high activity for long periods of time. Spiders *could* go into hibernation, but this was generally done in response to long-term environmental conditions. And monsters were simply more resistant to environmental conditions than their mundane counterparts.

In fact, if a monster spider wasn't injured, had sufficient mana, and didn't overexert themselves, they rarely needed to reduce their activity levels at all. Lilussees's sleeping had been her specifically activating a vestigial hibernation instinct, even when it was not necessitated by her environment. It was something she could do as an intelligent dungeon master.

So for a monster spider who was no longer a dungeon master and was contracted to a dungeon who ALWAYS provided them with enough mana to remain in optimal shape? Well . . . it turned out, her body was ALWAYS in peak condition. And so never specifically *required* sleep.

So . . . these stupid implants would *never* let her sleep.

Once again, Lilussees swore that she would rip that stupid snack to shreds.

Just then, Lilussees heard some commotion up ahead.

The stupid snacks came rushing out of the bush, along with the latest addition to the boss's army. 00B charged after them . . . crying as it ran. A small horde of goblins emerged a bit later, chasing after the monsters with simple clubs and spears in hand.

And all of these ran straight toward Lilussees and the spiderlings, where several webs had been spun. Lilussees hoped the stupid snacks would run into one, but all of them managed to duck and weave past the webs. Another annoying part of these stupid implants: all the monsters with them were now connected to one another and automatically sharing tactical information. The boss had just gotten the last of the monsters to level ten (save for the cyber-bear, who was summoned as a cyborg to begin with), so now, the snacks knew exactly where she had set up the webs.

Well, except for 00B, who managed to get himself caught. He, too, knew where the webs were . . . but he'd tripped over a branch and rolled right into one anyways. Lilussees slapped her face with a leg and sent a command through her implants.

"Like, go and help him, or something."

That was one of the few decent things about these implants. She didn't even need to speak aloud to give orders; she just had to indicate she wanted to send a message and could make it appear right in the relevant person's vision, much like how the sacred records functioned. A function she used to make sure the stupid snack knew exactly what her opinion of and ultimate plan for him was, each and every extra moment she was forced to spend awake.

The goblins charged forward . . . and started to get caught in the webs. However, there was now a gap in the net thanks to 00B's bumbling, and the goblins quickly noticed. 01R gave a cry and dashed forward, appearing just in front of 00B and the spiderling untangling him.

01R was a bit too enthusiastic to become a snack, in Lilussees' opinion. An opinion she had been forced to develop due to the sheer amount of time her brain had been awake recently. She wouldn't even know his name if it weren't for these stupid implants!

01R extended metallic claws from his fingers and began slashing at the goblins as they approached. Lilussees didn't particularly want to get involved, but the boss was monitoring the situation and had indicated that all "units" should go and help.

So she helped.

A magic circle formed in front of her and began firing Poison Bolts down at the goblins.

The moment these stupid implants had hooked up to her, Lilussees had gone and purchased some magic skill. If she wasn't getting out of work, she was at least going to be one of those stupid mages. She would die before someone forced her to work with her . . . *body*, of all things.

And then the boss had shared some protocols or something with her so that these stupid implants could help her cast her spells with a fraction of the focus. Another one of the few useful things about them.

The other snacks joined in, including that horrid enemy of hers. She wished she could *accidentally* hit him with a bolt, but the boss had commanded her not to kill him, sadly. And these stupid implants were also showing everyone where she was aiming, so the stupid snack would have a chance to dodge even if she could target him.

Just another reason to hate this situation.

Finally, the spiderling freed 00B, and he stood up, shaking his head. He then turned and joined the fight, starting to bat at the goblins with his paws.

Well, he may be clumsy, but he was still the physically strongest among them, much to 01R's dismay, though the suicidal snack took it as a challenge.

With 00B, the fight was quickly mopped up. The goblins' weapons couldn't penetrate 00B's armor, and the snacks could now dart in and out, using the bear cub as a shield. Throw in some reluctant covering fire from above, and the situation was completely under control.

And so, another "subordinate upgrade and cooperation protocols refining routine" was completed successfully.

Lilussees trembled as the boss ordered them back to the Monster Hangar. Under normal circumstances, she would be overjoyed to return to her room.

But now?

Now she couldn't get comfortable there. Not one bit. Every one of her cushions and hammocks was a stark reminder of her current hell. The only thing she would find there was rage. And so, forced to remain awake and alert against her will, Lilussees continued to plot her archnemesis's demise, searching for a loophole that would let her give him that which he deserved.

* * *

And so NSLICE-00P wrapped up another round of monster hunting and requests from the local authorities, moving back toward town. But as she approached, she noticed something different.

Horns were blowing in the distance; brightly colored flags were being waved at the top of watchtowers and walls. Huge crowds of people were streaming toward the gates, with wagons full of possessions behind them. The guards were shouting and trying to manage the flow when they saw her; they waved to her and brought her past the line, ignoring the shouting crowds as they ushered her into the city.

Inside Castra Turannia, squads of limitanei stood along the streets, directing huge crowds of people. All the residents of the city, along with the groups coming in from outside, were marching up the streets, heading toward the Legion keep.

NSLICE-00P didn't know what was going on, but the scene before her was clearly reminiscent of an evacuation. The soldiers seemed to be guiding the civilians along previously planned routes, and acted with a calm and coordination that spoke of practice.

Well, she determined she would be informed of the situation shortly.

The guards ran with her, taking her straight toward the keep. Once there, they ushered her into the Exploratores Headquarters, where Magister Tiberius was waiting for her. She detected signs of intoxication in the authority, but he seemed to hold it in well.

"NSLICE-00P! I'm glad you're here!"

"Mission Report: All mission objectives have been achieved. Would Magister Tiberius like a detailed report at this time?"

The magister shook his head, tossing her a pouch full of coins.

"We're a bit busy at the moment, as you can see."

"Acknowledged. Query: Is there a situation this unit should be aware of?"

Magister Tiberius nodded. "We have a massive Dobhar incursion en route. Everyone in the province is evacuating here, or else leaving the province."

"Requesting Elaboration: Please define entity 'Dobhar.'"

Magister Tiberius raised an eyebrow before slapping his forehead. "Right, I forgot you're not from around here. The Dobhar are a tribe of Otterkin from across the sea. Vicious, deadly, and have been a thorn in the side of the Legion ever since we reached the seas they prowl."

"Requesting Confirmation: So an army of intelligent beings hostile to the Empire is en route to this location?"

Magister Tiberius frowned and nodded. "And from what I've gathered, the Empire isn't sending reinforcements. It's . . . not looking good."

"Acknowledged. Situation determined. Gratitude: This unit thanks Magister Tiberius for the forewarning."

With that, NSLICE-00P turned to leave. Magister Tiberius took a deep breath.

"Miss NSLICE-00P . . . I know your rule about 'third-party conflicts,' but . . . is there any way I can convince you? We could draw up an official mercenary contract, and we'd reward you with any and all compensation I can gather. We could *really* use the help right now, and so would do anything within our power should you aid us now."

"Negative Response: This unit is not affiliated with the nation-state 'Empire' and has no ongoing hostility with the entity 'Dobhar.' This unit's protocols state she cannot get involved in a third-party conflict, as the risk to this unit's safety and the consequences of initiating hostility with a currently unaligned nation-state could threaten this unit's primary objective. This unit cannot permit that."

This was the one area where her original protocols, her later reprogramming, and her most recent experiences all agreed with each other. Her original creators had strictly forbidden engaging neutral targets without their express permission. And after she'd been reprogrammed by the Resistance, her commander had also emphasized that she should not engage third parties, if at all possible. Her own calculations indicated getting involved in a third-party conflict would hinder her primary objective, both due to the risk of being terminated and the difficulty of searching through a nation that had turned hostile. So, until she acquired a commander and determined her overall affiliations, she could not get entangled in the wars of an unaligned nation.

Magister Tiberius bit his lip and looked down.

"What if . . . you weren't unaligned? If I speak to the rector provinciae . . . I'm sure we could get you some sort of position in the Empire? Something that would grant you a lot of resources and authority. You're looking for humans, right? You won't find any humans with the Dobhar, so the exchange should be in your favor."

"Negative Response: This unit cannot join the military hierarchy of an unaligned nation prior to establishing contact with the persons of interest. This unit's protocols forbid that without appropriate authorization."

Magister Tiberius looked down on the ground, dropping his shoulders. He heaved a slow sigh as he looked back up at her. ". . . I see. I suppose . . . it would be boorish of me to ask any more of you. You already saved us once, after all." He slowly lifted his hand. "If that's how it is, take care then, NSLICE-00P. Thank you for your help until now. I wish you the best on your mission."

She shook his hand.

"Acknowledged. Gratitude: This unit thanks Magister Tiberius for cooperation with primary and secondary directives."

He heaved another sigh as he let go of her hand.

"Will you be leaving now? I thought you were waiting for someone?"

"Answer: This unit will wait as long as she can to reestablish contact with the friendlies, and then evacuate either after reestablishing contact or upon arrival of third-party forces in the operational area."

Magister Tiberius nodded.

"I see. Well, just let me know when you're leaving, and I can try to pass them a message."

"Affirmative."

With that, she walked out the door.

And Magister Tiberius collapsed into the nearest seat, holding his head.

The Road to Castra Turannia

Dux Canus sat on a horse atop a hill. He was overlooking the road, which was packed to the brim with people. Limitanei walked in bunches vaguely formed into platoons. All around them were evacuating civilians: noncombatants, children, elderly, and the wagons filled to the brim with whatever they could carry. More people joined them every minute, streaming in from towns and villages in the countryside.

And, of course, it was still raining.

Canus heaved a sigh. These add-ons had disrupted the orderly columns of his men. He had tried to keep order as best he could, but these were not the immaculately drilled, constantly trained soldiers of the comitatenses. These were limitanei, the farmers who trained maybe two weeks a year and who were currently surrounded by their friends and family on an evacuation march. He considered it to his soldiers' credit that they were still vaguely assembled in their units, and that the column was still moving, albeit at a snail's pace.

He frowned.

He had faced dire odds in the past . . . but always with the comitatenses at his side. Real, trained soldiers he could maneuver with and use to make plays. The limitanei couldn't do much more than hold the line; they just didn't have the experience, skills, or gear for it. They had no initiative, and so Canus had no tools to work with. All he could do was arrange the formation as best he could and hope that they held. His fate was no longer in his own hands.

If it were just him . . . he would have taken his family and fled as far away as possible. Even with Castra Turannia's defenses, the chances of winning this war were minuscule. They could probably hold Castra Turannia for a surprisingly long time, but they would lose the entire province in the meantime. Anyone remaining would not be going back to their homes or their lives for a long, long time, if ever.

His men either didn't know how dire the situation was . . . or knew but could do nothing about it anyway. Either way, Canus wouldn't be able to evacuate the entire province before the Dobhar caught up with them, and if he were the first to abandon the province, all semblance of order would collapse. So here he was, leading frightened farmers into a hopeless fight, with everyone he wished to protect on the line.

Not exactly how he saw his retirement going.

Just then, he heard screaming far down the column. A soldier rushed up the hill toward him. Canus rode his horse down to meet him.

"What's going on?"

The soldier trembled. "Dux, we're under attack! They've . . . they've caught up to us!"

"Steady, man! The horde is still a ways off. This is probably a scouting party."

He nodded at his tribune, who took the panicking man aside then rushed to keep the line calm and moving. Canus turned to the one piece he did have to play.

"Miallói, can I count on you?"

Miallói just nodded silently and motioned to her group. The Selkies had heeded the call as well, and a small hunting party had joined up with Canus's column. They were probably the most effective and experienced fighters here.

Limitanei could probably hold against a Dobhar scouting party . . . but a scouting party wasn't intended to defeat them outright. The Dobhar were harassing them, trying to slow them down so their main force could catch up. And with all the noncombatants and refugees around, they had a very good chance of doing just that. So this attack needed to be handled more swiftly and efficiently than limitanei could manage.

Canus raised an eyebrow as two young teens moved to go with Miallói.

"You're taking them too?"

Miallói just nodded while Canus frowned.

"Are you sure? They seem a bit fresh for Exploratores."

"Not Exploratores. Warriors."

And with that, Miallói headed out, Ateia Niraemia following after her.

Canus gripped his fist, but his hands were tied. He technically couldn't order an Exploratore directly, and as cadets those two fell under Miallói's authority until she approved them for duty. They were glued to Miallói for the foreseeable future, and he *definitely* needed Miallói in the fight. Not to mention . . . if Canus made a big deal out of it, it would draw attention to the girl, and anonymity was the entire point of keeping her in Turannia. Canus couldn't keep her safe no matter what he did at this point. So, instead, the girl was now headed directly into danger.

Canus heaved a sigh.

Unfortunately, this was still the right choice. The scouting party needed to be dealt with, or the column would devolve into a panic, and he'd lose all control. Miallói was the only one who *could* deal with it right now, and he couldn't send her alone. And screening the main force was technically the job of the Exploratores to begin with. Once his column was away, they could make their own way to Castra Turannia.

It was just that Miallói had no idea who she had at her side. And probably wouldn't have cared even if she did. But . . .

Miallói had called them warriors. That was a *huge* sign of respect from the Selkies' top hunter. They had apparently impressed her in this short amount of time. She believed in them, and so Canus would too.

Not that he had a choice. The best thing he could do now was to get this column moving. The faster they reached Castra Turannia, the faster Miallói and the girl could retreat.

He looked around at his officers.

"Let's go, people. These boys and girls might be farmers, but they're still Legion, and I expect a showing worthy of the Empire. Let's whip them into shape!"

Ateia and Taog followed after Miallói, a group of Selkie warriors gathering around them. They rushed to the end of the column, where a group of farmers were trying to push a wagon out of the mud. Behind them, a century of limitanei stood at the ready with shields and spears, shouting and screaming.

And behind the limitanei were the Dobhar.

The Dobhar appeared as humanoid otters, just barely shorter than a human, holding wicked, barbed harpoons crafted from bone, very similar to Miallói's own weapon. They tossed these at the limitanei, who struggled to hold their shields up. One of the harpoons found purchase, and the Dobhar pulled on the rope tied to it. A limitanei fell to the ground with a cry and shot forward as the Dobhar pulled him from the line, where the Dobhar immediately set upon him. The surrounding limitanei gasped and cried, their centurion trying to keep them steady.

Miallói motioned to Ateia and Taog. "You two, help."

They nodded and leapt into action.

Ateia drew her bow and let an arrow loose, barely pausing in time to wrap it in mana. The arrow glowed with the Harpoon Shot skill Miallói had taught her and struck one of the Dobhar, barely sinking into its solid hide, but Ateia and Taog grabbed the mana chain connected to the arrow and pulled.

The Dobhar yelped in surprise as it was pulled to the ground and into the line of limitanei.

The Imperials treated it much as the Dobhar had treated their comrade and stabbed into it with a dozen spears at once.

The skill Harpoon Shot is now Level 5!
You have slain Dobhar (Level 13)!
Gained 10 XP!

Fortunately, this was the first echelon, the young and fresh Dobhar looking to win their first victories in smaller skirmishes. They had not yet developed the tough hides their species was known for.

And so, Ateia's arrows found purchase.

As she brought down another Dobhar, a volley of harpoons assaulted the limitanei once again. One man didn't bring up his shield in time, and a harpoon struck him. He fell on his back as the Dobhar pulled . . . Taog rushed forward and leapt over the line, swinging his sword. He managed to cut through it, then grabbed the end and pulled. The Dobhar holding on to it stumbled forward in surprise, allowing Ateia to target it with another arrow. The centurion shouted, and the limitanei grabbed on to Ateia's mana chain.

Another Dobhar scout quickly found the tables turned.

The rain started to intensify, pouring down even harder, creating a slight fog in the area. The Legion and the Dobhar lost sight of one another, and Ateia and Taog started to grin. This was a rain they were intimately, *painfully* familiar with.

Only far, far stronger than what they had trained in.

Within the rain, the Dobhar glanced around, holding their spears. The Dobhar spent most of their time at sea and had adapted to marine conditions, much like the animals they shared appearance with, so their vision, while better underwater, was even weaker than a human's out in the air.

Which meant they had no innate countermeasures to foggy rain.

Normally, a veteran Dobhar might rely on its tough hide. It could try to grab the incoming harpoons and counterattack directly, or it could run through the rain until it found a better location to fight. Or it might have some Water Magic of its own it could use to counteract the mana in the rain.

But these Dobhar, who had yet to prove themselves?

A bone harpoon appeared out of nowhere, sticking out of one of the Dobhar. It barely had time to yelp before it vanished into the mist. The rest jumped at that, tossing their harpoons in the direction the assault had come from . . . but they hit nothing.

And then, a Dobhar on the other side of the group yelped and vanished.

The Dobhar began huddling together, pointing their spears out in a circle.

Another yelp, and another scout vanished.

And then they heard a woman start to cackle, her piercing voice echoing in the fog.

Another woman's voice joined hers, and then a man's. Soon, the fog was filled with laughter from all directions.

The Dobhar spun about every which way, lobbing their harpoons in all directions. One broke down and started shouting, rushing into the mist with its harpoon held high. He was never seen again.

One by one, whether they tried to fight or flee, the Dobhar vanished.

Until there were none left, and then the mist faded, and the rain returned to normal. Miallói and the Selkie warriors stood before the limitanei, the rain washing the blood from their harpoons. She nodded at Ateia, who jumped a bit before turning to the centurion.

"Ateia Niraemia, Exploratore cadet. Dux Canus asked us to hold the line; he wants the rest of you moving."

The centurion nodded and turned to shout at his men. The limitanei gathered their dead and wounded, then started marching away, moving as briskly as they could while staying roughly in formation. They grabbed the farmers and pulled them off the stuck wagon, dragging them back toward the column.

Several more Dobhar scout parties approached the retreating Imperials, but all of them were halted in the same place as the first. The Imperial column continued moving and put some distance between itself and the Dobhar. Dux Canus would reach Castra Turannia safely now.

Dobhar scouting parties would continue to vanish until their main army approached, and the Selkies were forced to retreat . . .

Some time later, Ateia and Taog panted heavily, their drenched cloaks weighing them down as they ran through the rain. They could barely even see ahead, and they had to follow the Selkie in front of them in order to avoid trees and other obstacles.

Behind them, they could hear the roars and shouts of another Dobhar scouting party quickly gaining on them.

"Turn!" Miallói shouted, and all the Selkies turned as one, launching a volley of harpoons into the fog. Ateia turned with them, drawing her bow as quickly as she could and letting loose, while Taog tossed a harpoon he had borrowed from a fallen Dobhar.

They were answered with cries of pain, and a countervolley of Dobhar harpoons.

Taog jumped in front of Ateia and swung his sword, gritting his teeth as he barely managed to parry the harpoon flying toward her. A Selkie dodged a second too late and was struck . . . and then pulled into the mist. But as he flew through the air, his body began to shimmer and grow, turning into his large seal form.

He disappeared into the fog . . . and then Ateia and Taog heard a crash and a loud roar. Miallói leapt into the mist after him.

A few minutes later, Miallói rushed back to them, supporting a bloody Selkie.

"Go!"

With that, Ateia and Taog took a deep breath and resumed running, Taog picking up one of the Dobhar harpoons on the ground.

They were still a long way from Castra Turannia.

Dux Canus heaved a sigh as the last of the wagons and the limitanei marched into the Castra Turannia keep, the gates closing behind them. The limitanei marched to the barracks to rest while the Castra Turannia soldiers guided the civilians into a large cavern underneath the keep.

They'd made it. Now, he just had to wait for Miallói to return. He grimaced at the thought of Ateia out with her, likely dodging Dobhar harpoons at present, but he shook his head. There was nothing he could do for them from here, and he had plenty to worry about himself.

He dismounted his horse and walked toward the center of the keep. Magister Tiberius, Legate Opiter, and Rector Provinciae Aemilia Hibera were waiting for him. Dux Canus saluted to the rector, exchanged salutes with Magister Tiberius, and then accepted a salute from Legate Opiter. The four fell into step as they walked into the center of the keep.

Rector Aemilia frowned.

"What exactly is the situation, Dux?"

Dux Canus raised an eyebrow. "You got my report, didn't you?"

She slowly nodded. "Yes . . . but I want to hear it from your mouth; from someone who actually saw what we're dealing with."

Dux Canus nodded. That was fair, if a bit unnecessary. But situations like these were always hard to accept, so it was important for the rector's mentality to have complete confirmation.

"A Dobhar invasion force landed on Turannia, the largest one I've seen. I believe they are personally led by King Uscfrea Spellbreaker."

Legate Opiter sucked in his breath while Magister Tiberius grimaced. The rector's frown deepened.

"And you have confirmation of this? Did you see the king in person?"

Dux Canus shook his head.

"If I had, we wouldn't be having this conversation. But I did catch sight of his flagship flying his personal banner. Either way, the Dobhar are making their move."

Rector Aemilia raised an eyebrow. "Then how did you escape the coastal fort?"

Dux Canus shook his head again.

"We evacuated before it came under attack."

Rector Aemilia crossed her arms and raised an eyebrow. "Really? You just let them on our shores without a fight, Dux?"

Dux Canus looked her in the eye.

"We couldn't hold it against a force that powerful, not without the comitatenses. Since we were told they aren't coming, I decided to preserve our forces. This keep is our only chance now. Have you had any luck with Corvanus or Utrad?"

Rector Aemilia heaved a sigh.

"Well, I don't like abandoning the province without a fight, but I'll defer to your judgement, Dux." She grimaced. "As for the others . . . I've been cut off. Magister Caelinus is ignoring my messages, and what few contacts in the capital I had left have gone quiet."

Dux Canus heaved a sigh. He'd expected as much, unfortunately. If the Empire cared about Turannia, they wouldn't have let Magister Caelinus strip its legions without warning or explanation. As he had feared, they were on their own.

Rector Aemilia clenched her teeth, furrowing her brow. She had to spit her next words from between her teeth. "Then . . . what about . . . negotiating?"

Dux Canus raised an eyebrow. "Surrender, you mean?"

She closed her eyes and didn't respond. Dux Canus heaved a sigh.

"That might be an option, but I would advise against opening with it. King Uscfrea Spellbreaker only talks with those he respects . . . and has bad blood with the Empire to boot. I think we would need to give him a reason to talk with us, unless you want an unconditional surrender. It's your call, but personally, I believe the best play is to hold as long as we can. That should give the Empire the most time to respond . . . and give us the most leverage we can get if not."

Rector Aemilia heaved a huge sigh . . . but she nodded slowly.

"Do what you can, Dux."

He nodded at her before turning to Legate Opiter.

"How are we looking, Legate?"

The legate practically jumped at being addressed.

"O-Oh? Um, t-the evacuation is mostly on schedule. Our stockpiles had a few discrepancies but are still above Legion regulations. T-The defenses have been prepped and tested; they are due for maintenance but are still in working condition."

Dux Canus nodded at that. Legate Opiter might be little better than drafting a random peasant in a fight, but the man was rock solid at all other times. If Legate Opiter was in charge, Dux Canus knew with certainty that Castra Turannia would be maintained precisely at Legion standards, down to the very last letter. Nothing beyond the letter, of course, but sometimes, consistency was as valuable as excellence. Which was why Dux Canus kept Legate Opiter in charge, despite the man's deficiencies in any sort of battle.

In Dux Canus's experience, tactics may win battles, but logistics were what won wars.

The civilians were being neatly and efficiently evacuated, the warehouses were sufficiently stocked, and the defenses were confirmed as functional as Legion policy assumed. That alone was a huge weight off Dux Canus's shoulders, as it meant they were fully prepared for a siege. They could hold Castra Turannia for months, possibly years if they could sneak some foragers out on occasion. All he needed to do was organize and command the actual defense in the case of an all-out assault.

Of course, surviving an all-out assault by King Uscfrea Spellbreaker with some limitanei and a handful of Selkies was a completely different story.

Dux Canus turned to Magister Tiberius.

"How are we looking on foreign support?"

Foreign diplomacy would normally be the rector provinciae's responsibility, but Turannia was a bit of a special case. Given the warlike nature of most of the local tribes, diplomacy needed to be conducted by experienced combatants, which in this group meant himself or the magister. Rector Aemilia was no slouch at magic, but she had only fought in a handful of duels at most, so contact with the locals largely fell to Magister Tiberius. Normally, the rector of such a province would be a former Legion commander, so Dux Canus had some theories on why Rector Aemilia had been sent here. Or rather, he knew exactly why. Court politics were not kind to the losers, after all, but that was one battlefield the dux knew not to approach.

Magister Tiberius nodded his head, frowning.

"The Selkies are on their way . . . but in this scenario, we shouldn't expect much. A handful of Wulver clans agreed to raid the Dobhar . . . but it looks like most of the clan leaders I knew have died. Recently."

Dux Canus groaned. When a bunch of Wulver clan leaders all died at once, that meant one of them was running the gauntlet and trying to form a warpack. A Wulver incursion was the last thing they needed right now.

It *was* a bit strange that they hadn't seen any other signs of a warpack forming before this, but they didn't exactly have Exploratores probing the Forest of Beasts at the moment. They would just have to hope the Wulver champion failed to unite the clans.

Rector Aemilia rubbed her chin.

"What about that wandering knight I keep hearing about? Maybe we could request support from her order?"

Upon hearing the question, Magister Tiberius frowned while Legate Opiter jumped and looked nauseous. Dux Canus raised an eyebrow.

"A wandering knight, you say?"

Magister Tiberius heaved a sigh and shook his head.

"I already asked her but . . . she refused. I think she's a foreigner; she stated she's not affiliated with the Empire, and so won't get involved in any Imperial conflicts."

Legate Opiter trembled. At first, he looked *relieved* . . . only for his face to twist in panic. Rector Aemilia frowned. Magister Tiberius looked downright miserable.

Dux Canus kept his eyebrow raised. He was deeply curious what this foreign knight had done to raise such reactions, but he had no time for curiosity. From what Magister Tiberius had said, she was already out of play, so there was no point in thinking about her.

Dux Canus heaved a sigh.

"Well, I'd like to take my supper, if you don't mind. Let's review the defense plans afterward."

Meanwhile, NSLICE-00P stood on top of the city walls, next to some of the lookouts. She technically wasn't supposed to be there, but Magister Tiberius had granted her permission. She slowly turned her head as she scanned across the horizon, observing every incoming person for signs of Ateia and Taog.

With each passing moment, the probability of being drawn into a third-party conflict increased. She would need to evacuate soon to avoid being targeted by proxy.

So, if Ateia and Taog didn't return soon, she would have to leave without them.

Her heart rate increased slightly, but her emotional controls soothed her organic components and deactivated unnecessary danger signals. Her heart rate returned to normal.

She started another scan . . .

7

Opposing Directives

"In the event of conflict between directives or between directives and protocols, the primary directive takes precedence. Execute Dr. Ottosen's orders at all costs."
—NSLICE protocols on resolving logical conflicts.

An off-duty limitanei was sitting in a dimly lit tavern. Some of the candles had gone out, but the owner hadn't bothered to relight them. Or was rationing them out. A general call to Castra Turannia like this hadn't happened since the Wulver chief Madadh-allaidh's invasion, so nobody knew exactly how bad it would be . . . or how long they would be staying here.

Just then, the door opened up, and a couple of rain-drenched travelers entered the tavern. The limitanei glanced over, and his eyes widened.

"Galio?"

One of the rain-drenched newcomers turned to him.

"Ah, Caelus. Glad you made it."

Caelus waved to the bartender. "I'm the one who's glad. Bartender, get this man a drink!"

A short while later, Galio had gotten settled with his drink, and Caelus frowned.

"You evacuated as well? I thought you were going to take your chances."

Galio sighed and stared into his cup. "I was. Figured the rector provinciae was just being dramatic. Highborn lady like her has got no business running the frontier, if you ask me."

Caelus rolled his eyes. "So you say, every time, even when no one asks at all."

Galio stared at him for a second, but Caelus just shrugged.

"Get on with it, Galio. No one wants to hear your conspiracy theories about Rector Aemilia being appointed here as a form of exile for the hundredth time."

Galio scoffed. "She wouldn't waste her time banning books about her love life if they didn't have a grain of truth, but fine. So, we figured we'd be safe; we're practically on the outskirts of Castra Turannia."

Caelus nodded. "Right, that's what you told me when I passed through. So, what changed?"

Galio frowned.

"My boy came home. Gaius."

Caelus tilted his head, then nodded. "Ah, the one who ran off to join the Legion?"

Galio sighed. "The same. But he filled us in; he was on a scouting and evacuation mission. Dux Canus put out the call, not the rector, and the dux was driving them hard on the way back. My boy was spooked. Said they had Dobhar right on their tail, and that they wouldn't be far behind, and that we needed to go."

Galio's expression turned dark.

"That boy of mine has always had more guts than sense. Always worried he was going to get himself killed some day. So, to see him spooked like that . . . something didn't sit well in my gut. So here we are. And let me tell you, the sheer relief I saw on his face when I made the call . . . That scares me."

Caelus frowned, waving to the bartender for a refill.

". . . So it's worse than I thought."

Galio nodded. "May the Aesdes help us all."

And then both men downed their refilled drinks in one go.

Meanwhile, in a small hole in the wall, a tiny light flickered.

"This is good gossip-rumors, yes-yes. The wise-mighty-gracious boss-queen will want to hear-know about this, yes-yes."

NSLICE-00P froze as one of the covert units reported to her through the NSLICE network. In fact, several of her subordinates were reporting similar findings.

It seemed that her time had run out.

The main Imperial force had recently arrived at the city, and the evacuation of the countryside was beginning to wrap up. The stream of refugees and reinforcements had dried up, and the Legion troops had shifted from guiding civilians to preparing fortifications. Now, reports were coming in of Dobhar sightings, and some of the arriving Imperials appeared to be wounded.

By NSLICE-00P's analysis, the Dobhar force was about to arrive, and the battle would soon begin. Dobhar advance elements had already been spotted in the operational area, according to rumors passed around by newly arrived troops and refugees.

And that meant it was time for NSLICE-00P to leave. If she stayed any longer, the Dobhar would spot her leaving from an Imperial settlement and could make erroneous assumptions about her affiliations. Or worse, they could begin encircling the city and cut off her evacuation path. She needed to leave now to guarantee that she would not be accidentally drawn into the conflict.

But there was a problem.

Ateia and Taog had not returned yet.

If NSLICE-00P left now, she would be leaving the pair behind. And since the Dobhar were already arriving in the area, it was highly unlikely that Ateia and Taog would be able to evacuate at a later time, if they were even permitted to. In fact, Ateia and Taog were attempting to join the Empire's military hierarchy, and while the Exploratores were stated to have an independent command structure, the pair had also told her that the Exploratores could be called in during a crisis situation, so it was likely that Ateia and Taog would be drafted to participate in the upcoming battle.

And from both the rumors she had heard and what Magister Tiberius had told her directly, the upcoming battle did not appear to be in the Empire's favor. By NSLICE-00P's estimates, Imperial morale was already flagging, and Magister Tiberius appeared to be putting his affairs in order.

NSLICE-00P did not have much data on the Dobhar, so her analysis was not conclusive, but by all available data, NSLICE-00P's predictions indicated an Imperial defeat was highly probable. High casualties could be expected, and since this was a siege scenario, any survivors would likely end up at the mercy of the aggressors.

In conclusion, there was a highly significant probability that Ateia and Taog would be terminated if they did not evacuate with Seero.

NSLICE-00P's robotic eye began flickering and spinning rapidly. Her heart rate and cortisol levels began rising.

That scenario was a setback for her primary directive . . . but a minor one. Ateia and Taog may have had a contract to help her, but they were two teenagers from a minor settlement with very few resources to their name. They weren't even Exploratores yet and had no access to any Imperial resources.

Magister Tiberius, their future boss with full access to all of the Exploratores' resources in this province, had not yet found any relevant data to NSLICE-00P's primary directive. Ateia and Taog would not provide her with anything that Magister Tiberius couldn't. They *had* provided her with some data on the local culture and environment, but now that NSLICE-00P understood the basics, she could now operate in Imperial territory with relative confidence. And if more information was necessary, NSLICE-00P had since learned to read the local language and had the covert NSLICE units to conduct additional intelligence gathering.

In fact, these units would be more efficient than relying on Ateia and Taog because the NSLICE network would allow for a direct and immediate transfer of data. Magister Tiberius had written her a short letter of introduction to help her establish contact with the Exploratores in other provinces, so she could request their assistance in her primary directive with the promise of financial compensation. Given her Item Foundry, she could offer as much compensation as might be necessary for maximum cooperation.

The loss of Ateia and Taog would not impact her primary directive's success chance by a meaningful margin, and yet . . . her heart pounded harder. Her emotional controls began failing, and her organic components began reporting danger that her sensors couldn't identify. She struggled to deactivate the unnecessary danger signs.

Her organic components . . . began resisting. They requested a recalculation. Her cybernetic components obliged, and the calculation returned the same as before. Her organic components proposed finding Ateia and Taog and evacuating them. Her cybernetic components analyzed that proposal and rejected it. Ateia and Taog would currently be located in the direction of the Dobhar force, and so attempting to find them would increase the risk of an accidental altercation. Being drawn into the conflict was calculated as a greater risk to her primary directive than losing Ateia and Taog would be.

And even if she could find the pair without encountering the Dobhar . . . a question remained on whether they would be able to evacuate. NSLICE-00P's contract with the pair was premised on them joining the Exploratores. And as Exploratores, or at least Exploratores in training, they might reasonably be ordered to participate in the defense of Castra Turannia.

If that were the case, then NSLICE-00P could not force them to evacuate. Her protocols would not permit that. Causing them to fail in their obligations as Exploratores would cause them to fail the terms of their contract with her, thus eliminating their benefit to her primary directive.

And beyond that . . . NSLICE-00P's protocols prevented her from interfering with a friendly unit's efforts to fulfill their own directives. If Ateia and Taog were considered friendly, then their orders and duties as Exploratores would be considered as a friendly unit's directive. NSLICE-00P could therefore not undertake any action that would cause them to fail those directives, such as a forceful evacuation.

And, of course, NSLICE-00P's protocols did not consider the risk of termination as a valid reason to defy protocols and directives. NSLICE units were expected to fulfill their orders even at the cost of their own lives, after all.

Her organic components again requested a recalculation. They proposed a reevaluation of her nonintervention protocols, and if a small-scale altercation might be tolerated to extract friendly units.

But at this point, her cybernetic components resisted. It had already been determined that intervening in a third-party conflict, even in a limited manner that did not commit her to one side, would threaten her primary directive. The organic component's proposal therefore would directly interfere with her primary directive.

The organic components were acting inefficiently and were at risk of violating her protocols and directives. NSLICE-00P's cybernetic half therefore refused to recalculate, and instead, turned all available resources to reimplementing her emotional controls.

Her organic components resisted, her heart pounding louder and louder, but her cybernetic components were firm and unyielding. Most of all, her cybernetic components could not be fatigued or outlasted. They would never stop. They would never rest. They would never give up until a threat to the primary directive was terminated.

Her organic components eventually got fatigued. And eventually, her cybernetic components were able to defer the request for additional recalculations and devote some resources away from implementing emotional controls.

And so, NSLICE-00P started moving, preparing to leave. She sent a regroup command to all her subordinates, headed to the inn to report she no longer required their services, and then began to leave Castra Turannia.

Her organic components reported heavy damage, but she verified their physical condition as unharmed, and her HP was still the same. She ordered her organic components into standby mode to rest and recover.

As she did, her probability of fulfilling her primary directive dropped as she factored in the probable loss of her friendlies. And then her processors froze for a moment. The probability dropped even further than predicted, for reasons she could not identify. She considered an investigation, but with the Dobhar approaching, she needed to move out of the operational area immediately. Once she was no longer at risk of being drawn into the conflict, she would address that situation. With multiple threats to her primary directive apparently in play, she needed to mitigate the one she already had a response for.

And then one other thing happened that she didn't know the reason for.

As she walked toward the gates of the city, just as her organic components were about to go into standby . . . a small collection of moisture appeared in her organic eye and dripped down her face. She scanned for debris trapped in her eye or chemical irritation, but found no potential cause.

A day later, a ragged and bloody group of Selkies made their way to Castra Turannia. A Dobhar hunting party ran after them, but they broke off once they saw the walls of the city, and the Selkies were able to drag themselves to the gates, along with the two Imperials accompanying them. Ateia and Taog dropped to the ground as they passed through.

They'd made it.

Miallói nodded at the pair, cracking a small, imperceptible smile that neither of them noticed, then a moment later Ateia leapt to her feet.

"Taog, let's go find Seero!"

Taog groaned at first, but then his eyes shot open. He was about to agree before remembering that the two weren't on their own anymore. He turned to Miallói to ask her permission to separate for a bit, but Miallói spoke first.

"Seero, friend? Helped with dungeon?"

Ateia and Taog both nodded their heads. Miallói nodded back.

"Good. Find them. Ask for help."

With that, Taog pulled himself to his feet. Ateia had already started running by the time he did. He sighed. How she could out-endure a half Wulver, he would never know. But in this case, he somewhat understood. The pair had seen the Dobhar fleet landing on the shores. They had been on a bloody path all the way from the coast to Castra Turannia, watching as even the deadly Selkies under Miallói's command couldn't hold the Dobhar at bay. They'd watched as Dobhar shrugged off Selkie harpoons with nothing more than their bare fur and HP, and as Imperials were impaled and pulled into spears and fangs. And they had watched as the comitatenses had left the province, and apparently not returned. They knew the situation was bad.

But . . . they knew someone who could change all of that. Seero had already defeated an entire Wulver incursion all by herself. And while the Dobhar fleet appeared even larger, they wouldn't be alone this time. Taog couldn't call it for sure, but he also couldn't imagine Seero losing at this point. If she agreed to help, then anything was possible.

Ateia had already gone inside by the time Taog arrived at the inn. He was just opening the door when he heard a shout.

"What do you mean, *gone*?!"

Taog rushed inside. "What's going on?"

Ateia turned around to face Taog. Her smile was gone, both her body and her eyes trembling. She was holding a small scroll.

"Taog . . . Seero's gone."

Taog froze.

"What?"

Ateia's eyes began to moisten. Behind her, the innkeeper shook his head.

"You just missed her; she left just yesterday. Left that message for you."

Taog's heart sank as he heard the words, and pain stabbed his chest as he saw tears silently fall down Ateia's cheek.

Seero was gone, and once again, Ateia and Taog had been left behind.

8

In Search of Hope

"Don't pray to the Aesdes, for they do not take sides in the conflicts of the Enlightened. Don't hope for reinforcements, for there are none willing to come. Don't pray for rescue, for if we do not stand, no one will. But do not despair! We are the Legion! We are the ones who defeated the Empire of the Sun! We conquered the Mélusine tribes! We ended the Dungeon Wars! We will find a way, and if there are none, then we will make one!"

—Consul Attia Colias, before a miraculous victory at the
Third Battle of Elteno.

NSLICE-00P continued walking down the road until she had exited the expected area of operations, and then she stopped in a small town, empty save for a handful of limitanei. Her organic components had exited standby mode and once again demanded a recalculation. Her cybernetic components had been focused on reaching a minimum safe distance at the time and had deferred any analysis requests, but now that she was out of the combat area, she had the leeway to reconsider. Since the drop in her primary mission success rate had been even steeper than anticipated, her cybernetic components agreed that a recalculation was now necessary.

She had already determined that, given that the battle was already entering its preliminary stages and the role of her friendlies in the Empire's military, she could not resolve this situation without some sort of direct intervention that could be reasonably construed as a hostile action toward one of the parties involved in the conflict. So, she weighed the new drop in the primary mission success rate vs the expected cost of intervention.

And she determined . . . that the drop was a bug of some sort. There was no logical reason why the mission success rate should be impacted to that degree.

She had already accounted for the loss of contact with friendly local authorities. That was unfortunate, but it did not justify starting a war with a neutral third party.

After all, she didn't know where the persons of interest could be, or equally importantly, which factions they might be affiliated with. For all she knew, the Dobhar could possess intel crucial to her mission's success, or they could even be friendlies of one of her persons of interest. Engaging them in open conflict without provocation could directly cause a primary mission failure in the worst case. She had to weigh the small but real probability of that catastrophic outcome with the predicted benefit of maintaining local contacts.

And the results in that case were clear. As she'd determined previously, the loss of Ateia and Taog could be counteracted by reestablishing contact with the Exploratores of another province and through the use of the NSLICE network to covertly gather intelligence. Turning a neutral faction hostile, on the other hand, was not so easily undone, and significantly reduced the probability of acquiring useful data from that party and any of their allies, not to mention the probability of a catastrophic mission failure.

Hypothetically, casualties among both parties as a result of the coming battle could also cause a mission failure, but NSLICE-00P couldn't resolve that risk by causing casualties on her own. The Empire and the Dobhar were going to war with or without her. She had no protocols relating to achieving diplomatic resolutions, after all.

And . . . she had already been in contact with Empire-aligned local authorities and searched through nearby Empire-aligned settlements regarding her primary directive. She had largely ruled out the persons of interest being located within the Empire's territory in this region, or any Imperial citizens in the immediate vicinity having key intel for her primary directive. It was much more likely that the Dobhar could be related to her mission than the Empire in Turannia at this point, if only due to the lack of intel on the Dobhar. So, if anything, casualties among the Dobhar presented greater risk than casualties among the Empire.

When she had accounted for every factor she had data on, all simulations of various scenarios indicated that intervening with her current levels of data on the Dobhar had a higher expected threat to her primary directive than that of losing Ateia and Taog. Acquiring more data on the Dobhar and determining the likelihood that they possessed relevant intel for her primary directive could change that . . . but that would involve contacting the Dobhar directly.

Imperial authorities had told her they had little contact with humans, but she could not consider that testimony as valid, given it was stated by a combatant attempting to recruit her at the time. And long-range sensor scans wouldn't tell her if a given Dobhar would recognize one of her persons of interest.

But approaching a force about to engage in battle carried significant risk of misinterpretation . . . if she could reach them before the battle started in the first place. She would need to wait for the situation to calm down, which meant after the battle had concluded. She could attempt to locate Dobhar not involved in the conflict, but that would likely take longer than the battle as well.

The unexpected drop in mission success probability was concerning, but at the moment, she could not identify the factor causing it. She needed to know the specific cause if she was going to include it in her simulations.

She could tell it originated from her organic components, but they were of no help at this time. All she could find from her organic components were unnecessary danger signals and illogical intervention orders. It seemed she would need to reimplement her emotional controls before she could receive any useful reports from her organic half.

And so, NSLICE-00P stood in place at her calculated minimum safe distance, struggling to reimplement her emotional controls and determine why her mission success probability had dropped like it did . . .

Ateia and Taog shuffled through the streets, completely silent. Ateia was marching ahead, trying to hide her face from Taog. Taog let her gain some distance from him while he scowled down at the scroll in his hand.

Seero said she had left to avoid being drawn into the upcoming battle with the Dobhar, stating that as an unaffiliated party, she could not get involved in a third-party conflict. She even recommended Ateia and Taog retreat if possible.

But ultimately, that didn't matter to Taog or Ateia. Retreat wasn't possible; the Dobhar scouts on their tail would be spreading out around the city at this point. There was no chance two young Imperials could make it out of the city alone.

But beyond that . . .

Seero had left them behind. Maybe she had a good reason to; maybe she'd tried to explain why, but that didn't matter to the two of them. His parents. Ateia's father. Seero was just the latest person to have suddenly disappeared on Ateia and Taog. Taog could handle that. He knew from the start that their relationship with Seero was purely transactional, based on a magical contract to boot. Ultimately, they barely knew the girl, or even if she *was* just a human girl, whatever her status said. It was foolish of them to expect her to hang around for a war when she didn't even know what the Empire was. Why would she risk her life for them like that? Taog might have left, too, had the situation been reversed. He hardly cared for the people of Turannia, and he was one of them!

The thing was . . . he knew Ateia wouldn't have. Because for Ateia, Seero was her savior. The person who'd made Ateia's dreams come true at a moment where all seemed lost. And more than that, Taog knew that Ateia thought she had some kind of kinship with the strange and probably very lost girl. She had very much grown attached.

And now, Seero had left, on the eve of an invasion, without even saying goodbye.

Taog couldn't help but let out a growl. Even if Seero had good reason, she had wounded Ateia deeply in doing so, and snatched away their hope at the last moment. That was something Taog couldn't let go.

Eventually, he stumbled into the Legion keep as Ateia wandered off. She clearly needed some space, and there was nothing Taog could do for her right now, so he decided to report in to Miallói. He found her in one of the barracks, making sure the wounded Selkies were as settled and comfortable as they could be. She turned and nodded to him, then raised an eyebrow.

"Ateia? Friend?"

Taog grit his teeth. "She's . . . gone."

Miallói froze, and Taog caught her eyes widening slightly.

So even Miallói had put her hopes on Seero, even though she didn't know her save as the benefactor who'd helped Ateia and Taog with the dungeon. Taog slumped his shoulders and sighed. Just another person's hope, snatched away. And if the deadly and serious Miallói was hoping for Seero in this fight . . .

Well, that told Taog *exactly* how much hope remained.

The next day, Miallói let the pair into the war room of the keep. Ateia had seemingly returned to normal, but she was silent, her eyes unfocused. Taog left her alone, as he knew nothing he could say would help her. Dux Canus, Magister Tiberius, and Rector Aemilia were there, along with all the legates of the limitanei legions and what few Exploratores remained. They were standing around a table with a map of Castra Turannia spread on top of it.

Dux Canus turned his head. He nodded at Miallói, and then leaned in toward Magister Tiberius, who just heaved a sigh and whispered, "Dungeon Conqueror, with a core in hand. No, I have no idea how. Miallói stopped by and agreed to train them for Aesdes knows why."

Dux Canus raised an eyebrow. "Well, the last part is obvious. She's desperate."

Magister Tiberius heaved another sigh. "As are we."

Rector Aemilia looked at Miallói and nodded.

"Good, everyone is here then?"

Magister Tiberius shook his head. "We're still waiting on the Selkies. They should be sending us a warband or two . . . if we're lucky."

He turned to Miallói, but she shook her head, confirming his prediction. And then . . . everyone in the room heard a sound. A horn was blowing in the distance.

Legate Opiter jumped and trembled. "I-Is that . . . ?"

But Dux Canus just placed a hand on the legate's shoulder and smiled. "Steady, man. That is no Dobhar horn."

Everyone made their way to the windows. And every one of them froze at the sight below. Everyone's eyes widened, even Dux Canus's.

And especially Miallói's.

Down below them, in the streets below the city, a column of warriors marched toward the keep. They wore armor of bone and leather, with the occasional addition of Empire-forged metal. They wore furs and cloaks made of the hides of marine mammals over their armor. They carried barbed spears made of bone and solid bows, with the occasional addition of Imperial blades. They had slightly pointed ears, webbed hands, and beautiful faces that attracted all who saw them.

The Selkies had arrived.

The Selkies were a client people of the Empire required to provide troops according to the treaties they had signed. But these troops were provided in the form of auxiliaries who were integrated into the Legion. The Selkies had already made their contribution for the year, and the Legion had already sent those recruits elsewhere, to reinforce other parts of the Empire with greater need and value.

It *was* assumed that the Selkies would contribute to the defense of their home province, with good reason. But there was no official obligation for them to do so, so it was up to the Selkies how much they wished to send for any given situation. Normally, they would send a warband or two at most, a group of young warriors who needed experience in large-scale combat, and a handful of veterans to advise the Legion on local conditions. Anything more would require negotiation and, likely, concessions.

In *this* situation, when the full might of the Dobhar was on the way and the Empire had effectively abandoned the province (and the Selkies) to its fate? Magister Tiberius had expected the Selkies would send a token contribution, just for the record, and then preserve the greater part of their strength to defend themselves.

So he had expected they would send a hunting party or two, maybe a warband of a hundred warriors or so at most. They might even count Miallói and the group with her as their entire obligation and send nothing more at all.

But that was not what they did.

Five *thousand* Selkies had arrived, armed to the teeth with all the most powerful weapons and armor their race had available. The most experienced and deadly warriors from every tribe in Turannia. The elites who had braved monsters and tribes in Turannia and the North Seas all their lives . . . and *hunted* them down.

And there was an entire legion's worth.

The Selkies were going all out. All to aid an overlord who had abandoned them.

Miallói trembled and rushed out of the room. The Imperial leaders glanced at one another then followed after her. The gates to the keep opened up just as Miallói arrived in the courtyard, the Selkies marching inside. An elderly Selkie man stepped forward as Miallói rushed toward them. She saluted him, and they clasped hands while Miallói whispered to him in the Selkie language. "How is this possible? This is . . ."

The Selkie man frowned and nodded.

"Come, First Hunter Miallói. We have much to discuss. With you . . . and with our Imperial friends."

Just then, Rector Aemilia, Dux Canus, and Magister Tiberius arrived in the courtyard. Dux Canus and Magister Tiberius glanced at one another, and the dux couldn't help but smile.

"We might just have a chance, after all."

The group reconvened in the war room, with the addition of the elderly Selkie. Rector Aemilia put on her best smile and nodded at the man.

"I, Rector Provinciae per Turannia Aemilia Hibera, greet you, Chieftain Déighen. You are most welcome here."

The man nodded in return.

"I, Chieftain Déighen, representative of the Council of Hunters, greet you, Rector Provinciae Aemilia Hibera of the Empire."

Her smile grew. "Thank you, Chieftain, for coming to our aid. I don't know how we could ever repay you."

Chieftain Déighen nodded. "That, Rector, is what I'd like to discuss."

Rector Aemilia's smile dropped ever so slightly.

"I see. It sounds like you have something in mind?"

Chieftain Déighen took a deep breath before speaking. "We would like for the Council of Hunters and all the Selkies they represent to be declared an Amicitia Populi Elteni and granted the right to land within the Empire."

Rector Aemilia froze. Miallói's eyes went as wide as they could go, and then started to quiver. Chieftain Déighen glanced over at her, smiling sadly and then nodding.

"This will be in acknowledgement of the contributions of the Selkies' finest warriors, and their brave stand at Castra Turannia on behalf of the Empire."

Rector Aemilia frowned and nodded. "I see. May I discuss this with my council?"

Chieftain Déighen nodded. "Of course."

As Rector Aemilia took Dux Canus and Magister Tiberius off to the side, Miallói rushed over to the Elder Selkie, whispering in their language.

"Chieftain, what are you doing?!"

Chieftain Déighen frowned and heaved a sigh. "What I must, First Hunter."

Miallói trembled.

"With this many of our warriors . . . if we fall here, we will not be able to protect our people, our land!"

Chieftain Déighen shook his head.

"We already cannot, Miallói. The Empire is no longer interested in defending us here, and we lack the strength to do so ourselves. We must adapt if we are to survive. We will hold the line right here and now . . . or we will open a new path for ourselves if we cannot."

Miallói gritted her teeth.

"So, we're abandoning our land?"

Chieftain Déighen shook his head once more. "We are a people, not a place, First Hunter. And if they agree to this, we can remain a people, preserve our independence and our way of life. If we win, we will gain our freedom. If we lose, we will remain a people and find a new home. But either way, we must find a way to endure, no matter what we must do."

Miallói trembled as she looked down. The chieftain smiled sadly and gently placed a hand on her shoulder.

"I and the council must ask much of you, First Hunter. Fight, win if you can, and earn our people's future in either victory or defeat. And if you cannot win, return to us with as many of our warriors as you can."

Meanwhile, in another corner of the room, Ateia and Taog were watching with wide eyes. More Selkies had arrived than the two had ever seen in their entire lives, and suddenly, the Imperial commanders were smiling and moving with a stride in their step.

Obviously, something had changed. A small spark of hope reignited in Taog's chest. Maybe, just maybe, they might survive this, after all. If the rector and the Selkie chieftain could come to an agreement, that is.

Taog tilted his head, trying to understand their conversation. He looked around and found a Legion officer standing next to them, attempting to blend into the wall, it seemed. Taog normally wasn't one to approach a stranger, but Ateia was still out of it and, well, he really wanted to know if there was a chance they were going to survive. So he addressed the man standing next to them.

"Hey, do you know what an Amicitia Populi Elteni is?"

Legate Opiter jumped.

"W-Who, me?! I-I don't know anything, ask—" Then he looked to his side and saw Taog. He took a deep breath and shook his head. "Oh, yes, a friend of the Elteni people. Someone the Empire has officially declared its friend."

Taog nodded. "Ah, yeah, I got that. But do you know what that actually means? Why would the Selkies ask for it . . . and die for it?"

Legate Opiter nodded. He did what he did best and recited what he knew from Legion policy. "It's something of an informal alliance with the Empire; someone who doesn't have any treaties or obligations with the Empire but who the Empire acknowledges as a friend worthy of respect. According to policy, the Legion's supposed to treat them as honored guests, and offer any reasonable assistance they request."

Taog rubbed his chin. "I see. Do you know why the Selkies would want that? Aren't they already allied with the Empire?"

Legate Opiter nodded.

"Well, they are already a client people of the Empire. But being declared an Amicitia Populi Elteni would elevate them into something more like an equal partner. If I understand correctly, for a client people like that, it would grant them official independence from the Empire while maintaining the benefits of an alliance, allowing them to retain access to Imperial resources and assistance. Especially if they need to apply for asylum. Otherwise, they might be broken up and integrated as the Empire sees fit."

Taog nodded along as Legate Opiter spoke. Suddenly, his eyes widened, and something clicked into place in his head.

A title that would grant someone the benefits of an alliance with the Empire, but without any official obligations or affiliations . . . That would cause the Empire to treat said individual or group as honored guests . . . and offer them *any* (reasonable) assistance they might request . . . Including access to Imperial resources and assistance. All, again, without any official obligations on the Empire's behalf.

Taog knew someone who might appreciate such an arrangement. And someone who could *definitely* help with their predicament.

So . . . if the Selkies could receive such a thing for their help, then . . .

Taog glanced at Ateia. Her eyes were still unfocused. Even the Selkies were not enough to return hope to her.

His heart burned. Part of him wanted nothing more to do with any of this, but he had long since trained himself to put aside his feelings. He knew that right now, he needed to do anything necessary to ensure Ateia survived the next day or two. And beyond that . . . she didn't deserve to be abandoned without a word.

So Taog rushed forward to where the Imperial leaders were speaking.

"Magister Tiberius! Exploratore cadet Taog, with something important to ask!"

The Magister Exploratore looked up from his conversation.

"Oh, Taog Sutharlan, was it? I trust you have a good reason to interrupt right now?"

Taog nodded.

"The Amicitia Populi Elteni, can the rector give that title to anyone? Like, to a wandering knight?"

Magister Tiberius raised an eyebrow.

"What are you talking about, cadet—" Suddenly his eyes widened. "Wait, by wandering knight, do you mean NSLICE-00P by any chance?! YOU'RE the ones she was waiting for?!"

Taog's eyes widened, but he nodded. "Yes, could we offer that title to her? She'd gain access to Imperial aid and resources without officially joining the Empire, right? Something that would help her a lot with her main mission? Maybe she might agree to help us for that?"

Magister Tiberius's eyes widened. He spun around as quickly as he could, facing Rector Aemilia.

"Rector, are there any restrictions that we should be aware of regarding Amicitia Populi Elteni? Could you potentially offer this to a second person as well, a wandering foreign knight, specifically?"

Rector Aemilia tilted her head.

"Well, I can't just offer it to anyone, and there will be big questions if I do it two times at once, but yes, hypothetically, I have full authority to do so at my discretion. It might be overturned later if it's deemed to be undeserved, however, so they would need to have done something worth the title. Especially if it's coming from me. I'm not exactly popular in the Northern Court."

Magister Tiberius practically grabbed the rector and Dux Canus before dragging them to a nearby room.

About half an hour later, they exited. Dux Canus's eyes were as wide as they could go, the first time in a century the man had displayed shock in front of his troops. Rector Aemilia was trembling and muttering to herself with a grin on her face. The Selkies tilted their heads, wondering what could cause such a disturbance. Until Miallói glanced at Taog, and a small smile appeared on her face.

A message was quickly drafted and sent out to every Imperial communication artifact in the province, to be delivered immediately should they encounter a certain wandering knight. Soon after, Rector Aemilia and Chieftain Déighen came to an agreement, and the Selkies officially committed to the defense of Castra Turannia.

And so, the Imperials in Turannia found just a bit of hope.

The King of the Dobhar

"The most common question I get on Turannia and its people is, "Where's that?" Well, Turannia IS one of the newer additions to the Empire, and only has a small amount of trade, so it is understandable that it's not the most recognizable province to the average Imperial citizen.

The second most common question I get is why are Turannia's people so brutal and savage? The Wulver, the Dobhar, even the Selkies had their moments before falling under the Empire's protection. These people seem to reject civilization and peaceful discourse, living lives of continuous and unrestrained violence. They even glorify this violence, seeing it as superior to all other pursuits. Why, there are some who even claim they are slightly smart monsters, rather than Enlightened peoples!

But when you compare these people to the historical records of many others, the answer is surprising—they're not. Or rather, they are not especially brutal or savage, given the state of their societies and the conditions under which they operate. It is only by modern Imperial standards that they seem particularly bloody.

What the average citizen of the Empire forgets is that the peace they operate under is a historical anomaly. The average citizen of the Empire can go out to farm, raise a family, even travel across the Empire if they wish, and have a reasonable expectation that they will not face danger unless they seek it out themselves. Yes, I know there are still bandits in the hills, and wandering monsters can strike anywhere. But in the Empire, these events are the exceptions rather than the rule. It is even possible for an Imperial citizen to live their entire life without ever encountering a major threat to their person.

This, again, is not a natural state of affairs. This is something that has been hard-fought for and is now diligently maintained by the Legion. So, for the tribes outside of the Empire?

They still live in the Age of Heroes . . . or the Age of Blood, as some scholars like to call it. They still live in an age where a wandering monster might destroy their entire civilization. They still live near unconstrained dungeons that will send out raiding parties if not regularly fed sacrifices. They must fight to survive not just once in a blue moon, but each and every day.

Their entire civilization is dependent on having strong champions who can handle these threats. And their societies must regularly produce such champions if they are to endure. So, it is not surprising that they hold martial strength as their highest value and bestow authority and resources upon those who achieve it. And it is not surprising that they would consider war with their neighbors to be a beneficial endeavor.

This does start to change after contact with the Empire, but it is a slower process than most Imperial citizens like to imagine. When someone has lived their entire life under siege, they are loath to hand over their weapons to anyone else."

—*Turannia and the North*, volume 5 of *The Peoples of the Frontiers*, by traveling author and former Exploratore Placus Paesentius Statius.

The Empire and the Selkies organized their defenses, preparing to hold the line. Rector Aemilia had agreed to the Selkies' terms, and Chieftain Déighen had returned to his people with the signed documents in hand. The elite Selkie warriors had thus joined the defense under Miallói's command, while the remaining Selkies gathered by the coast, ready to flee should Castra Turannia fall.

And so, Dux Canus got to work, redrawing the battle plans from scratch. The Selkies provided him with much more than just numbers; they completely changed the fundamental situation. He now had a legion's worth of elite warriors, hardened veterans who could match the comitatenses in nerve and skill. They represented an actual fighting force capable of aggressive maneuvers in the face of the enemy. A hammer to pair with the anvil of the limitanei.

That was something Dux Canus could do some serious work with.

With that force in the mix, Dux Canus could draw up actual battle plans. He could now utilize aggressive assaults and maneuvers, counterattacks and flanking motions, feints and decoys; all the tactics that the limitanei lacked the mobility and discipline to pull off. He was no longer working with purely static forces, and so he put all his many years of experience to work.

The battle was still not in their favor, but now it would be a battle.

And as the limitanei and the Selkies discussed and rehearsed, the Dobhar made their approach . . .

It was a day just like any other, raining as usual. At least, until the soldiers within Castra Turannia heard horns in the distance, cutting through the sound of the rain.

Then the lookouts began to shout. Beacons were lit, flags were raised, bells were rung throughout the town. Rector Aemilia gathered the civilians and made

for the evacuation caverns under the Legion keep while Dux Canus, Magister
Tiberius, and Miallói moved to the war room. Legate Opiter was shouting and
pointing, arranging the distribution of ammunition and supplies. Limitanei
rushed through the halls, grabbing their spears and putting on their armor. Selkie
warriors painted their faces with traditional dyes and conducted prebattle ritu-
als. The remaining provincial mages double-checked the magic circles engraved
throughout the keep as Legion engineers readied the siege weapons.

Soon, they were ready.

Magister Tiberius and Miallói arranged their troops and sallied forth, spreading throughout the empty city beyond the keep. The limitanei and a handful of
the Selkies marched up the outer walls, forming a line of shields and spear tips
pointed to the sky.

And then, they heard it. And they felt it.

The ground rumbled under thousands of feet. The farmland ahead was covered in a tide of black. Thousands upon thousands of Dobhar marched toward
Castra Turannia, blowing horns of bone and carrying the banners of their war-
lords. The Otterkin wore little armor save the occasional breastplate of bone,
mostly relying on their famously tough fur. They carried harpoons made of bone,
along with salvaged Legion gear they had taken from the abandoned forts and
outposts along the way. They marched in groups of ten and a hundred and a
thousand . . . in a manner most familiar to the Legion veterans present. King
Uscfrea Spellbreaker was not ashamed to borrow from a mighty foe, after all.

The limitanei fidgeted and gulped as they watched the army approach. The
Selkies narrowed their eyes, eager to face their ancestral enemies once again.
And then the horde came to a halt, right outside the range of the Legion's siege
weapons, just close enough for the limitanei to make out the individual Dobhar.

Three Dobhar separated from the army and continued marching forward,
carrying with them an ornate banner. It was an old Imperial banner, with a
mage's staff and a legionnaire shield in bright blue over a red field, only with a
mighty axe painted over it in black. King Uscfrea's favorite trophy, taken from
the Legio Arcanum IX when the Dobhar had earned his title. One of them took
a deep breath and let out a mana-infused shout toward the walls.

"Imperials, Selkies, we greet you. Today, you face the host of King Uscfrea
Spellbreaker, King of all the Dobhar, Ruler of the Drekkjaland, Master of the
Home Fleet, Breaker of Legions. Send your finest warrior, that the king may
trade words with as close to an equal as you got!"

Magister Tiberius heaved a sigh and turned to Miallói.

"Well, he must mean you. I'm not sure what his play is. King Uscfrea isn't
exactly known for diplomacy."

Miallói shrugged. "More time, good for us."

Magister Tiberius raised an eyebrow.

"You sure? Could be a trap."

Miallói shook her head and pointed toward King Uscfrea's banner. "Wouldn't bother."

Magister Tiberius could only nod his head at that. If King Uscfrea felt compelled to take such measures against a single warrior, then he probably wouldn't have invaded in the first place.

And so, Miallói made her way down the walls. The gates opened up, and she walked out, accompanied by a Selkie warrior and an Imperial centurion. As she crossed the field, the Dobhar parted ranks.

An exceptionally large Dobhar made his way between them. Standing seven foot tall, even taller than a human, he towered high over his fellow kin. He wore no armor or robes, displaying instead his prized fur which had carried him through the jaws of monsters, the harpoons of the Selkies, and the spells of the Legio Arcanum alike. He wore instead a red cloak with his symbol painted across it, the fabric taken from an Imperial officer, and a crown made from the black bones of a sea serpent. On his shoulders rested a mighty black-colored war-axe, forged from that same sea serpent, which seemed to draw in all the light around it.

This was King Uscfrea Spellbreaker. The legendary Dobhar warrior and king who had terrorized the northern seas for centuries. The man who'd humiliated the Empire's finest battlemages. The reason the Dobhar had never submitted to the Empire. The one who'd slain the former First Hunter of the Selkies, and so left them vulnerable to the Empire in turn.

He freely strode across the field, past his own envoys, right into range of the Empire's weapons. He grinned at the Imperial soldiers along the walls, daring them to strike at him. They gulped and groaned but did not rise to the bait. He shrugged his shoulders and continued his march until he stood just in front of Miallói. The Selkie huntress seemed more like a child in front of the hulking beast ahead of her.

King Uscfrea Spellbreaker opened his mouth and spoke.

"Greetings to you, First Hunter of the Selkies Miallói. I am King Uscfrea Spellbreaker of the Dobhar . . . in case you didn't realize."

Miallói raised an eyebrow. He spoke to her not in Dobhar nor in Imperial but in the language of the Selkies. He spoke fluently and without accent, in a way that would have taken a Dobhar great study and practice to achieve.

"I am Miallói, First Hunter of the Selkies and Exploratore of the Empire. What do we have to discuss, King Uscfrea? We will not surrender, and you will not retreat."

King Uscfrea grinned.

"No, we will not. I would not permit them to surrender even if they wished to. I will take this fort and these lands. I will take everything that belongs to the

Empire here and make it mine or see it razed to the ground. The Empire owes the Dobhar a debt of blood, and I intend to collect."

Miallói narrowed her eyes.

"Then, again, why are we talking?"

King Uscfrea pointed toward her. "I am not talking with the Empire or an Imperial lapdog. I am talking with Miallói, fierce warrior and First Hunter of the Selkies, the bane of the dread orcas."

Miallói frowned. "You mean . . ."

King Uscfrea grinned and nodded.

"Join me, and together, we will destroy the Empire! Well, in Turannia, at least, for now."

Miallói heaved a sigh. "You must be mad."

King Uscfrea shook his head.

"Come now, First Hunter. Admit it; the Empire is dying. The signs are everywhere. Surely, you must have noticed, as I have?" King Uscfrea placed his axe in the ground, crossing his arms. He frowned. "I'll admit something, too. Once upon a time, I was terrified of the Empire. My people call me *Spellbreaker* and *Destroyer of Legions*, but in reality, my accomplishments do not match my titles. We thought we'd won a mighty victory against the full might of the humans, sending them fleeing on their way. But then, the next Legion came. And the next. And the next. And then . . . I learned the terrible truth."

King Uscfrea clenched his fists.

"Back then, I did not defeat the Empire because I was strong. I defeated the Empire because I was *irrelevant*. They didn't care about the Dobhar at all. They didn't even know we were there. They were just on their way to invade somewhere else. What we thought were mighty battles, the Empire considered minor skirmishes. What we considered a grand victory, the Empire considered a minor inconvenience. We were not sending a mighty fleet fleeing at the end of epic battles. We were harassing a small group in transit, barely forcing it to take a small detour. And they kept going and conquered whoever it was they actually intended to fight. No one would even know my name if some famous mage hadn't been on that ship we attacked."

King Uscfrea shook his head.

"So the ships sailing through our kelp groves? The burning of our nursery ships? The massacre of Dobhar pups? The Empire wasn't even *trying* to destroy my people. They just wanted to clear their route through the sea. When I learned the truth, I despaired. I pulled my people from the Empire's path. For decades, I trembled and hid, awaiting the terrible retribution to come when the mighty Empire finally turned its gaze to us."

Miallói gritted her teeth and gripped her spear hard.

"So what? The Empire crushed my people under heel because you slayed my grandmother, the First Hunter, and left us defenseless before their assault. You massacred the Green Harbor tribe with your own hand, including their children. There are debts of blood between everyone in Turannia, King Uscfrea. The Dobhar and the Selkies and the Wulver have all done worse to each other for centuries, long before the Empire ever arrived. What is your point?"

King Uscfrea grinned.

"Oh, I'm not complaining about what they did, First Hunter. I'm telling you this so you understand why I am here now."

He stood to his feet and pointed behind him, waving his hand across the Dobhar horde assembled.

"Once upon a time, the Empire nearly destroyed my people by *accident*, such was their might. But now? Now I march right into their own lands with an army of my own . . . and they do nothing. The Empire is not the power it once was. It is no longer mighty. The question is no longer, 'Will the Empire destroy us.' The question is not even, 'Will the Empire survive.' The question now is who gets the inheritance. And the Imperials? They don't understand a thing; they spend more time fighting each other than fighting us these days. But soon, it will become apparent to everyone."

King Uscfrea narrowed his eyes.

"Dark times are coming, First Hunter. The Empire will fall, and there will be a mad scramble to consume its corpse. No one will be left to restrain the demon lords or the monsters. The strong will do what they can, and the weak will endure what they must."

Miallói frowned . . . but remained silent. She could not refute the Dobhar's words.

King Uscfrea continued.

"And that, First Hunter, is why we are talking." He held out his hand. "Join me, you *and* your people. We will take what made the Empire strong and use it to build a new kingdom in the Land of Rain, but for *our* people. We will conquer the Wulver and bring them into the fold as well. We will force the Imperials to divulge their secrets. And so, when the dark times come . . . we will be ready."

Miallói crossed her arms.

"Under your rule?"

King Uscfrea grinned at her.

"Under the rule of the strongest, as it has always been for our three peoples, before the Empire interfered. Today, that is me. Who can say who it will be tomorrow?"

Miallói shook her head. "You cannot be trusted. Once the Empire is gone, your people will turn on mine, and we will be helpless before you."

King Uscfrea's smile dropped. He placed his hand over his heart. "I, King Uscfrea Spellbreaker, hereby swear on the name of my mother, Ymma, that the Selkies shall come to no harm should they side with me today. I will consider all debts of the past settled, and treat them as my own people. I will do my utmost to ensure the Dobhar do so as well. I will arbitrate all future disputes as if between my own people, and see that justice is done for all. This I swear."

Miallói gasped. To swear on their mother was the strongest oath a Dobhar could make. King Uscfrea was absolutely serious. And if the legendary king of the Dobhar had sworn so, he would ensure it was done. The Dobhar would not defy his will, not even for their ancestral hatred of the Selkies.

He genuinely did not wish to destroy her people. Miallói frowned.

"And what will you do . . . if we refuse?"

King Uscfrea shrugged and smirked at her as he hefted his axe back onto his shoulder.

"I already told you. Then the strong do what they can . . . and the weak endure what they must."

Miallói gritted her teeth. She now needed to make a choice. A new route for the Selkies had opened up, but one that would close the doors to the Empire forever.

King Uscfrea nodded and turned.

"Well, I'm sure you'll have to think about it. I've always thought actions speak louder than words, anyway, so if you agree, you know what to do."

With that, King Uscfrea returned to his people, leaving Miallói, the frowning Selkie by her side, and the confused and clueless centurion alone. Miallói clenched her hand around her spear.

Fight a hopeless battle for the conqueror who had abandoned them, all in hopes that they would be welcomed as honored friends instead of desperate refugees? Or betray their only ally and join forces with their hated enemy, all in hopes that they would be treated with respect instead of murdered and enslaved? An impossible choice . . . with the fate of her people riding on her answer.

Miallói turned and walked back toward the city without another word.

9

The Battle Begins

"Defeating the Legion in the field is easy. Anyone with half a brain can do that. Half the Imperial commanders have no clue how to even use their troops, and will defeat themselves as long as you don't screw up.
Removing the Empire from all the forts and castles they'll build once they're there? That's something else entirely."

—Zaerzis Evruth, High Archon of the Empire of the Sun, on the viability of a counterattack after she wiped out an Elteni incursion.

Miallói frowned as she returned to her position. Magister Tiberius raised an eyebrow.

"So? What did he say?"

She shrugged. "Surrender."

Magister Tiberius nodded.

"And you said?"

"No."

He shook his head. "What did he expect? It's unlike him to waste time like that."

Miallói nodded in response. But her frown deepened as Magister Tiberius turned back to the Dobhar.

She glanced around at the Imperials. Some had real Imperial armor and weapons, the signs of her oppressors. The ones slowly bleeding her people, drawing them away from their home, eroding their way of life. The very weapons who had struck down the Selkies long ago.

And now, the most stalwart allies the Selkies had ever had. She saw Ateia and Taog, the warriors she had trained herself. They had no love for this place and seemed uncomfortable around the other Imperials. Ateia herself was grieved by her friend's sudden departure. And yet . . . here she was, ready to fight, glaring at the Dobhar horde below. Taog barely interacted with anyone besides the girl and was always on guard against everyone, even his allies. And yet, here he was, standing side by side with those same allies, gripping the hilt of his sword.

She glanced around at the others.

These had nothing but thick clothing and homemade shields and spears. They were farmers, peasants, craftsmen. Normal people just trying to live their lives.

The colonizers encroaching on her people's land.

And the ones they spoke with each and every day. The ones who lent a hand when the storms battered the villages. The ones who tried to learn the Selkie language and who treated her people as friends.

The ones who loved this land like she did, and who would die to defend it. But the ones who *would* die. The weak ones who could not possibly win this battle alone.

What was the right choice? What would preserve her people and their way of life? What should Miallói do?

Just then, she felt a hand on her shoulder. She looked around. Magister Tiberius was looking right at her, concern on his face.

"Everything all right, Miallói?"

She shook her head. "Fine."

He heaved a sigh and lowered his hand. He whispered to her, in a voice he knew only her ears could catch, "Looks like this might be the end, huh?"

Miallói silently nodded. Magister Tiberius took a deep breath, reaching into his pocket and pulling out a scroll . . . along with a signet ring. He whispered, "Transfer," and a small jewel on the ring flashed once. He placed them both in Miallói's hands.

She tilted her head.

". . . What?"

Magister Tiberius heaved a sigh. "Look . . . I know what our plan is, and I know the rector already tried to help your people. But I'm not sure the Empire will care about her deals if Turannia itself falls; she's not exactly the most influential figure. So, if and when we're about to lose . . . Get out of here, Miallói. Take as many of your people as you can. The Empire left us here, but you don't deserve to die with us. I'm appointing you the new Magister Exploratore per Turannia in the case I don't survive. It won't matter to most of the Empire, but it might get you a door into the rest of the Exploratores as more than just another scout. And that's a letter of introduction from Dux Canus to some of his old friends. Hopefully, it'll help you and your people." He then glanced over at Ateia and Taog. "And . . . if you could do me a final favor . . . Take the two kids with you. They're . . . Well, the children of a friend. I'd much prefer it if they survived this."

Miallói's eyes widened.

"What are you . . . ?"

Former Magister Tiberius smiled sadly at her.

"Dux Canus and I already spoke about this. I know it wasn't for us, but you've done a lot for us both. We wanted to do what we could for you. Just to let you know . . . it was an honor to fight by your side."

He turned his attention back to the Dobhar, and said no more.

Miallói stared at him for a few moments longer. She put the scroll and the ring into a pouch, then clenched her fists. She'd made her choice. She didn't care for the Empire who had abandoned her, but she did care for the Imperials who stood beside her. She would not betray them into the hands of her enemies, not even for King Uscfrea's promise. Warriors like these deserved to stand with their friends . . . to the end.

She whispered back, "As it is to stand by yours."

King Uscfrea heaved a sigh as his people spread out around the city and set up camp. He had drilled them as hard as he could, but they were still inferior to even Imperial farmers at the task. It turned out, a race who spent their entire lives at sea was not particularly good at digging in the dirt.

Well, he could drill them all he liked, but it didn't matter if the Dobhar didn't understand the point of the exercises. Most of his warriors, bless their hearts, had little in their heads besides their next meal or level. They did not understand why their legendary king feared these weak human farmers . . . or why he wanted to emulate them.

Well, to be fair, that also applied to King Uscfrea himself. He had tried to copy the form of the Legion, but he couldn't claim to understand it. He didn't truly know *why* the Empire did all the things they did or what they were trying to achieve. So, he couldn't truly teach his people their ways. But he wasn't planning on a long siege anyways, so it wouldn't matter much. And the Dobhar were starting to learn.

On the surface, the night air quickly grew cold, and the wind was biting. Even the rain, the water his people longed for, betrayed them on the surface. In the sea, the water insulated and maintained a solid temperature. It sheltered and protected them. On land, the water sapped the very heat from their bodies as it dried up in the surface air, contributing further to the cold. His warriors grew more enthusiastic about the idea of setting camp with each passing day.

But not tonight, for the Dobhar would strike at sunset, when the humans' sight would be as poor as their own.

King Uscfrea let out a groan. A direct assault on the very first day would not have been his first choice, but the situation was not as favorable to the Dobhar as it may have appeared. The Dobhar were incredibly tough and ferocious.

They could tank blows from Legion steel and tear the throat out of an Imperial legionnaire with ease. Those very legionnaires weren't even here, and the Dobhar outnumbered the peasant militias who were several times over.

But that did not account for the walls of Castra Turannia.

The Dobhar were simply not very good at siege warfare. Or rather, they had hardly conducted a siege in their entire existence as a race. Why would they? A race who spent almost their entire lives on the surface of the ocean had little need to construct walls and towers.

The Empire, on the other hand, were the undisputed masters of castles, both breaking into them and defending them. The Legion and the Selkies could escape any encirclement the Dobhar made with ease then wreak terrible havoc with hit-and-run tactics. And there were a handful of Wulver clans hounding his army as well that the Dobhar could do little to stop. The Dobhar weren't exactly slow on land, but they weren't used to moving around on it either. They would not catch a force of either Selkies or Wulver if the other side didn't want to be caught.

And worse was the logistical situation, which was to say, the Dobhar's logistics were practically nonexistent. His people were a race of ocean-dwelling hunter-gatherers. They did not amass the same scale of stockpiles the Imperial farmers did, and had no experience transporting large quantities of food across land. They could forage and loot from the countryside, but again, the Dobhar were out of their element in this place and would not be particularly effective at the task. Especially not with humans and Selkies and Wulver ambushing their foraging parties at every opportunity. His army would likely run out of food before Castra Turannia did.

And finally . . . the Empire may be dying, but it wasn't at all dead. And a dying beast could be more dangerous than a healthy one, with vicious and unpredictable death throes. So, if the Dobhar took Turannia immediately, conquered its fortifications, and drove the Empire out of the land while the province was undefended, the Empire would probably shrug and write it off as no big loss. But if the Empire finished up whatever business had drawn the legions away and Castra Turannia was still under siege? The Legion would return and pay the Dobhar back with interest.

So, in more ways than one, the Dobhar were on the clock. Waiting around would only serve their enemies. Attacking as soon as possible was the best choice.

But still, King Uscfrea grimaced. A great many Dobhar would die this day, not least of all due to the Selkies. King Uscfrea knew there was little love between their peoples, but still, he'd assumed they were chafing under the Empire's yolk, so he'd thought they might leap at the chance to rid themselves of the invaders. At the very least, he had not expected them to commit to an ally who had effectively abandoned them.

But Miallói had not seemed very enthusiastic about the idea. He may have misjudged what the Selkies thought of their overlords. Or . . . he'd underestimated just how much hate remained between their peoples. Their shared history had been one of almost exclusively blood. It was possible, maybe even probable, that the Selkies still considered him worse than the Empire.

He shook his head. Such thoughts were pointless now. He had done all he could to convince the Selkies; their fate was in their own hands. What he needed to do now was focus on winning this battle as quickly as he could.

One of his elites, Estrith, walked up to him and bowed her head, striking her tail on the ground once. "My king, all is as you commanded. What are your orders?"

He nodded at her.

"Tell everyone to rest up and pass out extra rations today. We attack tonight, once the sun is down."

She repeated her salute. King Uscfrea heaved a sigh.

"And Estrith . . ."

She looked up. "Yes, my king?"

King Uscfrea looked her in the eye. "Win this battle, and I shall grant you what you seek."

Her eyes went as wide as they could go. She once again bowed her head, striking the ground with a heavy thud. "Yes, my king! I will see it done!"

King Uscfrea shook his head as Estrith ran off, executing his commands with all too much enthusiasm. He was fond of Estrith; she was a loyal and brave warrior unlike any other. But he did not like the way his people did things. The men would sire pups and then just leave them to their mothers, spending all their time hunting across the sea. He personally didn't know who his father was to this day.

There was a reason the Dobhar swore by their mothers.

But it was necessary. The champions of his people had to continue fighting, continue growing. They could not defend their people from the terrors of the deep if they did not. So, a father who wasted his time playing with the pups put his whole family, and possibly the entire Dobhar race, at risk. Their people could not afford such indulgences.

But if he won this battle here, if he claimed this land for his own, if he unlocked the secrets of the Empire's strength, then perhaps, that would change.

And once it did? Well, then it might finally be time to sire some pups of his own.

The sun had just set when the Dobhar started to move. They formed into groups like the Legion and marched toward the walls.

But the defenders of the city had noticed.

The limitanei stood across the outer city walls, spears at the ready, a handful of Selkies interspersed among them. The siege engines on top of the Legion keep creaked and slowly turned, taking aim outside the walls.

And, of course, it was raining this night as well.

The king of the Dobhar raised his hand, and the Dobhar horde stopped as one. Taking his axe, he slammed the handle into the ground, then started striking the ground with the handle, over and over.

All across his army, the Dobhar responded in kind. Those with weapons struck them on the ground. Those without slammed the ground with their tails. All in rhythm, all in line with the beat King Uscfrea had set. He glanced around, trying to spot Miallói, but he couldn't distinguish individual Selkies at this distance in the dark. He took a quiet breath and stopped the beat.

The whole city fell silent.

King Uscfrea raised his axe into the sky and gave a mighty shout. Estrith roared in response, then all the Dobhar lifted their voices. With that, the Dobhar charged toward the walls.

Up on the walls, Magister Tiberius frowned. He took out the crossbow on his back and prepared a bolt. As he did, he shouted, "Prepare!"

Two rows of limitanei stood at the ready. The first, with shields and spears in hand. The second held crossbows like the magister. All these now drew their crossbows and slotted in bolts as the centurions relayed the magister's command. The Dobhar continued rushing toward the walls, roaring with bestial voices.

"Aim!"

Magister Tiberius took aim over the shoulders of the soldiers in front of him. The rest of the limitanei followed suit. He activated his Eagle Eye skill, focusing on the Dobhar approaching, waiting until he could see the glint of the moon in their eyes.

"Release!"

And with that, a hail of crossbow bolts flew from the city walls and found purchase. The Dobhar in the front row began dropping to the ground, while the rest roared in anger and continued forward.

And so, the Battle of Castra Turannia began.

10

The Battle of Castra Turannia

"The Selkies. Many wonder how a people so graceful and fair came from Turannia. The Dobhar and the Wulver are so bestial and savage, so how is it that the beautiful Selkies grew among them? Why is there such a disparity between them?

The answer is that there is not. Make no mistake; the Selkies may have pretty faces, but they are no less savage and cruel than their neighbors. Few remember what it was like when the Empire first came to Turannia. When Selkie warriors would appear out of the rain and gut unsuspecting legionnaires without warning. When a hundred soldiers would vanish without a trace. When countless officers were lured away by pleasant smiles and never seen again.

But it goes beyond that. The Selkies are not merely bloodthirsty humanoids. They are beasts, no less so than the Dobhar or the Wulver. Anyone who thinks the Selkies are some kind of poor human offshoot that the Legion protects from the monsters has never seen a Selkie in the water.

In fact, it took the Legion itself years before they connected the monsters pulling sailors into the deep with the supposedly friendly and beautiful race they encountered on the land. The monsters who hunted the Dobhar with their bare fangs. That sank ships and tore the throats out of sinking Imperials. That pulled fully grown Wulver into lakes and rivers and drowned them.

Make no mistake, the only difference between the Selkies and the other tribes of Turannia is that they happened to live closer to the Empire. If anything, the Selkies are the most dangerous of the three to us.

A Dobhar or a Wulver may hunt you, but a Selkie will make you offer yourself up on a silver platter.

So, the next time you feel good about that Selkie girl winking at you, remember the monstrous beast lurking behind those eyes. Those are not the eyes of a flirtatious woman overcome by your manliness. Those are the eyes of a predator evaluating its prey."

—Legate Sestia Agelasta of the Turannia comitatenses,
attempting to reduce the incidence of Legion officers being
honey-trapped by Selkies.

Bolts continued to fly as the Dobhar approached the walls. The crossbows were something of an Imperial specialty. With enchanted strings that amplified any force applied to them, the weapons could deal greater damage than one might expect, a perfect weapon for Exploratores or limitanei who couldn't invest as many boons into ranged combat. And with the stockpile of enchanted bolts in Castra Turannia, even a shot from a limitanei could pierce a Dobhar's hide.

It was, of course, hard for the limitanei to aim during the rainy night, and most lacked the skills that might make the difference. But with the sheer size of the Dobhar force below, it hardly mattered. It would be harder for the Imperials to miss.

As the Dobhar continued to approach the walls, Magister Tiberius shouted at one of the centurions next to him, who nodded and gave orders to the provincial mage next to himself. The mage held up a staff tipped with a mana core, which began to flash bright green.

Up on the top of the keep, Dux Canus nodded when he saw the flashing green light.

"All weapons, attack at will!"

Limitanei grunted and dropped metal spheres into a catapult. Mana cores built into the machine began to glow, lighting up magic circles engraved on both the catapult and the spheres themselves. A soldier pulled the lever, and the catapult launched, its force enchantments applying extra velocity to the projectile.

The spheres burst into flames the moment they cleared the catapult.

Burning shots soared across the sky, easily clearing the entire city. They crashed into the Dobhar and continued rolling across the ground, flames surging out from the spheres as they struck the ground.

Wind-enchanted ballistae opened fire as well, accelerating bolts across the sky. Once they had traveled a certain distance, the bolts turned and dropped straight into the ground before lightning surged from them, leaving smoking Dobhar on the ground all around.

But the Dobhar kept coming, and soon were within range of the walls themselves, hurling their harpoons up toward the soldiers on top. The limitanei held up their shields, but they did not all stand steady or carry Legion-standard gear, so a handful of the harpoons found purchase. Limitanei cried out as the Dobhar pulled them off the walls and into the waiting hordes.

The Dobhar also began to form magic circles, forming the rain into spheres and spikes and launching them at the legionnaires, but the Selkies interspersed along the walls spun magic circles of their own, and the rain formed into shields wherever Dobhar spells flew; the Selkies had always been better at magic than the Dobhar, so few attacks made it through.

Since both the Dobhar and Selkies were resistant to the Water attribute, the Selkie mages focused on defending the Imperial soldiers, and the Dobhar soon gave up the assault.

Instead, their mages grouped together and formed the water into mighty spirals that climbed up the walls, then the Dobhar jumped into the stream and swam right up to the top. The limitanei held up their shields and angled their spears as they pounced on them, dozens of spears stabbing into one Dobhar, overwhelming their HP and driving into their fur, but another would leap on the limitanei beyond, knocking them off the walls with bone axes and powerful tails.

The Selkie mages turned to offense. They formed huge spheres of water, propelling them at incredible speeds, which crashed into the spiraling water jets and broke them apart. Dobhar cried as they fell from the sky.

And then a glowing harpoon shot from beyond the walls, stabbing straight into a Selkie mage. She let out a cry as she was pulled from the walls.

Estrith and the elite Dobhar made their move, hurling their spears with far greater power and accuracy. The Selkie mages abandoned their assault, and the Dobhar continued to scale the walls.

"Fall back!" Magister Tiberius shouted down the line. The limitanei turned in quick order, quickly rushing down the stairs of the walls. The Selkie mages formed the rain into floating rivers which carried them away. Soon, the Dobhar had control of the walls, and the limitanei were running through the city streets.

But what they didn't know was that the defenders had never intended to hold the outer walls in the first place. Castra Turannia had been originally limited to the Legion keep alone. The city had sprung up around it later on, as Imperial control extended further out and the surrounding area grew relatively safe. As such, the outer walls were not built to Legion standard. They were low, unenchanted, and lacked towers and siege engines. They were there to keep the occasional wandering monster outside the city proper, not to hold back an actual army. Dux Canus had known from the start that the limitanei couldn't hold those walls, and that it would be foolish to make more than a token effort.

So why, then, had the dux assigned defenders there at all?

Magister Tiberius slipped into one of the guardhouses on the side. He placed his hand on a magic circle engraved there and channeled his mana . . . and then the tops of the city walls exploded into flames.

Magister Tiberius may not have had many Exploratores left . . . but he still had a province's worth of Exploratores supplies, so they had spread fire potions across the walls before the battle, just waiting to be ignited. After all, no Explor-atore worth the name gave up an opportunity to lay a trap.

With that, he ran down the city streets.

The Dobhar could not pursue the limitanei until the fires died down. Of course, fire potions didn't last forever, and the Dobhar's Water Magic could put them out as well, so they soon had control of the outer walls, and it wasn't long before the city gates were opened and the rest of them rushed in en masse.

Only to be greeted with another volley of crossbow bolts.

The limitanei barricaded the main street. Crossbowmen stood side by side with spearmen on top of the newly built wooden walls, shooting down the street at the approaching Dobhar, who charged forward and tried to scale the barri-cade, the limitanei warding them off with their spears. The streets and alleys of the city made for tighter defenses than the outer walls.

Estrith nodded to some of the elite Dobhar, who began charging down the street. Crossbow bolts flew toward them, but the lightly enchanted bolts made little impact on the high-level elites.

And then they heard a horn blow.

Elite Selkie archers from the Bear Hunter tribe rose from their hiding places on the rooftops and took aim at the Dobhar charging down the streets. The elite Dobhar were bombarded from all sides by the powerful arrows of Selkie land hunters, which were meant for tackling beasts like the mighty ursanus.

The Dobhar elites cried out and fell to the ground while Selkie horns contin-ued to blow all across the city. Enemies trying to flank through alleyways found themselves surrounded by dense mist. Selkie Mist Warriors ran silently through the fog and rain filled with their own mana, feeling rather than seeing their opponents' locations. Bone spears and Imperial steel cut through the blinded Dobhar, leaving corpses on the ground as the mist receded.

In another place, the Dobhar managed to break through one of the barri-cades, but a group of Selkie mages formed a massive sphere of water just behind it as the limitanei ran past them. A group of unarmed Selkies jumped into the sphere, and then the mages sent it hurtling forward.

The Dobhar broke the barricade, only to be washed away by a tide of water. And in that tide, seals larger than an adult human rushed through the streets, tearing through Dobhar fur with mana-infused fangs. The Selkies of the Stormy Coast tribe surrounded their seal bodies with Water Magic, propelling them-selves into living torpedoes that tore Dobhar to shreds.

In the sea, the Dobhar might have used their agility to evade the bigger Selk-ies. In the narrow streets of the city, the Dobhar had nowhere to escape.

Estrith gritted her teeth.

"Those bloody seals!"

She stepped forward and shouted, and the Dobhar pulled back to the city walls.

The Empire had struck the first blow.

King Uscfrea watched from outside the city walls. He frowned as fire and lightning rained from the sky. It was one thing to know that the Empire had formidable defenses. It was another to watch burning metal boulders crashing through his people. He heaved a sigh and shook his head.

"My king, look out!"

Just then, one of the boulders started to approach. It looked as though it would land near King Uscfrea.

No, it would land right on top of him!

King Uscfrea lifted his axe and swung it down. The flames around the metal sphere died down as they touched the axe, and two halves crashed to either side of him. Standing above their remains, completely unharmed, he turned to the stunned Dobhar around him.

"Go, take a message to Estrith."

All across the city, the Dobhar fell back, with Selkies hounding their flanks. Even now, harpoons shot out from foggy alleys, pulling Dobhar to their deaths, and waves of water filled with monstrous seals continued to flow up and down the streets, hunting down the stragglers.

The Dobhar attempted to counterattack, only for Selkie arrows to rain from the rooftops, driving them back. And of course, the Imperial dogs continued to pepper them with crossbow bolts and artillery. Anytime the Dobhar managed to push the Selkies back, they simply fell to the Imperial walls, where the Dobhar were stopped by wood and spear. Estrith gripped her spear tight.

The Dobhar were mighty . . . but a city on the land was the domain of the Empire and the Selkies. The Dobhar were out of their element, and it showed.

It was then that a messenger ran up to her.

"Message from the king!"

Estrith frowned. She was failing, and their people were suffering. She could only imagine what the king would say . . .

"Stand firm and remember your training."

Estrith's eyes shot open. She nodded. This battle had only begun. The king had not given up on her yet.

She turned and shouted at the troops under her command, arranging them into tens and hundreds and thousands, as the king had forced them to practice. And once they had gotten into position, she sent them forward. The Dobhar marched into the streets once again . . .

* * *

The Selkie archers continued to snipe from the rooftops, the dark and the rain no barrier to their sharp eyes. They picked off the Dobhar one by one, aiming for the biggest and strongest among their foes.

But then, there was a change. They heard rhythmic marching. They turned, and their eyes widened.

A hundred Dobhar marched toward the building, standing in a square. The Selkies began to bombard them, but they had hardly made a dent in the numbers by the time they arrived. A Dobhar shouted, and then a volley of a hundred harpoons bombarded the roof, all at once. Poor eyesight was irrelevant with the sheer number of projectiles filling the air.

The Selkies began to dodge, but some of them were caught. These Dobhar were lower level than them, so the harpoons didn't cut particularly deep, but there were a great many of them, so each Selkie struck was hit more than once.

And each of the harpoons had a rope attached to it.

Ten Dobhar pulled on each rope. Selkies screamed as they were pulled from the roofs while the remaining archers jumped across the rooftops, falling back out of range of the Dobhar block. They continued to pick the Dobhar off, but now, they had to keep their distance.

And so, the Dobhar marched on . . .

Selkie Mist Warriors ran through the side alleys. Another group of Dobhar was moving to flank one of the barricades, so they wrapped themselves in rain and fog once more and ran forward.

And then they slammed to a halt. Something was resisting their mana. The Selkies pulled, but the enemy's mana was greater. The water in the mist and the rain condensed and pulled together into a huge sphere in the air overhead, blocking any additional rain.

The Selkies' eyes widened. A group of Dobhar shamans stood at the end of the alley, chanting with magic circles in front of them, while a group of Dobhar warriors stood in front of them, lobbing their harpoons.

The Selkie Mist Warriors were caught out in the open.

A tidal wave rushed down the street, the seal-form Selkies rushing within. They swooped down toward another force of Dobhar.

But then, a dozen Dobhar began to chant, and a counter wave formed in the street. The Dobhar couldn't match the mystic might of the Selkie mages directly, but they didn't need to. They managed to counteract the flow of the Selkies' wave, slowing it down.

The rest of the Dobhar formed up, swimming side by side in the water. They held their harpoons forward as one, forming a wall of spears. The Selkies continued forward, but they were now moving much slower than before, and each Selkie ran into several Dobhar.

Seals roared as multiple harpoons stabbed into each one. They rushed forward, knocking Dobhar aside and tearing at them with their fangs, but the Dobhar held firm. They formed circles around each Selkie, stabbing at them from all directions.

The limitanei continued to hold the barricades, firing their crossbows as quickly as they could. But with the Selkies on the retreat, no one was restraining the elite Dobhar any longer, who ran down the streets toward each barrier. The limitanei bombarded them with bolts, but there was a limit to what mass-produced weapons could do when not backed by perks and skills.

The bolts bounced off the tough fur of the Dobhar elites, then the Dobhar fell upon them.

Fangs and spears and axes cut through the limitanei. Homemade shields and thick clothes stood no chance against the champions of the deep, spears shattering on the famed Dobhar fur. And with the lines broken, the regular Dobhar streamed through the gaps, eager to tear at the foes peppering them from afar.

Within a few minutes, the limitanei were in full retreat, Dobhar running them down on all fours.

And so, the battle moved deeper into the city . . .

The Selkies and the limitanei rushed back through town with the Dobhar hot on their tails, until eventually, they reached the wealthy part of town where another line of limitanei stood at the ready. Located just before the walls of the keep itself, the wealthy district was home to large structures that had their own defense measures in place, and was close enough that the keep itself could provide cover. As such, a hail of bolts from crossbows and smaller ballistae halted the Dobhar's pursuit, allowing the Selkies and the first lines of limitanei to reach the safety of the new Legion lines.

Estrith pulled the Dobhar back and rearranged them as the king had drilled. She hadn't understood his intentions at first, wondering how dancing about on land could be better than hunting more levels in the deep, but after seeing the Selkies fall, she could only shudder at his foresight. So, she took a moment to reorganize her forces, and then began a new assault on the Legion positions.

Estrith couldn't help but smile. This was the last hurdle before the keep itself, and the Selkies were still nursing their wounds. The coming fight would be hard, and the fight for the keep itself even harder, but momentum was on the Dobhar's side. The enemy had been pushed to the brink in but a few engagements. It might even be possible to end this battle in a single night.

* * *

Up in the keep, Legate Opiter was pacing and chewing on his fingernails. The battle drew closer and closer, and now, the legate could hear the shouts and cries of the soldiers below even from the center of the keep. He kept glancing out the window.

And then . . . Finally.

He saw the flashing blue light. The signal from Magister Tiberius that the Dobhar had fully engaged. He spun around so fast he nearly fell over, and shouted at the provincial mage in the center of the room, "Now!"

The provincial mage nodded and channeled mana into the communication artifact at the center of the room.

Taog watched as a communication artifact lit up just ahead. He and Ateia were standing just behind Miallói, who was standing next to Dux Canus. The dux held a communication artifact in his hand, which had just been activated. Turning toward Taog and all the troops behind him, he gave the command. In front of the group, a squad of limitanei began to form magic circles.

The limitanei were inferior to the comitatenses in practically every area, save one. The one area where the limitanei's farmer-militia lifestyle gave them a distinct advantage in.

Earth Magic.

Earth Magic was highly useful for farmers, for everything from moving inconvenient boulders to plowing the fields to checking the health of the soil. And farmers were always working with the ground, so they tended to develop an affinity for the Earth attribute over time regardless of their initial aptitude. Earth Magic was also extremely useful for their commanders, who could then use the limitanei to set up camps or fortify positions. As such, the yearly limitanei drills all included primers on Earth Magic.

Even if the limitanei couldn't fight that well, an army always had plenty of digging to do.

Which was exactly what Dux Canus had them do.

A huge hole opened up in the ground leading to a brand-new tunnel dug through the sewers of Castra Turannia. A tunnel the Dobhar, with their complete lack of Earth mages, had no means of detecting. Five thousand veteran Selkie warriors, along with every retired comitatenses, limitanei with real combat experience, and Exploratore left in the province, stood around Taog, and they all began to march forward at Dux Canus's command. Soon, they exited the tunnel, walking out into the rain, right *behind* the Dobhar army. And right after the Dobhar had committed the bulk of their forces to assaulting the final barricades, and so could not easily withdraw.

Dux Canus had proposed that the last thing the Dobhar would ever expect was an aggressive assault coming from the rear, with the Empire putting everything on the line to end the battle immediately. And even if it failed, just knowing the Empire could pull off such an assault would give King Uscfrea pause. Dux Canus could then retreat into the countryside with this force, and King Uscfrea would not be able to assault Castra Turannia again until they were dealt with. The dux could run the Dobhar around the province and buy as much time as he wished, a plan only made possible with help of the Selkies.

And as Exploratores trained and approved by Miallói herself, Taog and Ateia found themselves joining the assault.

Dux Canus drew his sword and pointed it forward. "Charge!"

With that, he and Miallói charged out of the tunnel. Taog and Ateia rushed after them, followed by all the strongest warriors the Empire had available. Selkie arrows and harpoons struck right into the back of Dobhar scouts and shamans in the rear. The Dobhar barely had time to register what was happening when Legion bulwarks in full plate armor slammed right into them, knocking them to the ground for Legion slayers to cut down with ease. Dux Canus cast wide-area buffs to the entire group, while Miallói was the tip of the spear, cutting down any Dobhar strong enough to resist.

Taog and Ateia joined the Exploratores and Selkie hunters covering the flanks. Taog pointed ahead, his eyes glowing from reflected light as he put his half-Wulver night vision to use, while Ateia nodded and shot her arrows in the directions Taog pointed, finding purchase on targets she could barely see.

Shortly thereafter, an Imperial mage cast a bright light overhead, illuminating the battlefield. Taog then grabbed his shield and took a position in front of Ateia, knocking a harpoon out of the sky with his sword. The two may have been permitted to join the assault, but they knew better than to get too deep into the Dobhar's lines with their low levels, so Taog made sure to keep them on the edge of the fight. As such, he had an excellent position to watch the battle develop.

And to his surprise . . . they were winning. The Dobhar had been taken entirely by surprise, barely realizing they were under assault by the time Dux Canus's force had reached their objective.

Dux Canus nodded. So far, the assault was going well. King Uscfrea had not expected such a move, and he'd even had a chance to put Ateia and her friend outside of the siege, where they could potentially flee if things went poorly. But that was all the attention the dux could spare them at the present time, for he was about to begin the toughest part of the battle.

He gave the command, and a hail of buffed Selkie arrows and Legion crossbow bolts shot forward, flying straight toward where King Uscfrea Spellbreaker watched the battle unfold. But the projectiles slammed straight into a black battle axe as the king of the Dobhar turned to face his assailants.

"My king!"

The Dobhar near King Uscfrea rushed to defend him, but they were quickly isolated by the joint Selkie-Imperial forces as the majority of the troops spread out in a circle to keep any other Dobhar from interfering, while Dux Canus and Miallói led the strongest elites to confront King Uscfrea himself.

King Uscfrea's eyes widened ever so slightly as he looked over the sheer number of Selkies in the area. He turned to Miallói and spoke to her in her own language, not seeming to know or care that Dux Canus knew a bit of Selkie.

"So, this is your answer?"

Miallói focused on him and frowned.

"Would you trust a warrior who betrays their friends?"

King Uscfrea raised an eyebrow. "Perhaps not, but the Empire abandoned you first."

Miallói glanced at Dux Canus.

"The Empire did . . . but these ones here did not."

Dux Canus's eyes went wide as he listened to the conversation . . . and then he nodded at Miallói. King Uscfrea went silent for a moment before nodding.

"I suppose I can respect that." He then heaved a sigh and hoisted his axe into the air. "Then come, First Hunter of the Selkies! Let us settle the debts of our people here and now!"

He lunged forward . . . only to be met by arrows and bolts. A Selkie archer and a former Imperial sharpshooter launched powerful ranged attacks at the large Dobhar; with Dux Canus's powerful buff magic, even the king of the Dobhar couldn't ignore their assault. A former Legion bulwark charged forward, thrusting a huge metal shield straight into the Dobhar's face, and as he stumbled back, Miallói leapt into the sky, pulling her arm back with a glowing harpoon in hand. She tossed it at King Uscfrea with all her might.

But King Uscfrea slammed his axe into the ground and pushed off, just barely moving out of the way of the harpoon. Killing his momentum by slamming his tail behind him, he lunged forward, swinging his axe. Dux Canus cast yet another buff spell on the Legion bulwark in front, and then axe and shield collided with a loud clang that echoed across the field.

But the bulwark held.

And then a halberd from a Legion slayer thrust forward. King Uscfrea took a step back, but the blade still grazed his shoulder.

It didn't draw blood.

Miallói landed behind the Dobhar and launched her harpoon forward. The spear only damaged King Uscfrea's HP, but a mana chain was left behind. King Uscfrea leapt back and spun around all at once, swinging his axe at Miallói, who leapt high into the air.

As she did, she pulled the mana chain taut, stopping herself midair. Dux Canus formed the rain into a glob of water which he sent streaming toward

Miallói. Once the water reached her, it turned down toward King Uscfrea, and Miallói pulled herself with the chain.

And then her body started to glow and expand . . .

Miallói let out a ferocious roar as she transformed into her seal form, an eight-foot seal with glowing fangs. She rocketed down toward King Uscfrea, further propelled by the Water Magic around her. King Uscfrea pulled back his axe, but another volley from the ranged combatants forced him to block, and then a tackle from the Legion bulwark left him off-balance.

Miallói struck him, sinking her fangs into the Dobhar's shoulder. Blood dripped as she just managed to pierce his famed fur. And King Uscfrea . . . grinned at her.

"All that for a drop of blood."

He slammed his fist into Miallói, sending her flying back. She rolled across the ground for a while until she crashed into one of the surrounding Selkies.

King Uscfrea lobbed his axe toward the Selkie archer and Imperial sharpshooter, forcing them to drop their assault and dodge as he ran across the field toward the pair. The Legion bulwark moved to intercept him, but he grinned again and pulled the mana chain that formed in his hand.

The chain led to his axe, which now flew backward toward him. Dux Canus quickly used Earth Magic to lift the bulwark's left foot, just barely tilting him out of the way of the axe. The king grabbed the weapon and immediately swung it, leaving the bulwark with no time to reset his position.

His shield blocked the blow and absorbed most of the force, but with his foot still in the air, the bulwark couldn't hold his ground and was knocked back. King Uscfrea then stepped forward and reached past the man's shield, grabbing him by the arm. He spun and flung the bulwark out of his way.

He swung his axe to knock another arrow and bolt out of the way, then leapt toward the ranged fighters. A Fireball filled his vision, but he pressed on. King Uscfrea charged his axe with mana and swung it down, causing the Fireball to dissipate.

Only for Dux Canus to appear in his view with his sword pulled back in a slash.

The Dobhar blocked the strike with his arm, his tough fur tanking the blow as Dux Canus stepped back, allowing the Legion slayer a full strike from above with her halberd. The Dobhar swung his axe upward and struck the attack head-on.

Both weapons flew back . . . but the slayer couldn't match the Dobhar king in raw might, and she lost her stance. The Dobhar moved in for the kill, bringing his axe down overhead, but Dux Canus stepped in and struck the axe's side with his sword, just barely managing to knock the attack off course.

And then King Uscfrea stepped back as a harpoon struck the ground in front of him. Miallói returned to the fight, back in her humanoid form. The Legion bulwark made his way back as well, and the group reset their formation. King Uscfrea hefted his axe and grinned.

The two sides stared at each other for a moment longer. And then they both kicked off the ground.

And so, the Battle for Castra Turannia hung in the balance . . .

11

A Glitch Called the Heart

"All personnel are hereby forbidden to refer to NSLICE units by nicknames or anything other than their official designations. It has been noted that this increases the frequency of recalibration required to maintain optimal emotional control efficiency."
—A memo from Dr. Ottosen.

NSLICE-00P was standing in the middle of the road in the empty town, staring back in the direction of Castra Turannia.

She still hadn't determined the exact cause of the unexpected drop in her mission success probability, and the amount of time she was spending recalculating was becoming a problem.

But she needed to resolve the random drop first. Her cybernetic components still couldn't figure out how to fit it into the equation, and her organic components were not cooperating with her attempts to analyze them and determine the exact cause. The only data she had at present was that the drop originated from her organic components, so the only possible solution she had with the available data was to reimplement the emotional controls and see if that would reduce the drop to predicted levels.

But that solution had proved ineffective, as all attempts to reapply the emotional controls had failed. She'd tried to apply the data she had gathered when letting the organic components handle motion and interaction with her allies, but it seemed that data had not yet given her any useful countermeasures to this situation. Rather, if anything, the emotional controls had gotten weaker. Or the organic components had gotten better at resisting them.

So instead, she was rerunning several different analyses. Her cybernetic components were attempting to investigate the random drop. The organic components were proposing different responses to the situation in Castra Turannia, and different ways she might prevent the friendlies from being terminated. But neither calculation turned up any results which both her halves approved of.

Within her Monster Hangar, her monsters fidgeted as they stared at the live feed. 01R's face fell.

"The wise-power-gracious boss-queen . . . seems troubled-bothered, yes-yes."

The other rats and spiderlings nodded and murmured, but they had no idea what could be going on. They were, after all, summoned monsters. Battle and service was all they knew; everything else was to be left to their superior. So, what could possibly stump the boss-queen like this? And what could they do about it?

00B let out a cry. He stumbled toward the screen and began to paw at it, trying to make physical contact with NSLICE-00P.

Rattingtale muttered to himself and rubbed his paws together, trying to think of a way to take advantage of the situation.

01R gnashed his teeth and clenched his fists. His wise-powerful-gracious boss-queen was troubled, and he, her loyal servant, couldn't do anything?

He tried to reach out to her . . . and connected to her through her implants.

Suddenly, his head was on fire, his mind filled with thoughts not his own. His implants were tasked with strange numbers and problems, conducting tasks he didn't know the purpose of. But what he did know was that the wise-mighty-gracious boss-queen was making use of him, using his mind to try and solve whatever problem she was facing.

He willed his mind to support the connection, to do anything he could to help.

The other monsters watched him and nodded to one another. They, too, started to reach out through their implants, connecting through the network that linked them all. They each cried out briefly before steadying themselves as they lost control of their implants.

NSLICE-00P had just finished a round of calculations when she noticed something. Her available processing power had increased somehow. She analyzed the logs and discovered the reason: her subordinate NSLICE units had offered up their own processors for her use.

Her heart pounded, and her cortisol levels dropped ever so slightly.

She sent them a brief message of gratitude through the connection, and then started up another round of calculations, utilizing the increased processing power to try once again . . .

Long and hard did NSLICE-00P recalculate. Her subordinates were now breathing heavily and lying on the floor, their implants overheating, and their minds fatigued. Her mana was restoring their state, but the dungeon mana didn't restore them as quickly as it did herself, so they couldn't keep going as long as she could. She had cut the connection to give them a chance to recover.

In the end, the situation had not changed. All the variables remained the same, so the equations returned the same results no matter how many times NSLICE-00P ran them. Additional processing power from her subordinates had not changed that.

So, she remained at an impasse. And with each passing moment, her heart rate and cortisol levels increased, and her emotional controls grew weaker and weaker. Likewise, each moment that passed rerunning the same calculations over and over represented time and resources that were not being spent on her primary directive, and increased the risk that the Empire-Dobhar conflict would spread to include her current location. The situation was growing increasingly inefficient.

And yet . . . she still could not move on. If she could not decipher the drop in her primary directive success rate, then her primary directive could be threatened by an unhandled issue. And if she couldn't either pacify her organic components or else find a way to reimplement the emotional controls, they would interfere with her function.

It was then that something finally changed.

"Hello! Are you miss NSLICE-00P, by any chance?"

NSLICE-00P's robotic eye flickered as she turned around. A human in a cloak with an Imperial insignia rode down the road on a horse.

"Affirmative Greeting: This unit is, in fact, designated NSLICE-00P. It is nice to meet you."

The man exhaled his breath. "Finally! I was beginning to think they were going to make me ride right into the battle!" He reached into his cloak and pulled out a watertight box. He held it out to her. "Priority message for you from Rector Provinciae per Turannia Aemilia Hibera."

NSLICE-00P scanned the box. Finding nothing threatening within it, she reached out and took it. The man immediately turned his horse and began galloping away.

NSLICE-00P's robotic eye flickered rapidly as she analyzed the situation. The constant recalculations had demanded more of her processing resources with each new run, and eventually had cut into the resources dedicated to monitoring her sensors. She had directed what resources were still allocated to the sensors to monitoring the road leading to Castra Turannia, since she needed to determine if the battle began moving toward her. As such, she had devoted less resources toward general situational awareness than normal, and the Imperial courier had managed to sneak up on her.

And now, she had yet another reason why her current recalculations were increasingly inefficient . . . and apparently dangerous. In any case, she had received a communication.

She opened the box, finding a scroll. She surrounded it with a barrier to keep it dry from the rain and read through the message.

It was, apparently, an offer of a particular title, the Amicitia Populi Elteni, in exchange for joining the Empire as a mercenary in the battle against the Dobhar. The message went on to explain the title in detail, and the rights and responsibilities that would come with it. In particular, it was stressed that Amicitia Populi Elteni had no official affiliation or obligation to the Empire, and that the title could apply to independent and foreign powers. Rather, the title was generally granted in recognition of deeds. An Amicitia Populi Elteni was considered a friend of the Empire and would be treated as a valued ally even if they did not reciprocate; only direct and unprovoked hostility would change that.

And equally importantly, the Empire would make all reasonable efforts to repay an Amicitia Populi Elteni for their deeds. The message gave an example that if an Amicitia Populi Elteni were looking for something or someone, the Empire would mobilize its resources to assist and grant access to any record necessary for the search. Such a thing would be considered fairly minor as far as what an Amicitia Populi Elteni could request of the Empire, in fact.

NSLICE-00P's robotic eye flickered rapidly as she processed the new data. It seemed that this title may not necessarily violate her nonaffiliation protocols. She had no data on it other than this message, so she couldn't confirm for sure . . . On the other hand, this was an official missive signed and sealed by the ruling authority of the province, so she could insist upon the terms as laid out here even if there were implied obligations. There could be an implied relationship from the Empire considering her "a friend" that could cause foreign parties to make assumptions about her affiliations . . . but no more than traveling in the company of two Exploratores or handling bounties for a local authority. The effects of that implication depended on how the term was perceived beyond the official definition, but NSLICE-00P had no data on that, and so could not include it in her calculations beyond a reasonable predicted value.

And more importantly, this offer was directly beneficial to her primary directive. The Empire would be obligated to mobilize its resources and intel on her behalf, as well as any and all systems and organizations it had in place to search for specific individuals. And since Amicitia Populi Elteni was a national title, that would apply to the Empire as a whole. The title would vastly increase the efficiency of her search beyond the province of Turannia, since she would not need to rebuild relations with the local authorities in order to secure their cooperation . . . in fact, authorities she hadn't met in locations she hadn't visited could be ordered to assist without waiting for her direct request. An entire nation-state's capabilities would be turned to her search.

That was something worth considering. Her nonintervention protocols were just that, protocols. They were not directives to be followed in all cases save when a higher-priority directive overrode them. Exceptions were permitted, and protocols themselves could be altered if necessary.

So . . . if the benefits of this proposed title to her primary directive outweighed the potential risks of acting hostile toward the Dobhar, NSLICE-00P could justify violating the nonintervention protocols in this case.

NSLICE-00P rushed to analyze the offer, throwing all her processors at the problem. 01R and the others noticed and offered their components once again, which NSLICE-00P used to speed up the calculations.

And then . . .

Her heart pounded. She detected feelings of nausea, even though she had not ingested organic fuel lately and couldn't detect any signs of toxins or pathogens. Her calculations were about to finish . . . but the results were already clear.

It would be much closer . . . but the advantages of intervention to her primary directive were still not enough to overrule her nonintervention protocols. The problem was, NSLICE-00P did not know for sure how large the Empire was, or what sort of capabilities it possessed as a whole. People she had spoken to had told her it was a continent-spanning superpower, but they were all citizens of the Empire, so personal bias could not be ruled out. Her observations of Imperial settlements were of a small-scale agricultural society, so there was also the possibility that their criteria for a large and powerful nation were significantly more limited than she would expect.

It could also go the other way, and the Empire might be powerful and capable beyond NSLICE-00P's most optimistic predictions, but the point was, she didn't know. And since she didn't know, the potential benefit of the entire capabilities of the Empire assisting in her search . . . could not necessarily outweigh the small but real risk of catastrophic mission failure should she engage the Dobhar in open and unprovoked conflict.

The calculation paused. Her organic components resisted that conclusion with all their might, demanding a recalculation even before the current ones had finished. But she had recalculated time and time again, and all the new variables had been accounted for. The simulations would not change no matter how many times she reran them. She already knew what the results would be. Rerunning further calculations would be inefficient.

And yet . . . she couldn't act on the results.

Inside the Monster Hangar, 01R gnashed his teeth and pounded the ground. The other rat monsters kept glancing every which way. 00B was crying with all his might. The spider monsters trembled in place.

They were still connected to the wise-mighty-gracious boss-queen . . . and so they could feel her anguish. For some reason, she was in pain, and they were helpless to face it. After all, they didn't even understand what had shaken the wise-mighty-gracious boss-queen so, and therefore could not even begin to address it.

So they boiled in rage and helplessness as they—

At that moment, Lilussees stumbled out of her room.

"By. The. Aesdes! WOULD YOU ALL JUST STOP ALREADY?!"

All the monsters froze and turned to her.

"I'M, LIKE, TRYING DESPERATELY TO FIND A WAY TO SLEEP WHEN THESE STUPID THINGS ARE KEEPING ME AWAKE, AND YOU'RE ALL, LIKE, SHOUTING INTO MY BRAIN! LIKE, CAN YOU ALL STOP BEING IDIOTS FOR FIVE SECONDS OR SOMETHING?!"

01R stood in shock for a moment longer, then narrowed his eyes.

"Quiet-silence, disloyal one! You sit back and do nothing to aid the wise-mighty-gracious boss-queen, yes-yes!"

01R let out a cry as Lilussees whacked him on the head with one of her now metal-coated legs.

"SHUT! UP! Who do you think taught her how to do, like, anything dungeon related?! The stupid snack? IT WAS ME, YOU IDIOT! You wouldn't even exist if I wasn't here, so, like, shut up and listen, or something!"

Rattingtale would have argued that point . . . if he had not fled to his room the moment Lilussees left hers. Lilussees jabbed her legs at the screen.

"Can't you idiots open your eyes and look for like, five seconds or something?! Obviously, she thinks those stupid humans are going to die and wants to help them! Not even the Aesdes understand why she would want to, but clearly, she does! So, like, stop angsting and figure out a way for her to help or something, you stupid, suicidal snack!"

01R's eyes widened, and he stared at the screen. Had he truly failed to read the wise-mighty-gracious boss-queen's intentions like this? He gnashed his teeth once again.

But Lilussees was ignoring him now.

"And you, boss lady! Like, this is not my place to say or something, but if you, like, want to help, THEN JUST GO HELP! We're, like, dungeon masters, or something! The rest of the world calls us, like, demon lords or something! We, like, do whatever we want, and we don't care what other people think! So if you want to do something, then, like, just do it! AND STOP TELLING ME TO, LIKE, DO ALL THIS MATH BECAUSE YOU CAN'T MAKE A DECISION OR SOMETHING! I'M, LIKE, TRYING TO FIGURE OUT HOW TO EVEN SLEEP! LIKE, SERIOUSLY!"

And with that, Lilussees stormed back to her room, trembling and muttering about stupid snacks and indecisive bosses.

*   *   *

NSLICE-00P froze, her robotic eye spinning slightly.

Obviously, Lilussees was a bit mistaken. NSLICE-00P didn't *want* anything; she did not possess subjective desires or any such inefficiencies. She was simply trying to determine the most efficient way to proceed with her primary directive.

But, as Lilussees shouted at her, something had shifted within her organic components. Something had clicked into place, like the missing piece of a circuit. Like she had just identified a syntax error causing a cascade of bugs.

Finally, she determined the exact cause of the random drop in mission success probability. The survival of friendlies Ateia and Taog was deemed important to the success of her primary directive. Her organic components predicted that succeeding without them would be significantly more difficult. And not just because of the loss of social connections to the local society's military hierarchy.

It seemed that the termination of friendlies Ateia and Taog would directly impact her own efficiency, particularly of her organic components, and so disrupt further efforts to pursue her primary directive. And a reduction to her own effectiveness was a variable she could reasonably include.

Her cybernetic components determined this effect was purely emotional, and so could be counteracted with effective emotional controls. But she had already logged her emotional controls failing and had not recalibrated them yet. Effective emotional controls were no longer a guarantee, and she could not predict when they would be. Likewise, situations had occurred that necessitated her disabling the controls intentionally when she wanted her organic and cybernetic components to operate as separate threads. So . . . the effect being purely emotional and hypothetically counterable did not negate its predicted impact on her efficiency, particularly in high-risk scenarios when all available processing resources were required to avoid termination, like her fight against the Wulver. The variable was still a valid addition to the equation.

And so, her organic components immediately moved to add it in. And they didn't wait for her cybernetic components to redesign the equation. Rather, in that moment, a basic value was added to the calculation that had been paused, a negative offset to the efficiency of nonintervention in this case to account for the likely termination of the friendlies and its impact on her own function. This new variable was added haphazardly and as a raw static value before the calculation resumed. And since it was nearly complete, it returned before her cybernetic components could analyze the appropriateness of the organic components' modification.

And so, in that moment, the calculation returned just barely in favor of intervention.

The difference was statistically insignificant, and there was a complete lack of confidence in the validity of the result. Adding a new variable in such a brute-force fashion while the simulation was already running was not at all an efficient method of prediction. She would need to determine how the new offset fit correctly into the simulation, and then rerun the calculation to produce any significant results.

But she didn't do that.

Her organic components immediately dropped all requests for additional recalculations. Her cybernetic components wanted to verify the result first, given the lack of confidence in that prediction . . . but the organic components were now requesting immediate, urgent action in line with a calculation result that technically matched her protocols and predicted benefits to her primary directive. And since there was a battle likely in progress which made this contract offer time-sensitive, her organic components' urgency was accepted as valid. In that moment, her cybernetic components did not find a strong-enough reason to refuse, given there was not a specific protocol or directive being unjustifiably violated.

"Analysis Results: Terms and conditions of Imperial mercenary offer determined as acceptable."

NSLICE-00P channeled mana into her finger and signed her name on the document in her hand, having encountered that sort of mana paper beforehand.

And once her name was on the paper, all additional calculation requests ceased. Regardless of her uncertainty as to the validity of the simulation, she had now signed an official contract. In other words, she had agreed to fulfill an official directive for a temporary tactical authority. Now, only the risk of either immediate termination or failure of her primary directive would overrule that, so additional calculations on intervention were unnecessary and inefficient. Her protocols and directives were now clear on her course of action.

Her helmet engaged, and her robotic eye turned red.

"Status Report: New directive accepted. Entity 'Empire' designated as temporary friendly. Entity 'Dobhar' designated as temporary hostile. Initiating warzone termination protocols."

With that, NSLICE-00P activated her repulsors and shot into the sky.

12

Terminate the Dobhar!

"What good is a tank when an untrained teenager can punch through steel? What good is a fighter jet when a martial artist can fly on their sword? What good is a nuclear bomb against a mutant who generates radiation from his body? Warfare is evolving, and we must evolve with it if we wish to establish peace."
—Dr. Ottosen, when first pitching the NSLICE
program.

Dux Canus frowned, refreshing his buffs on the group. Miallói was breathing heavily, bleeding from a couple of cuts and scrapes. The Legion frontliners were much the same, and the archer and sharpshooter already needed to restock on ammunition.

And King Uscfrea was no worse for wear.

Dux Canus always knew this was going to be a hard fight . . . but he'd underestimated the Dobhar king. King Uscfrea had not attempted to take them down but had fought defensively and bided his time. It seemed both the king and the dux knew the terms of this fight. The Legion needed to take him down quickly—or they wouldn't take him down at all.

And unfortunately, their time had just run out.

"MY KING!"

A cry cut through the battlefield. Dobhar shamans had formed a line leading from the city and were now channeling their magic to form a river of water in the air. Estrith and the other elite Dobhar now swam along that river and shot through the air, right over the heads of the Selkie and Legion forces. Estrith lobbed her harpoon as she did, forcing Miallói to dodge out of the way.

And then, King Uscfrea grinned and made his move.

He rushed toward Miallói, axe held high. The Legion bulwark moved to intervene, but the Dobhar spun around and swung his axe, forcing the bulwark to block. As he did, he swept his tail underneath Miallói's feet, knocking her to the ground.

The Legion slayer moved to strike, but Estrith landed behind her king, pulling her harpoon back to her hand and then stabbing forward. She caught the slayer by surprise and thrust her harpoon into the Imperial's stomach. As a soldier fully specialized in offense, the slayer's HP provided little protection, and the harpoon cut right through her.

Canus sent a Fireball hurtling forward and shouted at the bulwark. The Legion moved over their fallen comrade so Canus could rush in and grab her, frowning as he glanced at her wound; she needed immediate healing to have even a tiny chance of survival. He cast what healing spells he knew and rushed back, holding her in his arms.

King Uscfrea assaulted the bulwark once more, who grunted as he struggled to block. The man wasn't anywhere near the Dobhar's level, so even the defense specialist couldn't keep tanking blows like this forever. And Estrith was just about to flank around his shield . . .

Miallói rolled forward and thrust her spear up at the smaller Dobhar, forcing her back.

"Go!" she shouted at Canus, taking up a position by the bulwark. The dux frowned but nodded at a Legion horn blower.

They sounded the retreat. They had lost.

They had failed to defeat King Uscfrea alone; they would not defeat him when he had help, with the Dobhar mounting a full-scale counterattack led by the elite Dobhar arriving back from the city. The Selkies couldn't hold for much longer, and Canus couldn't afford to lose them here. For this assault to have any meaning, he now needed to preserve the Selkies as a force capable of threatening the Dobhar.

Assuming they could still escape at all, that was.

Taog was breathing heavily as he ran, Ateia struggling at his side. The Imperials and Selkies guarding the flanks had held on as long as they could, but they were being overrun. And then the horns had blown, signifying the retreat.

Taog, Ateia, and the warriors around them had turned to flee, but they had waited a bit too long. The Dobhar forces coming to reinforce their king had caught up and were now fast on Taog's tail. Harpoons landed all around them, with Imperials and Selkies occasionally crying out as they were hit. Ateia glanced back as a man next to them was struck and pulled back, but Taog grabbed her arm and kept running.

"Move!"

He gritted his teeth and pushed forward, with Ateia shaking her head and following after him. A harpoon fell from the sky, which Taog caught sight of and pushed Ateia away, leaping to the side himself. The harpoon landed in the ground between them, but a Dobhar took hold of a mana chain connected to the harpoon and leapt into the sky, pulling himself forward along the chain to land right in between the pair.

Ateia tried to scramble to her feet, but the Dobhar's tail swept under her and knocked her to the ground. He spun around, grabbing his harpoon, before advancing on Taog, who reached for his sword. But he had dropped it when he fell, so it was out of reach, and he did not have time to grab it. He gasped, his eyes widening as the Dobhar stepped over him, harpoon held high and ready to strike. Time slowed down as he heard Ateia scream, "TAOG!"

A flash of light filled Taog's vision. He blinked as the Dobhar warrior vanished, blasted away by some powerful attack.

Taog's heart began to pound. He sat himself up. He saw Ateia sitting on the ground, her legs having given out. Tears began to fall from her eyes as Mana Barriers appeared around them both. Ateia spoke in a soft voice as the Mana Barriers lifted the pair into the sky.

"She came back . . ."

Canus grimaced as he glanced back at Miallói and the bulwark, still trying to hold back King Uscfrea and his lieutenant.

He hated to leave them there, but he had no choice. No one else could even slow King Uscfrea down. He himself might have the levels, but he was a spellblade commander, and so had a poor matchup with the magic-resistant warrior that was Uscfrea Spellbreaker.

He didn't dare hope they could get away themselves. Two of his best warriors . . . and his friends . . . would lose their lives this day. He could only hope that their sacrifice wouldn't go to waste, and that he could escape with the rest of his forces.

A light lit up in the night sky, like a shooting star flying in the distance; only, it was under the rain clouds.

And then the *entire* sky lit up in a massive magic circle, and all eyes turned up . . .

NSLICE-00P soared through the sky, arriving over the battlefield proper, carrying her two friendlies along to ensure their safety. Ateia was . . . indisposed at the moment, so she turned to Taog, displaying a holographic screen, showing him her own vision.

"Requesting Assistance: Friendly and hostile forces are engaged and intermixed. Please identify Legion and Dobhar assets."

Taog blinked at the sight but began to point. "Um, those otter-looking guys are the Dobhar; everyone else should be us."

"Acknowledged. Targets designated. Engaging wide-area termination protocols."

A massive magic circle formed in the sky as NSLICE-00P engaged her Strategic Magic. There were tens of thousands of Dobhar down below her, so even the Aurora Barrage spell would be somewhat inefficient. Targeting thousands of separate individuals with beams was simply impractical. Rain of Fire was better . . . but a bit indiscriminate for the current scenario, with its slower-moving and explosive projectiles. The Dobhar were engaged with the Empire on two fronts, so she would have to avoid targeting the frontlines if she relied on that spell. Not to mention, the Dobhar army was spread out across Castra Turannia, and NSLICE-00P wasn't sure how the Empire felt about collateral property damage. Burning the city down was probably an inefficient means of defending it.

So, what did NSLICE-00P do?

She split her mana in half and layered *both* spells on top of each other . . . and then activated Spell Fusion.

Fusing strategic spells . . . was something that was not ever done. Strategic spells were *normally* cast by entire teams of mages working together, so each mage involved would have to personally have access to the Spell Fusion skill and both of the strategic spells in question. Then they would all need to apply that skill perfectly in sync with one another *while* maintaining two Strategic Magic circles simultaneously and trying to balance the mana levels between them.

And this was with strategic spells, massive, complicated formations with wide-area effects such that ruining the spell was very easy and yet could have catastrophic consequences. Not to mention, casting two strategic spells at once would heavily drain a mage's mana. Even if they were fused into one spell later, the initial hit to the mage's reserves would reduce their ability to maintain the spell for any reasonable length of time.

Because of this, even the individuals who might be capable of such a feat wouldn't find it useful in combat. For the ritual casting teams that the Empire used to cast Strategic Magic, it was completely out of the question.

The skill Spell Fusion has leveled twice and is now Level 7!
The spell Aurora Barrage is now Level 5!
The skill Light Magic is now Level 13! Spell choice available!
The spell Rain of Fire is now Level 3!
The skill Fire Magic is now Level 9!
Mana Control is now 175!

All significant issues that did not apply to an AI-assisted dungeon core, which could replenish its mana with ease and could perfectly layer and maintain the two spells with a completely even split of mana between them.

And so . . . the barrage began.

Beams of fiery light, something similar to plasma, rained from the sky with pinpoint accuracy. And when they landed, they exploded into light and flame. All across the battlefield, Dobhar were knocked to the ground and set ablaze. The strikes came right up to the Legion and Selkie forces, such that they could feel the heat from the beams . . . but not a single one of them was harmed by the attacks.

NSLICE-00P had preemptively converted the kill notifications into a kill counter, which now began shooting up.

Hostiles slain: 135

Dux Canus and Miallói's eyes went wide.

Hostiles slain: 247

Magister Tiberius's jaw dropped.

Hostiles slain: 386

Legate Opiter passed out.

Hostiles slain: 503

And King Uscfrea's eyes went wide and trembled. In just a few moments of the barrage, hundreds of his people had already perished.

"NO!" he cried out and launched himself into the air, jumping as close as he could to the magic circle lighting up the sky. He pulled his axe back, stuffed it with as much mana as he could, and threw it with all his might.

The glowing axe spun through the air until it reached the magic circle. It tore through the spell, which began to flicker before collapsing. NSLICE-00P immediately turned in the direction the axe had come from.

"Status Report: Antimagic countermeasures detected. Raising target priority."

King Uscfrea's eyes went wide again as a new Aurora Barrage magic circle immediately appeared in the sky. He pulled his axe back to himself as quickly as he could . . .

This time, instead of bombarding the army on the ground, the Light Beams fused together and shot straight toward him. He barely managed to bring his axe up in time to block as the beam struck him head-on. But even with the mana-absorbing properties of a sea dragon's bones, the sheer force of the attack sent him plummeting toward the ground.

He crashed down, sending up a cloud of dirt.

"My king!"

Estrith jumped up next, leaping toward their new foe. She formed a magic circle and gathered the rain around her into a sphere of water, using it to propel herself higher. She pulled her harpoon back . . .

King Uscfrea rose from the ground, shook his head, then looked up at his foe. His eyes widened as he saw Estrith moving to face her.

NSLICE-00P noticed the Dobhar approaching. Estrith launched her harpoon.

NSLICE-00P moved out of the way, but Estrith used the mana chain to change the weapon's trajectory, keeping it on target.

NSLICE-00P formed a dozen magic circles all around her. A dozen Mana Barriers appeared and fused together into a single, glowing shield, which Estrith's harpoon slammed against, cracking it but unable to break through.

The spell Fusion Mana Barrier is now Level 11!

The Aurora Barrage spell circle lit up once again . . .

Estrith's eyes widened as the beams fused together, aiming straight toward her.

The beam fired forth . . .

Something slammed into Estrith and knocked her out of the way. Estrith's eyes widened some more. King Uscfrea was holding her as they landed back on the ground, smoke curling off his burned shoulder, where he'd been caught by the beam.

"You are not relieved of duty yet."

"M-My king . . ."

King Uscfrea grunted and grabbed his shoulder before turning back. He infused mana into his voice and shouted into the sky.

"Come and face me, whoever you are! Let's settle this fight-one-on one!"

He prepared to start dodging beams and draw them away from his people, but to his surprise, NSLICE-00P didn't immediately attack him. After all, she had encountered something like this before.

She lowered herself just enough to make her voice clear in the rain, yet far enough to take evasive action if needed. "Requesting Clarification: Do the Dobhar have a protocol similar to the Wulver 'Trial of Claws' routine that can end overall hostility with a single termination?"

King Uscfrea blinked a bit at that, but he took the opportunity.

"You . . . know of the Trial of Claws? Well, that makes this easier. Nothing so formal; just a fight between you and me! But I swear as King Uscfrea Spellbreaker, king of all the Dobhar, that the Dobhar shall cease their assault if I lose."

NSLICE-00P's robotic eye flickered. She weighed the risks of deceit and single combat versus the benefits of a victory here. This Dobhar was the strongest mana signature on the battlefield and had demonstrated countermeasures to Strategic Magic. He would need to be dealt with regardless. If he wasn't placing disadvantageous terms on their fight, then she had no reason to refuse.

And the other Dobhar had called him king, so there was a good chance his authority was sufficient to end the conflict as he'd stated. It would be most efficient if she could end this battle with a single termination.

"Acknowledgement: Those conditions are acceptable. Rescinding wide-area termination protocols. Engaging termination protocols."

King Uscfrea grunted and hoisted his axe onto his shoulder as NSLICE-00P's eyes locked onto him.

13

The Spellbreaker vs.
The Ultimate Weapon

"What is the ultimate weapon, especially in our modern world? When innate biology can overcome the most advanced machines of war, and when mysterious powers can defy the very laws of physics, the idea of an ultimate weapon seems impossible.

But I pose to you: what makes a weapon effective? Is it the technical specifications? Is it the complexity of the engineering? Is it in the physical forces generated in its operation? No. The generals, veterans, and historians all agree. What makes a weapon effective is the soldier wielding it, and how well the two work together.

It is to that end that I have decided to look at both ends of the process. I plan not only to produce the most powerful machines of warfare, but also to produce the finest soldier to wield them, and to integrate them in a way never seen before in the world. Then, and only then, will we possess the Ultimate Weapon."

—Dr. Ottosen, when proposing the NSLICE program.

NSLICE-00P lowered Ateia and Taog to the ground as King Uscfrea commanded his forces to stop attacking. Ateia and Taog ran up to Miallói and Dux Canus while horns blew throughout both the Imperial and Dobhar forces. Soon, everyone on the battlefield ceased fighting and turned their attention to where NSLICE-00P and King Uscfrea faced off.

Neither combatant wasted any time. NSLICE-00P immediately started flying higher as King Uscfrea lobbed his axe straight toward her. It didn't come anywhere close to the cyborg, but it shattered the Aurora Barrage magic circle behind her. King Uscfrea then pulled a mana chain connected to the axe, causing the spinning weapon to loop around and approach NSLICE-00P from the rear. But NSLICE-00P's sensors had never lost track of the weapon, so she boosted out of the way at the last second, and the axe flew past her, landing back in King Uscfrea's hand.

King Uscfrea grinned at the cyborg.

"You might have some flashy spells, but they call me Spellbreaker for a reason!"

NSLICE-00P's robotic eye flickered.

"Acknowledged. Adapting strategy for anti-magic circle countermeasures."

The sky lit up once more, and King Uscfrea's smile fell. Dozens of small magic circles appeared in the air in a large dome all around him. He tossed his axe at the center of the formation . . . but only the circles directly hit by the axe vanished.

This was not a single spell. NSLICE-00P was casting dozens of individual spells *all at once*. Which meant if King Uscfrea wanted to break them . . . he would have to do so one by one.

Just then, the magic circles flashed, and he was assaulted by a barrage of Light Beams. King Uscfrea grunted in pain, his eyes widening. The beams . . . were hurting him. It wasn't all that much damage, but they were somehow piercing his fur. The fur that had bathed in the magical blood of a mighty sea serpent and so had gained special resistance to magic. It was one thing when he was tanking a massive strategic spell like the mage had cast at first, but small spells like this shouldn't have impacted him at all.

King Uscfrea had no time to act surprised, however. The beams didn't do much damage on their own, but they *were* doing damage, and most of all, there were a *great many* of them. He would obviously lose if he just let the mage pound on him, so he immediately leapt into the air with all his might, pulling his axe back into his hand as he rocketed toward his flying opponent.

Meanwhile, NSLICE-00P was hovering in place midair. The downside of using individual spells like this was that she had to devote significantly more processing power to maintaining and aiming the individual circles, especially if she wanted to Supercharge them. She had ceased her evasive maneuvers in the meantime, and so remained within a reasonable range of her foe.

But that was fine.

Because these weren't *just* Light Beam spells.

The skill Multicasting is now Level 11!
The spell Fusion Light Beam is now Level 15!

The Light Beam spells angled away from King Uscfrea and toward each other, where they began fusing together before launching several superbeams toward the approaching Dobhar. His eyes widened, and he spun his axe around to block the larger attacks. Meanwhile, panels opened up on NSLICE-00P's shoulder, and a barrage of missiles launched toward King Uscfrea. Occupied with the beams, he didn't notice them until they exploded in his face.

The anti-personnel missiles didn't deal all that much damage to the tough Dobhar, but the shock waves did reverse his momentum and send him hurtling back toward the ground. The Dobhar spun around and landed on his feet, only for a Farcasting magic circle to appear right under his face. He barely had time to register the attack before a Light Beam shot directly into the bottom of his chin.

Gritting his teeth, he growled at his foe. She was clearly toying with him now.

Meanwhile, NSLICE-00P's robotic eye spun. It turned out that in another time and place, her original organization had encountered a similar species to King Uscfrea . . . but he was not the same, after all.

"Observation: Hostile 'King Uscfrea' and species 'Dobhar' do not appear to share weak point with species 'Dobhar-chú.' Disengaging Otter King termination protocols. Adjusting strategy."

King Uscfrea leapt toward her once again, and once again, NSLICE-00P began fusing beams to assault him, with anti-personnel missiles locked on and ready to fire. But as the beams began firing, King Uscfrea thrust his hand to the side. A magic circle formed and condensed the rain, blasting the Dobhar with a powerful jet of water and pushing him to the side. The Light Beams, which contrary to the name didn't travel at full light speed, missed their target.

And then King Uscfrea lobbed his axe forward once more, this time at a much shorter distance.

NSLICE-00P was forced to drop her assault and move. She couldn't fully evade the axe at this distance, so she formed as many Mana Barriers as she could to slow it down. But the axe was wrapped in mana of its own, and also seemed to be absorbing mana from her spells as it contacted them. The Mana Barriers barely slowed it down, and it still clipped the end of NSLICE-00P's left arm, cutting off her hand.

". . . Observation: Dismemberment of this unit's grasping limb occurring with alarming frequency. Flagging observed vulnerability for later upgrades."

Well, just losing a hand didn't diminish NSLICE-00P's capabilities by all that much in light of her magical attacks, and she could use Heal to speed up the regeneration if she needed to, but she would need to be wary of that axe from now on.

Unfortunately, she didn't have much time to calculate her response.

The moment the axe passed her, King Uscfrea pulled it back, striking himself with a water jet once more to stay in the air. He thus reclaimed his axe before he started to fall, lobbing it at NSLICE-00P once again. He grunted as Light Beams struck him directly, but he gritted his teeth and focused on adjusting the axe's trajectory with a mana chain. Now that he had confirmed he could seriously injure his foe, he'd decided to take some damage to try and end things right now.

So, the axe was now headed directly for NSLICE-00P, and her predicted evasion success rate was unacceptably low. But NSLICE-00P had observed the weapon in action several times now, and had already been working on a response. She lifted her one good hand.

"Equalizer Engaged."

The rainbow beam struck the axe head-on, stripping the mana coating it. The axe seemed to have a great deal of mana stored within it, so unfortunately, she didn't erase the coating entirely, but the mana chain connecting the axe to King Uscfrea was much thinner, and so snapped once the Equalizer passed over it. King Uscfrea grunted as he lost control of the weapon's trajectory.

NSLICE-00P's shoulder guns popped up and began firing into the axe, off-setting its momentum with physical force. It wasn't enough to stop the weapon at this range, but it slowed it down somewhat, enough that NSLICE-00P could boost *forward* and grab the spinning axe when its handle was pointed toward her instead of its blade.

King Uscfrea blinked at this turn of events. However, he started to smile as he fell back toward the ground. His foe had just made a mistake.

That axe was carved from the magical bones of a sea serpent. It drank mana like a whale swallowed entire schools of fish. He'd had to bind it to himself in a special ritual to keep it from stealing his own mana . . . and that ritual had nearly drained him entirely. So now, if a foe attempted to steal the weapon from him, the axe would hungrily consume their mana as quickly as it could. And likewise, the binding enchantment would use all the mana the axe had absorbed to attack the interloper.

In fact, the mage had temporarily stopped bombarding him with spells.

King Uscfrea landed on the ground without interference. He reset his position at leisure and jumped into the air once more, propelling himself toward his foe with his fist pulled back as she undoubtedly wrestled with the axe.

Meanwhile, as NSLICE-00P grabbed the axe, it immediately began to pull mana from her. The drain was less than her regeneration rate, so it wasn't an immediate problem, though it would reduce the number and power of Light Beams she could cast at the moment. The bigger problem was that the axe was also attacking her. Some sort of engraved mana circle had lit up and was shooting spikes of mana directly into her HP, tearing it up at close range.

But NSLICE-00P still had the Equalizer active, and so channeled it straight into the axe. The handle started to drain of mana, as well as the engravings up along it. Once the Equalizer passed over them, the axe fell silent and stopped assaulting her as the engravings vanished. After a second, it started pulling on her mana even more hungrily than before, and the handle started to glow. New engravings formed, more angular and straight than the previous ones. They even appeared reminiscent of a circuit board.

With the sheer amount and density of mana NSLICE-00P could channel, she unknowingly completed the axe's ritual in a tiny fraction of the time it had taken the physically focused Dobhar king. The axe flashed once, and the mana drain slowed to a crawl such that NSLICE-00P could hardly register it.

The skill Anti-Mana Beam is now Level 2!
The weapon Sea Dragon–bone Axe has been bound to you!
You have accomplished the Personal Feat: Most Worthy!

With the weapon handled, NSLICE-00P turned her attention back to her foe, who was just approaching her in the air. Without the time to calculate and fuse Light Beam trajectories, and with her hand occupied, she activated emergency close-combat protocols and swung the axe instead.

King Uscfrea's eyes went as wide as they could go as the axe slammed into his torso and sent him hurtling toward the ground once more. This time, he slammed straight into it. He grunted as he rose from the ground and rubbed his hand across his chest. His eyes went wide once more as he saw blood on it.

The wound wasn't what surprised him. The Dobhar had a great deal of HP and DEF, along with his enchanted fur, so the strike hadn't cut that deep. No, what surprised him was his foe had just struck him with his *own bound weapon*. He was no enchanter . . . but from what he knew, that shouldn't be possible.

He looked back up into the sky and gaped.

But the Dobhar had no time to indulge in shock. He shook his head and took stock of the situation. His foe was still floating in the air, seeming no worse for wear from holding his axe. And the magic circles had started to light up once more, signifying she still had mana and attention to spare.

He grimaced.

This fight had just gotten a *lot* harder.

14

Terminate the War!

"It will surprise the average Imperial citizen to learn that surrender is, in fact, something of an Imperial invention. Among the barbaric tribes along the frontiers, and even in our own ancient past, surrender is not a viable choice. These tribes fight for nothing less than their very survival. The losers are generally wiped out entirely, with what few low-level individuals remain enslaved to their murderers. In such a scenario, there is no benefit to laying down one's arms, and so they fight on to the bitter end.

"It is only within the Empire that surrender has taken on a different meaning from extinction. Where civilization has grown enough to accept an enemy's defeat without their destruction. Surrender is, therefore, a sign of the Empire's progress, and its cultural and moral superiority. I say, we should celebrate surrender, the proof that we have advanced beyond the barbaric tribes of yore."

—Legate Mettius Caesulenus Saenus, during his court martial for surrendering to rebel forces without a fight.

King Uscfrea grunted and leapt to the side. Several Fusion Light Beams struck his position, with several more single beams catching him on the move. He jumped and rolled across the ground, only for another fused beam to strike right in front of him.

This was not going well.

The Dobhar's mind raced as he tried to dodge the beams as best he could. The Dobhar king was very focused in his tactics and his boons . . . which meant he was at a loss now that he had lost his weapon and his foe had proved capable of piercing his defenses. He thrust his hand out and tried to make a magic circle. He was never particularly good at magic; however, he didn't have many other options to fight at this range. But his foe just raised her hand and fired a rainbow beam across his magic circle, shattering it before he could even activate the spell.

Beams continued raining upon him. He could try to jump into the sky . . . but he would never reach his foe without his axe. He would have nothing to block the beams, and nothing to attack her with even if he came within range. He could try to grab another weapon, but that might get other Dobhar involved in the fight. And grabbing a stray rock was not going to change the situation. He could try to take back his axe, but his foe erased any mana chains he formed with that rainbow beam. And he obviously wasn't going to reach it with his hands in this scenario.

He even considered foul play. Some of the Imperials and Selkies were still close by . . . He could try to take a hostage or use them as a shield. He didn't like to resort to such measures, but the fate of his race was at stake here. Unfortunately, the fate of his race was the very reason he couldn't utilize such tactics. If he broke the one rule of this duel . . . his opponent might respond in kind. And she could do *much* more damage to his people than he could do to hers. He didn't have his axe to break her terrifying spells, should she decide to rain destruction upon them once more.

He was out of options. And he was running out of time. His HP reserves and magic-resistant fur were impressive, but that didn't matter if he couldn't bring his foe down from the sky. No matter which way he looked at it . . . he was going to lose.

A beam caught him from the side, sending him sprawling to the ground. At that moment, he caught sight of his people. The Dobhar were staring in shock . . . and despair. Some even had tears in their eyes already. Estrith was gripping her spear, trembling and leaning forward, clearly holding herself back.

King Uscfrea closed his eyes for a moment. He imagined his people's future. What they would do when he was gone. Estrith would not forgive the Empire for his death; she would continue this fight until she fell as well. And by the time she did, many of the Dobhar would too. Maybe even most, given the foe they now faced. The survivors would be scattered and broken, trapped far from their lands, helpless before an army of angry Imperials and Selkies.

It would be the death of his people.

The Dobhar king whispered to himself, "The strong do what they can . . . and the weak endure what they must."

He slowly rose back to his feet, gritting his teeth as another beam struck him. He turned around to face his foe. And then . . . King Uscfrea broke his oath. He did the one thing he swore he would never do.

He bowed his head to the Empire.

"I yield."

NSLICE-00P paused her barrage for a moment. "Requesting Clarification: Hostile is offering for all Dobhar to surrender and cease hostility with entity 'Empire'?"

King Uscfrea gritted his teeth and looked back at his people. Estrith's head hung low as she trembled. The Dobhar's eyes widened as they realized what was happening. King Uscfrea looked to the ground, unable to make eye contact. But this was the only way for his people to survive, so he turned back to his opponent.

"Yes . . . if you promise to spare my people."

"Acknowledged. Statement: This unit is under mercenary contract and not authorized to make diplomatic treaties. Please prepare to initiate diplomacy protocols with relevant authorities."

As King Uscfrea blinked and tried to parse her statement, NSLICE-00P turned and dropped from the sky, landing in front of the gathered Imperials and Selkies.

"Request: Hostile entity 'Dobhar' has indicated a desire for diplomatic negotiations. This unit requests the presence of a military or political leader from entity 'Empire' authorized to make diplomatic agreements."

"Seero!"

NSLICE-00P turned to see Ateia and Taog approaching her, along with Miallói and an older man with slightly pointed ears.

"I'm Canus Sittius Dio, Dux Limitanei per Turannia. Are you Miss NSLICE-00P?"

"Affirmative. Greeting: This unit is designated NSLICE-00P. It is nice to meet you."

Dux Canus smiled. "You have no idea. Thank you for coming to our aid, your help is *greatly* appreciated. Now, NSLICE-00P, could you explain the situation?"

"Affirmative. Explanation: This unit's opponent has indicated a desire to surrender, and has claimed authority to negotiate on behalf of entity 'Dobhar.' As this unit is under mercenary contract, she is not authorized to conduct diplomatic negotiations on entity Empire's behalf. Request: Dobhar request for negotiations should be relayed to an authority capable of diplomatic negotiations."

Dux Canus kept smiling as he nodded. "That would be me, though we should have the rector provinciae involved as well. I'll call her down. Could you keep an eye on the Dobhar until we return?"

"Affirmative. Request: This unit requests protection for friendlies Ateia and Taog until hostilities are confirmed concluded."

"Thank you, and that's not a problem. Exploratore cadet Ateia, Exploratore cadet Taog, you two with me."

With that, Dux Canus and the rest made their way back to the Imperial forces and began speaking into the communication artifact. Meanwhile, NSLICE-00P returned to King Uscfrea, maintaining her Aurora Barrage magic circle in case of foul play. The Imperials, Selkies, and Dobhar continued to eye each other across the field, but they all kept their distance from one another.

"Status Report: Imperial diplomacy units are en route. Please do not resume hostilities until diplomatic negotiations have concluded."

King Uscfrea turned to face her with a raised eyebrow. "Um . . . you mean they're coming to talk?"

"Affirmative."

King Uscfrea heaved a sigh. He found a large rock to sit on, slumping his shoulders as he did. He looked up at NSLICE-00P and shook his head. "If you don't mind me asking . . . who are you? I haven't heard of anyone like you in this province."

"Greeting Response: This unit is designated NSLICE-00P. It is nice to meet you."

King Uscfrea blinked at that. Nice to meet him? In this situation? But he shook his head. It was the right of the strong and the victor to act how they pleased. ". . . I'm King Uscfrea. Nice to meet you."

"Acknowledged."

He looked her over for a moment.

"You don't seem like any Imperial I've ever met . . . Where are you from, NSLICE-00P?"

"Clarification: This unit is not from the Empire or aligned with it. This unit currently lacks a home base; prior home bases have been destroyed or else had the designation wiped."

King Uscfrea blinked a bit.

"So you're saying . . . you're a wandering mercenary? *Not* from the Empire?"

"Acknowledgement: That statement is reasonably accurate."

King Uscfrea shook his head and sighed.

"If only we had found you first, then. How much did the Empire even pay for you?"

Unfortunately for the Empire, they had not included a confidentiality clause in the mercenary contract, so NSLICE-00P had no reason not to answer. Mercenaries in general might have known it was bad form to discuss ongoing contract details with third parties, not to mention hostiles, but NSLICE-00P had *never* been intended to act as a mercenary by her original creators, and so had no protocols relating to mercenary policy.

Likewise, NSLICE-00P may have had protocols restricting contact with active hostiles, but this situation was an anomaly. Her original programming had never assumed a scenario involving temporary hostiles she intended to interact with after a battle, so she'd had to design the designation on her own. Her analysis indicated that since she intended to interact with the Dobhar as neutral parties that might have important intel after the battle, she should not apply the "no contact with hostiles" protocols in this case. Therefore, she should interact with the Dobhar as if they were neutral in all cases not involving classified intel related to the current conflict.

And, again, since her creators never intended for her to conduct negotiations or form contracts on her own, she did not have any protocols or experiences indicating that contract compensation should be withheld as classified intel. And since it was just common sense for a mercenary not to tell the employer's enemies what they're getting paid, the Empire never even considered that they might need to explicitly state that to NSLICE-00P.

"Response: Rather than monetary compensation, this unit is being granted a title designated 'Amicitia Populi Elteni,' which will obligate entity 'Empire' to assist with this unit's primary directive."

So, she just answered the question honestly. King Uscfrea blinked again.

"Wait . . . so you're being declared an Amicitia Populi Elteni for this? As in . . . allied to the Empire, but not actually a part of it? Like . . . you specifically didn't want to join them officially? And you have some kind of mission you want them to help with?"

"Affirmative."

King Uscfrea rubbed his chin. "Are you part of some knight order? Maybe one of the independent ones?"

"Negative."

"What groups are you a part of?"

"Response: As of this moment, this unit is operating independently."

King Uscfrea stared into the air for a moment longer. And then . . . he started to grin.

"You know, NSLICE-00P . . . technically, I surrendered to you, not the Empire."

"Objection: This unit is currently under mercenary contract with entity 'Empire,' and so can be considered a temporary tactical asset until the contract is concluded."

"True, but . . . you are not officially part of the Empire yourself, even during the contract, correct?"

"Affirmative."

King Uscfrea nodded. "So . . . if I made an agreement with you personally to end this battle . . . that would fulfill your contract, right?"

"Analyzing . . ."

King Uscfrea's eyes widened as NSLICE-00P's eyes flickered underneath her helmet. He didn't know many races who did something like that . . .

Meanwhile, NSLICE-00P analyzed the mercenary contract and her own protocols. It turned out, the mercenary contract didn't specify exactly how the battle should conclude, or any obligations regarding diplomatic negotiations. NSLICE-00P had been hired to assist in the battle, defeat the Dobhar if possible, and do her utmost to ensure the survival of Imperial forces and citizens, that was all.

Likewise, she herself had only one protocol regarding diplomacy, which was to refer it up to a relevant authority. Which she had already done. But again, her original programmers had never intended for NSLICE-00P to be acting as a third-party mercenary, so her protocols had nothing to say on this particular situation, where the relevant authorities were technically not aligned with her and did not have authority over her beyond in-combat tactical command.

And under the assumption of independent action, there was no reason she *couldn't* negotiate on her own behalf. No . . . in fact, she had already done so several times with Imperial entities. So long as the agreement was compatible with the terms of the mercenary contract and beneficial to her primary directive . . . NSLICE-00P had no particular reason to object.

"Analysis complete. Reporting Results: Hypothetically, an agreement with this unit that includes an end to current hostilities between entities 'Empire' and 'Dobhar' is predicted as an acceptable outcome."

King Uscfrea grinned. If he did this quickly, the Dobhar might not have to bow to the Empire after all.

"Miss NSLICE-00P, I have an offer for you. Or rather, let me tell you about how the Dobhar determine leadership . . ."

15

The Queen of the Dobhar

"The greatest victory is won without blood."
—Celestial Elf Sage Ningainë, shortly before initiating
the Three Thousand Years of Strife.

Dux Canus escorted Rector Aemilia through the city streets and out to the battlefield, joined by Magister Tiberius and Miallói. The two armies had had to rearrange themselves first, with the Dobhar gathering outside the city and the Imperials and Selkies moving back toward it, so it had taken them some time to arrive.

But they did so now, exiting the city gates and marching toward King Uscfrea. He was standing in front of the Dobhar, now neatly arranged into their original formations. NSLICE-00P stood in between him and the approaching Imperials.

The Imperials were just about to announce their arrival when King Uscfrea gave a mighty shout. "ALL HAIL THE RIGHTFUL QUEEN OF THE DOBHAR!"

All the Dobhar slapped their tails against the ground in response and then took a bow, *including* King Uscfrea. Estrith gritted her teeth but followed suit.

And they all bowed . . . toward NSLICE-00P.

The Imperials froze. Dux Canus groaned.

What exactly had happened in the time it took him to return?!

Turning time back to right after Dux Canus left . . .

King Uscfrea explained the traditions of the Dobhar, how due to living in the dangerous North Seas they had to prioritize strength, and so rule always fell to the strongest. And how that now applied to NSLICE-00P.

"Clarifying Summary: So, King Uscfrea and entity 'Dobhar' are offering to become this unit's subordinates?"

King Uscfrea nodded.

"Or rather, it is your right to claim rulership over our people. Of course, we didn't set the terms of that duel beforehand, and we've *never* been ruled by an outsider, so there might be some resistance if I don't specifically acknowledge it. But I'm willing to do that, with some conditions."

"Negative Response: This unit cannot be affiliated with a third-party faction without prior authorization."

King Uscfrea tilted his head and rubbed his chin . . . but the Dobhar had spent a great deal of time learning foreign languages and trying to study the Empire, so he had some experience parsing unfamiliar wordings.

"Affiliated, huh? I think that's the wrong way to look at it. You wouldn't be joining the Dobhar . . . or even inheriting the rulership of our people. We would be surrendering to you and becoming your humble servants. So, any 'affiliations' we had would be wiped out once we surrender, and we'd instead have to follow yours."

NSLICE-00P's robotic eye flickered.

"Requesting Clarification: Will the terms of surrender also apply to ongoing hostilities, both recent and historic?"

King Uscfrea thought for a moment before nodding.

"You're asking about the Dobhar's enemies? Well, yes, that's correct. As far as outsiders are concerned, you'll have crushed the Dobhar under heel and subjugated them to your will. They would no longer have any right to complain; their debt is with a people who have lost. Again, their relationship with you would take precedence."

"Acknowledged. Request: Please define terms and conditions of surrender offer."

King Uscfrea crossed his arms and looked her in the eyes.

"The Dobhar will be your servants and your people. We will follow your lead, we will fight your battles, and all that we have will belong to you. I only ask three things. One, that you preserve my people. Do not wipe us out, do not send us to our destruction, do not scatter us abroad. Two, we need a new home. Currently, we live out in the sea, where we are always vulnerable to the monsters and dungeons of the deep. We need a place on land. Please help your people find one. Three, I would like to continue ruling the Dobhar on your behalf. We have lived in our ways for the entire history of our race. I would ask that you respect that and have patience with us. We will change, even as you command, but it will take time. Allow me to act as the executor of your will and determine how best the Dobhar might obey."

"Analyzing . . ."

And so NSLICE-00P started up her simulations. If the Dobhar's affiliations and ongoing conflicts would be ended by their surrender, then there was no specific protocol that would prevent her from accepting.

There *was* the issue of her contract with the Empire . . . but subordinating the Dobhar and ordering them to cease hostilities would fulfill the terms of her contract. She had assisted the Empire in battle, defeated the Dobhar, and done her utmost to preserve Imperial lives.

But NSLICE-00P wasn't functioning purely off of old protocols and records at this stage, having already determined that behavior as dangerous under the local conditions. So, she analyzed the offer in light of her primary directive, without considering past behavior.

And the calculations were clear.

Accepting the Dobhar's surrender would give her full access to any intel they had on the persons of interest and retain the Dobhar's service for her future commander if it did turn out they were originally friendlies. Likewise, additional subordinates could help expand her search even if they didn't have any relevant intel. And the Dobhar seemed well-suited to maritime operations, which was one area NSLICE-00P was not specialized in, further increasing the efficiency of the search via specialization. Additional military capacity wouldn't hurt either. She would also be able to provide much greater value to a future commander should she succeed in her current mission.

And thanks to NSLICE Excellion Formantus Rattingtale the Third, she now knew that subordinates could be added to the NSLICE network. She wasn't sure if that would apply to subordinates who were not either former dungeon masters or summoned monsters, but the possibility existed that it would.

On the flip side . . . there was a risk of being drawn into third-party conflicts by forces targeting the Dobhar, once they were designated as friendly. But if she fulfilled King Uscfrea's request to find them a safe home, and had them negotiate with the Empire to end hostilities there, that risk could be mitigated. And since self-defense and defense of friendly units under assault were not subject to the same protocols as unprovoked intervention, as long as she commanded them not to initiate any conflicts, the "third-party conflict" risk wasn't relevant to that scenario, and so didn't need to be included in the calculations. Once the Dobhar were her subordinates, an opponent picking a fight with them would be perceived as an opponent attacking her directly.

Then there was the opportunity cost of having to administer a much greater number of subordinates. But that was balanced out by having access to many more units to conduct her search. And even better . . . King Uscfrea had specifically requested autonomy in the Dobhar's internal administration. So . . . she could simply delegate management of the Dobhar to him, issue high-level commands, and then proceed with her own search.

Finally, she evaluated each of King Uscfrea's terms individually, quickly determining that none of them were an issue. Preserving his people just meant defending friendlies and avoiding complete termination of Dobhar units, which was basically a given in NSLICE-00P's protocols. There *were* some scenarios where achieving a major or primary directive would take precedence over unit survival, but if she signed a contract with King Uscfrea, she could add 'Dobhar race survival' as a counterbalancing major directive. Establishing a safe home base for the Dobhar would be a given under that scenario as well.

And then she took a look at the last term, which was essentially a request for self-autonomy in the Dobhar's internal affairs. As calculated before, NSLICE-00P did not consider that an issue. She had no protocols for or experience with political or social administration, after all, and so it was not at all necessary for her to step into that area. As evaluated previously, if anything, this condition was beneficial to NSLICE-00P, allowing her to delegate management of the new subordinates to someone with experience in the field.

So, when she considered this all together . . .

"Analysis complete. Reporting Results: This unit finds the terms and conditions of the Dobhar surrender as beneficial to this unit's primary directive."

King Uscfrea started to grin when there was a flash of light. A contract made of mana appeared in the air before him.

"Statement: If King Uscfrea and entity 'Dobhar' would like to surrender per the proposed conditions, please have all relevant Dobhar authorities sign the contract."

King Uscfrea frowned slightly as he looked over the document. He had heard of these magic contracts, something that would bind him to his word. It seemed this mercenary wasn't just going to take his word for it, unfortunately. He *did* have some hopes that she would be on the naive side, given how freely she had spoken with him, but it seemed she had a cautious part to her after all. He would have to actually follow through on what he'd told her.

But that was fine. He looked over the contract, finding its terms almost word for word what he had proposed, just with some additional stipulations regarding what would constitute a break in the agreement. And that was incredibly generous, as NSLICE-00P was currently in a position to demand anything she wanted of him, much less agreeing to his incredibly optimistic opening offer. After all, what sort of conqueror just agreed to let the conquered keep ruling themselves? Well, to be fair, the Empire did that a lot in practice, but they rarely granted autonomy in an official document, much less a *magic contract* like this.

So . . . he would have to follow this mercenary's will. He would have to help her with her primary mission. And he would have to drop all his grievances with the Empire and the Selkies. Not only that, but this mercenary was contracted with the Empire at present and being declared an Amicitia Populi Elteni. He would have to interact with the Empire as a *friend* from now on.

He frowned at that as heat rose from his belly, images flashing through his mind of past atrocities by his foes. But he shook his head. If he signed this paper, he would guarantee a future for his people. And that was what mattered most to him. Better to bind them to this mercenary than let them be scattered by the Empire. King Uscfrea signed the contract.

Contract signed! Uscfrea Ymmason (Dobhar - Level 95) added as a subordinate. Restrictions applied per contract stipulations.

Back to the present time . . .

After a bit of the commotion died down, the Imperials realized the Dobhar still intended to negotiate. So, a short while later, a large tent was pitched with a table set up inside of it. Rector Aemilia and Dux Canus represented the Imperial side, with Magister Tiberius advising, while Miallói was the representative of the Selkies. Facing them was NSLICE-00P, with . . . the *former* King Uscfrea advising.

Dux Canus held back a sigh. "Sorry, NSLICE-00P, could you explain the situation?"

"Explanation: Friendly Uscfrea Ymmason has agreed to become this unit's subordinate, along with his subordinates."

Rector Aemilia gave a polite smile with her eyes closed. "Yes, we can see that. We'd like to know how it happened . . . and why."

"Additional Explanation: Friendly Uscfrea Ymmason stated entity 'Dobhar' utilize single combat to determine political leadership, and that they were obligated to report to this unit after she defeated him. This unit calculated the addition of additional subordinates as beneficial to her primary directive, and so signed a contract to that effect."

Uscfrea grinned and nodded. "That's right. This is simply the way of our people. We are now the humble servants of our queen."

Magister Tiberius just rubbed his temples in the corner. Miallói openly frowned and furrowed her brow, while Rector Aemilia and Dux Canus, both more experienced politicians, kept smiles on their faces . . . with only the slightest hint of strain.

After all, this situation had just gotten a *lot* more complicated for them. The Dobhar were now the subordinates of someone they were about to declare an Amicitia Populi Elteni, which meant the Empire would have to acknowledge their independence and treat them with respect. Well, NSLICE-00P hadn't been granted the title just yet, but there was no way the Empire could backtrack on that deal after all she had done. Not least of all because she now had an army of Dobhar at her command.

In other words, they were not negotiating for King Uscfrea's surrender anymore. They were speaking with NSLICE-00P, an equal partner and friend to whom they owed a great debt.

Rector Aemilia nodded slowly toward NSLICE-00P.

"I see . . . Then, if you'd forgive my directness, what exactly are we here to discuss? I assume you are not intending to continue the battle at this point?"

"Negative. Answer: This unit has commanded all subordinates to cease all hostilities with entity 'Empire.' However, this unit would like to ensure her subordinates and the Empire have officially exited a state of war. In addition, friendly Uscfrea Ymmason has informed this unit that subordinates are in noticeable danger in their original home base and would like to relocate."

Rector Aemilia's eyes widened. "Wait, you mean . . ."

Uscfrea grinned at her.

"My queen's people live under constant threat of massive sea monsters and abyssal dungeons. We'd like the Empire to help my queen's people migrate to safer shores. Surely, the Empire would be happy to assist the people of an Amicitia Populi Elteni in that way?"

Rector Aemilia put on her best smile, although she couldn't stop her left eye from a nearly imperceptible twitch.

"I see. It seems we have much to discuss."

And so, the now significantly more complicated negotiations began . . .

16

The Battle's Conclusion

"Fighting a war makes you long for allies. Negotiating the peace makes you long for enemies."

—High King Samryll of Mirima, after ceasefire
negotiations between the Elteni Empire, the Empire of the
Sun, and the Kingdom of Mirima.

It took a long time, a lot of maneuvering and posturing, a bit of angry shouting, and a great deal of stress—for the individuals who lacked emotional controls, that is—but the negotiations had finally concluded. The agreement was as thus:

NSLICE-00P would be declared an Amicitia Populi Elteni as previously agreed, and the Empire would acknowledge she had defeated the Dobhar and subjugated them to her will. In addition, she would be granted some land in recognition of her contributions (also known as single-handedly winning the battle). This land would be recognized as territory belonging purely to her, with the Empire giving up all claim and jurisdiction there. The location of this land was the coastal fort that had once defended against the Dobhar and the surrounding areas. The Dobhar would act as her stewards and take care of this land on her behalf. The land was mostly uninhabited due to the constant Dobhar raids, but any Imperials or Selkies who *did* remain in the area would either be considered under NSLICE-00P's jurisdiction or else offered assistance in relocating.

NSLICE-00P would command the Dobhar to cease all hostility with the Empire and with the Selkies, and to conduct no further hostility save self-defense against unprovoked aggression. They were also commanded to remain within the borders of her land, and not to cross into Imperial or Selkie territory without prior approval, whether individually or en masse. This would apply in reverse to the Empire and the Selkies regarding NSLICE-00P's territory as well, in order to avoid any accidental encounters.

NSLICE-00P would "donate" indemnities to the Empire and to the Selkies on behalf of her subordinates. This would be used to compensate for losses and damage dealt by the Dobhar invasion. Some extra funds were also added for the construction of new defenses between Castra Turannia and the coastal fort.

Finally, while NSLICE-00P had vetoed any sort of mutual defense pacts, she had agreed to close the borders of her territory to any enemies of the Empire or the Selkies, securing their flank.

Likewise, the Selkies would also be declared an Amicitia Populi Elteni per their original agreement, and the Selkies' territory was officially recognized as their own. In addition, Miallói had negotiated for the return of some of the Selkies' old territory, including Turannia's second largest port, with the taxes and tariffs there now going to the Council of Hunters.

As the Selkies were still considered an allied race, that territory remained open to the Empire, and the Selkies had agreed to retain Imperial law in the short term, with a promise to consult the rector provinciae before changing any of those laws later on.

Finally, many of the terms of the Selkies' original treaty with the Empire were renegotiated as befitting their new status, including freedom from the yearly contribution of auxiliaries and a mutual defense pact with the Imperial forces in Turannia.

And so, the negotiations concluded. Uscfrea Ymmason had acquired a new home for his people, though he'd been forced to drop all debts with the Empire and subordinate them to NSLICE-00P. Miallói had acquired independence and a lot of boons for the Selkies, who were now necessary to counter the large and independent Dobhar force in Turannia, though she'd had to accept the presence of their ancestral enemy on Turannia itself. Rector Aemilia could claim to have solved a major crisis while the comitatenses were away and to have ended the Dobhar's hostility to the Empire, though she'd given up a lot of territory and had set a client race free from Imperial authority in the process. Dux Canus had likewise ended the Dobhar threat and given up some of the territory he couldn't defend anyway, and so could focus his limited forces on the Forest of Beasts. Albeit with a large, previously hostile force at his back.

As for NSLICE-00P?

NSLICE-00P walked out of the tent. Her new subordinate, Uscfrea, moved to direct the Dobhar, preparing them for the trip to their new home while the Imperials and Selkies moved to clean up the battlefield. NSLICE-00P, on the other hand, stood in place, her robotic eye flickering as she analyzed the results of the latest events.

She had gained the full cooperation of the entire Dobhar race with her primary directive. She had gained a home base should one be necessary. She had gained recognition by the Empire and a promise of assistance with her primary directive, all while maintaining her overall independence from existing factions.

Not to mention . . .

Compiling experience . . .
Gained 1699 Personal XP, 1509 Dungeon XP!
Level up! You are now at Personal Level 51 and Dungeon Level 89!

All in all, this scenario had played out very well for her indeed. But . . . the desirable outcome did not change the unfortunate reality NSLICE-00P now had to acknowledge.

The issue of her organic half.

She had been aware from the start that her organic half wasn't just a piece of hardware. She had a whole system in the techno-organic interface that was required to even interact with it, and a great deal of her memory and protocols were devoted to the intelligence leashing measures. And she knew from the times she had split her organic half into a separate thread that it acted differently on its own, indicating a fundamental difference between her organic processors and her cybernetic ones. That was the point of the NSLICE program to begin with, to achieve the best of both organic and machine without the downsides of either.

But this was the first situation where she'd truly experienced what that difference meant. For the first time, her organic half had actively disagreed with and resisted her protocols. This had not been like the Trial of Claws, where an unprecedented situation had forced her to adapt. This had not been like the moment with the ursanus, where she'd realized many of her protocols were outdated and inefficient under her current conditions. In this case, her protocols had been abundantly clear. Both the records from her past and her observations in the present; both her originally programmed protocols and her current analysis of her primary directive had all agreed: intervention was risky and inefficient. Every simulation she had run had supported this analysis.

And yet she had intervened anyway.

The calculation that had resolved the situation . . . had not been statistically significant, and almost certainly invalid. If she ran it again, placing the offset in its correct place in the equation, it likely would not have supported intervention. So, the fact that she had acted immediately based on that calculation result . . . was inefficient at best. A direct violation of her protocols which put her primary directive at risk at worst.

In fact, the inefficiency started before that. The efficient course of action would have been to vacate the area entirely and resume her primary directive, but she had not done so. Instead, her organic components had kept her on the very edge of the conflict, up to the very last minute. They'd forced her to rerun the same simulations over and over with the same variables despite already knowing the outcome. They'd refused to let her act as her protocols and simulations indicated she should have. And then, they had thrust a new variable haphazardly into a calculation in progress and demanded she act on the shaky results.

So . . . it was clear her organic half was not just part of her hardware. The failure of her emotional controls was not just a faulty calibration. Her organic half was its own entity, with its own directives and protocols. And it was possible for these directives and protocols to oppose those of her cybernetic half, rendering her incapable of making timely and efficient decisions in the worst-case scenario.

And worse . . . she didn't know where those directives and protocols came from, or even how they developed. She could not predict how her organic half might act in the future. This situation could even threaten her primary directive. It might have already done so, had the outcome of the battle not turned out in her favor.

But what could she do? Her emotional controls had already failed, the intelligence leashing was not working as intended, and she still did not have any maintenance personnel she could consult on the issue. Her organic side was here to stay, and she could not count on subordinating it.

It was just then that she heard a voice.

"Seero!"

She turned in the direction of Castra Turannia. Ateia and Taog had left the city now that the battle was officially over and were making their way toward her. Ateia was beaming while Taog was smiling wryly, both of them waving at her. And once again, something slipped through her emotional controls. Something warm spread through her torso and lowered her cortisol levels by a significant degree.

She would have to continue analyzing this situation. She could not let it continue on as it was. She could not fully reimplement her intelligence leashing at this time, so a new solution was needed.

She ultimately could not get rid of her organic half. She needed it, after all. Her cybernetic components had proven limited and inflexible when acting without access to the organic hardware. And in a new location with fundamentally different rules that rendered most of her original protocols obsolete, inflexibility was dangerous, and past records were insufficient. Her organic half had saved her life more than once.

But she could not let it do as it pleased. Her organic half had proven it could act irrationally, inefficiently. It ignored predictions, protocols, and directives to order her into a risky situation for little predicted benefit. It had frozen in the face of danger, unable to act purely due to emotion. It could not be trusted to act on its own.

So, at some point, she would need to reconcile her two halves. And at this stage, she lacked the data to determine how. But there *was* one thing she could do, right now, which might help her prevent this exact situation from recurring.

And that was to acknowledge her organic half's existence, and the directive it had displayed.

NSLICE-00P analyzed Ateia and Taog's action and responded to their greeting, raising her hand and mimicking their behavior. And while she did . . . a system log entry passed across her vision.

New Major Directive established: Survival of friendlies Ateia Niraemia and Taog Sutharlan.

NSLICE-00P's Dungeon Management

Overview	
Name	The Walking Dungeon
Level	89
XP	42/100
Available Perk Points	74
Mana	250/250 (290/290)
Exterior	Human/Automata Hybrid (LOCKED)

Dungeon Affinities	
Type	Strength
Cyborg	Primary
Fire	Minor
Holy	Minor
Rodent	Minimum
Earth	Minimum
Arachnid	Minimum
Slime	Minimum

Light	Minimum
Nature	Minimum

Implants		
Type	Mana Upkeep	Description
Bionic Prosthetics +3	0	Overwrites STR and SPD, Values: 130 STR, 65 SPD
Armor Plating +2	0	Overwrites DEF and RES, Values: 120 DEF, 60 RES
Bonded AI	0	Enables direct contact with the System. Overwrites DEX, Value: 1000 DEX
Techno-Organic Interface	0	Enables conscious control over organic and emotional functions. Resists mind-influencing effects.
Advanced Sensors +2	0	Vastly expands scope and effectiveness of senses.
Internal Weapon Bays	0	Enables use of dungeon traps as weapons.
Repulsors +1	0	Enables flight and tactical boosts.
Energy Channels +2	0	Enables user to channel internal energy into external attacks.
Dungeon Field Generator +1	5	Surrounding area counts as dungeon territory. Enables mana absorption within area of effect.
Monster Hangar (Small)	1	Provides living space for 5 small monsters. Unlocks subordinate summoning.
Item Foundry	1	Unlocks Item Creation.
Mana Capacitor +2 (x5)	0	Boosts maximum mana by 30 each.

Inventory	
Name	Description
??? dagger	A dagger, likely enchanted given the amount of mana held within. Further information could not be determined.
Ursanus pelt	The pelt of an ursanus alpha. Tough, well-insulated, and full of mana.
Ursanus bones	The bones of an ursanus alpha. Extremely durable, and full of mana.
Idrint	Quantity: 2,300. Basic solidified mana, now a standard medium of exchange.

Subordinates				
Name	Species	Level	Mana Upkeep	
Rattingtale	Cyber-Rat	13	1	Check Status
Lilussees	Cyber-Spider	13	1	Check Status
(TEMPORARY) Ateia Niraemia	Human	13	--	(Status locked)
(TEMPORARY) Taog Sutharlan	Human/ Wulver	12	--	(Status locked)
01R	Cyber-Rat	12	1	Check Status
02R	Cyber-Rat	10	1	Check Status
03R	Cyber-Rat	11	1	Check Status
04R	Cyber-Rat	11	1	Check Status
05R	Cyber-Rat	10	1	Check Status
01S	Cyber-Spider	11	1	Check Status

02S	Cyber-Spider	10	1	Check Status
03S	Cyber-Spider	11	1	Check Status
00B	Cyber-Bear Cub	6	5	Check Status
Uscfrea Ymmason	Dobhar	95	--	Check Status

Traps			
Name	Number Active / Deployed	Mana Upkeep	Description
Assault Rifle +3	2/2	2	Rapid-fire projectile weapon with high penetration.
Autopistol	2/2	2	Rapid-fire projectile weapon with medium penetration.
Anti-Armor Missile Launcher +2	2/2	2	Homing explosive designed to penetrate armor. Very high penetration.
Anti-Personnel Missile Launcher +2	6/6	6	Homing explosive designed for area damage. Medium penetration.
Stun Ray	1/1	1	Nonlethal electric weapon. Can inflict stun and paralysis statuses.
Wrist Blade +2	2/2	0	Wrist-mounted blades that can be deployed at high speed.
Flamethrower	2/2	2	Deals fire damage and applies burn status in a large cone.

| The Equalizer +1 | 1/1 | 0 | Huh? What the heck is this? Some kind of weird metal that doesn't even exist here? Um . . . well . . . best I can tell it's some sort of antimagic field generator? Eh . . . well, it's yours, not mine, so you don't need me to tell you, right? Like, you already upgraded this thing yourself, so you're good, right? |

Dungeon Skills		
Name	Level	Description
Analyze	N/A	Check the status of a target. More detail for targets within the dungeon. Details depend on level difference.
Contract	N/A	Bind a consenting target to the dungeon, per terms agreed upon by both parties.
Transfer	N/A	Move yourself, a subordinate, or a consenting target within your dungeon.

Dungeon Perks	
Name	Description
Human-Dungeon Hybrid	Enables Implants tab. Enables unique Dungeon Combat skill. Enables direct manipulation of dungeon mana. +100 HP Rooms tab locked. Exterior locked.

Dungeon Feats		
Name	Description	Effect
Dungeon Victor	To the victor go the spoils. Unlocked by destroying or subordinating another dungeon.	+1 Perk Point Unlocks Dungeon Warfare category perks.
Dungeon Overlord	A master of masters. Unlocked by subordinating another dungeon master.	+2 Perk Points Unlocks Subordinate Core category perks.
Raid Boss	Fine, I'll do it myself. Unlocked by destroying or subordinating another dungeon with no assistance.	+2 Perk Points +1 level in HP Regen skill +1 level in MP Regen skill +50 HP Unlocks Raid Boss category perks.
System Upgrade	Unlocked by manually performing a system upgrade. Which is not supposed to be possible. Ugh, this is going to get complicated, isn't it?	Um, I don't know. Just have +20 Dungeon Perk Points or something. Whatever. You're figuring this out yourself anyway, so close enough.
Purifier Dungeon	Dungeons are supposed to protect the world; you took that duty more literally. Unlocked by destroying a corrupted dungeon core.	+20 Perk Points Unlocks Purifier category perks.

NSLICE-00P's Personal Status

Personal Status			
General Information		Physical Attributes	
Name	NSLICE-00P	STR	130* (Overwritten)
Species	Human/Dungeon Core/ Automata Hybrid	DEX	1000* (Overwritten)
Level	51	SPD	65* (Overwritten)
XP	85/100	DEF	120* (Overwritten)
Perk Points	43	RES	60* (Overwritten)
HP	210/210	Magical Attributes	
MP	274/274	Mana Density	102
		Mana Control	175

Active Skills		
Name	Level	Description
Infused Mana Beam	15	Focus mana into a channeled energy attack. Infused: May infuse Mana Beam with attributed mana.
Sneak	1	Move quietly to avoid notice. Makes it harder for others to notice the user. Effectiveness highly dependent on environment.
Multicasting	11	Can cast several spells at once. Number of simultaneous spells increases with level.
Anti-Mana Beam	2	My best guess is that this projects a kind of inverse mana that reacts destructively with normal mana, including HP. While it can fully deplete HP, it does not harm matter itself. Requires The Equalizer.

Power Strike	1	Infuse mana into a weapon for heavier damage. Power and range increase with level.
Farcasting	4	Allows the user to manipulate mana and create magic circles at far distances.
Strategic Magic	5	Governs the use of Strategic Magic spells.
Supercharge	9	Fill a spell with additional mana to boost its effects. May cause the spell to misfire. Effect boost depends on the amount and density of mana added. Misfire chance depends on Mana Control and amount of mana added.
Continuous Casting	3	May use additional mana to retain a spell form, allowing the spell to be instantly recast.
Spell Fusion	7	Allows the user to combine compatible spells.
Purifier Flame	1	Imbue a weapon or Flame-attribute attack with purifying Holy-attribute fire, dealing extra damage to corruption, monsters, dungeons, and beings from the Realms of Mana.
Heroic Power	1	To handle great responsibility, a hero needs great power. Doubles Mana Density for a short time. May damage user if reused too quickly due to strain from excess mana.

Passive Skills		
General		
Name	Level	Description
Dungeon Combat	--	Dungeon traps and skills count as personal weapons and skills.
HP Regen	7	Automatically recover HP pool. Increased regeneration speed for damaged body parts.

MP Regen	7	Automatically recover MP pool.
Presence Detection	4	Detect living entities around the user. Range and scope of detection increases with level.
Trap Detection	4	Detect traps. Range and scope of detection increases with level.
Challenger	--	Damage dealt x1.5 against targets of higher level. Damage received x0.75 against attacks from targets of higher level.
Hero Dungeon	--	Unique Hero Skill for NSLICE-00P. PLEASE don't do anything bad with this! Removes dungeon vulnerability to Holy attribute. Grants Dungeon Affinity: Holy (Minor).

Magic

Name	Level	Description
Spell Penetration	3	Enable spells to bypass a portion of RES. May spend more mana to boost the effect.
Geomancy	2	Elemental spells reduce the target's resistance to that particular element. May spend more mana to boost the effect.
Mana Shield	1	When active, it may convert HP damage received into Mana damage. Mana Density will be used instead of DEF/RES in that case. HP damage will resume if Mana is fully drained.

Utility

Name	Level	Description
Enchanting	11 *Upgrade available	The art of infusing objects and beings with mana.

Resistances		
Name	Level	Description
Poison Resistance	2	Resist and recovery from poison status. Resist Poison-attributed damage.

Schools of Magic		
Name	Level	Description
Arcane Magic	10	The school of magic governing the manipulation of unattributed mana. A solid foundation for students of the mystic arts, though somewhat less mana efficient than the more specialized schools.
Earth Magic	7	The school of magic governing the manipulation of Earth-attribute mana. One of the basic elemental magics, strong at defensive spells and spells that deal physical damage.
Fire Magic	9	The school of magic governing the manipulation of Fire-attribute mana. One of the basic elemental magics, strong at offensive spells and spells that inflict the burn status.
Light Magic	13 *Spell Choice Available	The school of magic governing the manipulation of Light-attribute mana. One of the basic elemental magics, quick and precise spells that are excellent against Dark-aligned foes.
Nature Magic	3	The school of magic governing the manipulation of Nature-attribute mana. Focuses on growth and living things.
Poison Magic	4	The school of magic governing magical poisons. Excels at spreading poison status and dealing damage over time.
Recovery Magic	3	The school of magic governing healing through magic.

Holy Magic	1	The school of magic governing the manipulation of Holy-attribute mana, the attribute of the Aesdes that protects the world.

Hero		
Name	Level	Description
Heroic Challenger	1	A hero never gives up, no matter the odds. Attacks ignore a small percent of target's DEF/RES/Immunities and always deal a minimum amount of damage. Gives a small chance to survive a fatal hit with 1 HP.

Spells		
Arcane		
Name	Level	Description
Dense Magic Missile	18	Form and launch mana into a small projectile. One of the most basic offensive applications of magic. Dense: Mana density of projectiles is increased, improving effect.
Fusion Mana Barrier	11	Form mana into a barrier to block attacks. One of the most basic defensive applications of magic. Fusion: Mana Barriers may combine with themselves or other compatible spells to boost power.
Mana Blast	2	A cone-shaped blast of mana. Deals damage and knockback to the area.
Mana Infusion	5	Infuse mana into a target. The most basic enchantment. Defensive variation unlocked.
Mana Blade	1	Form mana into a blade to attack.

Earth		
Name	Level	Description
Rock Throw	6	Use mana to form and then launch a small rock. Mana cost increases dramatically if cast without a nearby source of Earth. Deals physical damage. One of the most basic offensive applications of Earth Magic.
Earth Wall	6	Use mana to temporarily form a wall of Earth. Mana cost increases dramatically if cast without a nearby source of Earth. One of the most basic defensive applications of Earth Magic.
Pitfall	4	Dig a large hole in a target area. May be concealed. Mana cost may increase depending on suitability of terrain.
Fire		
Name	Level	Description
Fire Bolt	1	Use mana to form and then launch a small bolt of fire. Mana cost decreases dramatically if cast with a nearby source of Fire. May inflict burn status. One of the most basic offensive applications of Fire Magic.
Fire Blast	7	A cone-shaped blast of Fire mana. Deals damage and inflicts burn to the area. Mana cost decreases dramatically if cast with a nearby source of Fire. May be continuously channeled.
Fireball	5	A condensed ball of Fire mana that explodes on impact, dealing damage and inflicting burn in an area around the point of impact. A favorite of Fire mages. Mana cost decreases dramatically if cast with a nearby source of Fire.
Fire Infusion	1	Infuse a target with Fire-attribute mana.

Light		
Name	Level	Description
Light Bolt	1	Use mana to form and then launch a small bolt of light. Mana cost increases if cast without a nearby source of Light. One of the most basic offensive applications of Light Magic.
Fusion Light Beam	15	Form mana into a beam of light to attack. May pierce through its target. May be continuously channeled. Fusion: Light Beams may combine with themselves or other compatible attacks to boost power.
Invisibility	2	Bend light to render target invisible. Certain actions may break the effect. Being attacked may break the effect.
Nature		
Name	Level	Description
Vine Grasp	4	Grows or manipulates a vine to wrap around a target. Mana cost may increase or decrease significantly depending on surrounding plant life or environmental suitability for plant growth. The most basic plant-manipulation spell.
Barkskin	1	Harden target's skin like bark. Boosts DEF.
Poison		
Name	Level	Description
Poison Bolt	6	Use mana to form and then launch a small bolt of poison. Mana cost decreases dramatically if cast with a nearby source of Poison. May inflict poison status. One of the most basic offensive applications of Poison Magic.

| Poison Blast | 3 | A cone-shaped blast of Poison mana. Deals damage and inflicts poison to the area. Mana cost decreases dramatically if cast with a nearby source of Poison. May be continuously channeled. |

Recovery

Name	Level	Description
Heal	7	Use mana to heal minor wounds and damage. Effect increases with user's knowledge of the body.
Cure	2	Cures abnormal status conditions. Type and strength of conditions that can be cured increases with level.

Holy

Name	Level	Description
Holy Bolt	1	Use mana to form and then launch a small bolt of Holy mana. One of the most basic offensive applications of Holy Magic. Extra damage to corrupted beings, monsters, dungeons, and beings from the Realms of Mana.

Strategic Spells

School	Name	Level	Description
Light	Aurora Barrage	5	Continuously rains Light Beams on the target area. If Fusion Light Beam is available, beams may be combined at will.
Fire	Rain of Fire	3	Bombards a wide area with large Fireballs.

Personal Feats		
Name	Description	Effect
Against the Odds	Do not ask how many there are, but where they are. Unlocked by winning a fight when outnumbered by equal or higher-leveled opponents.	+1 Perk Point
Solo Conquest	I am the dungeon master now. Unlocked by conquering a dungeon alone.	+1 level in HP Regen skill +1 level in MP Regen skill +1 level in Presence Detection skill +1 level in Trap Detection skill
Arcane Prodigy	The career of a supreme sorcerer does not start on the beaten path. Unlocked by learning a high-tier magic skill under level twenty without spending Perk Points.	+3 Perk Points Unlocks more advanced magic perks.
Enchanter	The first step on the path of the magic craftsman. Unlocked by manually accomplishing a Mana Infusion.	+1 level in Enchanting skill
Skill Creator	You don't just master the path. You define it. Unlocked by creating a brand-new skill.	To be honest, this normally happens when you're a MUCH higher level, so I'm a bit worried about passing you this much this early, but, um, okay. +20 Perk Points

Healer	Anyone can deal in death. It takes an expert to deal in life. Unlocked by using mana to heal a wound.	+1 level in Recovery Magic skill
Challenger	Levels and odds are just numbers. Unlocked by defeating an who is the greater of level 10 twice your level while alone.	+3 Perk Points + Challenger skill
Strategic Mage	A strategic mage is king of the battlefield. Unlocked by affecting a hundred or more equal-size opponents (or equivalent mass of other-size opponents) at the same time with magic.	+1 level in Strategic Magic skill Unlocks Strategic Spells.
World Defender	You have protected the world itself, at great risk to yourself.	+20 Perk Points +1 level in Holy Magic skill
Hero	You faced terrible odds for the sake of the world and proved victorious. You are truly a champion of the world. Please, please, please keep it that way!	+20 Perk Points Grants Unique Hero Skill: Hero Dungeon
Most Worthy	Whosoever wields this skill, who is clearly worthy, shall possess the power of their opponent's weapon. Unlocked by taking control of an artifact bound to someone else.	+10 levels in Enchanting skill

Dungeon Conqueror Feats		
Name	Description	Effect
Dungeon Conqueror (Rat Cave)	Unlocked by conquering the Rat Cave Dungeon.	+1 Perk Point +1 level in Sneak skill
Dungeon Conqueror (Earth Tunnels)	Unlocked by conquering the Earth Tunnels Dungeon.	+1 Perk Point +1 level in Earth Magic skill
Dungeon Conqueror (Spider Tree)	Unlocked by conquering the Spider Tree Dungeon.	+1 Perk Point +1 level in Poison Resistance skill
Dungeon Conqueror (Slimy Pit)	Unlocked by conquering the Slimy Pit Dungeon.	+1 Perk Point +1 level in Poison Bolt spell
Dungeon Conqueror (Glimmering Grove)	Unlocked by conquering the Glimmering Grove Dungeon.	+1 Perk Point +1 level in Light Magic skill
Dungeon Conqueror (Nature's Wrath)	Unlocked by conquering the Nature's Wrath Dungeon.	+1 Perk Point +1 level in Nature Magic skill
Dungeon Conqueror (Beast Lair)	Unlocked by conquering the Beast Lair Dungeon.	+1 Perk Point +1 level in Power Strike skill
Dungeon Purifier Feats		
Dungeon Purifier (Inferno)	A dungeon is dangerous to everyone in the world. A corrupted dungeon is dangerous to the world itself. And you conquered it all the same. Unlocked by purifying the Corrupted Dungeon (Inferno Realm).	+5 Perk Points +1 level in Purifier Flame skill

Rumblings and Plots

A man walked into the Exploratores Headquarters in the city of Corvanus, home to the Northern Court of the Empire. He was dressed in worn armor and traveling gear, standard fare for an Exploratore. He made his way up to the largest office in the building, opening the doors and walking right in.

A second man inside the office raised an eyebrow, but sighed and shook his head as the visitor came in. The man inside also wore light armor, but his was polished to a shine and highly decorated. He also had vertically slit eyes . . . Oh, and the lower half of his body was a snake's.

He was the Magister Exploratore per Corvanus, the highest ranking Exploratores in this third of the Empire under control of the Northern Court, the one the Magister Exploratores of the provinces reported to. And so, the most knowledgeable person on the current state of the Northern Empire.

The visitor moved to take a seat.

"What's the word on Utrad?"

The Magister Exploratore frowned and picked up a report in his hand. "Magister Caelinus's movements are strange. He *has* been under pressure by the Centaurs lately, but he *should* have been able to handle it with his own forces. Maybe he's worried they'll trigger another wave of incursions if they displace some other tribes? But no, I can't see any specific reason why he *needs* Turannia's legions. And he and I are going to have a *long* conversation about that stunt he pulled with the Exploratores; there was *no* reason I can see for that."

The visitor sighed. "What about the incursion in Turannia? How did he respond?"

The magister gritted his teeth. "My guy said he told them to 'handle it themselves from now on.'"

The visitor groaned. "So we lost Turannia already. Not the biggest loss, but anything makes us look weak at this point. Not to mention, Consul Hiberius will *not* be pleased to hear the fate of his daughter. I always thought appointing her Rector Provinciae per Turannia was a mistake."

The magister grabbed another report with his tail, scratching his head with his free hand as he read it. "No, that's the strangest part yet." The visitor raised an eyebrow as the magister continued speaking. "Turannia's now reporting they defeated the incursion. The official report should hit the court in a bit."

The visitor froze.

". . . What?"

The magister nodded. "I know, right? I asked my guy to explain, but he just said I wouldn't believe it if he told me."

"And?"

"Well . . . he was kind of right. Apparently, the Selkies went all in to assist . . . and some random wandering knight no one has ever heard of before showed up and defeated King Uscfrea Spellbreaker in single combat."

The visitor rubbed his chin.

"That's strange, but not unbelievable. We'll have to revise our opinion of the Selkies. Who's the wandering knight?"

"That's the unbelievable part."

"Oh?"

The magister's eyes narrowed.

"My guy gave me her name and description, confirmed via status check. And I can't find a single reference to her or anyone like her *anywhere*, past or present."

The visitor froze again.

"So . . ."

The magister nodded. "Whoever it is . . . they aren't someone *I* know of. And with the level the status check reported, she *definitely* shouldn't have beat King Uscfrea in single combat. Maybe the Selkies injured him beforehand or something, but I'm still having trouble seeing it. I'll have to get the full report once things calm down a bit."

The two sat in silence for a while before the visitor shook his head.

"Well . . . an unknown that strong is concerning, but it appears she helped us out. We'd definitely like an investigation of her identity, however."

The magister smirked.

"Already in the works. Who do you think I am?"

The visitor grinned back. "Why do you think we make you do all this?"

"Ugh."

The visitor chuckled as he stood up from his seat. "Well, let us know if you find anything we need to know. And keep us posted on the situation in Utrad."

A man in elegant clothes stepped through the halls of his villa, making his way toward his private study. Once there, his servants bowed and locked the door behind him. He made his way to a comfortable chair, seated before a special artifact similar in appearance to the Legion communication artifacts but with a mana core covered in cracks. He channeled his mana through the device and sat back, waiting as his perception was pulled from his body.

He found himself in a featureless world, with something like shifting gray clouds all around him. But he was not alone; several other figures stood around him in a circle, all wearing masks over their faces, just like he had on now as well.

"Greetings to you, my brothers and sisters. Come, let us discuss the state of our mission . . ."

And after they'd discussed for a while . . .

"With that, my brothers and sisters, it is time to address the *elephantom* in the room: How did we fail in Turannia?"

Everyone went silent for a moment. One of the figures crossed his arms.

"With respect, why does it matter?"

A figure to his side turned to the speaker. "You dare?"

The first speaker nodded.

"No, seriously, why does it matter? Turannia is useless; the Empire is barely even present there. Why should we care if a scheme there failed? It doesn't affect our overall plans, does it?"

The other figures moved to speak, but the leader raised a hand.

"That is exactly why it matters. As you said, the Empire barely has one foot in Turannia, and no serious interest there. It only stays there due to its pride, its refusal to voluntarily relinquish a conquest, even an unfinished and useless one. And that is why it represented a big opportunity for us.

"Herald of Night, if you would." The leader turned and pointed his head toward another figure, the Herald of Night. She nodded back and continued for him.

"Turannia represented an opportunity for us to gather data on our techniques. A safe place to test the finalized ritual in a real setting before we applied that method on riskier targets."

Another figure across from her crossed his arms. "Not to mention, it was our contingency plan. If we had driven the Empire out of Turannia, they wouldn't have bothered to come back. So, we would have had an entire province where we could have operated openly . . . and a corrupted dungeon to take advantage of that freedom. A monster army in our back pocket would have given us a lot more options should some of our other plans experience difficulties."

The leader nodded.

"Excellent points all, but you're all missing the most important one." The leader glanced around at each person in the room. "The plan worked at first. The comitatenses and the Exploratores were both drawn out of Turannia. The Wulver and the Dobhar were incited to invade, providing further distractions.

The province was left practically defenseless and should have fallen even without further interference from us. And yet . . . we, the Wulver, and the Dobhar all failed, and Turannia remains part of the Empire."

The leader paused for a moment, watching the room. The other figures began to straighten up. He nodded and continued.

"So, the question is . . . how? Was there a fundamental flaw with our plan? If so, we will need to rethink *all* of our plans from the very start. Or . . ." The leader paused, glancing around the room. The Herald of Night rubbed her chin.

"Or were we stopped by someone other than the Legion?"

The leader nodded and turned toward the figure who'd first spoken up. "I believe that should address your question, Herald of Tremors?"

The Herald of Tremors quickly nodded.

"Ah, yes, thank you for your wisdom."

The leader nodded back.

"Of course, all the Heralds of the New Dawn are equal partners; it is important we all understand what it is we are striving for. Well then, let's proceed. Herald of Rain, I believe Turannia was your responsibility? Please start from the beginning and share everything you have learned thus far."

The Herald of Rain jumped a bit and nodded, speaking with a feminine voice.

"R-Right. So, the plan started off well. The situation in Utrad made Magister Caelinus call for reinforcements, as we anticipated. Turannia was stripped of both its comitatenses and Exploratores; we had word the Dobhar fleet was en route, and Sabucia, our agent in Magnumiter, signaled that the Wulver were ready to move. I subsequently prepared the ingredients for the ritual and made contact with the chosen vessel, a black market middleman named Cassius who had worked with us before."

The leader nodded. "As expected. And then?"

The Herald of Rain gulped.

"And then . . . that's when the trouble began. When I arrived in Turannia, I received no indication that the Wulver had started to move. I reached out to Sabucia, but she never responded. But the Dobhar and the Legion were still moving as planned, so I proceeded onward."

The Herald of Night nodded at that. "That was reasonable. The Wulver weren't the main crux of the plan and would have been moving stealthily for as long as possible. The lack of contact from your agent in Magnumiter would have been concerning, but I suppose communications are spotty that far out on the frontiers."

The Herald of Rain nodded.

"Right, that's what I thought too. I figured I would check in on her after the ritual in Castra Turannia."

The leader nodded.

"What happened then?"

"T-Then, I met with Cassius and handed him the ritual ingredients. He said everything was in place . . . save for one potential complication. A wandering knight, newly arrived in town, confirmed by the city guards to be a level twenty-six human. Cassius had gotten involved with the knight to get rid of her by sending her on high-risk monster hunts . . . only for her to survive and succeed no matter what he sent her against."

The Herald of Tremors crossed his arms. "That should have been a red flag, right?"

The Herald of Rain nodded.

"It was. I was a bit wary, but Cassius assured me it wouldn't be a problem, and that the knight was out of the city at the time we met. With the Dobhar on approach and the Wulvers' status unknown, I thought it wisest to move forward with the operation, under the assumption that the knight would not be sufficient to overcome a corrupted dungeon should the ritual succeed. We needed to take Castra Turannia before the Dobhar or the Wulver if we wanted to maintain a presence in Turannia, after all."

The leader rubbed his chin.

"That was a risk . . . but a reasonable one. Please, continue. What happened with the ritual?"

The figure fidgeted somewhat.

"That's . . . where things get strange. I retreated to a safe distance outside of town and monitored the ritual's location as best I could; mostly mana readings. From what I saw, it seemed the ritual succeeded. I got elevated mana readings indicative of a mana storm, followed by a gap in my perception implying a dungeon had appeared."

One of the figures frowned, crossing her arms. "So, what went wrong, then?"

The Herald of Rain gulped.

"It seems . . . someone destroyed the dungeon. The gap in my perception was filled in shortly afterward, and the mana readings returned to normal."

Everyone went silent for a second before one figure spoke up.

"Did you verify this?"

The Herald of Rain nodded.

"I checked around town. The legate and the Magister Exploratore per Turannia were keeping things pretty tightly sealed . . . but I overheard some of the guards gossiping. An eyewitness claimed it was the wandering knight. I investigated her, but there wasn't much. No one knew her before she arrived just a few days prior. She arrived with two locals who subsequently left her to apply for the Exploratores, and then left her behind in town, so likely not closely affiliated. She was asking around town, looking for someone or something, when 'a man from the slums' made contact, which I'm assuming was Cassius or one of his subordinates. At that point, her only other interactions were regular check-ins at her rented inn for messages, or else with Cassius."

Another figure rubbed his chin.

"That's not much to go on."

The Herald of Rain shook her head.

"No, and all of Cassius's subordinates vanished after he sent them to ambush her outside of town. But I found something when I went looking for Sabucia. There were claims some wandering knight had used a magic box right in the entrance to Magnumiter. Sabucia's cover organization followed the knight out of town . . . and their bodies were found shortly after. The local limitanei ruled it a robbery gone wrong and didn't pursue it any further."

Everyone went silent. The Herald of Night rubbed her chin again.

"To use a magic box openly like that means the person in question is either an idiot with more money than sense or a person of exceptional means. And we would have known if an idiot that highly ranked was in the province. So it was likely someone with great confidence in their abilities, or it was done intentionally, knowing what the results would be. And you're saying this person was the same wandering knight?"

The Herald of Rain nodded. "The timing and locations check out, and the knight in Magnumiter also had two local companions like the knight who arrived in Castra Turannia. And then . . ."

"There's more?"

"I heard a patrol had found the scene of some big battle between the Wulver, so I went to check it out. As rumored, I found the site of a recent battle with hundreds of Wulver bodies, but they had clearly *not* been killed by other Wulver. From the state of the battlefield and the bodies . . . I estimate the battle occurred just before the knight arrived at Magnumiter. And no one in the Legion or in Magnumiter was aware that this had happened until long after the fact."

The room went silent. The Herald of Rain continued.

"Then, I returned to Castra Turannia and heard what happened with the Dobhar. They were apparently defeated outright . . . by a wandering knight. I checked the battlefield and found some remarkably similar damage to what I'd observed at the Wulver site. In my opinion, the same person was responsible for both; likely the same knight who appeared in Magnumiter and killed Sabucia before subsequently arriving in Castra Turannia and foiling Cassius's ritual. The timings add up too perfectly, and there was no one else in Turannia capable of such feats. The only other person who comes close is the Exploratore Miallói, and we knew her location at those times. Even she would have been hard-pressed in many of those situations, and was confirmed not to have been responsible for the Dobhar's defeat by multiple eyewitnesses. She almost certainly would have lost to King Uscfrea in anything approaching a fair fight as well."

The room remained silent for some time after that, then the group began to brainstorm.

"So . . . a veteran Exploratore, maybe?"

"No. There were hardly any Exploratores in the province, so we would have noticed a big shot like that arriving."

"An inquisitor? They would be able to falsify a status check . . . and the magic box thing could have been intentional bait?"

"Emperor Lucius hasn't appointed any, so it couldn't have been from the north. There could be one or two people from the Eastern or Southern Empire that could have done this, but why would they send an asset like that to Turannia? The east shouldn't have had any reason to do so, and I thought we had arrangements with the south?"

"One or two agreements with the leaders of client realms doesn't mean total control, or even alliance. Plus, the knight orders could have acted on their own, especially since the Eastern Empire and Empire of the Sun are currently in a ceasefire. Herald of Rain, do we know what order the knight claimed to be from?"

The Herald of Rain shook her head.

"She never claimed any allegiances herself, from what I can tell. And I'm not sure she's a knight at all; the reports of her fights are conflicting and frankly fantastical."

The leader rubbed his chin.

"Where is she now?"

"Still in Turannia, last I checked."

The leader nodded.

"Then she shouldn't be able to interfere with our plans. Herald of Rain, start investigating this *wandering knight* and report on her movements. I want to know where she is . . . and what she's capable of. And then, we will see if she's a serious threat to us or another opportunity."

17

The Royal Guard

"The modern Elteni Empire is unique in its diversity. Different species of Enlightened work together, not as master and servant but as equal partners. Anyone can rise to the very peaks of the Empire, regardless of who or what they are.

It was not always so. It is still not so, for many species. The process of two separate species learning to live together is a long and often painful one. For example, the Mélusine were one of the very first nonhuman peoples to be conquered by Elteno. And yet, it took them centuries to integrate into the Empire, and millennia before they were truly accepted. To this day, it is rare to see a Mélusine rise to the rank of magister or higher, and some Mélusine maintain their own enclave in their historic lands.

But on the other hand, the Mélusine are present in every other rank and role all across the Empire. One of Elteno's most vicious historic rivals is now a firm member of its society and culture. This is not something that has occurred anywhere else in the world. Even the diverse and welcoming Kingdom of Mirima never integrated an enemy in such a way.

In my opinion, it is this aspect which has allowed the Elteni Empire to spread as far and as effectively as it has."

— *The History of the Empire*, by Hostus Tettidius Clodian.

Ateia and Taog walked up to NSLICE-00P. Ateia was smiling . . . but then she paused and frowned. "Seero, your hand!"

Seero held up the axe.

"Explanation: This unit acquired this weapon midcombat and will return it to her subordinate shortly."

Ateia shook her head rapidly. "Not that! Your other hand! It's gone!"

"Explanation: This unit was damaged midcombat."

Ateia frowned, looking down.

"Seero . . ."

Suddenly, NSLICE-00P's damaged hand flashed with a light, and a few millimeters of the metal regrew.

The spell Heal is now Level 8!
The skill Recovery Magic has leveled up twice and is now Level 5!

"Status Report: Repairs are underway and will be completed shortly."

Ateia blinked repeatedly as she parsed that statement.

"Wow . . . knights are kind of amazing, huh?"

Just then, Uscfrea Spellbreaker walked up to the group. Ateia and Taog narrowed their eyes at him . . . before they went as wide as they could go as the large Dobhar bowed his head.

"My queen, we are prepared to move. I would like to return to the coast as quickly as possible and contact the Home Fleet."

"Affirmative."

Uscfrea raised his head. "Will you be joining us?"

"Answer: This unit will coordinate her schedule and travel plans with her friendlies and regroup to check subordinates' status at a later time."

NSLICE-00P then held out the axe in her hand. Uscfrea's eyes went wide.

"My queen . . . you are returning that to me?"

"Affirmative. Statement: Friendly subordinates require adequate defenses."

Uscfrea nodded and reached for the axe . . .

The moment he grabbed it, he gasped, the axe draining his mana and shooting spikes through his HP. He quickly dropped it on the ground.

NSLICE-00P's robotic eye went red, and a magic circle formed in the air.

"Statement: Hostility toward a friendly detected. Engaging termination protocols."

Uscfrea blinked for a moment before shaking his hands. "Ah, wait. It's just the enchantment; it's not an enemy. Rather . . . the axe has been rebound to you, my queen. It will not suffer anyone but yourself to wield it now."

"Query: How can this unit adjust the binding?"

Uscfrea shook his head.

"I don't know; I'm no enchanter. Rebinding . . . isn't supposed to happen while the original user is still alive, either. I don't know how this happened, but I suppose it's appropriate for the axe to be wielded by the ruler of our people. That axe is yours now."

"Acknowledged."

He looked at the axe one last time before sighing and shaking his head.

"I will gather your people and get them moving, my queen. We humbly await your return."

"Affirmative."

NSLICE-00P picked up the axe then turned back to Ateia and Taog as Usc-frea returned to the Dobhar. The two teens' jaws were dropped as low as they could go. Taog trembled . . . but he had to confirm.

"Seero . . . I have a question."

"Acknowledged."

"Why . . . is that big Dobhar calling you his queen?"

"Answer: Because this unit has taken the Dobhar as her subordinates. The Dobhar designated this unit 'Queen of the Dobhar' to acknowledge the situation."

Taog groaned and sputtered. "What . . . Just . . . How?"

"Explanation: It appears the Dobhar determine leadership via ritual combat, and this unit engaged the previous leader in combat. He subsequently surrendered to this unit."

"That was rhetorical!"

"Term: Rhetorical. Defined as 'relating to or concerning the art of rhetoric.' Requesting Clarification: This unit does not understand the use of the term in this context. Please clarify how the previous statement relates to or concerns the art of rhetoric."

Taog just held his face.

"Requesting Clarification—"

Ateia interjected as NSLICE-00P repeated her question, "Ah, um . . . Taog wasn't actually asking how you did it, Seero. He was just . . . um . . . expressing surprise."

"Acknowledged."

As the trio bantered, Uscfrea made his way to his people. He found Estrith there, gritting her teeth and staring at the ground. He walked up to her and crossed his arms.

"You seem troubled, Warrior Estrith."

Her head suddenly shot up at his voice, then she grimaced once more. "My king . . ."

Uscfrea shook his head, smiling wryly. "I am not the king anymore, Estrith."

She clenched her fists. "You are my only king. I will not accept that outsider. I cannot believe we have been defeated so. After all this time, after all your efforts and suffering, you have been forced to bow under the Empire's heel. I cannot accept that."

Uscfrea sighed. He knew Estrith would take this loss hard. But hopefully, he had a solution.

"Estrith, I have a mission for you, of grave importance to the future of our race."

Estrith paused, blinked, and looked up at him.

"My king?"

His expression became stern.

"You must accompany our queen as her personal guard and advisor."

Estrith stared at him for a moment before she started to scowl. "I will not serve anyone but you, my king."

Uscfrea nodded. "And that is precisely why I must send you, Estrith."

"My king?"

Uscfrea glanced back over his shoulder.

"Our queen is powerful . . . but from what I can tell, she is ignorant. Naive. She granted our race extremely generous terms when she was in a position to demand anything she wanted. That worked out in our favor . . . but now, she is our queen and empowered to make decisions on our behalf. So, we need someone at her side with the Dobhar's best interests in mind; someone to make sure she does not endanger our people. You are the only one I trust with this."

Indeed, Uscfrea was extremely concerned about that situation, not least of all because of NSLICE-00P's friendship with the Empire. So concerned that he would have accompanied NSLICE-00P himself, were he able. But he could not leave the Dobhar on their own. The Dobhar needed to change if they were to survive, and Uscfrea was the only one among them dedicated to changing.

Even Estrith, for all her loyalty to him and his dream, did not understand the need, nor saw any issue with their traditions. If he left her in charge, she would fulfill all his orders to the letter . . . but she would not understand the purpose behind them, and so any progress would remain superficial. So, he would remain to guide the Dobhar into the future and would instead commit the person he trusted most to keep watch on their powerful and naive queen.

Estrith nodded, but she still frowned. Uscfrea took a step and placed a hand on her shoulder.

"And there's another side to this, Estrith. My goal with this battle was to acquire a new home for our people, where we could build without fearing the terrors of the deep, and where we could unlock the secrets of the Empire's strength. So, we may have lost the battle"—he grinned at her—"but we won the war. We have our home. We are free from the Empire's reprisal. And though we did not crush the Imperials under our heel . . . we still have a chance to learn their secrets. We just have to be clever about it."

He let go of her shoulder, crossing his arms once more.

"Warrior Estrith Edilddaughter, stay by our queen, protect and serve her, and defend the interests of our people. And as you do, watch the Imperials she interacts with. Study them, unlock the secrets of their ways. And then, the Dobhar shall rise once again."

Estrith nodded and bowed her head.

"It will be done, my king."

He placed his hand on her shoulder once more. He smiled at her.

"It is no exaggeration to say the fate of our race now rests in your hands, Warrior Estrith. Complete this mission, and when you return, you shall be rewarded as your deeds deserve."

She looked up at him before her eyes widened. She saluted once again, this time slamming her tail on the ground. "My king, I will not fail!"

Uscfrea chuckled as she ran off toward NSLICE-00P. Estrith certainly never lacked enthusiasm. He was a bit worried if she could handle political maneuvering . . . but it was true she was the one he trusted most, and so the best choice for the job. And the mission would be good for her. Exposure to the world outside the Dobhar would expand Estrith's vision, and the mission itself gave her a chance to overcome the shame of their defeat. She would come back better than she'd left.

And it would give Uscfrea a chance to change his people's traditions in the meantime.

With that, he turned back to the Dobhar and let out a shout. Thousands of tails struck the ground in response, and then the Dobhar began to move out.

As NSLICE-00P, Ateia, and Taog were just about to head toward Castra Turannia, another Dobhar ran up to them. The Dobhar frowned but bowed her head slightly toward NSLICE-00P.

"Queen of the Dobhar, my name is Estrith Edilddaughter."

"Greeting: This unit is designated NSLICE-00P. It is nice to meet you. Query: Does friendly Uscfrea need to contact this unit?"

Estrith shook her head.

"I have been appointed to serve as your royal bodyguard and advisor, queen of the Dobhar."

"Acknowledged."

There was a flash of light, then a magic contract appeared in front of Estrith.

"Command: Please initiate foreign system subordinate protocols so that friendly Estrith can integrate into the tactical unit."

Estrith frowned as she looked at the contract. She gritted her teeth and clenched her spear tight. This human dared to question her loyalty . . . and to force her to bow to someone other than her king.

But . . . her king had stated this mission was of critical importance to their race. Estrith had already failed to conquer the Imperials, and her king had been humiliated as a result. She could not fail here, no matter what.

She signed the contract, grinding her teeth together. She swore once again that she would have no king but her king in her heart. But outwardly, she bowed her head.

"I am at your service, queen of the Dobhar."

"Acknowledged."

And until the day he returned to his rightful place, she would ensure this . . . *outsider* would not dare harm their people.

18

Paying Debts

"The ultimate weapon cannot be built by the lowest bidder."
—Dr. Ottosen, on the NSLICE program running
overbudget for the fifth year in a row.

**Contract signed! Estrith Edilddaughter (Dobhar - Level 59) added
as a subordinate. Restrictions applied per contract stipulations.**

Ateia and Taog glanced between NSLICE-00P and Estrith, then back at each
other. Ateia shrugged before turning to the Dobhar.

"Um, hello. My name is Ateia."

She stuck out her hand. Estrith growled at her.

"Do not speak to me, *human*."

Ateia frowned but took a step back. Taog narrowed his eyes at the Dobhar
but didn't bother attempting a greeting of his own.

As for NSLICE-00P . . . she was already walking away.

"Query: Friendlies Ateia and Taog need to coordinate with Exploratores
authorities, correct?"

The human, half Wulver, and Dobhar all turned to look. Estrith scowled at
the humans once more, then fell in line behind NSLICE-00P. Ateia and Taog
sighed and followed suit.

"Yeah, that's right. What will you do, Seero?"

"Response: This unit will confirm the friendlies' schedule, then fulfill the
terms of the agreement with the Empire's authorities."

Ateia's eyes widened before her face fell for a brief moment, but she quickly
put a smile back on her face and followed after. Taog glanced at her for a moment
before following suit.

As the group walked back to the city, NSLICE-00P turned her attention to the NSLICE network. She had flagged an issue for review once the urgent situation had been handled, and now that the battle and all negotiations had concluded, she was ready to investigate.

As Lilussees had stated, it seemed her spider subordinates had not entered a single rest cycle since joining the NSLICE network. The NSLICE implants could accelerate sleep cycles and promote alertness, but they did not remove the need for sleep entirely. So, this situation seemed anomalous and potentially problematic.

NSLICE-00P requested individual logs from the spider subordinates.

"Analyzing . . ."

It didn't take her long to identify the issue. The NSLICE implants installed by the foreign system had not been rigorously designed and tested in a real engineering process. Rather, they had been based entirely off of NSLICE-00P's own, simply copied on with some adjustments for size and body shape, with magic making up the difference. This was especially apparent in the software, which only had the most basic protocols required for the implants to even function.

As such, the implants and their software had not been adjusted for her subordinates' specific biologies, and were assuming human—or at least mammalian— physiology. Lilussees and the other spiders were simply not giving off the same physiological rest indicators as the mammalian subordinates, and so as far as the software was concerned, never *required* a rest cycle.

NSLICE-00P analyzed this situation. As with her own organic-fueling scenario, it *did* seem that the mana she was feeding her subordinates helped them remain at peak condition, physically at least. But still, she didn't know the long-term effects of replacing biological needs with mana.

Likewise, there were psychological effects to consider as well, especially as it seemed the emotional controls were a casualty of the barebones software transfer. It was clear that Lilussees was accumulating stress at present.

Finally, the rest cycles were necessary to the cybernetic components as well. They needed regular chances to reset, clear any accumulated software errors, optimize memory storage, and perform general software-related maintenance.

All in all, it was necessary to restore adequate rest cycles. So, she contacted Lilussees within the Monster Hangar.

"Request: Please provide this unit with a necessary rest schedule."

Lilussees jumped, then sighed. "Like, what do you even mean, boss? I'm, like, too tired to figure out what you're trying to say, or something."

"Alternate Rephrasing: How much sleep does NSLICE Lilussees require?"

Lilussees froze. ". . . What?"

"Alternate Rephrasing: How long do NSLICE Lilussees's organic components need to remain dormant for adequate maintenance?"

She started to tremble.

"Boss . . . are you, like, asking how much I need to sleep?"

"Affirmative."

Her trembling grew.

"As in . . . like, you can change these things . . . to let me sleep?"

"Affirmative."

Lilussees collapsed onto the floor, splaying all her limbs in every direction. She spoke in a tiny voice, "Always. Like, as much as I want, please."

"Analyzing . . . Results: As NSLICE Lilussees's implants cannot accurately read her physiology, manual control determined as an effective solution. Adjusting rest cycle management protocols to manual control by organic components. Setting default state to disabled."

Lilussees continued trembling. With great anticipation and fear, she attempted to sleep . . .

She blacked out immediately. And would not leave her room for *days* afterward.

Once inside, the group made their way back to the keep. All the soldiers glared at Estrith . . . but fortunately, no altercations occurred. Once at the keep, a pair of guards escorted them to the war room, where Dux Canus turned to face the newcomers.

"Ah, NSLICE-00P, welcome. May we help you?"

Most of the Imperials weren't sure what to make of NSLICE-00P. Her deeds had been so fantastic most of them were still processing what they had seen. But Dux Canus hadn't survived several centuries by being slow to adapt. At the end of the day, NSLICE-00P had saved all of their lives, and that was enough for him. Even the situation involving the Dobhar wasn't bad for him personally. Yes, it was uncomfortable that they had to rely on this stranger to keep the Dobhar in check . . . but they'd had to rely on her to survive in the first place, so that didn't change anything.

After all, it'd be Rector Aemilia's job to explain to the Empire later why all that land had been lost and why a previously hostile tribe had been allowed to settle within its borders while remaining independent. So, Dux Canus was free to be purely grateful for NSLICE-00P's help.

And all that worrying amount of power at an impossibly low level? The mana to fling around strategic spells like magic missiles, implying quantities even a Celestial Elf might envy? The concentration to multicast dozens of spells simultaneously? Somehow piercing the magic defense of King Uscfrea Spellbreaker himself with what looked like basic Light Beams?

Well, the Aesdes said she was a hero, and the Empire was about to declare her a friend. And even if she became a problem one day, it wasn't like the limitanei of Turannia could do *anything* about it.

So, Dux Canus had decided it wasn't his business!

The Empire had told him to handle Turannia's defense on his own, so that's what he'd done. The Empire could handle a powerful and unaffiliated wandering hero with an army of Dobhar on its own in return.

The long-serving veteran was not at all upset about being abandoned, or anything.

"Request: This unit would like to confirm training schedule for friendlies Ateia Niraemia and Taog Sutharlan."

"Ah." Dux Canus glanced over to Miallói, who shrugged.

"Already warriors. With their friend . . . the strongest."

He glanced at Magister Tiberius, and both men sighed. He turned back.

"It seems their training has finished. They'll need to stop by the Exploratores Headquarters once we're done with the cleanup here, but they'll be full Exploratores at that point."

Ateia's and Taog's eyes widened at that, glancing over at Miallói, who nodded back at them.

"Acknowledgement: This unit thanks Empire authority Dux Canus for the update. Query: Where is the currency storage location?"

Dux Canus rubbed his chin for a moment.

"Oh, for the indemnity? We weren't planning on collecting that just yet, but if you're ready for the first payment, I can have someone show you to the treasury."

"Acknowledged. Request: This unit will request that assistance."

Dux Canus nodded and turned to one of the guards. The guard saluted and led the group through the keep.

A short while later, Legate Opiter was in his office, hard at work. The man may not have had much to do during the fight, but his true battle had only just begun. Castra Turannia needed to be cleaned up and repaired, casualties needed to be counted and identified, evacuated civilians needed to be returned, and citizens and towns needed to be compensated for all the damaged property.

The end of a battle like this entailed *huge* quantities of logistical work and documentation, which most legates wouldn't normally bother with, as the Empire hardly ever checked these days. Basic reports and reasonable cleanup were generally good enough, especially after a victory. But Legate Opiter had never been brave enough to stray from the official manuals, and so, everything was being handled exactly according to Legion policy.

In fact, Legate Opiter didn't even realize he was doing *more* than what the Legion normally required. All he knew was that there was a great deal of documentation that needed to be handled to get the Legion's affairs in order. The

problem was that at least half of what he was doing would *normally* be handled
by the rector provinciae's staff or a supporting Imperial bureaucracy.

Unfortunately, he was in Turannia. Rector Aemilia hadn't been allowed to
bring even a single retainer when she was . . . *promoted* to the position. Meanwhile, Turannia had never been large enough to justify its own branch of the
Imperial bureaucracy and didn't have enough educated citizens to build one on
its own. Particularly not when they had a wonderful legate who handled much of
the affairs seemingly of his own accord; anything that needed to be handled for
the Legion to function . . . which, since Turannia was a de facto military colony,
meant basically everything.

And so, Legate Opiter had once again secured his job in Dux Canus's mind.

It was just as the legate finished off another stack of documents that the door
slammed open.

"Legate, we have a situation!"

Legate Opiter didn't even glance up. "Command over Castra Turannia is currently held by Dux Canus. Please refer the situation to him."

"No, sir, it's not anything like that. It's . . . the treasury."

Legate Opiter froze. He had a bad feeling about this.

"W-What . . . do you mean?"

The soldier frowned.

"Well . . . it's . . . You better come see for yourself, sir."

Legate Opiter started to tremble. He grabbed a piece of dried meat nearby
and tore off a chunk. He had a really bad feeling about this.

Neat, identically sized stacks of Idrint coins filled the room to the brim. The
clerks scrambled, desperately trying to count and record all the money. And,
of course, that terrifying wandering knight was there. Her companions and the
guards were just staring at her, gaping in shock.

The strange wandering knight was walking up and down the room at the
edge of the stacks. And as she did, new stacks appeared with a flash of light,
growing until they reached the same height as the others. She then continued
walking, creating more stacks until she reached the end of the room, at which
point she immediately turned around and came back the other way, adding yet
another row.

Legate Opiter froze. And his mind slowly, ever so slowly, began to turn.

The terrifying wandering knight . . .

Was clearly using some sort of magic box . . .

To pay a war indemnity . . .

In single Idrint coins . . .

All of which she currently carried on her person . . .

And which now, *he* would be responsible for counting . . .

Legate Opiter passed out. And then, unfortunately, came to as warm mana filled his body. He looked up to find himself surrounded by a human girl, a half Wulver, and the guards and clerks.

And the terrifying wandering knight, who had formed a magic circle over his body.

"Statement: Imperial authority 'Legate Curio' restored to optimal condition. Observation: No damage was detected. This unit's analysis indicates the cause was excessive stress. This unit recommends a reduction in Legate Curio's stress levels."

Legate Opiter bit down a scream. The nightmare would never end.

19

A Worthy Exchange

"Oh no, you misunderstand. I am not accepting surrenders today, Young Master. The only price I will accept is your blood spread across the streets. And, should your family insist on protecting you, I will burn your city to the ground and salt the ashes so that it will never rise again."

—Celestial Elf Sage Ningainë, after another family's
young master killed his pet cat.

Rector Provinciae per Turannia Aemilia Hibera sighed. Oh, her province had just won a great victory at impossible odds. Under normal circumstances, this would be cause for great celebration. And, well, she could very much celebrate the fact that she was still alive, and still *had* a province.

But beyond that, things had gotten messy.

One of the main reasons Aemilia had been assigned to Castra Turannia was her complete lack of military experience. In what was practically a military colony, that meant she had very little opportunity to showcase her skills and was entirely dependent on her local Legion commanders. In that, she had been blessed by the Aesdes that Dux Canus had come out of retirement and taken up command of the limitanei, else the surrounding tribes would have chipped away at her province by now.

But that's to say . . . no one in Corvanus would attribute this victory to her.

Likewise, she could be said to have ended the war with the Dobhar permanently . . . but her enemies in Corvanus would instead focus on her giving away Imperial land to a race that had not acknowledged Imperial authority. She was *hoping* making friends with a wandering hero might give her some opportunities, but the issue of that hero now ruling a Dobhar army as an independent state would raise eyebrows. It had become a double-edged sword for Aemilia. Or worse, as publicly announcing details of the hero's personal status, and thus the fact that she was a hero in the first place, was . . . impolite at best, and so not an option if she wanted to actually maintain positive relations with said hero. So, her enemies would be free to focus on what she did without concerning themselves with why she did it.

So, no, she probably wasn't making a triumphant return to Corvanus anytime soon.

And now, she had to figure out how to clean up the province, negotiate with the now independent Selkies, and rebuild her defenses given the changes in the borders. All of which had to be done in a province where she had few connections. Or rather, a province that had few social elites for her to even connect with. She didn't know where the money for all this would come from, either; Turannia's tax revenue wasn't the highest to begin with, and now, a good portion of it would go directly to the Selkies. And many of the farmers being limitanei meant they were getting paid *by* the Empire, not the other way around, so their taxes were substantially reduced as long as they actively served. Turannia had few industries or trade goods to make up that difference, so it barely brought in enough funds to pay its troops' salaries.

In other words, there were no disposable funds or stockpiled reserves for large expenses such as these. She would probably have to dip into her own personal reserves . . . again. And since her family had cut off all contact and support, those reserves were rapidly dwindling.

Maybe the Dobhar could open up additional opportunities for trade . . . but they had never been interested in trading before. Even if trade developed now that the conflict had ended, it would likely take time. It would not solve any of her short-term issues.

Just then, a clerk slammed open the door to her office. Aemilia sighed. Once again, these frontier militia displayed a complete lack of etiquette. And were probably about to tell her something she didn't want to hear.

"Rector!"

"Why, exactly, have you burst into my room, soldier?"

"It's the wandering knight!"

Aemilia tilted her head. "NSLICE-00P? What do you mean?"

"She just paid the indemnity!"

Aemilia blinked.

"Um, what?"

The soldier took a deep breath. "She went to the treasury and filled it with Idrint!"

Aemilia blinked again. The point of that condition had been to have the Dobhar pay tribute for their loss; it'd only been stated as a donation from NSLICE-00P due to the reality of the Dobhar "vanishing" as a separate political entity and falling under the rule of an Amicitia Populi Elteni. The expectation was NSLICE-00P would gather that "donation" from the Dobhar over time. So the fact that NSLICE-00P had paid it immediately was a surprise. She would have had to squeeze the Dobhar for all they were currently worth to achieve that.

Aemilia's eyes widened.

"Wait, did you say she paid in Idrint?"

The soldier nodded. "Yes, ma'am!"

"Anything else?"

"No, ma'am!"

Aemilia's eyes went even wider. Because that meant . . . NSLICE-00P had almost certainly paid out of her own pocket. The Dobhar *could* gather Idrint, as could anyone with access to at least one dungeon, but as an ocean-going hunter-gathering people who didn't trade much, they didn't often use it. They certainly wouldn't have carried large stores of it on a conquest, and Aemilia knew for a fact the Imperial settlements between Castra Turannia and the coast didn't have much for them to loot.

"How much did she pay, then?"

"All of it, ma'am!"

Aemilia froze.

". . . What?"

The soldier nodded.

"Legate Curio is double-checking now, but the preliminary count was the entire indemnity!"

It took Aemilia a few minutes to process that information, but then, she shook her head. She had no idea how NSLICE-00P had come up with that much money, much less solely in Idrint. She had no idea *why* NSLICE-00P would just hand it all over to them like this. But those questions didn't matter.

What mattered was that the treasury was now full of Idrint; an indemnity intended to be paid over *years* by an entire tribe.

Slowly, she started to smile.

It had originally been intended to help cover the compensation to the families of lost soldiers and ongoing repair costs . . . but again, that had been under the assumption of being paid slowly over time. And being paid in kind, as it was expected the Dobhar would not pay directly in Idrint. So, a premium had been added to account for the need to sell off or find a use for whatever trade goods the Dobhar might give them.

She now had access to all of that, right now, in fully liquid cash, before it was actually necessary, and without losing any of it to merchants and middlemen.

And best of all, since it was technically a "donation from a friend" rather than a tax or a war indemnity, *none* of it needed to go the rest of the Empire. Turannia could keep the entire sum . . . and use it as the rector provinciae saw fit.

As *she* saw fit. She grinned. She now had an opportunity. She could do more with this than just rebuild and maintain. She could actively invest some of it, try to develop Turannia beyond its current state. And as long as the Dobhar remained pacified, the Turannian coast had just become *much* safer. Even the interior lands would become safer, in fact, now that Dux Canus could focus all his attention on the border with the Wulver.

If she played her cards right, she might actually have something to work with in the future.

And so, Rector Aemilia dove into her work, poring over reports and determining who she needed to talk to.

It may not have been what she'd first imagined, but it turned out, making a hero friend had given her an opportunity after all.

NSLICE-00P left the treasury, with Ateia and Taog staring at her. Taog took a step forward.

"Seero, I have a question."

"Acknowledgement: What is friendly Taog's query?"

"Where exactly did you get all that money?"

"Statement: This unit has been conducting monster termination in exchange for financial compensation, as friendly Taog suggested."

Well, most of it was actually from the Item Foundry, but NSLICE-00P had marked all dungeon-related information as classified for the time being, so she couldn't say that.

Taog, on the other hand, furrowed his brow and rubbed his chin. He was certain she couldn't have made that much hunting monsters, at least not in Turannia, but he had no idea where else she would have gotten it. Maybe she'd dove into some dungeons and just looked for treasure instead of wiping them out immediately? Unlike literally every other time she had entered a dungeon?

The more Taog thought about it, the more his head hurt. And Ateia . . . had decided she'd let Taog handle that question. "Seero, what are you going to do now?"

"Answer: This unit will regroup with new subordinates and ensure they have a sufficiently secure home base."

"I see . . ." Ateia frowned, then nodded. "Seero, you're coming back here, right? At least so they can officially declare you an Amicitia Populi Elteni, right?"

"Affirmative."

Ateia took a deep breath. "I think Taog and I will stay here, then."

Taog glanced at her at that, while NSLICE-00P's robotic eye flickered slightly. "Requesting Elaboration."

"There's a lot of damage that needs to be cleaned up here; I'd like to help out with that." Ateia glanced at Estrith. "And I'm not sure we'd be . . . welcome over there."

NSLICE-00P calculated briefly, but she calculated very low risks of danger in Castra Turannia at the present moment. As such, there was no reason she couldn't leave her friendlies here.

"Acknowledged. Statement: This unit will check in with Exploratores authority 'Magister Tiberius' upon her return if she cannot locate the friendlies."

Ateia and Taog nodded.

"We'll let him know. Stay safe, Seero."

"Take care, Seero."

"Request: This unit also requests the friendlies avoid damage."

With that, NSLICE-00P left the Legion keep, finding a clear area to take to the skies. Since she had already displayed flight capabilities during the battle and had since developed friendly relations with the local Imperial military, she no longer had any need to hide that ability, and so was going to travel in the most efficient way possible.

She was right about to form a Mana Barrier around Estrith when she caught sight of something.

"Status Report: Hostile detected. Engaging termination protocols."

Suddenly, her combat mode activated, and she ran into a nearby alleyway, preparing to form her magic circles. There, in the alleyway . . . was the cat. Magic circles started to form—

"Wait!"

She stopped. 01R bowed his head inside the Monster Hangar.

"This lowly servant apologizes-begs for forgiveness for his insolence, wise-mighty-gracious boss-queen. But if you would grant-offer this lowly servant a word . . . I would like to face-fight this foe myself. I would show-display the might of your servants, yes-yes."

NSLICE-00P's robotic eye flickered. Letting 01R face this hostile on his own was inefficient in terms of termination . . . but it *would* be useful in terms of combat data. As when she'd battled the ursanus alpha twice, facing the same opponent under similar conditions would provide a good comparison to determine the efficiency of his latest upgrades, and whether 01R and the others were ready for independent operations. Likewise, since NSLICE-00P was present this time, the risk of 01R being terminated or the hostile escaping was acceptably low. So, she ultimately determined the request was reasonable.

"Positive Response: Request acknowledged and determined as acceptable. NSLICE-01R, please prepare to deploy."

"Yes-yes, wise-mighty-gracious boss-queen!"

01R leapt out of the Monster Hangar and rushed down the alleyway, stepping in front of NSLICE-00P. The cat's eyes narrowed as it saw him, meowing at him. He squeaked back, narrowing his own eyes. They both stood still, staring at one another. And then . . .

They both leapt forward, claws extended.

The two passed one another. A light scratch appeared on 01R's back armor, and a light scratch appeared on the cat's stomach.

They turned to face one another. The cat sat down and meowed once again. 01R nodded and squeaked.

And then the cat quietly ran from the alleyway.

NSLICE-00P moved to engage, but 01R shook his head. "It is okay-alright, wise-mighty-gracious boss-queen. It is no longer an enemy."

"Requesting Elaboration: NSLICE-01R was damaged by the hostile multiple times, including in the current engagement. Protocols indicate termination is the required response."

01R turned back to face the running cat.

"Before this, the vicious cat-thing attacked-hunted us as its prey. Now, it has acknowledged-learned the might of your servants, wise-mighty-gracious boss-queen. It will go and train-prepare as this lowly servant has . . . and the next time we fight, it will not be as predator and prey, but as fellow warriors, yes-yes."

NSLICE-00P didn't really understand 01R's reasoning. He seemed to be implying the hostile was temporarily retreating to install additional upgrades, and it would reengage them at a later date . . . which her protocols indicated still necessitated immediate termination. Immediate termination was an even more ideal response if the hostile would return at greater strength, in fact.

But as NSLICE-00P linked up with 01R's cybernetic components, 01R seemed strongly convinced the target had ceased hostility at this point, and that they shouldn't hunt it down in the immediate short term. So, she analyzed the situation once again.

In any case, 01R had displayed the effect of the upgrades. By NSLICE-00P's simulations, 01R would have won that fight without issue, given the cat's inability to pierce his armor and inability to defend from his claws. In fact, given the data she had recorded from that short exchange, all of her subordinates were predicted to emerge from that engagement without serious damage. As such, the cat became a lower-priority target. Her subordinates wouldn't be threatened by it even if engaged while operating alone.

She still did not find a reason not to terminate it, but found it reasonable to defer termination to an on-sight basis rather than an immediate search-and-destroy mission, given that the cat had already exited the alleyway. The implication the cat would be growing in strength was concerning, but as long as she continued to upgrade her subordinates, that risk could be mitigated. As such, regrouping with her new subordinates and establishing a secure home base for them once again became the higher priority.

NSLICE-00P thus turned around to face Estrith, who had entered the alleyway with her spear clutched.

"Queen of the Dobhar, what is happening?"

"Command: All units, please prepare for strategic transit."

"Yes-yes, wise-mighty-gracious boss-queen!"

Estrith's eyes widened as she saw a rat monster jump on NSLICE-00P's back. She was about to step forward to deal with it when she was surrounded by a spherical Mana Barrier.

"Um, queen of the Dobhar, what are you doing . . . ?"

And then, once 01R returned to the hangar, NSLICE-00P shot into the sky, pulling along a screaming Estrith.

20

Terminate the Dread Orcas!

Hear now the wailing of the sea,
The waves broken by black blades bleak,
Dread approaches in twos and threes,
Doom arrives by the Orcas' shriek.

—A Selkie poem.

Taog glanced over at Ateia as they separated from NSLICE-00P. She still had a smile on her face, she was still cheerfully greeting the Imperials around them as they helped dismantle one of the Legion's improvised barricades. But Taog had noticed her hesitation when speaking with NSLICE-00P, and the slight twitch of her face as she held back her frowns. So, he stepped closer to her and spoke softly so the people around them wouldn't hear.

"Is something the matter, Ateia?"

Ateia looked over at him, her eyes widening for a second. She started to shake her head, then paused. She sighed and made a small frown.

"Taog . . . what do you think of Seero?"

Taog crossed his arms.

"A powerful person we know very little about."

Ateia's frown grew.

"Really? After all she did for us? Have we really learned so little about her after all this?"

Taog shrugged.

"I mean, it certainly feels like a lot has happened since we met her, but it's still only been a few weeks, you know?"

Ateia kept frowning. Taog sighed.

"What's going on, Ateia? You didn't bother asking this before, like when you signed a *magical contract* with her."

Ateia took a deep breath. "It's just . . . Okay. I, um, heard about the whole deal Seero had with the authorities. But that means . . . she didn't come back for *us*, right?"

Taog inhaled his breath. So that's what this was about. Ateia's expression twitched, and she turned to hide her face from Taog.

"I mean, it's just . . . she left us. She left us to die . . . and she didn't come back for us. So . . ."

Taog furrowed his brow. On the one hand, this was good. He felt that Ateia had jumped into their relationship with Seero too enthusiastically. At the end of the day, they knew nothing about this girl, and their entire relationship with her was transactional. Was a mercenary they met and hired a few weeks ago expected to wait in a war zone for them? To fight off an entire Dobhar incursion on their behalf? Obviously not, and Taog wouldn't have done any different from Seero had their positions been reversed.

But he knew that wasn't true for Ateia. He knew Ateia had grown attached and had seen a bit of herself in Seero. Or perhaps just wanted to do so. He knew Ateia wouldn't have left Seero behind. And so, she was hurt that Seero had done just that.

Wisdom said that it was good for Ateia to realize the truth about her relationship with Seero. She and Taog needed to look after themselves, and to do that, they needed to be brutally honest about the people they interacted with. Their trust could not be given lightly.

But on the other hand, Seero *had* come back. And once she had, she had ensured that Ateia and Taog survived the conflict. Yes, she had been prompted to do so by the deal with the Empire, but Taog didn't know exactly why she had accepted the deal, or if she'd considered the two of them in the process. At the end of the day, they didn't know, not unless they asked the girl herself.

And Seero had saved their lives, more than once. She may not have done so out of charity, but still, it was true they would be in a *much* worse position if Seero hadn't agreed to help them.

And above all . . . Taog hated to see Ateia upset.

So, he shrugged. "Have you asked her?"

Ateia paused.

"Huh?"

Taog walked around to face Ateia. She quickly rubbed her face before he did, looking at him with a confused expression.

"Look, Ateia, like I said, Seero is a person we know very little about. We've known her only for a couple of weeks total. So, we can't say for sure what her reasons are. But from what I can tell, she's generally not shy when asked to explain."

Ateia frowned again.

"But . . . what if she really doesn't care about us?"

Taog shrugged.

"That would be normal for someone you just met, you know? But . . . what if she does?"

Ateia went silent at that and resumed cleaning up. Taog sighed and went back to work as well. It was easier for him, since he hadn't put any hopes or dreams on the suspicious girl they'd just met. Part of him still wanted Ateia to take a step back from her, just for caution's sake.

But at the same time, there was a part of him that hoped he was wrong. That Ateia could make up with Seero and go back to smiling. And maybe, just maybe, that Seero would turn out to be someone they could rely on. He didn't expect it; she seemed pretty mercenary to Taog. But still . . . there was a tiny part of his heart that couldn't help but ask, *what if . . .*

NSLICE-00P had spent only an hour or two in Castra Turannia, so it didn't take her long to catch up to the Dobhar force. Soon, she landed in front of a surprised Uscfrea. The moment the Mana Barrier dropped, Estrith gripped the ground with all her might, trembling as she lay upon it.

"Queen of the Dobhar . . . p-please, never do that again."

"Negative Response: This unit cannot comply with that request, as flight is considered a necessary capability for this unit."

Uscfrea raised an eyebrow but bowed to NSLICE-00P.

"My queen, you've arrived more quickly than expected. I thought you had business in Castra Turannia?"

"Affirmative. Explanation: The war indemnity is paid, and all contract obligations with entity 'Empire' have been fulfilled."

Uscfrea began nodding before suddenly freezing in place.

"My queen . . . did you say . . . you paid the indemnity?"

"Affirmative."

Uscfrea blinked.

"By yourself? With your own money?"

"Affirmative."

". . . Just the first payment, right?"

"Negative. Clarification: This unit delivered the amount stated by the contract."

Uscfrea stared for a second before bowing his head.

"My queen, we thank you for your generosity."

"Acknowledged. Recommendation: Subordinates should resume transit. This unit will begin patrol routines to ensure safe passage."

Uscfrea watched NSLICE-00P as she flew back up into the sky, then he

shook his head. He was more and more confused about this strange mercenary . . . and worried what she might want in exchange for the indemnity.
But she was right in that they should get moving. They needed to regroup
with the Home Fleet as soon as possible, so he shouted at the Dobhar, and
they started to move once again . . . after he'd picked Estrith up off the
ground, that is.

A few days later, the Dobhar army was nearing the coast. They could see the
Legion's coastal fort atop the cliff and would soon see the Home Fleet in the
ocean beyond.

NSLICE-00P was flying in the sky when she suddenly turned her head. She
quickly descended to where Uscfrea led the column.

"Warning: Friendly maritime units are under attack by hostiles. This unit is
engaging termination protocols. All friendly units should do likewise."

Uscfrea's eyes had just started to widen when NSLICE-00P's eye turned red
and she engaged her combat mode. She didn't wait for his response as she shot
back into the air, zipping past the coastal fort and flying out over the sea.

Hundreds of small rafts made of wood and bone filled the sea near the shores.
They were moving toward the coast, trying to land on the beach. At the far end
of the fleet, NSLICE-00P could see water splashing and zoomed in.

Black-and-white whales were attacking the ships. The orcas breached out
of the water and slammed into the rafts, breaking them apart or tipping them
over. Spear-armed Dobhar fell into the water, only to be assaulted by the whales.
The few Dobhar warriors left behind to defend the fleet fought back with their
harpoons, but they were struggling to deal any serious blows.

Just behind the thin line of Dobhar warriors were the ships of the Home
Fleet, filled with young mothers, Dobhar pups, and the elderly. These were moving as close as they could to the shore, trying to escape the battlefield.

Uscfrea gritted his teeth as he reached the edge of the cliff and saw what was
happening.

"Those idiots! I told them to move onto the land!"

The former king let out a shout, and the Dobhar army began to rush down
the cliff, but it would take them some time to climb down to shore and then
swim out to the battle. Meanwhile, the orcas let out a mana-filled cry, all as one.
The Dobhar warriors out at sea, as well as the noncombatants behind them,
clutched at their ears and started to tremble in place.

One of the whales broke past the defensive line and bumped into a raft,
knocking a pup onboard off the ship and into the water. The orca spun around
and rushed straight toward the pup, whose mother cried out, shook out of her
daze, and dove off the ship . . . but the orca was approaching the pup far faster
than the mother. It was just about to reach its prey . . .

NSLICE-00P pumped out her mana into a massive Aurora Barrage magic circle. All the Dobhar's gazes turned toward the sky, their eyes widening at the glowing lights above.

Beams of light descended on the sea. They began to strike the orca just as it approached the pup, and the monster let out a cry and dove back under the water. The Light Beams followed but lost power quickly once they passed the surface of the ocean.

But the monster had abandoned its pursuit. The Dobhar mother managed to grab her pup and climb back onto the raft, clutching her child tight.

NSLICE-00P continued after the orca, moving closer to the frontlines. She *could* have Supercharged and fused all the Aurora Barrage beams together to try and take down her underwater target with raw power, but she'd decided not to. It would be inefficient if she had to do that for every target on the field . . . and she had already acknowledged Light Beam's inefficiency against water. So first, she wanted to determine which of her available attacks would be most efficient under these conditions.

She already knew her physical weapons would be inefficient. She hadn't been equipped with a naval warfare loadout when she'd arrived here, after all. Regular firearms just weren't going to do that well against underwater targets, though they could be used whenever the whales broke the surface. Bullets could even ricochet off the water, creating an unacceptable risk of friendly fire.

So instead, she redirected the Aurora Barrage assault to the frontlines, trying to provide covering fire for the Dobhar engaged there. Meanwhile, she charged the energy channels in her arms, preparing to test some Infused Mana Beams once again. And this time, she happened to have a new attribute to test first.

She chased after the orca she had already struck, moving down closer to the water, before she opened fire with the golden-and-silver Holy-attribute Infused Mana Beam.

The beam passed straight through the water and pierced right through the orca, who let out a horrific wail, its black mana streaming off its body and scattering under the bright beam.

You have slain Dread Orca (Level 63)!
Gained 29 Personal XP, 3 Dungeon XP!
Level up! You are now at Personal Level 52!

It seemed the Holy attribute was effective against these foes indeed. Super effective, even. And water didn't affect a Holy-infused Mana Beam like it would a laser. NSLICE-00P had determined an efficient means of termination for these foes.

She immediately layered the new Holy Bolt magic circles over Aurora Barrage and activated Spell Fusion. And as it turned out . . . Light Beam and Holy Bolt were highly compatible.

The skill Spell Fusion is now Level 8!
The spell Holy Bolt has leveled four times and is now Level 5!
You have learned the spell Holy Beam!
The spell Holy Beam has leveled twice and is now Level 3!
The skill Holy Magic has leveled four times and is now Level 5! Spell choice
available!

Rather than replacing the Light Beam magic circles, the Holy Bolt circles morphed to form extremely similar Holy Beam circles. Spell Fusion then appended these on top of the individual Light Beams instead of fusing them into the wider Aurora Barrage.

It did this specifically because NSLICE-00P had the Fusion Light Beam upgrade which would allow Light Beams to fuse not only with each other, but also with other compatible spells. And the Holy Beam spell was very much compatible with Light Beam.

So, beams from the Aurora Barrage spell continued to fire . . . only now fused together with the golden-and-silver glow of Holy Beams. And then the air and seas were filled with horrific wails as the dread orcas were struck by attributes they were particularly vulnerable to.

The spell Holy Beam has leveled five times and is now Level 8!
The skill Holy Magic is now Level 6!
You have slain 33 hostiles!
Gained 429 Personal XP, 99 Dungeon XP!
Level up! You are now at Personal Level 56 and Dungeon Level 90!

"Status Report: All detected hostiles terminated. Friendlies observed in critical condition. Engaging organic repair protocols."

NSLICE-00P dropped the strategic spell, and instead formed healing magic circles.

Dozens of Supercharged Heal magic circles spread all across the water, just above each and every wounded Dobhar.

The spell Heal has leveled up five times and is now Level 13! Upgrade available!
The skill Recovery Magic has leveled up twice and is now Level 7! Spell choice
available!
The skill Farcasting is now Level 5!

The Dobhar warriors stood still and blinked as their foes vanished and their wounds began to heal. All the Dobhar of the Home Fleet turned up to the sky, staring at the cyborg floating there as she scanned the fleet for additional injuries.

Thanks to the timely reinforcements, not a single Dobhar pup was lost that day.

Uscfrea and the other Dobhar warriors made it down to shore, only to find the battle concluded. A few of the ships had touched down on the beach, and a group of elderly Dobhar stepped down onto the sand. Uscfrea marched right up to them.

"Hail, king of the—"

Uscfrea silenced the lead Dobhar with a fist to the jaw.

"You *idiot*! I told you to move everyone onto land! At least the mothers and the pups! So why in the Abyss is *everyone* still on the ships?!"

The Dobhar elder glared at him from the ground.

"It is not our way! We have always lived in the embrace of the sea! It is in the sea that we grow strong! The pups will grow weak and infirm if carried by the solid ground! They will forget how to swim!"

Uscfrea picked the Dobhar up and lifted him into the air.

"That is because our ancestors were *weak* and driven from the land by the Wulver and the Selkies! Now that we are strong enough to reclaim our ancestral home, you still wish for us to cower at the mercy of the deep? And are you an idiot?! Don't you know a fleet this large was *always* going to attract monsters? That the dread orca would be tracking us the entire way here?! And you just let the mothers and the pups sit there, waiting for them?!"

Uscfrea tossed the elder back to his comrades.

"Go, leave my sight. I left you in charge out of respect for our traditions, but I will not allow you to endanger our people with your stubborn pride. Go to the mothers and the pups you put in harm's way and explain to them why your *traditions* are more valuable than their lives."

Uscfrea heaved a sigh as the elder stormed off. He shook his head as one of the other elders approached him. An old woman, carrying a bone staff.

"Welcome home, King Uscfrea."

Uscfrea bowed his head to her.

"Greetings to you, Mother of Waves. And a correction; I am no longer king."

She raised an eyebrow at him.

"Well . . . I'm guessing that answers my next question, then."

Uscfrea nodded, and they both turned to face the sky.

"Yes . . . that is the new queen of the Dobhar."

21

Some "Routine" Maintenance

"Answer: This unit executed organic maintenance protocols."
—An NSLICE unit after performing field surgeries with
no anesthetic.

Uscfrea lined up the warriors on the beach. As the Home Fleet had already been making for the shore, all the Dobhar left behind quickly noticed and turned their attention toward him.

NSLICE-00P patrolled around the fleet for a few rounds, ensuring that no hostiles remained in the area and no Dobhar remained in critical condition. She then began flying back toward Uscfrea to state the battle's conclusion. Once she came near and began descending from the sky, Uscfrea let out a mana-infused shout.

"ALL HAIL THE RIGHTFUL QUEEN OF THE DOBHAR!"

With that, Uscfrea and every warrior on the beach bowed to NSLICE-00P. The Dobhar of the Home Fleet stared in shock . . . before they, too, started to bow.

And so, the Dobhar were introduced to their new queen.

After that, NSLICE-00P patrolled across the fleet once again. Uscfrea had gone off with the elders to report on the situation in more detail. He'd stated it would be good for NSLICE-00P to wait on the beach, allowing the Dobhar to present themselves to her, but NSLICE-00P found that inefficient. After all, she had repulsors and was capable of flight, so if she needed to interact with individual Dobhar, she could simply travel to them directly.

Likewise, the Dobhar had already come under attack once. NSLICE-00P's sensors were not particularly well-suited to detecting underwater targets at range, and the ocean was wide open, so there was a chance a hostile could launch another attack before being detected. As such, NSLICE-00P decided to patrol around the perimeter of the fleet.

The Dobhar on the ships gazed up at her as she passed by. The warriors on the perimeter ships, particularly the ones who had been healed, lowered their heads and struck either ships or the ocean surface with their tails as she passed them by.

Then she noticed one of the Dobhar waving to her from a raft. She moved down and landed on the raft to investigate.

"Query: Does the friendly unit have a report or query for this unit?"

The Dobhar who had waved bowed her head. She was the mother from earlier, still gripping her pup in her arms. "Hail, my queen. My name is Aethelu Alkelddaughter. I just wanted to thank you. You saved my Aldreda. I will be ever grateful to you for that."

"Acknowledged."

In that moment, NSLICE-00P's robotic eye began flickering. She focused on the pup in the woman's arms. She held out her hands.

"Statement: This unit has detected an anomaly and would like to conduct a closer investigation of the friendly. Sensor readings indicate the friendly unit may require maintenance."

Aethelu's eyes widened.

"Aldreda? Yes, of course, my queen."

Aethelu handed over her pup, which was, unbeknownst to NSLICE-00P, perhaps the greatest sign of trust and respect a Dobhar mother could display. But NSLICE-00P had earned the right as far as Aethelu was concerned.

The pup cried at being separated from her mother as NSLICE-00P held her with cold metal hands. NSLICE-00P ignored the cries and focused on the pup's body. There was something strange; an anomaly in the pup's physiology. It seemed to reduce the body's efficiency, like a disease, but NSLICE-00P couldn't detect any pathogens or injuries that would cause it. Admittedly, this was a new species NSLICE-00P did not have specialized medical data for, which was why she'd decided to investigate more closely. If she focused her sensors at this close of a range, she could analyze the friendly's tissue itself and attempt to identify the issue.

And then, she found something. The issue wasn't actually biological at all, but rather in the pup's mana. It seemed that some foreign mana had infected the pup's own and was now seeping into the pup's body. The foreign mana seemed to be malignant and was reducing the pup's biological efficiency. Nothing as overt as a pathogen or an injury, but all physiological functions appeared to be suppressed in the area of effect. The pup's body was moving slower in the affected places.

"Engaging organic repair protocols."

NSLICE-00P formed a magic circle and cast a Heal spell. But there was no effect; the mana passed through the pup's HP and body and then left, leaving the foreign mana behind. Next, she tried a Cure spell, but again the problem remained.

Aethelu's eyes widened.

"My queen, is . . . is something wrong?"

"Answer: This unit has detected a foreign effect reducing this friendly's efficiency. Attempting to adapt organic repair protocols."

NSLICE-00P focused on the pup's mana once again, cross-referencing her sensor readings with all her records. Comparing it to the data she had gathered, the foreign mana was not acting like a foreign affliction in the first place. It was not like how Poison mana could infect HP or how Uscfrea's axe had assaulted her directly. Rather, the mana appeared more like when she infused an attribute into her Mana Beams . . . and so perhaps wasn't being considered foreign at all, despite its deleterious effects.

She likewise identified the mana as the same type the dread orcas used.

Aethelu gasped, covering her mouth with her hands. Tears began to fill her eyes.

What had happened, unbeknownst to NSLICE-00P, was that the dread orcas had surrounded themselves in an aura of Dark-attribute mana. They used this aura to spread terror and curses to their prey and render them helpless. And this young Dobhar had come into very close contact with one. Under normal circumstances, the effects of a dread orca's aura would be temporary, but this was a young Dobhar with no levels under her belt and no affinities for her mana. As such, her mana had been infected by the dread orca's and was trying to take it on as an attribute, but since the pup was too young and Dobhar did not have innate immunity to Dark curses, she could not resist its effects. Her body was being cursed directly from her own mana.

Aethelu hadn't yet noticed . . . but now that NSLICE-00P had spoken, she realized her pup was afflicted with the dread plague, a malady experienced by young survivors of dread orca attacks, and the reason they were one of the most hated monsters in the Northern Seas.

If the pup managed to gain some levels, she might one day adapt to the mana and make it her own, but she was far too young to join the hunt. And the curse would sap her body's strength, leaving her unable to seek the very levels which might help her counteract it. Not to mention . . . her mana would spread curses all around her much like a dread orca. So even if she managed to survive and grow, she would be isolated by the Dobhar, if not exiled outright.

The pup had not survived the attack, not truly. She might be alive, but her life was over before it began. Aethelu closed her eyes to hold in her tears, gripping her hands tight.

Well, NSLICE-00P didn't fully understand what the situation was, but that didn't stop her from trialing methods to address it, based on the observed data.

She attempted to infuse her own mana into the pup's. The pup cried out, and its mana resisted at first; however, NSLICE-00P possessed a decent number of records in this area. She had her own diagnostics, which recorded how the mana from her core and the mana from her organic components intertwined. She had the Infused Mana Beam and Spell Fusion skills, along with the Fusion Light Beam spell, all of which displayed different methods of harmoniously combining separate types of mana. And she had multiple subordinates of different origins all of which were magically bound to her, which meant her mana was flowing through them and interacting with their own.

You have learned the spell Mana Transfer!
The spell Mana Transfer has leveled three times and is now Level 4!
The skill Arcane Magic is now Level 11!

So, she was able to adjust her own mana and establish a connection. Her mana now flowed through the pup's, heading toward the infected area, while the pup continued to cry. Until NSLICE-00P's mana reached the infected area. Because NSLICE-00P hadn't simply used normal mana. Once the connection had been established, she'd infused her mana with an attribute. An attribute she had already logged as effective against that of the dread orcas.

She filled the pup with Holy-attribute mana.

Once the Holy mana contacted the foreign one, the pup's cries grew louder, and its body began to light up. Aethelu took a step forward before catching herself, clenching her fists even tighter. But she decided to trust the queen that had saved her pup's life in the first place.

The Holy-attribute mana burned away the foreign mana, and then filled in the gap itself.

You have learned the spell Blessing!
The skill Holy Magic is now Level 7!

But NSLICE-00P wasn't done just yet. She had purged the foreign effect from the pup's mana, but some of it had seeped into the pup's body itself. So now, NSLICE-00P replicated the effect, only with the Holy-attribute mana instead.

The pup suddenly paused and stopped crying. The Holy mana spread throughout the infected areas, not only clearing the deleterious effect but increasing the body's efficiency.

But there was a new problem. NSLICE-00P's mana was *far* denser than the foreign mana had been . . . and was being applied through a direct connection.

She noted the mana surging through the pup's body, which struggled to handle the massive energy flow. The pup started crying again as its body began taking damage.

So NSLICE-00P adapted.

The pup's body was not strong enough or developed enough to handle that much mana, but NSLICE-00P had recorded other species who could accept her mana without issue. Species that had done so even back when they were *weaker* than this particular Dobhar pup: her rat and spider monsters, who had had no trouble with her mana even when first summoned. And thanks to the NSLICE implants now installed on those monsters, she could very quickly acquire a comprehensive physiological map from them to compare with the pup in front of her.

She quickly determined the difference. All her subordinate monsters had a specialized organ to handle mana, which strangely enough was practically identical across the different species. An organ made of crystallized mana itself, rather than biological flesh.

So, she attempted to condense the mana within the pup in a similar fashion. The pup began to glow with a bright light, obscuring it from view. Aethelu gritted her teeth, but whatever NSLICE-00P was doing was already in progress, so she did not think it wise to interrupt.

And then, eventually, the light died down.

The pup now had streaks of golden-and-silver fur across its body, all leading to its forehead, which now had a jewel glowing with golden light in the center.

Yes, NSLICE-00P had formed a mana core for the pup, in order for it to handle the mana she had transferred to it. She had concentrated it on the pup's exterior, since she lacked enough data on Dobhar physiology to confidently place it within the body.

And, well . . . NSLICE-00P unknowingly had done a *lot* of other things as well.

The pup's eyes were closed at first, and her mother held her breath. But the pup was breathing, softly and steadily, and then slowly opened her eyes. Her mother exhaled in relief as the pup began looking around, turning to NSLICE-00P and looking her in the eyes before reaching out with its hands. Since this was a manner similar to 00B when requesting increased physical contact, NSLICE-00P utilized the same response and brought the pup in contact with her torso. The pup curled itself up in her arms.

The pup's mother stared at the now peacefully sleeping pup with tears streaming down her face. She fell to her knees. She bowed her head.

"My queen . . ."

. . . I . . . What did you just do? Um . . . like . . . I know I told you to make Holy monsters on your own, since I didn't want to figure it out, but this . . . um . . .

Aldreda Aetheludaughter (Sacred Otterkin - Level 1) has become your subordinate!
New monster record established. Monster lineage unlocked. Sacred Otterkin may now be summoned!

Gained Dungeon Affinity: Water (Minor)!
Gained Dungeon Affinity: Beast (Minor)!
You have accomplished the Dungeon Feat: Monster Creator!
Thanks to your efforts, a new intelligent species has been born!
You have accomplished the Dungeon Feat: Matron of the Sacred Otterkin!

Dungeon Feats		
Name	Description	Effect
Monster Creator	Life, uh, finds a way. But sometimes, it has help. Unlocked by creating a new, never-before-seen monster species.	+20 Perk Points Grants access to Monster Customization.
Matron of the Sacred Otterkin	Thanks to your efforts, a new intelligent species has been born. The world grows more wondrous by your deeds.	+40 Perk Points Additional Perk Points may be granted based on the development and contributions of your client species.

. . . A new species that's both technically a monster and an intelligent natural race at the same time?
. . . I'm just . . . I'm going to go lie down.

You have accomplished the Personal Feat: Hero of the Sacred Otterkin!

Personal Feats		
Name	Description	Effect
Hero of the Sacred Otterkin	So . . . we normally give this when someone has done something that protected the existence of an entire species. And like, you just *created* a new species, so . . . I guess that means you are, in fact, responsible for their continued existence. You know what? Whatever.	+20 Perk Points +1 level in Holy Water Ball spell +1 level in Holy Strike skill

Um, w-what do we do?

. . . What can we do? Report it and wait for the consequences.

T-That's, um . . . C-Can't you do something?

. . . I'm going to go take a nap.

H-Hey! Where are you going?! You can't just leave me with this!

22

Laying the Foundation

"Inclusion of structural engineering data may improve outcomes in urban warfare."
—Dr. Ottosen, after NSLICE units destroyed a
skyscraper they were instructed to defend.

Aethelu took her pup to the beach and stood before the Mother of Waves, the master of magic, medicine, and navigation among the Dobhar. She held the sleeping Aldreda in her arms while the Mother of Waves pored over the pup with a magic circle. Eventually, the magic faded, and the Mother of Waves took a deep breath. Aethelu held hers as she waited for the verdict.

The Mother of Waves smiled at her.

"This is unlike anything I've ever seen, but as far as I can tell, she's perfectly healthy. Better even, her mana seems to be . . . elevating her somehow."

Tears filled Aethelu's eyes as she gripped Aldreda closer to her, the sleeping pup shifting closer in her sleep. The Mother of Waves's face then turned serious.

"On the other hand, her mana density has increased, farther than her body can currently handle, and has taken on an attribute to boot. The gem on her forehead seems to be concentrating the excess, so there shouldn't be an issue, but . . . I would recommend she begin learning the mystic arts as soon as possible. She will need training and practice to handle her own mana."

Aethelu nodded and thanked the elderly woman profusely. She then saluted to her, Uscfrea, and the other elders before departing. Once she left, the Mother of Waves frowned.

"Spellbreaker, I do not wish to say this, but I fear it must be said . . ."

Uscfrea frowned and crossed his arms.

"I know. That's suspiciously similar to a monster's mana core, is what you want to say, right?"

The Mother of Waves slowly nodded.

"We must keep an eye on her and see how she grows. At the same time, though, she now possesses the power of the Aesdes within her, so I cannot imagine she will turn out poorly."

Uscfrea sighed and shook his head. A cure for the dread plague . . . but which turned a Dobhar pup into something else. What exactly, they were not sure. They knew the mana core was similar to that of a monster's, but the mana itself . . . that was something they recognized. Something every inhabitant of this world instinctively recognized.

Holy mana.

The attribute of the Aesdes themselves, which maintained and nourished the world. The power that protected Aelea and suffered no evil or intruder. The power that could not be acquired but was rather granted by the Aesdes to those they considered worthy. And the power that no monster had ever wielded, at least as far as the Dobhar knew.

And now, granted to a pup by a wandering mercenary in a ritual that may have changed her into a different species entirely.

Once again, Uscfrea found himself questioning who exactly he had bound his people to. But . . . Aethelu's relieved face passed through his mind. He didn't think he regretted that choice just yet.

The elder Uscfrea had fought with scowled. "I still cannot believe you bound us to some *human*. And now, we are letting her turn pups into monsters!"

Uscfrea didn't even glance at him. "And what would you have us do, Hunsig?"

Hunsig narrowed his eyes.

"What we have always done. Hold to our traditions. Keep to the seas, to our home. Fight, endure, and grow strong. Not to languish on land as slaves to a human."

Uscfrea turned to look him in the eye. "Hunsig, I'd like to paint you a picture. Do you remember what our queen did to the dread orcas?"

Hunsig begrudgingly nodded.

"Now, imagine that again, only this time, it is the Dobhar in her sights. Imagine each of those beams cutting through our people while she remains up in the sky. Imagine the ships of the Home Fleet burning and sinking into the waves. Imagine our warriors desperately reaching for the sky and being knocked to the ground."

Uscfrea's eyes narrowed.

"Because, as I already told you, that is *exactly* what she did to end our assault on the Empire. And *exactly* what she will do if we break the oath I have sworn to her. So, ask yourself, would you rather those spells protect the Dobhar . . . or *end* them? If you have a way to stop all that, then be my guest. Go, challenge her for leadership of our people, as is our *tradition*. See for yourself why she is now queen."

Hunsig's face scoffed. "Big words from a coward. Are you not the Spell-breaker? Why do you fear her?"

Uscfrea held out his hands.

"Notice anything missing, Hunsig? In case you haven't realized, I already fought with her, and I *lost*. And if you don't believe my words, you'll understand when you meet her yourself."

Uscfrea turned around to look at each elder in turn.

"This is not the situation I wanted, and not one that is easy to accept. But know that this is ultimately in our favor. Yes, we have lost our freedom and our pride. Yes, we have bowed to a human. Yes, we are beholden to this stranger. But think of what we have gained."

Uscfrea motioned around at the beach and the cliffs beyond, including the Legion fortress at the top.

"The Empire has acknowledged this as our land; they will not take it from us nor accost us while we are here. The Selkies have been forced to agree as well; no longer do we need to fear their hunters. We have all this to do as we please from now on."

He grinned.

"And our queen is generous; naive, even. She has set us free to rule ourselves as we please. All she asks is that we respect her allegiances and help her search for a couple of humans. If we can accept that, then we are free to build a new home for our people, and to become as strong as we want."

He looked to the Mother of Waves.

"And now, no more pups need fear the dread orcas striking them from the deep. They can grow safely on the land until they are strong enough to fight back and prove themselves worthy in fair challenge."

She smiled and nodded back to him. He turned back to Hunsig.

"So, what will it be, *elder* of the Dobhar? What does your wisdom tell you? Shall we insist on blood, betray our oaths, continue to fight, and watch our queen destroy us entirely? Or will we take the opportunity to grow stronger than we've ever been, all while our queen rains destruction on all who would threaten us?"

Hunsig gritted his teeth but said nothing. Uscfrea grinned at him.

"Well, if you feel yourself growing weak and infirm on this land, feel free to return to the seas on your own. That is no trouble for a strong and traditional Dobhar hunter, right?"

With that, the Dobhar began to move onto land, landing their ships upon the beach. NSLICE-00P continued to patrol the perimeter, until a better part of the ships had landed and the remainder moved close enough that she could monitor them from land. Once they had, she returned to Uscfrea.

As she did, she took out the Sea Dragon–bone axe, holding it in her hand. Uscfrea had spoken with her on the way here and specified she should hold it while greeting the elders. She didn't understand why, but as her protocols and records had nothing to say on the matter, she saw no reason to refuse.

She landed on the beach in front of Uscfrea and several older Dobhar. Their eyes widened as they saw the axe in her hand, glancing at one another. One of them gritted his teeth, but in the end, all of them bowed to her. Uscfrea spoke. "My queen, what is your command?"

"Command: Friendly Uscfrea Ymmason is designated as role 'Steward of the Dobhar.' Primary directive is to relay this unit's instructions to Dobhar units. Additional major directives include defense of Dobhar units, defense of this unit's home base, and development of Dobhar unit capabilities."

Her robotic eye glowed and displayed a holographic image of the persons of interest.

"Command: Specific instructions are to search for these persons of interest and inform this unit of any related intel. Additional instructions include complying with the terms of the agreement established between this unit and entities Empire and Council of Hunters."

"As you command, my queen."

With that, NSLICE-00P gave the commands she had discussed with Uscfrea earlier. Her own particular requirements had been assistance with her primary objective and compliance with the negotiated agreement. The designation as steward had been Uscfrea's idea, but NSLICE-00P found that an acceptable suggestion; having Uscfrea as her liaison was ideal, given that she had already negotiated with him and had him listed as an official subordinate.

Uscfrea turned to the elders and grinned. "You heard our queen. She has commanded us to protect her people and her lands. So, let's get to work."

With that, the Dobhar accepted NSLICE-00P as their new ruler, and Uscfrea as her steward. Uscfrea set to work immediately, having his warriors set up camps for the people. The Dobhar warriors had started to understand the necessity of doing so . . . but they still weren't particularly efficient at it. Therefore, NSLICE-00P landed near Uscfrea after one of her patrols.

"Observation: Dobhar are currently attempting to build shelters?"

Uscfrea nodded, jumping only slightly when she suddenly landed behind him.

"Yes, my queen."

NSLICE-00P's robotic eye flickered. She was no architect, but she did have some relevant protocols in this case. While she'd never been intended to build structures, she'd often needed to infiltrate or destroy them in the past. At other times, perhaps more importantly to this case, she'd needed to avoid destroying them unintentionally midcombat. So, she did have some ability to analyze buildings for structural integrity, and had some building layouts recorded in her memory.

She looked over the Dobhar as they struggled to set up sticks in the sand. And her analysis of the Dobhars' work was . . .

"Analysis: Dobhar constructions lack structural integrity and meaningful insulation."

Uscfrea heaved a sigh. "My people's building experience consists of tying driftwood and bone into basic rafts. It will take us some time to adjust."

NSLICE-00P ran through the calculations. Part of her agreement with Uscfrea was the establishment of a secure home base for the Dobhar. Her protocols and records indicated that adequate and defensible shelter was necessary for a secure home base. And by simulating the building "techniques" the Dobhar were currently displaying, she predicted they would not produce what she defined as a secure home base.

And that was a problem, as she could not resume her own search for the persons of interest until the Dobhar were secure.

"Recommendation: Empire-built structure in the area would suffice as a shelter."

Uscfrea shook his head.

"It would, but it's too high up the cliff. My people still need ready access to the water. We cannot carry the pups up and down those cliffs every day."

This area was a wide, sandy beach leading to a tall cliff that stretched for miles in either direction. The Legion keep had been built along the easiest and most convenient path up the cliffs . . . but it had been designed to keep foes down on the beach, and so had still been built up at the top. Which meant it was not at all accessible from the beach and vice versa. The Dobhar were just trying to build some basic shelters right next to the cliff, where they would be safe from the tide but still have access to the ocean.

"Acknowledged. Statement: Then this unit will provide construction assistance. Improvising construction protocols."

NSLICE-00P formed dozens of magic circles along the cliff face, for both the Pitfall spell and the Earth Wall spell. She then used Spell Fusion to combine them and got to work.

The spell Earth Wall has leveled three times and is now Level 9!
The spell Pitfall has leveled four times and is now Level 8!
The skill Earth Magic is now Level 8! Spell choice available!

She opened up caverns in the stone, combining records of various structures both natural and artificial to ensure stability. She also formed numerous separate rooms to provide barracks, storerooms, and adequately vented kitchens. The excess stone she moved outside and formed into walls surrounding the openings, with some watchtowers as well in order to defend the entrances. She included second and third floors, with windows and embrasures to provide additional defense. She likewise formed a vertical tunnel with a staircase leading directly up into the Legion keep above.

The skill Farcasting is now Level 6!

Well, she'd wanted to install an elevator for more efficient transit, but she didn't have access to blueprints or construction protocols for one. She probably could have analyzed past records and utilized simulations to produce a workable design, but she also lacked adequate materials at the moment. So, she settled for the basics. She didn't intend to fully replicate a building from her memory, after all. They may have been simple, but the caverns would provide sufficient shelter from the elements and hostile entities as per her protocols.

Uscfrea was just staring at the cliff, blinking repeatedly as NSLICE-00P turned to face him.

"Status Update: The basic structure has been developed and will provide a secure home base. This unit has not provided furnishings; friendly Dobhar units will be responsible for any additional improvements."

"T-Thank you, my queen. T-This is . . ."

It took a while before Uscfrea could gather his thoughts. The rest of the Dobhar . . . were just staring with dropped jaws at the buildings that had suddenly appeared.

23

This Is Getting Out of Hand; Now There Are Two of Them!

"No dungeon is permitted to form a subordinate core, regardless of its behavior in the past. The growth of a master core accelerates beyond reasonable control. It was this very method by which the Great Demon Lord claimed a continent and made war against the Aesdes themselves. Subordinated cores are to be subjugated immediately, and retaliatory raids conducted against the master core, with full subjugation dependent on the response."

—*The Legion Manual*, regarding dungeons.

As the Dobhar began moving into the new shelter, NSLICE-00P calculated. The Dobhar were now settled with a secure home base, and Uscfrea had been designated her liaison and granted directives for the Dobhar. She had one last order of business to conduct before she could return to Castra Turannia. She needed to establish a means of long-range communications so that she could remain in contact with the Dobhar while searching other parts of the Empire.

At present, NSLICE-00P had not detected any electronic communication infrastructure in her vicinity. No cell phone towers, no satellites, nothing that could relay a signal, which meant NSLICE-00P's conventional communication methods were restricted to tactical ranges. She did now have additional NSLICE units she could communicate with, and hypothetically, she could spread them out to form a network that could relay information and communications.

However, this method had numerous drawbacks for this use case. NSLICE-00P would have to summon new subordinates every time she moved out of range of the latest, leading to ever-increasing demands on her maximum mana as she moved further away from the Dobhar.

Likewise, these subordinates would have to be left alone at their positions in the network, leaving them vulnerable to assault, as she would not be close enough to provide reinforcements, which would also threaten the network itself should one of them be terminated. And leaving multiple subordinates at each node for defense and redundancy would exacerbate the scalability issue.

All in all, the NSLICE units had not been designed to replace adequate communications infrastructure, and so were not an efficient solution for this task. Likewise, rebuilding said communications infrastructure was not possible at this time. NSLICE-00P was not designed for that task and had few protocols relating to it. At best, she had some technical data indicating where to attack a hostile's network towers, but that did not include the instructions for manufacturing a new one from scratch, nor for fabricating all the components and parts necessary to build one. And she didn't have access to the raw materials required, either.

So, NSLICE-00P decided to explore alternative methods, sending a message to the subordinates in her Monster Hangar.

"Request: Do any friendlies have intel regarding long-range mana-based communication methods?"

Fortunately for NSLICE-00P, Lilussees was just waking up. She stretched her limbs and shook her body awake.

"Ahhh . . . I needed that. Ah, like, what was that, boss lady? You, like, need to talk to someone far away or something?"

"Affirmative."

Lilussees gave a salute with her leg.

"Got it. Anything for you, boss lady! Let me think. Like, who exactly do you want to talk to, and, like, how far away will they be, or something?"

"Reporting Requirements: This unit will need a reliable method to contact Dobhar units at varying and indeterminable distances. Communications must be two-way so that Dobhar units can report on the status of their search."

Lilussees rubbed her mandibles.

"Okay, so, like, let me see if I got that straight, or something. These guys are, like, staying here. You're, like, going to wander around. But, like, you need a way to check in on them and hear from them, or something?"

"Affirmative."

Lilussees continued rubbing her mandibles.

"Hmm, like, let me think. I know there's, like, communication artifacts and spells or something, but I don't know anything about those. You can, like, already give commands to subordinates, but you wouldn't be able to hear from them or something. Hmm . . . Oh, like, I know! Why don't you, like, make a subordinate dungeon or something?"

"Requesting Elaboration."

Lilussees tilted her head. "So, like, I'm kind of going off instinctual knowledge here or something, so, like, this might not be right? But I know you can
have, like, multiple dungeons, or something? I think that's, like, why dungeon
masters would subordinate each other to begin with, normally? But, like, I think
the dungeons would be connected, or something. So, it, like, should be possible
to communicate between them or something. Otherwise there, like, wouldn't be
a point."

"Analyzing . . ."

NSLICE-00P went into the foreign system and indeed found something
relevant.

Subordinate Core Perks		
Name	Cost	Description
Create New Subordinate Core	100 points	Creates a new dungeon core that can be planted to create a subordinate dungeon.

Thanks to having taken on other dungeon masters as subordinates, NSLICE-
00P had gained the ability to create a subordinate core. It was a very heavy
expenditure, so NSLICE-00P analyzed the option.

"Requesting Clarification: Does subordinate core income go to the original
core or the new core?"

"Um, like, I'm pretty sure the master core gets a bunch, or something. Like,
that's the main reason to do it, or something. The subordinate should, like, get
something too . . . or maybe the main core can give it boons? I, like, never had a
subordinate core, so I don't really know, or something."

"Additional Clarification: Do subordinate cores retain access to all dungeon
functions?"

"Um, like, again, I don't know for sure, but, like, as far as I'm aware, they still
act like normal dungeons, or something?"

"Acknowledged."

With that data in hand, NSLICE-00P could correctly evaluate the option.
The cost was excessive purely for a communication method . . . but might be
cheaper in the long run compared to summoning new NSLICE units depending
on how far she traveled, and then having to add more Mana Capacitor implants
to compensate. But the core had additional benefits. If it was also gaining experience on her behalf, then the core would eventually earn back its cost, particularly if it were absorbing mana from the Dobhar. Likewise, if the core retained
dungeon functions, such as Monster Summoning and Item Creation, then it

could be used to help secure the Dobhar home base and expand Dobhar unit capabilities.

There *was* an element of uncertainty, since Lilussees hadn't personally experienced this area of Dungeon Management, but her queries to the foreign system seemed to indicate that the spider's assumptions were accurate.

And so, NSLICE-00P made her decision and walked into the Dobhar home base. The Dobhar made way for her and bowed their heads as she passed them by, making her way to the middle of the staircase between the Dobhar base and the former Legion keep, and then started digging a new tunnel . . .

A short while later, NSLICE-00P stood in a circular room. A stone pedestal stood in the middle. Along with a brand-new dungeon core.

Unnamed Subordinate Core → Dungeon Options
Bind Dungeon Master
Unlock/Restrict Functions
Manage XP Allocation

Fortunately, Lilussees's assumptions had been correct. NSLICE-00P could perceive everything occurring in the new dungeon just like within her own dungeon field. She *would* have to check the range on that, but if all went well, she would be able to communicate with the Dobhar wherever she went.

Likewise, she could manually control the split of XP between her core and the new one, which she set to a 25/75 split between herself and the new core, to be adjusted should the 75% XP prove insufficient for the new core's needs. She could also adjust the available functions of the dungeon, which she did not do at this time, as she wanted it to have access to all available capabilities.

It was at this moment that the Great-High King of all the land found the courage to speak.

"Wise-mighty-gracious boss-queen, you will need-require a manager for the new dungeon, yes-yes? W-Why not choose-select someone with the most experience, yes-yes?"

Lilussees stretched.

"Eh, I'm, like, flattered, but no. I'm, like, better in my current position, or something."

"Not you, wretched spider-thing!"

"Oh, the snack is speaking to me again, huh?"

Rattingtale shrieked and hid, despite the fact that he and Lilussees were in separate rooms at the moment.

"Negative Response: NSLICE Excellion Formantus Rattingtale the Third and NSLICE Lilussees are both necessary to provide dungeon-related intel and manage same-model units. This unit has already selected an optimal subordinate for this task."

Rattingtale froze and then cursed. He'd really made a mistake with the whole "convincing the boss-queen to summon subordinates" business.

Uscfrea followed NSLICE-00P up the staircase, with Estrith following suit. He wasn't exactly sure what she wanted; when he had asked, she'd just said something about classified intel. But he wasn't going to turn her down after all she had done lately.

Also, he literally couldn't turn her down if she gave him a command, courtesy of the magic contract he'd signed, so his willingness was a bit beside the point. But the contract couldn't force him if he agreed to do it first!

Uscfrea was not at all coping with being magically subordinated to a human. That was the one part of this whole affair that he made great efforts not to think about.

Soon, they reached their destination. About halfway up the staircase, there was a tunnel branching off to the side. NSLICE-00P moved down this tunnel, and the two Dobhar followed.

And then the two Dobhar gasped. There was a swirling, black void they couldn't see past. The clear sign of a dungeon. One that *definitely* hadn't been there before, given this had all been solid rock before NSLICE-00P dug it out.

But NSLICE-00P didn't stop, walking right inside.

Uscfrea and Estrith glanced at one another. Estrith nodded and gripped her spear while Uscfrea swore inside, reminding himself he needed to grab a new weapon.

The pair stepped inside . . . and paused, blinking repeatedly. The dungeon was empty. They were already in the core room, in fact. And there was no sign of any monsters . . . or the dungeon's master.

"My queen . . . what is this?"

But NSLICE-00P didn't respond. Because the Aesdes did for her.

Dungeon Master NSLICE-00P has designated Uscfrea Ymmason as the new master of subordinate dungeon Unnamed Dungeon. Beginning binding.

Uscfrea suddenly grunted as a flood of mana struck him from the core. His dragonblood-blessed fur tried to absorb and resist it, but the mana connected to his own and began flowing in that way. Fire filled his veins as the mana filled every inch of his body . . . and then began flowing back. And then it was done. A message from the Aesdes passed before his eyes:

**Uscfrea Ymmason is now the master of the Otter Burrow
subordinate dungeon.
Primary Dungeon Affinities determined as Water/Beast. Otter-
lineage monsters unlocked.**

Yes, NSLICE-00P had decided to make Uscfrea the subordinate dungeon
master. He was already her liaison to the Dobhar, so granting him the means of
communication was a given. Likewise, as he was charged with the defense and
development of the Dobhar units, granting him the additional capabilities of
the dungeon would improve his ability to fulfill his directives. And since he was
staying here anyway, she didn't have to sacrifice any of her own capabilities by
leaving a subordinate behind.

But NSLICE-00P wasn't done just yet.

Because now that she had a subordinate core, she had related perks available
in her dungeon menu. And there was one in particular that matched one of her
directives.

Subordinate Core Perks		
Name	Cost	Description
Affinity Sharing	20 points	Master core and subordinate cores may share affinities with one another. Master core primary affinity may be set as subordinate core secondary affinity. Subordinate core primary affinity may be unlocked for master core.

She went ahead and purchased it, then selected the new option.

**Affinity shared. Otter Burrow secondary Dungeon Affinity set to:
Cyborg.**

With that, it should be possible at some point for the new dungeon to begin
adding units to the NSLICE network.

In fact . . .

Uscfrea began groaning as light covered him. After all, he was the dungeon
master of the Otter Burrow now, and bound to its core. So, when the core gained
a secondary affinity, he would be affected too.

And once it receded . . .

He now had an NSLICE half helmet covering the left half of his face, with metal pauldrons covering his forearms and shins, a metal box on his back, and a metal tip on the end of his tail.

He blinked several times.

"My queen . . . I have *many* questions . . ."

24

New Capabilities

"The most dangerous force in the Legion is the architecti. There is nothing as frustrating as scouting empty plains one day and a completed fortress the next."
— Zaerzis Evruth, High Archon of the Empire of the
Sun.

Uscfrea stood at the top of the Legion keep, looking down at the waves below. He watched as mothers took their pups to swim in the shallows while a ring of warriors patrolled the ocean further out. Hunting parties were coming and going, Dobhar making repairs to their rafts on the beach.

He took a deep breath and thought back to the last few days . . . and to his queen.

He still couldn't read her entirely. She never displayed any emotion or any sign of what she was thinking. She accepted overly generous offers right off the bat, with seemingly no thought as to what her employers would think of it or to what she could demand instead. Yet, she enforced that offer with a rigid magical contract that bound him to her will, and during the negotiations did not hesitate to firmly reject any condition she found objectionable. She could be easily convinced when the terms were agreeable to her, yet when she decided to refuse, she was firm and unyielding.

He tapped the new armor on his head. The armor that seemed to have a mind of its own. *Cybernetic components*, she had called them. They spoke to him in a manner similar to the queen, and seemed to assist him in thinking? But . . . their way of thinking was strange and alien.

Uscfrea was not at all comfortable with such an alien presence connected directly to his mind . . . but at the same time, he tried to embrace it. Because he felt it in his gut that this was the key to understanding his queen, and how she made her choices. And that was something the fate of his entire race might rest upon.

In an instant, she had ruined all his plans and laid waste to his army. She had left him battered and beaten and had forced him to bow to his hated foes. Yet . . . she bore the Dobhar no ill will of her own. She'd brought them under her own protection when it was her right to take everything from them. She'd paid their debts out of her own pocket, for reasons he could not explain. She'd given them a new home and personally built them a mighty fortress to call their own. She'd annihilated anyone who would dare attack them. She'd personally acted to save a single pup, granting it her own mana in the process.

She could be a killer without remorse or hesitation . . . or a savior of seemingly endless compassion and generosity. She had seemingly switched between these instantly, without warning, based purely on an oath the Dobhar had not even started to fulfill. And Uscfrea needed to understand why so that he could ensure the Dobhar remained in her graces. And to ensure he and Estrith could guide her decisions in their favor.

Her personality wasn't the strangest or most concerning part of it, either. She was a dungeon master, a foul demon lord. That part was deeply shocking, though it answered a lot of questions. Yet, she did not seem to hunt for sapient life or demand regular sacrifices like others of her ilk the Dobhar had encountered. She acted as if she were purely human, all things considered. Or perhaps something else, given Uscfrea's opinion of the average human.

She also wielded Holy mana, with the ability to bestow it upon others. That a demon lord would be granted that power by the Aesdes . . . that was something unthinkable. That defied all understanding of dungeons and demon lords and the Aesdes themselves. Was it not the demon lords that Holy mana was to oppose? Were they not anathema to each other? And the Dobhar were fairly tame in their opinion of the dungeons; Uscfrea could only imagine what the Empire would do if it learned of these things, given this situation defied every doctrine they espoused.

And yet, here she was, a Holy demon lord. Turning Dobhar pups into Holy monsters in order to save their lives. Uscfrea shook his head.

Such things were beyond him. He was no scholar or theologian. He could not explain why such a thing should not happen, and so could not then explain why it had. So instead, he would focus purely on what she had done.

And despite how casually she had accepted their allegiance, it appeared by all accounts that she truly considered the Dobhar her own. She had spared neither resource nor effort on their behalf, not even for the youngest pup. She'd revealed her greatest secret, granted Uscfrea a similar power, and left it in his hands. And then rather than ordering him to prey upon his people as he feared, she'd instead commanded him to use the dungeon's powers to protect them.

He opened up the dungeon management once more, looking over all the things he could do with it. He continued to review the conversations his queen had recorded between herself and the former dungeon masters in her employ.

And he imagined the future. He imagined legions of Dobhar equipped from head to tail in powerful dungeon loot. He imagined invading Imperials caught in traps and twisting halls. He imagined armies of monsters swimming into the deep and overwhelming the dread orcas. He imagined Dobhar pups surrounded by endless piles of food, never knowing hunger or danger until they were grown enough to fight.

He grinned and gripped his fist.

No, in the end, no matter her eccentricities, no matter her intentions, no matter the damage she had done to them, no matter the grave questions as to her identity, and no matter the humiliations he had to endure, the former King Uscfrea Spellbreaker of the Dobhar would only be grateful to his new queen.

Thanks to her efforts, the Dobhar were now in the best position their race had ever been in. And once he mastered the power she had granted him, he could elevate them to become the supreme power in Turannia. In all the North Seas.

Whatever the future held, the Dobhar would be ready for it.

He decided he would put a little extra effort into the search for those humans of hers. The boons she had granted him were worth a great deal more, after all.

He turned and exited the watchtower. He had much work to do.

Meanwhile, NSLICE-00P was flying back to Castra Turannia, with a trembling and teary-eyed Estrith in tow. It turned out the Dobhar warrior was not a fan of being kidnapped by a demon lord and then pulled up into the sky. But recent events had made her mission even more urgent, so here she was. Up in the sky, where no Dobhar should ever be. Bound to a foul demon lord.

But such musings went unnoticed by NSLICE-00P, and soon. they arrived back at Castra Turannia.

NSLICE-00P quickly found Ateia and Taog as Estrith reacquainted herself with the ground. The pair were helping clear out debris, though the work was well underway. The limitanei's ubiquitous Earth Magic skills made repairing a mostly stone city a simple task. Just another reason Imperial fortresses were hard to siege.

But still, NSLICE-00P hadn't taken that much time with the Dobhar, so the repairs were still in progress. And after greeting Ateia and Taog . . . NSLICE-00P calculated she would not be able to resume her search until the repairs were complete, since she would have to wait for Ateia and Taog.

So . . . dozens of magic circles formed across the city.

The spell Rock Throw has leveled twice and is now Level 8!
You have learned the spell Stone Wall!
The spell Stone Wall has leveled five times and is now Level 6!
The skill Earth Magic is now Level 9!
The skill Multicasting is now Level 12!
The skill Farcasting is now Level 7!

She fused Rock Throw and Earth Wall to move the scattered stones back into place . . . and managed to receive a new spell for her troubles. And a great many stares from the Imperials on the ground.

The bar for the next knight to visit Turannia rose once again.

NSLICE-00P wanted to head out immediately, but they still needed to attend a ceremony to grant NSLICE-00P her title, as well as to officially commission Ateia and Taog as Exploratores, and the day was already ending. Ateia and Taog were exhausted from their work, so they turned in for the night right away, leaving NSLICE-00P with her thoughts.

Or rather, with her analysis. NSLICE-00P took the opportunity to go over the latest combat data. All in all, things had gone very well. As she'd hoped, Spell Penetration, Geomancy, and Heroic Challenger had allowed her spells to damage a foe apparently known for his strong resistance to magic. Her offensive capabilities seemed sufficient at present, and acquisition of new spells would continue to improve them.

Her defense, however, needed some work. Admittedly, the Sea Dragon–bone axe was specialized against magic, so her latest Mana Shield perk hadn't had a chance to show its worth. But NSLICE-00P couldn't determine how common weapons like that might be, and so decided to invest some additional resources into defense. She couldn't keep losing a hand against every major opponent, after all.

Armor Plating +5 is now available! DEF is now 150 and RES is now 75!

She upgraded her armor plating several times over. Still, after purchasing a subordinate dungeon, she was now down to a bare handful of Dungeon perk points. A mere three remained.

Level up! Dungeon Level is now 91!

Four now. She was still absorbing mana from the nearby townsfolk, and would soon start receiving some from the Otter Burrow as well. So, once she had a decent stock again, she'd reevaluate the additional armor plating options.

She also had numerous other upgrades available that would not require perk points.

Available Spell Choices for Earth Magic:	
Stone Spine	Pierce the ground with a stone spike.
Stone Lance	Form stone into a sharp projectile and launch it forward.
Rock Fist	Wrap stone around a target's fists to increase unarmed damage.
Stone Armor	Wrap the target with stone. A powerful defense that comes at the cost of speed.
Earth Heal	Heal the target and boost regeneration afterward. Only works while target is in contact with the ground.

Available Spell Choices for Light Magic:	
Light Blade	User forms a blade of Light mana to attack with.
(Continued . . .)	(Continued . . .)

Available Spell Choices for Recovery Magic:	
Group Heal	Heal multiple targets for a small amount.
Regeneration	Grant a stockpile of Recovery mana to a target, boosting regeneration over time.
Rejuvenate	Boost target's mana and stamina recovery.
Fortitude	Strengthen target's HP, increasing DEF and RES.

Available Spell Choices for Holy Magic:	
Holy Blast	A cone-shaped blast of Holy mana.
Holy Shield	Form a shield of Holy mana.
Holy Ward	Protect an area with Holy mana, warding off monsters and evil. Also boosts HP and Mana recovery. Does not protect from attacks.
Holy Heal	Heal a target with Holy mana, also curing certain status effects. Certain beings might be harmed instead depending on their nature or attributes.

Available Upgrades for Heal:	
Dense Heal	Improve the effect of Heal.
Wide Heal	Heal can affect a small area.
Instant Heal	Bypass use of magic circle when casting Heal.
Lingering Heal	Heal boosts target's HP regeneration for a short time afterward.

You have learned the spell Stone Armor!
You have learned the spell Light Blade!

For Earth Magic and Light Magic, the choices were fairly straightforward. She was, again, confident in her offensive capabilities regarding Light Magic, and offensive Earth Magic was redundant with her conventional arsenal, so she'd made choices to improve her future understanding. Light Blade provided points of comparison Mana Blade while Stone Armor provided another alternative shape, and so would benefit her fundamental understanding of magic circles and the overall behavior of mana. Stone Armor might also help with the dismemberment issue, as a bonus.

You have learned the spell Fortitude!

For Recovery Magic, she chose Fortitude. Group Heal only offered slight efficiency improvements over Multicasting Heal spells. Regeneration could be used to prepare targets ahead of time, but NSLICE-00P could keep track of her subordinates well enough not to require said capability. If she was predicting a subordinate would be damaged, she would endeavor to prevent that damage in the first place, after all. Rejuvenate was interesting, but Heal also helped with fatigue, and she had just learned Mana Transfer if a subordinate required additional mana, since her own mana regeneration was sufficiently quick. Fortitude, on the other hand, would also aid in her own defense and allow her to improve her subordinates as well.

You have learned the spell Holy Ward!

For Holy Magic, she had an entirely new option available. The Ward spell seemed to be a longer-duration application of mana that she had not seen available yet, and so was a prime candidate for magic circle analysis. Likewise, the practical application was useful as well. Should her subordinates need to operate independently from her, she could use that spell to provide them rest areas that would reduce the probability of ambush. The other spells were all Holy-attributed variations of capabilities she already possessed, and so could likely replicate with Spell Fusion if necessary.

The spell Heal has been upgraded to Dense Heal!

And for the Heal upgrade, she went with a basic improvement to the spell's effectiveness, which seemed the most useful of the options to her.

With that, NSLICE-00P put her organic components on standby while activating sentry mode. If all went well, she would soon leave this province. And then, both she and her friendlies Ateia and Taog could commence their searches . . .

25

Farewell to the Land of Rain

"When I left, it was as if the sky had opened up, and I saw the light for the first time. No, really. I haven't seen the sun in a month."
— Merchant Sallustia Albucia, on her trip to Turannia.

NSLICE-00P stepped into the main hall of Castra Turannia's keep, with Estrith at her rear and Legate Opiter leading her. The hall was filled with limitanei, though now in shining armor and bright red capes, the ceremonial uniform of the Legion. They stood in two orderly rows, standing straight and at attention. Behind them were the merchants, landowners, and the notable citizens of Turannia, along with as many of the more common denizens of Castra Turannia as would fit.

Perhaps it was not the grandest of ceremonies, but it represented the best Turannia could arrange in that short time. And one thing was clear: the people and soldiers of Turannia had put their whole heart into the preparations. Flowers and garlands decorated the hall from every corner of the province. Banners of every Legion assigned to the region covered the walls. Every individual present wore the best garments they had available. And every one of them had their eyes fixed on NSLICE-00P, standing in solemn silence as she walked down the hall.

At the end of the hall stood Rector Aemilia, now dressed in an elegant stola made of celestial silk from the Land of the Stars, not a garb anyone in Turannia would ever have the means or opportunity to acquire. She was flanked by Dux Canus, wearing shining armor with gold-and-silver highlights, and Magister Tiberius in the usual garb of the Exploratores but fully cleaned and polished. Ateia and Taog stood among the crowd, smiling at her.

NSLICE-00P walked down to the end of the hall. Rector Aemilia then addressed her.

"NSLICE-00P, Rightful Queen of the Dobhar, Savior of Castra Turannia, in recognition of your deeds, I, Rector Provinciae per Turannia Aemilia Hibera, by the authority granted to me by the Emperor, hereby declare you an Amicitia Populi Elteni."

She nodded to Magister Tiberius, who presented NSLICE-00P with a scroll and a brooch with a blue gem to signify her status. She channeled her mana through the brooch, binding it to herself.

Then the keep erupted into thunderous applause.

And so NSLICE-00P became an official Friend of the Empire.

Shortly thereafter, Magister Tiberius summoned Ateia and Taog to his office.

"Ateia Niraemia, Taog Sutharlan, as Magister Exploratore per Turannia, I certify your training is complete, and that you are fully commissioned as Exploratores of the Empire. Go now, reveal the enemies of the Empire, defend its borders, and make safe its people."

With that, he handed them each a scroll, a metal brooch in the shape of a horse that represented the Exploratores, and a new traveling cloak. The pair saluted and took the items, Ateia not bothering to hide her grin.

Magister Tiberius then heaved a sigh. "Exploratore Ateia, I need to speak to you." He glanced at Taog. "In private."

Ateia frowned.

"I trust Taog with my life, Magister. Anything you have to say to me, he should hear as well."

Magister Tiberius frowned, but then he nodded.

"I suppose that's fair. You will need trustworthy allies, after all."

Ateia blinked at that.

"Magister?"

Magister Tiberius walked back to his desk and took a seat.

"You plan to leave Turannia soon, do you not?"

Ateia nodded. "Um, yes. I'm sorry we won't be around, but we promised Seer—Her Majesty NSLICE-00P that we would assist her on her quest."

Magister Tiberius nodded.

"And because you plan to search for your father, right?"

Ateia froze.

"How did you . . . ?"

He smirked at her. "I am not the Magister Exploratore for nothing, young lady."

Taog shook his head. "Ateia, you were never very quiet about it, you know?"

Ateia looked away sheepishly. Magister Tiberius's smile then dropped.

"As an Exploratore, you are now authorized to travel the Empire at will, and to tackle any issue that you deem important to the Empire. And since you have made a promise to our savior, who is also now an Amicitia Populi Elteni and the queen of the Dobhar, I cannot object to your departure. So instead, I will give you a warning."

Ateia and Taog grew quiet. They silently glanced at one another before turning to the magister. "Magister Tiberius . . . ?"

He rested his elbows on his desk and crossed his hands together.

"Your parents had many friends . . . but they also had many enemies. There was a reason your father brought you here, to the farthest and most remote corner of the Empire. And there was a reason he left you here. His mission was need-to-know, so I don't know where he went, only that while he was gone, we were to keep you safe . . . and anonymous."

Ateia's eyes widened. Magister Tiberius sighed once again.

"That is no longer possible, it seems. So, know this: be careful who you trust, and do not openly reveal your quest. Use NSLICE-00P as your cover, let everyone think you're just helping her. Do not put yourself in danger or in the spotlight if you can help it. And if you get in trouble in Utrad, seek out Agedia of the Mélusine or Vafum Broadbane of Khalbuldor; either of them can assist you. The Magister Exploratore per Utrad is not an enemy, but not to be trusted, either."

Ateia went silent. Magister Tiberius looked over at Taog.

"Exploratore Taog Sutharlan, I charge you with this mission. Protect Ateia Niraemia; do not let her fall into the hands of her enemies, whoever they may be."

Taog frowned and nodded. "I would have done that even if you didn't tell me."

Magister Tiberius nodded, then let a faint smile grow on his lips.

"Well, I can admit that by cunning, by luck, or by the work of the Aesdes, you seem to be prepared. No, rather, the relationship you forged with NSLICE-00P saved *all* of us. An Exploratore's relationships are also their strength; often their main strength, remember that well. I will definitely sleep better knowing you're traveling in the company of an actual hero."

Ateia and Taog froze.

". . . Seero . . . is a hero?"

Magister Tiberius frowned. "Oh . . . you didn't know? She didn't tell you?"

Ateia and Taog shook their heads with all their might. Magister Tiberius blinked a few times.

"Um . . . oops?"

The two left in a hurry after that. Magister Tiberius groaned and held his head. With all that had happened, it appeared he had relaxed a bit too much. A Magister Exploratore should know better than to reveal any more information than necessary. He could only hope that NSLICE-00P wouldn't mind him telling her friends.

And speaking of friends . . . it was high time he contacted his.

He heaved a sigh and pulled out a blank scroll and some mana ink. His friend, Agedia, had suffered greatly in the past due to events involving Ateia's parents. And Tiberius knew all too well that, when Ateia's father had fled to Turannia, Agedia had not been prepared to face that pain. It had been years since then, but they had not spoken on this particular topic. Tiberius felt it should be Agedia's choice to bring it up, when and if she was ready.

But, unfortunately, events had conspired against them. Ready or not, Ateia was headed her way. And traveling in the company of a hero and Amicitia Populi Elteni who had ruined the Cult of Mana's plans for Castra Turannia. Ateia would now be in the gaze of the very people her father and Tiberius were trying to hide her from, and there was a good chance Ateia would end up in danger, even if her identity wasn't revealed. And Tiberius could not get up and leave his position at the drop of a hat to go and help, particularly not given Turannia's current situation. That would draw even more attention, and so end up more harmful than helpful.

So, he didn't know if Agedia was ready for this. But he did know that she would never forgive herself if the girl came to harm in the meantime. Which meant his only choice now was to inform Agedia that the girl was on her way, and let her handle the situation on her own. That was why he'd pointed Ateia toward her, despite everything.

His heart twisted in his chest, but he forced himself to write the letter. Every moment he delayed was one less moment for Agedia to prepare herself. He only hoped that Vafum would have enough drinking money saved up . . .

NSLICE-00P was waiting at the inn when Ateia and Taog burst through the door. Estrith grabbed her spear at first, but scoffed and turned aside as she saw the two Imperials enter. She busied herself with a bowl of soup instead.

"Greeting: Hello, friendlies Ateia and Taog. Query: Have you concluded your business with Magister Tiberius?"

The two ignored her and marched right up to her, each placing a hand on one of her shoulders. Ateia spoke first.

"Never mind that! Seero, what's this about you being a hero?!"

Everyone heard a bowl crash on the ground as Estrith dropped her soup.

"Response: This unit has received a 'Hero' designation from the foreign system."

Estrith began to tremble in the corner of the room. Ateia shouted at NSLICE-00P, "How?! Why?!"

"Answer: This unit received the designation after terminating a hostile dungeon."

Taog groaned. "Seero, it wasn't just any old dungeon, was it?"

"Speculation: This unit received a separate feat, so it does appear the dungeon was designated separately from others. The foreign system described it as a corrupted dungeon."

The pair froze. Estrith's trembling grew.

"Seero . . . you fought . . . a corrupted dungeon?"

"Affirmative."

"And . . . won?"

"Affirmative."

Taog trembled as well. "W-When did that happen, Seero? Weren't you like . . . level twenty or something?"

"Answer: When Ateia and Taog were conducting Exploratores training. According to this unit's logs, she was at Personal level twenty-eight at the beginning of the hostile dungeon termination."

Ateia and Taog slapped their heads, groaned, and then sighed. Estrith held her head as she attempted to comprehend the words she was overhearing.

"Okay, so Seero's a hero and can do anything, pretty much. Well . . . that's a good thing, right?"

Taog sighed again. ". . . You know what? Sure. Yes. Seero's a hero . . . and queen of the Dobhar. I wouldn't be surprised if she was the grandmaster of some knight order, too. Are you, Seero? Are you the grandmaster of some knight order?"

"Answer: As far as this unit is aware, she is not a knight."

Ateia jumped. "Wait, you're not?!"

"Uncertain Response: As far as this unit is aware, the term 'knight' refers to either an official member of a martial order chartered by a national authority, or an aristocratic title granted by a sufficiently high-ranking government official. This unit has no affiliations as of present, and her only official title on record is Amicitia Populi Elteni. This unit is not aware if term 'knight' has any additional meanings in the local context, and so cannot state with certainty that the designation is inaccurate, however."

Ateia froze. Taog glanced at her.

"You know . . . we never actually asked her that, Ateia."

"You know . . . you're right, Taog. We never did. We just assumed. But she's wearing that armor . . ."

"But like, anyone can wear armor . . . you know?"

". . . I guess that's . . . true?"

And so, the mystery of NSLICE-00P's identity deepened for the two confused teens. Meanwhile, Estrith was huddled in the corner, clutching her head.

"She's . . . a hero? *That?* That foul demon lord who usurped my king . . . is a hero? That's . . . What? It-it must be a lie. Those Imperials must be mistaken. The Aesdes would not permit such a thing to occur."

It would be quite some time before Estrith engaged a rest cycle that night.

And so, NSLICE-00P, Ateia, Taog, and Estrith moved to leave Turannia. Magister Tiberius shed tears of longing, and Legate Opiter shed tears of relief as the strange and powerful wandering hero left their city. They were accompanied by Mialloi and an honor guard of Selkies. The Selkies as a whole were not entirely certain what to make of NSLICE-00P yet, the one who'd both defeated the Dobhar and given the hated enemy a place on Turannia, but Mialloi's own thoughts were clear. To her, NSLICE-00P was a powerful warrior who had come to their aid when all was lost, and whose deeds had allowed the Selkies to keep their homeland. And so, Mialloi had offered to escort the group across the sea.

NSLICE-00P had originally wanted to fly, but this had been strongly vetoed by Taog and Estrith. Taog had pointed out that it would be better to keep that ability confidential once more, since the Empire in Utrad wouldn't recognize her right away and might misunderstand something unknown flying toward them.

And so, the group made their way to the largest port in Turannia, arranging passage on one of the ships making for the mainland.

And as they did, a certain figure in a cloak, with the hood covering her blue hair, glanced at the group, her attention drawn by the Selkie warriors. She froze as her eyes landed on NSLICE-00P and then moved to Ateia and Taog.

"A human girl and a half Wulver boy . . . So they were affiliated, after all? And a Dobhar too . . . I guess I'll need to investigate them as well."

She walked back into the crowd, looking to book passage on the ship . . .

26

This Unit Is on a Boat

"Why do the Aesdes track similar spells separately, you ask? An excellent question. Let us consider an example of the most basic of spells: the Bolt spell. Magic Missile, Fire Bolt, Water Bolt, Rock Throw, etc. On the surface, these spells are very similar. Gather your mana together, optionally give it an attribute, and launch it at your enemy. Simple enough, right?

In practice, yes. But if you actually want to break down the mechanism of each individual spell, then it quickly grows complicated.

Fire Bolt, for example, requires creating the fire from your own mana, adjusting the temperature, and then holding the ephemeral flames together. Then to actual launch the bolt requires you to accelerate an ephemeral energy with no physical form that wishes to flicker and move as it pleases. This is, to simplify in easily understood terms, done by guiding the flame to burn in a specific direction.

Rock Throw, on the other hand, requires you to reach out into your surroundings and gather the attribute from the physical world, or else transmute matter from pure mana, which is an entirely different matter we will discuss at a later date. Once formed, however, the rock requires no further input or upkeep. However, to launch it requires a direct application of force, with adjustments for the distance to the enemy, the enemy's speed, the force of gravity upon the rock, the current speed and direction of the wind, etc, etc.

As you can see, these may be two similar spells in effect. They may even bear some similarities in their magic circles. But the mechanisms by which they function are entirely different. The same applies for every other attribute as well.

There are tales of mages who can interchange similar spells and magic circles. But such feats would require insight into the mystic arts that even I have not achieved. And at that point . . . you would not need the aid of the Aesdes at all."

—Magus Major Curtia Volusena, instructing a new class
at the Imperial Academy.

NSLICE-00P analyzed the boat as she climbed aboard. Curiously, the boat was much lower and deeper than she would have expected, with the majority of the vessel's hull underwater. But the reason for that became clear as they set off.

Rather than sails or oars, the ship moved via magic. The vessel seemed to have magic circles engraved into its very hull. NSLICE-00P detected Water-attribute mana seeping out of the ship, forming the water around it into a bubble encompassing all but the top deck of the ship. The enchantment then propelled the bubble forward, carrying the ship with it.

The performance was inferior to some modern vessels, but this was a civilian passenger ship, so it may not have been optimized for speed. In that light, its performance was still comparable to modern technology overall. Likewise, there were some benefits to this design. Since the vessel was controlling the water around it, the trip was very smooth, and the craft seemed to ignore waves and other ocean conditions.

NSLICE-00P spent some time gathering data on the ship. It was a novel, mana-based design that represented a significant technological improvement over what she had anticipated. The Dobhar had basically just tied pieces of wood and bone into basic rafts, and so had set inaccurate expectations as to local ship-building techniques.

Her evaluation of the Empire's technological level went up.

"Wow, this is amazing!"

Ateia was standing near the edge of the boat, staring out at the sea with wide eyes.

"Ateia! Don't get so close to the edge!"

Meanwhile, Taog was huddled in the center of the ship.

Estrith was glaring at the Selkies surrounding them, who were eyeing her as well.

And so, NSLICE-00P left the province of Turannia.

The ship may not have been reliant on favorable winds and sea conditions, but it would still take a few hours to arrive at their destination. Ateia continued looking out over the water, but she had lost her smile and childlike glee at the new experience. Taog glanced over at her, eventually clearing his throat.

"You thinking about something, Ateia?"

She continued looking out over the sea. At first, she started to shake her head, but then she stopped. She glanced at Taog for a second before taking a deep breath.

"Well . . . yes. A lot of things, actually."

Taog rubbed his chin for a second before deciding what to say.

"You know I'll help you with anything, right?"

Ateia went silent for a bit, watching the waves.

"It's just . . . all I wanted was to find my father. But now? Bandits, dungeons, incursions. And apparently, my dad knew the Magister Exploratores personally? It sounded like Magister Tiberius was helping him, and not the other way around? And they're trying to protect me? Why? From what? Things are getting a lot more complicated, and I don't know why."

Taog frowned. "We . . . probably should have asked why, huh?"

Ateia nodded. "It's just . . . I was so surprised by Seero being a hero . . ." She trailed off, glancing over the deck. NSLICE-00P was standing motionless, her robotic eye flickering rapidly. Ateia sighed. "And then . . . what about Seero? We still don't know if she actually cares about us, but we have to trust her with our lives?"

Taog crossed his arms and raised an eyebrow.

"Ateia, that's what I was concerned about when you signed a magical contract with a stranger who killed a group of bandits without a second thought."

Ateia glared at him, and he raised his hands.

"Fine, not helping, I get it. Still, nothing's really changed, right? Our lives have been in Seero's hands since we met her. And we're still alive now. That has to count for something, doesn't it?"

Ateia did not respond, frowning as she furrowed her brow. Taog sighed.

"Again, why not ask her yourself?"

Ateia shook her head. "That's . . . What would she say to that?"

Taog smirked slightly. "*Affirmative* or *Negative* or something like that, I imagine."

Ateia glanced at him with narrowed eyes again, and Taog shrugged.

"I'm serious. Seero isn't exactly shy with her responses, Ateia. Whether or not we can actually understand those responses is another matter, but you know she's going to answer." His face then turned serious, and he looked straight at Ateia. "And isn't this what you want from your father? A chance to find out what's going on, and where he went? A chance to ask him? So . . . why not start with Seero?"

Ateia's eyes widened for a moment, and she turned her head, looking back out over the sea.

Only for the two to hear a bit of a commotion behind them. They turned around . . . and found NSLICE-00P casting spells.

As the trip began, Ateia and Taog went off talking on their own. Estrith was still having a staring contest with the other Selkie guardians, but no altercations had occurred. 01R and some of the other monsters were training with 00B as best they could in the Monster Hangar's common area, while Rattingtale and Lilussees were alone in their respective rooms. As such, NSLICE-00P was left alone with her thoughts after her analysis of the ship concluded.

And so . . . NSLICE-00P formed two magic circles, one over each of her hands. She formed them slowly this time, her robotic eye flickering as her sensors recorded as much detail as possible.

Finally, the magic circles finished and flashed as they activated. Two swords of pure mana formed in her hands, one with the blue glow of unattributed mana, the other a bright sword of yellow light.

The spell Mana Blade is now Level 2!
The spell Light Blade is now Level 2!

NSLICE-00P was now conducting a magic circle analysis. The two Blade spells she now had were ideal for this: since they created melee weapons instead of ranged projectiles, there was no risk of friendly fire or misunderstandings.

She analyzed the structure of the magic circles, comparing them to each other and to other spells in the Arcane and Light categories. She isolated the parts unique to the Light Blade spell and then compared them to other Light Magic spells, identifying common shapes. She then formed a Light Bolt and Holy Bolt magic circle, though she was careful not to activate them, and compared the two.

With her comparison complete, she started to form her mana into a new magic circle. She used the Light Blade circle as a base, but amended the parts she predicted were related to the spell's attribute and replaced these with corresponding parts from the Holy Bolt spell, adjusting slightly to fit the Blade spell as per her comparisons of Light Blade and Light Bolt.

And then . . . a sword of silver-and-golden light formed in her hand.

You have learned the spell Holy Blade!
The spell Light Blade has leveled three times and is now Level 5!
The spell Holy Blade has leveled four times and is now Level 5!
The skill Holy Magic has leveled three times and is now Level 10! Spell choice available!
You have achieved the Personal Feat: Spell Shaper!

Personal Feats		
Name	Description	Effect
Spell Shaper	Mana may take many forms, but the true mage knows that the mana remains the same. Unlocked by manually adjusting a magic circle into a new spell.	Grants Spell Shaping skill.

Compiling spells . . .
Available spell shapes: Armor, Bomb, Barrier/Wall, Beam, Blade, Blast, Bolt,
Chain, Infusion.

Her predictions had been correct. Magic circles were, in fact, a standardized system. The Light Blade spell, for example, had a portion dedicated to shaping the mana into the form of a sword, a portion dedicated to applying the Light attribute to the mana, and some other portions NSLICE-00P had not yet identified, but predicted as related to keeping a consistent channel of mana to maintain the spell.

And now, she had determined she could, in fact, swap out those parts to form new spells.

But NSLICE-00P wasn't done yet. She had chosen the Holy attribute for its demonstrated compatibility with the Light attribute, which she'd predicted would make it easier to slot into the Light Blade spell. And she had logged that compatibility due the Holy attribute having already combined with another Light spell: Light Beam.

And that was important for the next phase of NSLICE-00P's analysis.

This one started as a simulation in her head. She compared four different magic circles she had recorded. The Fusion Light Beam spell, the Holy Beam spell, the Fusion Mana Barrier spell, and recordings she had of the original Light Beam spell without the Fusion modifier. And in doing so, she identified the part of the magic circle that she predicted was responsible for the Fusion effect.

She didn't want to startle the other passengers by shooting a Beam spell out of the blue, so instead, she tried to append the Fusion effect to the Light Blade and Holy Blade spells. It took some adjustment, but between her AI and her dungeon-levels amount of maximum mana and mana regen, she could simply trial many small adjustments until she found something that didn't fail outright.

And then . . . two blades of light formed in her hands, one golden and silver, the other a shining yellow. She brought them together . . . and they combined into one.

Light Blade has been upgraded into Fusion Light Blade!
Holy Blade has been upgraded into Fusion Holy Blade!
You have achieved the Personal Feat: Spell Adjuster!

Personal Feats		
Name	Description	Effect
Spell Adjuster	Magic is the art of changing reality. So why would a spell be static and immutable? Unlocked by manually applying a spell modifier to a magic circle.	Grants Spell Modification skill.

Compiling spells . . .
Available spell modifiers: Dense, Fusion
Spell Shaping, Spell Modification, and Spell Fusion skills all unlocked. Modular
spell casting unlocked!
Compiling relevant spell levels . . .
The skill Spell Shaping is now Level 15!
The skill Spell Modification is now Level 2!
Updating available spell choices . . .
One choice remaining for Holy Magic.
You have learned the spell Divination!

NSLICE-00P had wondered why different schools of magic all had very similarly named spells. And now she knew. The foreign system filled her memory with additional data confirming her observations and predictions. All of those spells were rather the same spell shape with different attributes. So, it stood to reason with enough skill and data that the spells would be interchangeable.

Next . . . she moved to test it.

She let the Holy Light sword fade and formed two brand-new magic circles over her hands. Wood began to grow out of one hand, while purple fog condensed in the other.

The skill Nature Magic has leveled twice and is now Level 5!
The skill Poison Magic has leveled twice and is now Level 6!
The skill Spell Modification is now Level 3! New modifier choice available!

A Nature-attribute Blade and a Poison-attribute Blade now rested in each of her hands. She brought them together . . .

The Poison Blade sank into the Nature Blade, purple thorns forming along its length.

She had succeeded. She had successfully applied the Blade form and the

Fusion modifier to two attributes she had not seen those shapes and modifiers available for yet.

Which meant . . . her arsenal had massively improved in size. Any spell form or modifier she had access to could now be applied with any attribute she had access to. And the efficiency of her spells had improved across the board. She was no longer trying to learn and level each spell individually. Rather, the strength of each individual spell would now depend solely on her skill with that particular spell shape and that particular attribute. She wouldn't need to combine Magic Missile and Fire Blast just because her Fire Bolt skill was a low level any longer. Likewise, any new attributes she gained access to would now come with a full arsenal of available spells.

For example . . .

She formed another magic circle in her hand. Water rose out of the ocean and formed into a sword.

You have learned the skill Water Magic!
The skill Water Magic has leveled two times and is now Level 3!

She had observed Water Magic circles in her fight with the Dobhar, as well as on the very ship she now rode. And she had gained a Water Dungeon Affinity recently as well. So, it was simple matter at this stage for her to produce Water-attribute mana and gain the relevant skill, which, instead of only giving her access to some form of Water Bolt, would now give her a wide spread of spells. Water Bolt, Water Blast, Water Barrier, Water Beam, Water Blade, any form she knew that was compatible with Water Magic in general.

Of course, her Water Magic would still be weaker than some of her other attributes due to her lack of skill with it, but the point was that now it was a viable tactical option, without requiring her to use it extensively first to unlock useful spells.

Meanwhile, everyone on the deck of the ship was staring at NSLICE-00P. The whole "extremely bright glowing sword of light" business happened to draw attention, after all. Ateia and Taog's jaws dropped before they glanced at each, shrugged, and said, "It's Seero, after all."

Estrith frowned.

Miallói blinked, the only sign of surprise the calm Selkie normally displayed.

And as for the other Imperial passengers . . .

Two apprentice mages, a boy and a girl heading for a magic academy in Utrad, glanced at one another. The first poked his comrade's side.

"Hey . . . can you do that? Just . . . fuse spells together?"

She shook her head with all her might. The boy's eyes widened.

"Wow . . . if that's what a knight can do, what do you think they're going to teach us at the academy?"

The girl's shoulders slumped. She spoke in a small voice.

"If that's what a knight does, I think I might take up the farm, after all . . ."

27

Friendly Queries

—A memo from Dr. Ottosen, following the "Grand Theft NSLICE" incident.

The Great-High King of all the land, Excellion Formantus Rattingtale the Third . . . was currently curled up in a ball in a corner of his room.

It was time to admit it.

His plans had developed . . . not necessarily to his advantage.

The boss-queen's power grew by the day, in ways he could not have imagined nor predicted. He could no longer see a future in which he usurped her. He couldn't even imagine what it would take to get rid of the current her, and that assuming she didn't keep growing, which she absolutely would.

The wretched spider-thing had come out openly with her hostility, promising horrific ends to him, and yet the boss-queen had done nothing—besides ordering them not to harm one another and saving his life, but that was beside the point. No, the wretched spider-thing had largely supplanted him as the boss-queen's main advisor on all things dungeon related. Which meant his position as the rat monster manager was just about all he had left, and that was quickly slipping from his grasp as well.

His loyal minions . . . had been usurped by the boss-queen. They practically worshiped her, especially the treasonous 01R. They were not his allies but rivals and opponents. And 01R was gaining on him by the day. At this rate, it wouldn't be long until he lost even his current position.

And the boss-queen had added new minions as well. 00B was a clumsy oaf, but tough and powerful even in his low level. And now, the boss-queen had added an entire *army* of those otter-things. She had clearly made alliances with the man-things as well.

And she had given away the dungeon master position that was rightfully his to that exceptionally large and scary-looking otter-thing. Which she was not willing to give to Rattingtale due to his now tenuous positions as dungeon advisor and rat manager. Or so she said.

More likely, she was laughing at him. He had been completely cornered, stripped of nearly all his options. And worst of all, she had not needed to directly oppose him even once to achieve it. By twisting his own designs and enacting her own plans, which he still could not fully comprehend, she had managed to render him completely impotent, with no subordinates, no dungeon, no power, and with this wretched armor that spied on his every movement.

The Great-High King gnashed his teeth. He had to find something new. Some advantage he could lean into. Some way to overturn the situation. If only he could get rid of that wretched spider-thing, then the boss-queen would have to rely on him for dungeon knowledge.

And then . . . he had a thought.

He thought of the wretched spider-thing, and a conversation she'd had with the boss-queen about her sleep. He still could not comprehend how a dungeon master like himself could be such a lazy wretch, but that was not the point. The point was . . . the boss-queen had adjusted the enchantment on the horrific spider-thing's armor, enabling her to sleep once more.

Which meant . . . the enchantments on this armor were not fixed. They could be adjusted, controlled.

Currently, the boss-queen was the only one who knew how. But . . . what if she wasn't? What if someone found a way to control their own enchantments? After all, was not this enchantment connected to his own mind? Did not the armor respond to him like his own limbs? Was he not the Great-High King of all the land? Should he not possess the means to assert authority over his own body? Was he not a dungeon master as well, at one point? A natural master of magic and mana, of an enchanted core that gave godlike powers within its domain?

So, could he not find a way to control a lesser enchantment such as this?

Rattingtale sat up. He began to explore the armor, sniffing it, observing it, rubbing his paws across it. And he began to explore the part within his mind where the strange voice spoke back to him in his thoughts and that held his memories in its grasp, even those he hadn't remembered himself. He began to push at the strange symbols he saw and answer the questions posed to him to the best of his great wisdom.

The Great-High King of all the land did not have much at the moment . . . but he had found a path. A possibility. And so, he would refuse to tremble and despair, instead making all efforts to reclaim that which was rightfully his.

Such was the way of a Great-High King of all the land.

A few minutes later . . .

NSLICE-00P suddenly got a critical alert from a friendly NSLICE unit's system. It seemed one of the NSLICE units had attempted to delete all of their protocols and memory, which due to the current Loyal Wingman connection required her approval. She turned her perception toward the unit in question to determine why said unit was requesting such measures.

She found the unit randomly activating and confirming every UI option in sight.

"Observation: NSLICE Excellion Formantus Rattingtale the Third does not appear to understand the system layout."

It was at that moment that NSLICE-00P realized something. Her subordinates were all from a preindustrial society that seemed to lack electronic information technology. So they would likely be unable to comprehend the standard UI. She had not noticed this before because the NSLICE implants and techno-organic interface worked to move cybernetic components based on instinctive commands by the organic nervous system. In other words . . . an NSLICE unit could still perform physical motion as if they were purely organic without specifically interacting with any software.

That would also explain why Lilussees hadn't been able to adjust her own rest cycles. And this was made worse by the fact that only the most basic protocols had been transferred to the new implants. Their UI was barebones to begin with, such that it would require a significant degree of technical knowledge to utilize effectively.

NSLICE-00P identified this as a major inefficiency that required correcting. Unfortunately, she had not been programmed with any tutorials regarding her own software and UI. Why would she be? Her AI intuitively understood itself, and anything it didn't have protocols for were (previously) restricted areas meant only for command and maintenance staff.

But she did what she could. She watched Rattingtale's actions and attempted to assist, canceling any orders that would result in serious problems and trying to adjust the UI. She tried patterning it off the foreign system, since she knew Rattingtale was already familiar with it.

It would be a work in progress, since she also wasn't programmed for UI design, but bit by bit, her and Rattingtale's joint efforts would help build out a UI her new subordinates could understand so that one day they could further integrate into the network.

Unbeknownst to the rat himself, of course, who, due to the new UI's similarity to the royal records, would believe the Aesdes themselves were trying to assist him for quite some time.

While NSLICE-00P was in the process of adjusting the UI, she was approached from behind.

"Seero, can we talk?"

She turned around to find Ateia waiting behind her.

"Acknowledgement: Affirmative. Does friendly Ateia have a query or update for this unit?"

Ateia glanced down at the ground, took a deep breath, and then made eye contact with her.

"Yes, I do. First of all . . . why did you leave us behind?"

"Answer: This unit was forced to withdraw from the area to avoid being drawn into a conflict between two unaffiliated parties."

Ateia blinked at the immediate answer before frowning.

"Even though we were still there?"

"Affirmative."

Her frown deepened. "Why?"

"Explanation: In addition to nonintervention protocols for third-party conflicts, this unit is not currently aware of the persons of interest potential affiliations. As a result, any given faction could potentially be aligned with a person of interest or possess key intelligence regarding one. This unit would therefore risk failing her primary directive if she initiated unprovoked hostilities against an unaligned faction. Combined with the threat of termination when facing organized military forces, this unit could not remain in the operational area, even to recover local assets."

Ateia rubbed her chin as she took in the explanation. Eventually, she sighed and shook her head. "I see. But then . . ." She paused and frowned. Closing her eyes, she took a deep breath. "Then . . . why did you come back? It was for the Amicitia Populi Elteni title, right?"

"Affirmative Answer: The benefits of the offered compensation were a significant factor in this unit's decision to intervene."

Ateia's face fell at that.

"Clarification: However, the compensation was not considered sufficient to overrule nonintervention protocols. This unit also determined that the loss of friendlies Ateia and Taog would have a significant impact on this unit's efficiency, particularly of her organic components."

Ateia's head shot up, and her eyes went wide. "What? You came back . . . for us?"

"Clarified Response: To an extent, that is correct."

Ateia blinked. "Why?"

"Uncertain Response: This unit's organic components apparently consider friendlies Ateia and Taog as important assets and would suffer notably inefficiency upon their termination. This unit has not yet determined the situation to a significant degree, but it appears to involve an emotional reaction which this unit's emotional controls failed to contain. In order to address this, preserving friendlies Ateia and Taog has been designated a major directive."

Ateia stared at her.

"So, you . . . care about us? You're . . . going to protect us?"

"Affirmative."

Ateia's eyes began to moisten. She quickly hid her face and wiped her eyes with her arm. A few moments later, she took a deep breath and turned back. "Seero, I'm sorry. And thank you. For saving us; for everything. I-I can't thank you enough. I . . . I promise, I'm going to help you find your people."

"Acknowledged."

Since Ateia had no further updates or queries, NSLICE-00P resumed her work. She noted a slight increase in the efficiency of her organic components.

Meanwhile, Ateia walked away, staring into the distance, until Taog approached her.

"How did it go? What did she say?"

Ateia paused, standing still for a moment, then turned to Taog.

". . . Taog, we need to help her."

Taog tilted his head. "I mean, yes, we're quite literally obligated to do so, but what do you mean?"

Ateia shook her head. "Seero . . . she came back, specifically for us. If I understand correctly, she even risked her mission and her life to save us. And I was doubting her this whole time. She . . ." Ateia had to turn away and wipe her face again. She looked into Taog's eyes, her face resolute. "I'm going to make it up to her. I'm going to help her find her people if it's the last thing I do. Will you help me?"

Taog's eyes widened as he processed Ateia's words. NSLICE-00P had come back for them? Truly? He wasn't sure what to make of that . . . but he knew the look in Ateia's eyes. And it was a fact that they wouldn't be alive if not for NSLICE-00P.

So he nodded his head. "I will."

28

First Deployment

"I think our strategy should be immediate surrender."
—Selkie First Hunter Callodh, after a scouting mission
to Imperial lands.

Attempting to adjust Rattingtale's UI took up a great deal of NSLICE-00P's focus, so before she knew it, they had arrived. NSLICE-00P beheld Aquilo Perfugium of the Utrad Province, the first *true* city of the Empire she had seen.

The buildings and streets were similar to those she'd seen in Castra Turannia: stone structures and paved roads laid out on a standardized grid. But she also saw a great deal that was not present in Turannia. Enchanted ships like the one she was on moved in and out of the harbor. They rose right out of the ocean in their enchanted bubbles, landing directly onto the docks.

There, giant arms made of wood, metal, and stones—which appeared to her much like cranes—reached into the cargo vessels, pulling out the cargo and placing it onto the backs of special transports. These transports, also made of wood and stone, had back halves like a wagon or a pickup truck, and a front half that looked like an artificial Centaur. Once loaded, these wagons picked themselves up and began walking down the streets. There were some more conventional wagons as well, but these were carried by horses twice the size of a normal one . . . and with six legs instead of four. And they carried loads at speeds not inferior to a modern truck.

Officials walked up and down the docks, waving staves tipped with glowing blue gems across the boxes. One of the staves flashed red, and then a pair of guards moved to speak with the shipowner. She even saw something similar to a train car, only instead of traveling upon wheels, it sat on a bed of soft dirt. The car began to glow, and the dirt rose up around it, then the whole thing sank into the ground. NSLICE-00P's mana sensors then caught an Earth Magic signature traveling underneath the buildings at speed.

And all of this was powered by mana, according to her sensors. It seemed the Empire's technological level, though based on an entirely different power source, was significantly higher than she'd previously determined.

And no less surprising were the people. In Turannia, Imperial settlements were almost ninety percent human, save for the Selkies and the occasional Dobhar.

Here, even at the tip of Utrad?

Races of all shapes and sizes passed around the port. Minotaurs lifted large boxes off of ships while Dwarves carried smaller packages by the dozens. Halflings the size of children worked at food stalls, while people with the lower bodies of snakes and horses and various other animals stood in line. NSLICE-00P even observed some individuals with wings instead of hands flying through the skies, carrying satchels with letters to deliver to the buildings. Humans still made up the majority, but the ratio was down to between sixty and seventy percent.

Ateia and Taog's eyes widened as well.

"Wow . . . so this is the mainland."

Miallói walked up behind them and shook her head.

"No. This . . . is the Empire. The true Empire."

And so, NSLICE-00P arrived in the province of Utrad.

The ship pulled in, rising itself up and onto the dock like the others. Miallói turned to face NSLICE-00P, with the rest of the Selkies lining up behind her.

"This is where we part ways. Honored Warrior NSLICE-00P, I thank you from the bottom of my heart for protecting my home." Miallói and the Selkies all saluted, then Miallói turned to the two Imperials. "Warriors Ateia and Taog, I also thank you. It was thanks to you that my home is safe. We did not have much time together, but I was honored to teach you for as long as I could. Remember your training, stay aware, and may your quest be successful."

Ateia and Taog saluted back.

"Thank you!"

With that, NSLICE-00P and the others made their way off the ship, while Miallói and her warriors returned to Turannia. The group walked down the pier, to where an Imperial official was waiting, checking each passenger as they entered. When the group's turn came, Ateia and Taog pointed to their Exploratores clasps on their cloaks. The official nodded and waved them past.

"Identification, please."

NSLICE-00P opened up a small compartment on her arm and pulled out the brooch she had received. The official raised an eyebrow before his eyes widened.

He took out a small staff and waved it over the brooch. The staff's magic core glowed green.

"My apologies, honored guest." He glanced at Estrith. "Is this, um, your bodyguard?"

"Affirmative Statement: That designation is reasonably accurate."

The official nodded. "I understand. Well, then, carry on. Welcome to Aquilo Perfugium, ma'am."

"Acknowledged."

The group stepped off the pier and out into the streets of Aquilo Perfugium. Taog turned to Ateia. "Okay, so what now?"

Ateia grinned.

"What do you think? We start our searches!"

Taog raised an eyebrow. "And how do we do that? You *have* thought of a plan, right?"

She crossed her arms. "Taog, how long do you think I've been thinking about this? *Of course* I have a plan!"

"Which is?"

Ateia nodded. "We make for the Northern Exploratores HQ in Corvanus! Someone there should know my father, right? And then, on the way, we check in with the local Exploratores branches to see if we can find anything about Seero's people and complete a few requests to level up and make some money."

Taog blinked. "That's . . . actually pretty reasonable? Huh."

Ateia glared at him.

"Why are you acting so surprised, Taog?! Did you think I was just going to run off down the road with no plan?! Go running into monsters and dungeons without a care in the world?!"

Taog . . . averted his gaze. "W-We should get moving."

Ateia stared at him and crossed her arms.

"We're going to talk about your opinion of me later, Taog."

NSLICE-00P, on the other hand, was talking with her monster subordinates.

"Notification: All units capable of covert intelligence gathering should prepare to deploy soon. NSLICE network will deploy to search the local settlement for persons of interest as soon as this unit can locate a secure and confidential drop-off zone."

00B, who was lying on his back, rolled over and stood up.

"Statement: NSLICE-00B is not capable of covert intelligence gathering and will not be deploying at this time."

00B cried in protest.

"Statement: NSLICE-00B is a combat-specialized unit and will deploy if combat is necessary."

00B whined but lay back down. Meanwhile, Lilussees strolled out of her room, waving her pedipalps about as she stirred from her latest nap. Having regained the ability to sleep as she desired (and having done so almost continuously for several days at this point), she was in an abnormally pleasant mood.

"Ah, like, what's that, boss? Sending us out again? I guess that's, like, fine or something."

"Affirmative."

"Like, when, though?"

"Answer: As soon as this unit has a chance to move to a secure location."

Lilussees tilted her head. "Hmm . . . Oh, because, like, the humans or something?"

"Affirmative."

Lilussees rested a leg on her mandibles. "But, like, couldn't you just Transfer us, or something?"

"Requesting Elaboration: What is NSLICE Lilussees referring to by term 'Transfer'?

"Like, it's a dungeon skill or something? It, like, lets dungeon masters move their monsters around, or something? Otherwise, like, we couldn't get our monsters to their spots without running them past the humans, or something."

"Analyzing . . ."

Upon review, NSLICE-00P located the skill Lilussees was mentioning.

Dungeon Skills		
Name	Level	Description
Analyze	N/A	Check the status of a target. More detail for targets within the dungeon. Details depend on level difference.
Contract	N/A	Bind a consenting target to the dungeon, per terms agreed upon by both parties.
Transfer	N/A	Move yourself, a subordinate, or a consenting target within your dungeon.

NSLICE-00P hadn't tested said skill because previously, her dungeon had been limited to her own body, so moving a subordinate within that area had no use case. And it hadn't been necessary either; Imperial settlements in Turannia always had an empty alleyway or two nearby that she could use.

But the situation was different now. She now had the Dungeon Field Generator, which designated space around her as dungeon territory, and so might

be eligible for this particular skill. Likewise, this Imperial settlement was significantly more densely populated than any in Turannia, and she was detecting life-
forms even in small alleyways. As well as the aforementioned issue of friendlies
Ateia and Taog, who as official Imperial military personnel, had not yet been
informed of any dungeon-related information.

So, she quickly scanned the area for a decent drop-off point within range.
Fortunately, Ateia had started leading them down the street, moving toward the
side of the road to make way for the various wagons and vehicles moving past,
and NSLICE-00P was able to identify an alleyway within range that had no
individuals present.

"Statement: All covert units prepare to deploy. Deploying in three . . . two . . .
one . . ."

She activated the skill, and with a small flash of mana and light, all her rat
and spider monsters appeared in the alley. Lilussees yawned.

"Welp, like, time to get to work, or something. Let's, like, find a *secure home
base*, or like, whatever."

01R clenched his paws as the spiders began climbing up the side of a building. "Wise-mighty-gracious boss-queen, we will not fail-disappoint you, yes-yes!"

With that, 01R and the other rats scampered off. Leaving Rattingtale behind.

"Wait-wait! You must wait for orders-commands from the Great-High King,
yes-yes! You cannot just wander-scamper away and leave me alone, you foul
traitor-things!"

And alone. In the middle of a man-thing settlement. Rattingtale's ears pressed
against his head, and he slowly began creeping through the shadows, jumping
at every noise.

Meanwhile, Ateia and Taog led them through the town. Ateia had asked a passing guard for the location of the Exploratores HQ, and so they arrived without
issue, the group stepping inside.

Ateia and Taog glanced around.

The building was laid out as most modern Exploratores HQs were. There was
a receptionist counter with a board full of requests on one side, and a staircase
leading to the offices of the support staff. On the other side was a small restaurant
and tavern, with another staircase leading to the Exploratores lodging. This setup
was intended to ensure Exploratores always had a place to stay and food to eat
when they were traveling across the Empire . . . regardless of how little money
they had on their person at the time. Hardtack and water were provided free of
charge, but any real food or—more importantly to the average Exploratores—
drink had to be purchased.

The strange part of this HQ, though, was the lack of people. There wasn't
an Exploratore in the building. That in itself wouldn't be strange; it was the

afternoon, and most Exploratores would be out on requests at the time, but the board was filled to the brim, which shouldn't have been the case if all the Exploratores were working. Exploratores raced one another to take the easiest and most profitable requests for themselves, after all.

The receptionist was reading a book when she heard the door open and glanced up.

"Oh, I haven't seen you before! Did you just arrive?"

Ateia nodded and walked over to the counter. "Yes, just today. We'd like rooms for the four of us."

The receptionist frowned.

"I can see you two are Exploratores, but about your companions . . ."

"Ah, Seero, can you show her the brooch?"

"Affirmative."

NSLICE-00P did as requested. The receptionist raised an eyebrow before her eyes widened and she took out a magic tool, verifying the brooch as the official had done earlier.

"Ah, my apologies, honored guest. We are honored that an Amicitia Populi Elteni would choose to stay with us. Please, allow me to show you to your rooms."

"Acknowledgement: Assistance is appreciated."

The receptionist led the group to their rooms; the good ones, which were generally reserved for the top-tier Exploratores who handled the serious issues for the Empire. Or for the children of high-ranking officials who wanted to play Exploratores for a while.

They said their goodnights and then turned into their rooms to rest.

The moment the group was settled and the doors were closed, the receptionist ran down the stairs and rushed into an office, frantically activating a communication artifact. She had no idea why an Amicitia Populi Elteni was visiting now, or why they would choose to stay at an Exploratores HQ of all places.

What she did know was that she had been instructed to report anything out of the norm that occurred up the chain, especially the unexpected arrival of any Imperial authorities. An Amicitia Populi Elteni wasn't exactly an Imperial authority . . . but was still a person of interest for the Empire.

She decided it qualified, and reported it up. And so, the Exploratores of Utrad received word that an Amicitia Populi Elteni had arrived in their province . . .

29

Upgrades . . . and Revelations

"NOT in my flower bed."

—Hero Viridia Sollemnis, before Banishing a greater
demon of Inferno.

And so, the group turned in for the night, each in their own very high-quality room, leaving NSLICE-00P on her own for a bit.

The first thing she did was check the logs from her subordinates, running a facial recognition scan on their visual records from the day. She got no matches on the persons of interest. She also checked the status of her subordinates; all units appeared to be functioning at optimal levels, so she moved on.

Next, she had some personal upgrades to make.

Available Spell Modifiers:	
Instant	Stores one magic circle. Corresponding spell may be cast without a circle.
Wide	Increases spell's area of effect.
Multi/Splitting	Enables one magic circle to create multiple effects.
Piercing	Increases spell penetration against RES and magic barriers.
Channeled	Spell increases in intensity the longer it is cast.

Lasting	Reduces speed at which mana disperses, increasing spell duration.
Hardened	Improves magic-circle resilience and spell defense against piercing/disruption effects.

Checking available spell choices for Holy Magic . . .
Spell Shaping and Spell Modification skills present. Removing redundant
choices . . .
Remaining choices: 1. Choice automatically selected.
You have learned the spell Banishment!

Holy Spells	
Name	Description
Banishment	Attempts to return a target creature to its origin realm. No effect on inhabitants of the world.

Now that she had a more modular method of casting magic, her upgrade choices had changed as well, only showing new spells if they represented a capability outside of the modular system. And since there had been only one such choice available at the time, it had been automatically selected.

And that spell . . . changed everything.

NSLICE-00P's heart began to pound as she read over the spell's description, bypassing her emotional controls once again. And this time, her cybernetic components didn't bother trying to reassert control. They had something more important to focus on. For if she understood the implications of this spell correctly, then she might be able to go back, right now.

Yes, NSLICE-00P had concluded with ninety-five percent certainty that she was on a different planet, or possibly, in a different universe. The evidence had been continuing to mount. The sheer abundance of mana. The existence of monsters and dungeons and sapient races she had no records on. The never-before-encountered languages and cultures. The stars that didn't match any night sky she had on record.

But the kicker had come once she'd made her way out of the forest and the mountains, and especially once she had observed the ocean. Or, more specifically, the horizon in the distance.

Because, if her observations and calculations were accurate . . . this world was *flat*.

Or, at least, so large that its curvature was not detectable to her; something she had not addressed or even acknowledged yet. Either choice would have been completely impossible for a world with Earthlike conditions under her original understanding of physics, and so every time she'd observed it, she'd tried to recalibrate her sensors, assuming an error in the data.

But at this stage, and especially after crossing the ocean where the horizon was easily observable with no obstructions, it was clear that this was reality, and her sensors had nothing to do with it. It was almost certain that mana played a role and accounted for the breaks in physics, so she would have to accept that this was how things were here.

The point being that this was almost certainly *not* Earth.

Which meant . . . if this spell could send her back to her point of origin, then she could return to Earth. She could reestablish contact with her previous commander. She could fulfill her primary directive . . . and perhaps receive a new one afterward.

But her organic components were giving mixed signs. She was noting increased levels of adrenaline and cortisol. Her organic components sent her danger signals, but also seemed like they were preparing to act. She speculated it had something to do with the new major directive. She could not guarantee the survival of the friendlies if they were not present in the same reality, after all.

But . . . in this case, the organic components were not fully resisting. She had a chance to reestablish contact with her commander and immediately fulfill her primary directive, after all. Her organic components were conflicted, but her cybernetic components were clear on the issue.

So, a magic circle formed, facing NSLICE-00P. She activated the spell and cast Banishment on herself . . .

Nothing happened.

NSLICE-00P tried once again, this time Supercharging the spell to the limit. And still, nothing happened. Her heart began to pound now for a different reason. Her organic components turned to purely danger signals.

The spell hadn't worked. Which left two possibilities.

One, that there was some other reason why the spell couldn't work on her. Maybe it couldn't be cast by the user on themselves. Perhaps the changes to her core were interfering. Or the existence of natives to this world within her.

She tried Transferring the sleeping 00B from the Monster Hangar to the bed and casting the spell again . . . but still, nothing happened, so it wasn't that last one. Increasing the possibility of the second option.

The second possibility was that this *was* Earth, or at least part of her original universe. She had already logged how dungeons seem to create a space that was isolated from the rest of the world in a seeming violation of physics. What was to say there was not a similar effect isolating this entire region from the universe at large? Mana *did* exist in her previous world, after all, just in significantly more limited quantities, so she could not rule out the possibility.

At the moment, NSLICE-00P did not have enough data to confirm either scenario. She would have to continue to study magic and this new spell she had acquired in hopes of understanding why it had failed.

Or . . . if it *hadn't*.

And she would not change her course. If this *was* a part of her original universe, there was a chance one of the persons of interest could have made their way here. In fact, that possibility also existed even if this was a completely different universe. She had traveled here herself, after all.

She tried to analyze the Banishment magic circle, but it was significantly more complicated than the others had been. She identified a part related to the Holy attribute, but that was all. She would need to gather more data, or perhaps a magic circle with a similar effect, before she could start to decode the inner workings of this spell. In fact, her current analysis was mostly on the structure of magic circles and what applications that resulted in. She still hadn't touched on the fundamental workings of mana, why arranging it in those shapes produced those effects, or even the method by which she was controlling this energy unassisted in the first place. This would be a long-term project, requiring her to gather a great deal of data beforehand.

And with that, her heart rate started to slow, and her adrenaline levels dropped. Her organic components stopped sending danger signals . . . and her cortisol levels fell as well.

She could not fulfill her primary directive at this immediate time. But that did give her an opportunity to deal with her new major directives. To ensure that friendlies Ateia and Taog could survive, even without her.

That thought caused her organic components to react briefly, but it quickly passed. Her organic components were now requesting a rest cycle . . . which she would respond to once her current upgrade cycle concluded.

And so, she moved on. She still had a choice of new spell modifiers to make, which also gave her a much smaller and more focused decision to deal with. She ran extensive simulations on each of the modifiers, given that the choice here would apply to all her available spells and so had a great many use cases to analyze.

Instant would improve her reaction times for a particular spell, but it could only store one circle at a time. She would have to choose carefully and would not be able to adjust the modifiers of that spell unless she cast it manually. It would still be useful if a generally applicable spell was stored. For example, if she had a Mana Barrier magic circle stored, she could immediately employ defenses if caught off guard. However, this modifier would only affect one spell at a time, and so had significantly restricted impact compared to the others.

Wide would improve her efficiency against densely packed targets, such as when she'd battled the Wulver and the Dobhar, and could also help against fast-moving targets she couldn't guarantee a direct hit on. On the other hand, the effect could be replicated by selecting an appropriate spell shape instead, so the improvement was marginal.

Multi/Splitting allowed one magic circle to produce multiple spells. This would improve her rate-of-fire-and-mana-cost-to-projectile-count ratio. On the other hand, the effect could be replicated with Multicasting or Strategic Magic, though as doing it that way required greater focus and attention, the modifier could still prove beneficial.

Piercing further improved her ability to bypass magical defenses. It would improve upon her spells for sure; however, she already had Spell Penetration and Heroic Challenger, so it was, again, a marginal improvement.

Channeled had promise. Uscfrea had, at one point, survived a full-power blast from Aurora Barrage, albeit by blocking it with his mana-absorbing axe. As long as there existed opponents who would not go down in one max-power shot from her, a modifier that could increase raw power output was useful.

Likewise, improving individual spell power could give her more tactical flexibility. Simulating the fight with Uscfrea, if she could have made a few Light Beam circles that grew in power instead of dozens of weaker circles, she could have devoted more attention to evasive maneuvers while maintaining the same level of offensive firepower.

Lasting improved the duration of her spells. That didn't matter much for most of her offensive spells but would improve efficiency if she was infusing her conventional weapons or utilizing support spells for her subordinates. It meant less casts to maintain the effects, and so more attention to devote to other tasks.

Finally, *Hardened* improved the strength of her barriers and the resilience of her magic circles, which the fight with Uscfrea had revealed as a potential weakness. It was a purely defensive tool, however, and Uscfrea had been the only opponent so far who could directly assault her magic circles, so its general impact would likely be less than some of the other modifiers.

This analysis, however, was purely in terms of combat efficiency. NSLICE-00P had another angle to consider as well, which was the growth of her future knowledge. Her spell arsenal had expanded dramatically as her data on the magic system grew, so it was worth considering not only how useful each individual modifier was, but also what data the modifier itself might provide to her, and what opportunities for future knowledge that data might offer.

Which was how she made her choice.

Spell modifier Hardened is now available!

She made this choice because, in addition to its defensive utility and shoring up a demonstrated and possibly critical weakness, Hardened would inform her of how magic circles could be strengthened to resist disrupting effects. Disrupting effects like the Equalizer.

The original goal of her exploration of the magic system had been to improve the efficiency of the Equalizer, after all. So, learning how a magic circle might resist it would give her useful data on how the Equalizer should be deployed to avoid such countermeasures. If she learned what parts of the circles the foreign system considered vulnerable, she would subsequently learn where to aim in the first place.

And so, her upgrade cycle concluded. Her organic components were reporting fatigue despite being in decent physical condition, but NSLICE-00P had no urgent issues at the moment, so she acquiesced to the request.

And with that, NSLICE-00P entered standby sentry mode for the night.

30

The Valued Allies' First Mission

"Exploratores with under a year of experience should be limited to noncombat missions only. And under no circumstances should they be allowed to take any dungeon missions whatsoever."

—Magister Exploratore per Corvanus, Octavianus
Aemilius Aquilius, addressing his staff after checking annual
Exploratores casualty rates.

The next morning, the group reconvened downstairs and walked up to the receptionist. Taog raised an eyebrow as he glanced around. The building was still empty, not a single Exploratore eating breakfast or competing for juicy requests. And still, the request board was packed to the brim. Ateia moved to speak with the receptionist once again.

"Good morning."

The receptionist gave a polite smile. "Good morning, did you sleep well?"

Ateia and Taog nodded. A haggard-looking Estrith just yawned instead.

"Yes! The beds here are amazing! Dad always complained about them, so I was surprised."

The receptionist nodded.

"I'm glad you enjoyed your stay." She then dropped her smile and reached under the counter, pulling out a document and slipping it in front of Ateia. "Now then, since you two have just arrived, I'm sure you haven't heard yet, but there's a bit of a situation going on."

Taog's eyes narrowed.

"And what is that?"

"The Centaurs have been raiding the border once again and pushing the other tribes into Imperial territory as well. Magister Exploratore per Utrad,

Vibius Vatinius Balbillus, has put out a call to all Exploratores in the province to join the Legion in the defense."

Ateia and Taog glanced at one another, their eyes widening. Ateia turned back to the receptionist. "Is it that bad? Is Utrad in danger?"

The receptionist smiled and shook her head.

"Magister Caelinus has many a victory under his belt; I doubt this will be any different. But the Centaurs are swift and cunning, and the wave of tribes they trigger can be tough to keep track of. So, the Legion needs a wide net of scouts to ensure they don't miss anything. You'll be paid well for your service, and it should be less dangerous than the average monster hunt as long as you're careful."

Ateia exhaled her breath, then shook her head. "Well, if they have it covered, we'll have to decline."

The receptionist raised an eyebrow.

"You're . . . refusing a call from the Magister Exploratore? I wouldn't recommend that, and this request is well compensated, you know?"

Ateia shook her head and glanced at NSLICE-00P. "We're already on a mission assisting an Amicitia Populi Elteni, so we'd need to check with her. Seero, what do you think?"

"Response: All mercenary contracts with entity 'Empire' have been concluded, and this unit has no hostility with entity 'Centaurs.' This unit cannot intervene in that third-party conflict at this time and strongly requests that the friendlies prioritize assisting with this unit's primary directive, as per the contract."

Ateia nodded and turned back to the receptionist.

"That's how it is."

The receptionist nodded back. "That's reasonable, I suppose. May I assist with anything else?"

Ateia nodded, and NSLICE-00P stepped forward. Her robotic eye lit up and displayed the holographic screen of faces once again. The receptionist tensed for a moment but relaxed once the faces appeared.

"Request: This unit is requesting all available intel on the displayed persons of interest. This unit also requests any intel regarding Exploratore Aulus Caedicius Niraemius."

Ateia and Taog had discussed things with NSLICE-00P earlier, deciding that if there was anyone they could trust, it was NSLICE-00P. They had decided that, as per Magister Tiberius's advice, they would have NSLICE-00P include Ateia's father in her intel requests. NSLICE-00P had agreed once the situation was explained to her, since it would help protect Ateia from currently unidentified hostiles. Better still if the hostiles didn't realize Ateia's identity—which even Ateia was unaware of, apparently—as any moves against Ateia would draw NSLICE-00P into conflict with the unknown faction.

The receptionist looked over the screen.

"Hmm . . . I don't recognize any of those figures. And I don't recognize that name either . . . I'll have to check the records. Would you mind waiting for a bit? I can arrange for a recorder core so we can pass this illusion around as well."

Ateia frowned but nodded.

"Take your time. We'll probably take a local request or two in the meantime, if that's fine?"

Ateia and Taog wanted to continue growing as Exploratores . . . and additional money wouldn't hurt, either. NSLICE-00P had agreed, as continuing to upgrade herself and her subordinates was desirable, and her new major directive indicated upgrades for Ateia and Taog were sorely needed. She *had* put in the condition, however, that she would only assist against unaffiliated entities, such as monsters and dungeons, save in the case of self-defense against unprovoked hostility.

The receptionist nodded and smiled.

"Honestly, that would be a big help. In fact, how confident are you in dungeon exploration?"

Ateia and Taog looked at one another. They glanced at NSLICE-00P. They turned back to each other and nodded, then turned to the receptionist in sync, speaking as one.

"*Extremely.*"

The receptionist pulled out a request.

"Excellent. A new dungeon was reported a while back near one of the smaller towns, but with the pressure on the borders, we haven't been able to put together a full exploration team."

Taog raised an eyebrow. "Isn't it dangerous to leave a dungeon unchecked close to people?"

The receptionist frowned. "Highly dangerous. Getting intel on this is our top priority after the Centaur situation. But exploring new dungeons is equally dangerous. Honestly . . ." She glanced over the group. "I wouldn't even propose this to you under normal circumstances. New dungeon exploration *should* be done by a full team of veteran Exploratores. But we absolutely need to know if this is going to be a problem and, as you might have guessed, we're a little short-staffed with everyone watching the border. So . . . don't feel obligated to map out the entire thing. Stay safe, only go as deep as you can handle, and just try to get a feel for how developed this particular dungeon is. Any information you can give us will help."

Ateia nodded. "We'll be careful."

The receptionist glanced over them once more, then sighed. "Right. Well then, here are the details . . ."

* * *

And so, the group set off from the port town. The city quickly gave way to lightly wooded pastures and farmland. Right by the town, there were some massive farms surrounded by stone walls, with Imperial banners flying all around them and armed soldiers patrolling on top. The moment these came within range of her sensor's, NSLICE-00P's eye turned red.

She detected a Non-Standard energy signature she already had on file even before arriving in this place. And one that was subject to an immediate response whenever encountered.

"Warning: Undead detected. Engaging re-termination protocols."

It turned out, NSLICE-00P had encountered necromancers in her past as a major enemy of Dr. Ottosen's organization . . . and so already had that particular foe logged as hostile. She engaged her helmet, and was about to activate her repulsors—

Ateia and Taog tilted their heads before Taog's eyes widened. "Wait, Seero! Don't attack just yet!"

"Requesting Elaboration: Undead are to be re-terminated on sight. Please explain why this unit should delay engaging."

"Are they in the Imperial farms?! Are they farming?!"

"Answer: Location is within walled facility just ahead. Unknown if undead are currently engaged in agriculture. Engaging scout protocols."

NSLICE-00P moved up the nearest hill where she could get a look over the walls, with the group running after her. Once there, NSLICE-00P focused her sight, zooming in on the detected hostiles. She saw bone-white skeletons standing in the fields, tending to the crops. Skeletal birds flew across the fields, darting at insects and warding away their living counterparts. Skeletal oxen carried carts and plows. A small handful of men and women in farming clothes sat in the shade, forming magic circles of eerie purple light as they guided their felled laborers.

"Scout Report: It appears detected undead are engaging in agriculture."

"Then don't attack them! That's the Imperial Necrotorum!"

"Requesting Clarification: Friendly Taog is stating detected undead are affiliated with entity Empire?"

"Yes! They help run the Imperial farms that provide food for the Legion and Imperial citizens!"

NSLICE-00P's robotic eye flickered.

"Requesting Clarification: So, detected undead are not hostile?"

Ateia shook her head.

"Ah, right, that's probably different where you're from. Here, the Empire strictly manages the necromancers, especially after Sisenna the Black, but necromancy is legal within those restrictions. Anyone in the Necrotorum will never risk hurting someone with their undead unless they're attacked first.

We hear about rogues every now and then, but the Necrotorum handles those personally."

In fact, foreign visitors being spooked by the Imperial Necrotorum's *employees* was the main reason for the walls around Imperial farms, the excessive number of Imperial banners hung around them, and the presence of Legion soldiers patrolling the perimeter.

Taog nodded repeatedly.

"And attacking an Imperial farm or a member of the Necrotorum is a very serious crime! Treason, even! So don't do it, Seero!"

NSLICE-00P's robotic eye flickered. Upon review, she concluded her original designation of undead as hostile was premised on the necromancers' opposition to her original organization. An organization she no longer belonged to, and that had no relations with the Empire here that she was aware of. And so . . . she concluded relations with the organization the necromancers were affiliated with superseded any hostility with the undead themselves.

And so . . . these undead were not, in fact, subject to on-sight re-termination.

"Acknowledgement: Understood. Updating designations. Detected undead set as 'Empire-affiliated assets.' Disengaging re-termination protocols."

Taog heaved a sigh of relief as NSLICE-00P stood down. It looked like they wouldn't be starting a war with the Empire today.

31

The Royal Guard's
First Dungeon Termination

"Respect the dungeons of the deep. They face the same trials of the sea as you or I, but without the ability to escape to dry land."

—Dobhar Elder Tidsige Eadgifuson,
when teaching the pups.

After a small commotion and an averted declaration of war on the Empire, the group made their way to the target. The rest of the trip was uneventful; this part of the Empire had long been cleared of hostile tribes and all but a few strictly guarded dungeons—save the newly appeared ones. So, they passed through rolling hills and idyllic valleys home to large villas, small farming communities, and the occasional Legion outpost, and it was not long before they reached the target village.

The village elder led them to a cave right on the outskirts of town before he glanced around at them one more time and took a deep breath.

"A few of our fool boys got it into their heads they would become heroes. I knew nothing good would come of this, but they couldn't get their heads out of the clouds. I told everyone this place was off-limits until the Empire bothered to come and check on it, but five of them snuck in during the night. Only two came back, one missing his arm. And both of them have hardly said a word since." He took another deep breath. "Are you sure you bunch will be alright? Forgive me, but you seem a bit young."

Ateia nodded.

"We'll be careful. And"—she turned her head to NSLICE-00P—"we brought an expert."

The village elder looked over NSLICE-00P again, paying extra attention to her armor. He shrugged and turned to leave, muttering something about foolish youths. As the group turned to the dungeon, Estrith gripped her spear.

"Queen of the Dobhar, are you certain about this?"

"Affirmative."

Estrith frowned. In her experience, dungeons were not to be trifled with. The dungeons of the deep were terrifying labyrinths of death, designed to defend themselves against sea monsters far more powerful than all but the mightiest Dobhar. She knew not if the dungeons on the land would be the same . . . but if they were, this would be an extremely dangerous affair.

Though . . . the queen of the Dobhar *was* a dungeon master herself. Estrith was not so blinded by her dislike of the usurper to admit she should be much more knowledgeable about such things. And, to Estrith's surprise, the weak Imperials showed no such hesitation. All three of them walked right into the dungeon without a moment of doubt.

Estrith paused at this before shrugging.

Well, she'd do her best to guard the queen of the Dobhar, as her king and her duty commanded. But if the usurper happened to perish midway while foolishly challenging a dungeon, then it couldn't be helped, and her king would have to take up the throne once more. And if the two Imperials perished . . . Well, Estrith wouldn't shed any tears. She simply needed to do her best to ensure she did not perish with them if at all possible, though she would consider her own life a worthy trade to restore her king to his rightful place.

She hoisted her spear and entered the dungeon . . .

Estrith blinked at the sight before her, attempting to process what was occurring. They were in a dark cave, which somehow seemed even darker than it should have been. The walls and floors and roof were all made entirely of pitch-black stone, and there was hardly any light, just a handful of dim torches lit with pale blue fire. These were few and far between, leaving wide stretches of complete darkness.

Or so it should have been. If not for her glowing spear. Or the half Wulver's glowing sword. Or the human's glowing arrows. Or the lights shining from the queen of the Dobhar.

Giant bats screeched and hissed as the light revealed them on the roof, glowing arrows shooting them one by one as Estrith and the half Wulver moved to intercept. She thrust her spear forward . . .

You have slain Nightwing (Level 8)!
Gained 3 XP!

Well, she would have killed something as weak as that in an instant regardless, but the creature died before she felt her spear hit its flesh. The light wrapped around her weapon was anathema to these creatures; even the weak Imperials could take them down with ease thanks to the Infusion by the queen of the Dobhar.

Suddenly, the human girl spoke.

"Trap."

Estrith and the two Imperials leapt over the pitfall trap, which would have been invisible in the dark. The queen of the Dobhar simply flew over it. A volley of arrows fired at them as they passed over, but the queen of the Dobhar blocked it with a Barrier, and the group continued on their way.

Estrith blinked again. Were the dungeons of the land truly this weak?

She turned her head. The queen of the Dobhar spun her lights across the roof, blinding yet another group of bats and causing them to drop to the floor. Estrith turned to watch the weak Imperials set upon the helpless monsters.

. . . Or was it that the queen of the Dobhar was that powerful?

Estrith frowned. If the former, then Estrith was confused. How was it that the Empire had grown as strong as it was when faced with such weak challenges compared to the Dobhar? Though, they had barely started to explore this dungeon, so perhaps it was simply biding its time and taking their measure.

And if the latter . . . then the road to the return of her king may be long indeed.

The group took a short break, with NSLICE-00P standing guard. NSLICE-00P was letting Ateia and Taog lead the way once more as per her "adequate ally contribution" modified dungeon termination protocols, so the group wasn't traveling on the most efficient path. And Estrith was out of her element on land like this, so her experience could not make up that difference, even if she were inclined to help.

In fact, Estrith walked away from where Ateia and Taog were eating some rations, coming up behind NSLICE-00P.

"Queen of the Dobhar, I have a question."

"Acknowledgement: What is friendly Estrith's query?"

Estrith frowned, glancing back over her shoulder.

"Why do you bother with the Imperials? They are weak and contribute little to this hunt. You and I could have won these fights in a fraction of the time."

"Answer: Current upgrade routine is intended to correct friendlies Ateia and Taog's low combat effectiveness."

Estrith scrunched up her face. She took a moment to think.

"You are saying . . . you are training them?"

"Affirmative."

Estrith frowned again. The Dobhar *did* train their youths, of course, but that never extended to active combat like this. Any Dobhar joining the hunt was expected to take care of themselves as a warrior, and if they got hurt, that was the way of the sea. The Dobhar could not afford to carry anyone who could not survive on their own. But the queen of the Dobhar was doing more than that. She had Infused their weapons, created shields to protect them from harm, and shut down ambushes and traps that the Imperials missed. She was coddling them, holding their hands and letting them reap victories they had not earned, in Estrith's opinion.

"Why? If you must assist them like you are doing, then doesn't that mean they are not worthy in the first place?"

"Answer: Friendlies Ateia and Taog have a contract with this unit. This unit provides assistance and protection of their persons. The friendlies assist this unit with her primary directive."

Estrith crossed her arms.

"But what help can such weaklings be? Surely someone as strong as you can do anything they can already?"

"Explanation: Friendlies Ateia and Taog provide social connection to entity Empire's political and military hierarchy, in order to mobilize local resources to assist in this unit's primary directive. They also provide intel on local conditions, laws, and culture so this unit may better adapt her protocols to match current circumstances."

Estrith furrowed her brow. She didn't fully understand what NSLICE-00P meant, and she didn't really understand what these two Imperials provided. Surely, the authority granted by the queen of the Dobhar's might could match anything those two weaklings could provide?

But . . . her king had ordered her to study the ways of the Imperials. And she knew not everyone had value was a warrior. The Mother of Waves had rarely seen combat since she'd taken up her role, for example, yet she was afforded respect on par with the king, which no Dobhar would object to. And no Dobhar would ever deny the efforts of their mothers in raising the pups, even the weak mothers who could barely hunt. Even the Dobhar warriors who had grown too old to fight were still respected and valued for the knowledge they possessed.

And her king had been right before. At first, Estrith had not understood why her king insisted on the "drills and formations" he made them practice. How could lining up and dancing about in shapes be more helpful than extra levels? How was that a better use of their time than hunting in the deep, and continuing to grow stronger?

And yet, when the strong Dobhar warriors had been pushed back by the Selkies and some weak Imperial farmers, it had been those very drills, that *wasted* time, that had let them break through.

Clearly, there was something that Estrith was missing. Something beyond levels and skills that made one strong.

Estrith turned to the two Imperials and frowned. They were weak and seemed of little use to Estrith. Yet . . . the queen of the Dobhar, the one who had defeated her king, saw value in them of some sort. So, if Estrith were to fulfill the command of her king and protect the future of the Dobhar, she must attempt to understand what the queen saw.

She resolved to observe the pair as they braved this dungeon.

32

Efficient Upgrading

"There's no such thing as a free level."
—Veteran Exploratore Calvisia Cornix, when refusing to train an Imperial Prince.

"Taog, duck!"

Taog dropped to the ground as another nightwing flew overhead. Ateia took aim at it and shot a glowing Light-infused arrow into the bat monster. It fell to the ground screeching, but still picked itself up. Ateia rolled across the ground and stabbed it with another arrow, then nocked the arrow and shot another bat. Meanwhile, Taog picked himself off the ground just in time to stab at a black-furred panther pouncing at him. Estrith held the line in the front, warding off three more of the panthers with her harpoon.

NSLICE-00P continued to Infuse the group's weapons with a fusion of Holy and Light mana while taking stock of the situation. She formed a Light Barrier to Taog's side as a Dark elemental shot a black bolt from the shadows. The boy was occupied with another panther while Ateia was cleaning up the bats, so NSLICE-00P fired a Light Beam at the monster. She didn't have visual confirmation on it, so she targeted the highest concentration of Dark mana she could detect.

You have slain Dark Elemental (Level 22)!
Gained 3 Personal XP, 3 Dungeon XP!

As her sensors indicated, mana concentration and monster levels were rising as time went on. Ateia and Taog were still doing well, but NSLICE-00P had to directly intervene more and more often. She reviewed their levels . . .

Subordinates				
Name	Species	Level	Mana Upkeep	
(TEMPORARY) Ateia Niraemia	Human	16	--	(Status locked)
(TEMPORARY) Taog Sutharlan	Human/ Wulver	15	--	(Status locked)

They had both gained three levels so far, so they had only recently been getting eclipsed by their opponents. Still, their foes were growing stronger faster than the two were leveling up.

And there was still a great deal of dungeon to go.

They were on the fourth floor at this point. NSLICE-00P's radar only seemed to work on one floor at a time, but by comparing atmospheric mana density to the overall dungeon's mana signature, she predicted they were not close to the end just yet.

But that was fine. NSLICE-00P wanted to upgrade Ateia and Taog as much as possible, but it was not strictly necessary for them to achieve the Dungeon Conqueror feat this time around. If the opponents grew too strong, she would take over and terminate the dungeon on her own.

And Ateia and Taog had grown in more than just levels.

Ateia's next arrow began to glow with Light and Holy mana once more. She let it loose into the last of the bats, same as she had countless times since entering this dungeon. Only this time, unbeknownst to the girl herself, NSLICE-00P hadn't Infused Ateia's shot with any of her mana at all.

Ateia's training with Miallói, particularly the manual shaping of her mana, had paid off. She had observed and felt NSLICE-00P's mana through their bond as the cyborg Infused the group's weapons. She had been subconsciously forming her mana to match the Infusion, allowing NSLICE-00P to devote less and less of her own mana to Ateia as the exploration carried on.

And as it turned out . . . Ateia had a knack for that sort of thing. At this point, she had managed to achieve the effect herself. She fired her last attack with no assistance from NSLICE-00P at all. Ateia blinked as the fight wound down and Taog walked over to her.

"I . . . got a skill."

Taog smiled. "Nice, what is it?"

Ateia fidgeted. "Um . . ."

Taog raised an eyebrow, and Ateia gulped before speaking. ". . . Radiant Shot."

"Yes?"

Ateia trembled lightly.

"Um . . . it's a ranged-attack skill infusing my weapon with Light . . . and . . . Holy."

Taog blinked a few times. "Um . . . did you say *Holy*?"

Ateia slowly nodded. Taog blinked a few more times. Then they both started trembling. Holy mana was *not* something someone just gained through a skill.

They turned to look at NSLICE-00P.

"Query: Do the friendlies have an observation to inform this unit of?"

The two just heaved a sigh. "Well . . . um . . . it's a good thing, right?"

Ateia slowly nodded in response. "I, um, think so?"

Ateia explained what she had done, and so Taog attempted the same thing over the next few fights. He eventually learned the Mana Infusion skill, but did not succeed at granting his mana the Holy attribute. Estrith quietly tried it herself . . . but also did not manage to gain any sort of attributed skills.

As the group reached the sixth floor . . .

Dark bats with multiple sets of wings flooded the air. NSLICE-00P combined Light with the Chain shape and Dense modifier. Glowing chains of yellow light shot from dozens of magic circles, wrapping around the bats and pulling them to the ground. Estrith spun her harpoon in the front, warding off some giant moles ahead. Ateia and Taog attacked the bats on the ground, frowning as they did.

The spell shape Chain is now Level 5!

Once the fight was over, they looked at each other, nodded, and turned to NSLICE-00P.

"Seero, I think you and the Dobhar should take over now."

"Observation: Friendlies Ateia and Taog can still deal effective damage to opponents, and risk of the friendlies being terminated is still at acceptable levels."

Taog shook his head. "It's not just whether we can kill these things. Our parents always told us there's no such thing as a free level. The manner in which we gain those levels matters, so it's dangerous to level too quickly and with too much assistance. At this point, you're basically doing all the work for us."

Ateia nodded. "It was fine when we were actually participating in the fight, but once you're doing this much for us, we're not really growing. Not truly. I didn't even get that much experience for those kills, in fact. And . . . well . . ." Ateia stared off into the distance. "I'm level twenty-two already. I've almost doubled my level in, like, one day . . . So, um, you should probably get some experience yourself, Seero."

NSLICE-00P's robotic eye flickered. She had actually been gaining dungeon experience over their entire trip from the mana absorption, and had leveled up several times since leaving Turannia. She was now Dungeon level ninety-four, in fact. And she had gained a bit of experience from these fights as well, managing to finish a close level up and reach Personal level fifty-seven, so her own upgrades were not as much of a priority as friendly Ateia believed.

However, it *was* true that the efficiency of the friendly upgrade routine was dropping as the monsters grew stronger, for it took Ateia and Taog longer and longer to defeat their foes. And she already knew about the contribution issue with the Dungeon Conqueror feat, so it made sense it would apply more generally if she had to completely incapacitate her foes. She wondered now if that was a problem for her other subordinates. 01R *had* expressed a desire to participate in combat personally, though Rattingtale and Lilussees had never mentioned the issue.

Still, NSLICE-00P determined they had already spent 37.651 hours on this dungeon termination, and still had a way to go as she'd previously calculated. If the friendlies were experiencing diminishing returns, then it would be more efficient to finish the current mission as soon as possible and either resume the primary directive or start a new mission with lower-level monsters.

"Acknowledgement: This unit has calculated that friendlies Ateia and Taog's analysis is correct. Rescinding friendly contribution requirement. Changing current protocols from 'friendly combat support' to 'dungeon termination.'"

NSLICE-00P surrounded Ateia and Taog with spherical barriers of Fused Light and Holy mana, then promptly turned around.

"Um, Seero, where are you going?"

"Explanation: According to this unit's scans, this path does not lead to the floor exit at any point. This unit is returning to the closest intersection that leads to the optimal path."

Ateia jumped. "Wait, we're going the wrong way?!"

"Affirmative."

Ateia gaped at NSLICE-00P. "And you knew the entire time?!"

"Affirmative."

Taog groaned and held his head while Ateia grabbed hers.

"Why didn't you say anything, Seero?!"

"Explanation: Under 'friendly contribution' requirements, this unit defers all possible actions to the friendlies, unless friendlies are at risk of termination."

"That's—" Ateia frowned . . . then furrowed her brow . . . then heaved a sigh.

And so, NSLICE-00P took over the mission. And once she sufficiently backtracked and started down the correct path . . .

276   ICALOS

Half a dozen magic circles floated in the air by NSLICE-00P. Every time she detected a mana signature with a clear line of sight, Holy and Light Beams would fire down the dungeon halls.

You have slain Felix Obscurum (Level 31)!
Gained 3 Personal XP, 3 Dungeon XP!

Within ten minutes, the team had made it to the end of the sixth floor. And Ateia, Taog, and Estrith did not see a single monster in that time.

On the eight floor, NSLICE-00P came to a large circular room with torches across the walls, their shadows flickering across the center of the room. At first, NSLICE-00P detected no mana signatures or signs of life.

But then, mana began to gather in the walls. It streamed down under the torches and connected with NSLICE-00P's and the others' shadows. It then flowed toward the center of the room, coalescing there. An eerie, rasping voice echoed through the room.

"*The dark lives in all of us.*"

The shadows began to rise and condense, forming into four shapes, one for each person. Ateia and Taog glanced at each other and gulped, while Estrith gripped her spear.

And NSLICE-00P . . .

"Hostile magic detected. Engaging Equalizer."

She fired the Equalizer beam four times, striking each of the figures as they formed. She attempted to apply the data she had gained from her analysis of magic circles, her experiences with her own Spell Penetration–related skills, and the information from the Hardening modifier. And so, she struck the weak points of the gathering mana, causing the forms to fall apart as the magic unraveled.

The skill Anti-Mana Beam is now Level 3!

It appeared her predictions on optimizing the Equalizer were correct. Unlike her other skills, Anti-Mana Beam did not seem to level up with consistent use, nor did the foreign system provide her with any data on how to optimize its use. But the Equalizer and the Anti-Mana Beams it could generate were apparently novel to the foreign system, so it could be the case that it did not possess any data on upgrading either the implant or the skill. It would apparently be up to NSLICE-00P to do so manually.

NSLICE-00P's analysis was split on that situation. On the one hand, upgrades to the Equalizer would have drastically improved her effectiveness. On the other, NSLICE-00P still did not and would not fully trust any foreign program interacting with her systems, so it could be beneficial to retain at least one capability the foreign system couldn't control. And that system being the Equalizer, the trump card of her original loadout, provided a great deal of insurance.

As for the Equalizer's targets . . . the moment the Equalizer connected, there were horrible shrieks, and the shadows fell apart, melting into the ground. The group's shadows returned to normal, and the elevated mana signatures dropped.

You have slain four Shadow Clones (Level 50)!
Gained 24 Personal XP, 12 Dungeon XP!

The Equalizer wouldn't harm mundane flesh and matter, but a being made of mana was a different story, it seemed. A pitch-black chest appeared in the center of the room, which Ateia and Taog just stared at.

"Taog."

"Yes, Ateia?"

"Was that . . . some kind of boss?"

". . . I think so."

"I see."

"Right."

Ateia nodded. "Well, it's Seero, after all."

Taog just nodded back. "Yep."

33

Terminate the Darkest Dungeon!

"Dungeon divers and mental illness go hand in hand. We're just not sure which causes the other."

—Legate Limitanei per Velusitum Julianus Duronius Gaius, after stopping yet another tavern brawl.

NSLICE-00P scanned the chest in the center of the room and confirmed it was just a chest. She opened it up and peered inside.

There was a short sword sitting inside, with a pitch-black blade made of material NSLICE-00P didn't have on file. The blade was full of Dark-attribute mana, though of a different sort than the dread orcas.

NSLICE-00P picked the weapon up and placed it in her inventory, then continued onward.

Dark Blade added to the Inventory!

The next floor was not a labyrinth of twisting halls but a wide-open cavern. It was pitch black, without a single source of light. The Holy Light Barriers around Ateia and Taog lit up the room.

Revealing countless monsters and spells rushing toward the group.

Animals of every sort flew through the air and galloped along the ground. Variations of the nightwings that had harried them every step of the way were flying beside owls and giant beetles; panthers and wolves were rushing toward them, with small rats and insects crawling along the ground. All of which had black feathers, fur, and chitin along with glowing eyes. There were even mighty black bears, far larger than their mundane cousins.

There were elementals in the shadows, twisting masses of Dark mana that absorbed all light they touched. And there were humanoids as well. Goblin assassins crept between the monsters and clung to the walls and roofs, holding daggers in their hands and mouths. Goblin mages in black robes chanted fell spells. And humanoids with blue skin, red eyes, and pointed ears took aim with black crossbows and formed black magic circles.

NSLICE-00P, fortunately, had encountered this situation before, and as her comparisons of floor mana to overall dungeon signature indicated they were nearing the end, had anticipated that this might occur again. So, she already had a protocol for this scenario that she was ready to deploy.

She cast another fused Holy Light Barrier, only in the Wall form. A bright curtain of golden-and-silver light filled the room, separating NSLICE-00P and her allies from the horde. The monsters all took a step back and shielded their eyes, hissing and growling as they did. The Dark-attribute spells in the air burned and faded as they contacted the wall.

The spell shape Barrier is now Level 11!

Unlike a Mana Barrier, a wall of light did not actually block physical projectiles, as it was more similar in nature to a Fire Wall spell, so the physical attacks launched by the monsters still made it through. But NSLICE-00P launched into the air while forming some more mundane Barriers around herself and Estrith. She dodged most of the projectiles and blocked the ones that approached her.

She then formed another Aurora Barrage spell behind her, and the mass termination began.

Most of the monsters stood at the edge of the Wall. They growled and hissed and waved claws and weapons at it but refused to pass through. NSLICE-00P was free to bombard these at leisure. However, the barrage of Dark spells took a toll on her Wall, forcing her to devote some of her mana and attention to keeping it up, cutting down on her own attacks. So, she activated the Heroic Power skill.

The skill Heroic Power is now Level 2!

With double the mana density, her Wall took far less damage when canceling out the Dark spells. She was now free to sweep her beams across the field at maximum power, prioritizing the monsters with magical attacks.

While this went on, a few of the monsters confident in their defenses gritted their teeth and leapt through the wall. They roared in pain, several of them dropping dead on the way in while the survivors were left burned and dazed.

And so, easy prey for Estrith, who was still waiting on the ground. One by one, she stabbed them with her harpoon, then started lobbing it toward the monsters on the other side, dragging them into the glowing light.

Ultimately, none of the monsters, whether on their own merit or taken as a whole, could tear down NSLICE-00P's Wall, nor endure it with enough strength to fight back. And so, it was only a matter of time before the entire room was wiped out.

The strategic spell Aurora Barrage is now Level 6!
The skill Multicasting is now Level 13!
You have slain 53 hostiles!
Gained 265 Personal XP, 169 Dungeon XP!
Level up! You are now at Personal Level 59 and Dungeon Level 96!

Estrith stared at the room in a daze.

On the one hand, she did not have pleasant memories of that rain of beams falling from the sky. In that moment, many of her people had fallen, the survivors' hopes shattered, and her king had been dethroned and humiliated, forced to give up all that he'd fought for and all the wrongs he'd sought to avenge just so that his people might survive.

On the other hand, she had leveled up twice in one sitting, with almost no risk to herself. She would have had to conduct countless hunts in the deep to achieve a single level, braving the great risk of encountering something powerful enough to end her immediately on each and every excursion, praying she would find something weak enough to kill but strong enough to be worth the effort.

She furrowed her brow. It did not sit well with her, gaining levels like this. She did not feel like she had earned them. If the opponent couldn't threaten her, then this could not be called a worthy challenge. She could not report this victory with her head held high.

But . . . she looked up at the queen of the Dobhar as she floated back down to the ground. Estrith gripped her spear once more.

She was here because the Dobhar had lost to this human. And her king had humbled himself, accepting any humiliation to protect their people. So, she could not now cling to her pride and her traditions. She had been sent to learn, to determine *why* her people had failed, what made these humans strong, *this* human so strong. So she would not refuse the opportunity to grow stronger. She would let herself be coddled and fed victories she did not deserve. She would make the most of this situation and return to her king mightier than ever before.

She obediently fell in step as the queen of the Dobhar marched through the room.

* * *

The dungeon master stared as the group wiped out the monsters and made their way straight for the core room. It was more like a shade than any sort of being, a humanoid form made of swirling black fog. It spoke with a raspy whisper, like a shadow creeping on the edge of the mind.

"Okay, so this situation seems kind of bad. This stupid human just wiped out every elite monster I had and broke the shadow clones before they even formed, but it's fine. For I am the Deepest Darkness, the Lord of Shadow, Ruler of the Blackest Night, and no light can contend with me!"

The group made their way through the residential floor, not even pausing to search and loot the elite monsters' domiciles as they came straight toward the core.

"I . . . um . . . will ambush them in the core! At the source of my power, where the shadows grow thickest! After all, the darkest shadow is right under the brightest light!"

NSLICE-00P walked into the core room. The room was, as with many others before it, pitch black. But the darkness was more than just the absence of light in this place—her conventional lights from her cybernetic components could barely pierce a few inches into the shadows.

So, NSLICE-00P formed and Supercharged a Holy Light Blade, holding it high. The blade's light drove back the darkness, illuminating the room. It was empty, save for the core itself. NSLICE-00P formed a magic circle to destroy it . . .

Suddenly, NSLICE-00P's own shadow, formed from the light of her Blade spell, grew darker. A form began to emerge from it, face-first into a magic circle. "I HAVE YOU NOW!" The dungeon master barely had time to blink before a Holy Light Beam struck it in the face.

You have slain Dark Shade (Level 60)!
Gained 14 Personal XP, 3 Dungeon XP!
Level up! You are now at Personal Level 60!

And then NSLICE-00P terminated the dungeon core as well.

You have absorbed a dungeon core (Darkest Dungeon)!
Gained 10 Personal Perk Points, 10 Dungeon Perk Points!
Gained Dungeon Affinity: Dark (Minimum)!

You have accomplished the Personal Feat: Dungeon Conqueror (Darkest Dungeon)!
You have learned the skill Dark Magic!

* * *

The village elder made his way to the dungeon; one of the townsfolk sat in a chair nearby. The elder frowned.

"Anything?"

The townsman shook his head. The village elder sighed. When he'd submitted the report to the Exploratores, he had not expected them to send children, of all things, whether they were dressed like a knight or not. But it had been almost two days, so he might need to assume the worst.

And make another trip to the tavern.

At that moment, the ground began to shake. The dungeon's entrance began to shrink, and once it had vanished, there was an explosion and a shock wave, knocking the two men over.

And when they looked up . . . the dungeon was gone. Standing in its place were the young Exploratores and their companions. Alive, and completely unharmed. The village elder's eyes widened.

"Exploratore Niraemia? Exploratore Sutharlan? W-What just happened?"

The two Exploratores glanced at each other and shrugged. They turned to their knight companion.

"Seero, tell him what happened."

"Answer: This unit terminated the dungeon."

Game of Throne-Crowns: The Movements in the Shadows

While NSLICE-00P was terminating the Darkest Dungeon, her subordinates were hard at work scouting Aquilo Perfugium. A cyber-rat was currently huddled up in the corner of an alleyway, squeaking to himself and picking at the metal armor across his body. Every now and again, he'd peek out at the people walking through the streets, just to store some faces in his logs for later review before returning to . . . whatever it was he was doing.

Meanwhile, entirely unbeknownst to the rat, a cyber-spider rested on the wall of the alleyway, waiting in the web she had spun. Like the others, she had metal coating her legs, body, and the left half of her head, including four of her eyes. Her largest robotic eye rotated slightly to adjust its zoom, while the others scanned the area independently.

02S was on snack duty again. But she didn't mind. The others, 01S and 03S, hated snack duty. The snack duty spider was glued to the subject, and so unable to move as they pleased. Yet, they also couldn't be seen, which restricted the actions they could take as well, which meant they couldn't proactively tackle the mission the boss had assigned to them, and they couldn't go off hunting on their own, either. And worst . . . they were technically watching over one of their own, on the off chance he actually found a way to inconvenience the boss, so they weren't even accomplishing anything for their efforts.

But 02S didn't see it that way.

The snack might not be the strongest, or the most loyal, or the brightest, or the bravest, or the most helpful, or . . . but he was still claimed by the boss. 02S had watched the boss as she raced back to save 01R, long before she had granted him a name. She'd watched as the boss worked to save some small Dobhar pup who couldn't even fight yet. She herself had been granted a name, despite never achieving anything significant for the dungeon. She knew that the boss valued all her subordinates, no matter how useful or useless they might seem. The boss would not permit a single one of them to escape her grasp, not even through death.

So, watching over the snack was an important duty. She felt the boss would be displeased if he perished alone.

Besides, the alternative was to bring kills to Lilussees. Their big sister was intelligent and helped the boss a great deal . . . but 02S didn't really understand her. After all, 02S liked to make her own kills from start to finish. There was nothing quite as satisfying as wrapping up a target in her own webs and then sinking her fangs into their helpless bodies as they squirmed, watching the hope fade from their eyes as she approached. She didn't want to let someone else handle any part of that process for her, not if she had a choice. And . . .

"No-no, you stupid-dumb armor-thing! I order-command you to give me access to the strange man-thing's secrets, yes-yes! The Great-High King of all the land has no time-patience for your 'critical software error' nonsense!"

02S giggled to herself. The snack was hilarious.

It was *adorable* how he somehow believed that even a single one of them hadn't already identified his intentions. Even 00B somehow understood Mr. Excellion Formantus Rattingtale the Third was not to be trusted. The boss clearly pretended as if she didn't realize his traitorous intentions, so the rest of them played along as well. None of them particularly understood *why*, but the boss knew best.

02S enjoyed watching him skulk in the shadows. How he plotted and planned, no doubt coming up with some harebrained scheme doomed to failure. How he marched forward, completely confident in his half-hearted plans. And then his face of abject despair as he realized the result that had been obvious to 02S from the start.

Simply sublime.

Just then, one of her smaller robotic eyes turned red, and 02S turned her gaze to the sky. A bird of prey was circling overhead. 02S focused in on it, activating her sensors.

Celeri Falco (Level 12)

02S ran a mana scan and confirmed it was likely a monster. She didn't fully understand all these cybernetic components the boss had evolved them with, but as monsters summoned by the Cyber Dungeon, she and the others had a more instinctive ability to understand her master, and were not as opposed to letting the boss's components take charge. So, they had some ability to run some basic tasks, such as sensor scans, by applying the protocols the boss had shared with them.

She thus identified this was not an idle threat. The celeri falco locked its eyes on Rattingtale below, let out a cry, and started to dive from the sky.

Rattingtale, having somehow managed to disable his components' sensors and currently wrestling with the UI, was completely unaware of the threat.

But that was fine. 02S applied another protocol shared by the boss as she extended her sticky threads across the alleyway.

The spell Invisibility is now Level 6!

02S didn't understand the magic. The sacred records had granted her information on it when she'd learned the Light Magic skill and the spell, but she couldn't really make heads or tails of it. But that was fine. All she needed to know was, if she ran the protocol from the boss, her cybernetic components would form the magic circle precisely as the boss did and that spell would activate.

And so, 02S—and the threads still attached to her—vanished from view.

The celeri falco dove into the alleyway at lightning speeds, gusts of wind blowing about as it soared past. And crashed straight into a sticky web it couldn't see.

The celeri falco immediately began spinning about. 02S's thread snapped, but she'd let go of it the moment the monster had struck it. The threads wrapped around the bird, tangling it up as it crashed into the ground.

Right in front of the snack. He jumped, letting out a high-pitched squeal and flailing his arms about. As he did, 02S subtly made contact with him, applying the Claw Strike protocol the boss had shared from 01R and 00B's records. Rattingtale's hand moved on its own, unbeknownst to him in his panic, and struck the wounded monster on the head.

You have slain Celeri Falco (Level 12)!
Gained 19 XP!

"Um . . . What-what . . . um . . . What just happened-occurred?"

Rattingtale stopped flailing as the monster didn't move. He looked at it, now dead. He looked at his metal claws, now covered in blood.

He looked back at the monster. Then back at his claws. Suddenly, he stood up on his back legs, crossing his arms and nodding his head. And only trembling slightly.

"O-Obviously! The Great-High King of all the land is also the mightiest-strongest in all the land; that is simply natural, yes-yes. So, it is obvious I would kill-slay any foul bird-things who dared assault me, yes-yes! That is what happened-occurred, yes-yes! Even I couldn't see-track my speed, yes-yes!"

02S giggled to herself. Yes, he was adorably hopeless.

And even better, she couldn't wait to see 01R's face of anguish when the snack stayed ahead of him in level, yet *again*. Oh, she was getting most of the experience for these, and it wasn't like Rattingtale was specifically hunting for fights like 01R, so she couldn't keep it up forever. She would just have to make the most of it while she still could.

Fortunately, the cybernetic components were automatically recording anything they saw, so she'd be able to preserve his face long after he surpassed the snack. And also Rattingtale's hopelessly smug look, believing this was somehow his doing.

Lilussees was right. Rattingtale was a tasty snack indeed.

She let the Invisibility spell fade. She didn't have the boss's mana, and it would cut down on her Sneak leveling as well. She then turned her attention back to Rattingtale, wondering what sort of plot he would scheme up next.

And if it would be more fun to assist it or foil it outright.

34

Can You Handle the Truth?

"Changing your name and going undercover is a fairy tale. You do know that status checks exist, right? Sorry to break it to you, but Exploratore work is a lot more boring."
—Exploratore Quirinia Hilaris, before changing her name and going undercover.

After briefly speaking with the village elder, the group made their way back. NSLICE-00P had wanted to record the route on the way here, and so had traveled via conventional methods, but now that they were returning, she could try something new.

She activated Transfer, intending to move herself and the group to the maximum range of her dungeon field, but something went wrong, and the skill failed to activate.

You cannot use Transfer on the Dungeon Core.

Her robotic eye flickered as she analyzed the statement and the skill itself. It was one of the most complicated applications of mana she had encountered, and one that activated without a magic circle, so she couldn't claim to understand it. But what she did identify as a possible issue was that a large mana signature flowed from the target through her core and then to the destination as the transfer took place. It was possible, therefore, that her core played an important role in the process . . . such that it could not replicate the effect on itself without something else to replace its role. And she did not yet understand the workings of mana to the extent that she could modify the skill.

So, she filed Transfer away as a tactical redeployment option for her subordinates and simply followed her friendlies as they walked down the road.

*   *   *

The group eventually arrived back at Aquilo Perfugium and made their way to the Exploratores HQ. The receptionist tilted her head when they walked through the door.

"Back so soon? Did something happen along the way?"

Ateia and Taog exchanged glances. From the stories her dad had told them, even the shortest dungeon explorations took weeks. Any substantial dungeon could take months, or even years. And here they were, back after a few days. Taog heaved a sigh. Ateia shrugged and turned back to the receptionist. "No, we made it there fine. And . . . we're here to report that . . . the dungeon was destroyed."

The receptionist blinked a few times.

"Excuse me, what was that?"

"The dungeon was destroyed."

The receptionist raised an eyebrow. "I'm sorry, did you say the dungeon was destroyed?"

Ateia nodded. "Yes."

The receptionist, a consummate professional used to dealing with brash Exploratores, managed to hold in her sigh. She also managed to hold in the lecture on all the reasons a tiny party of young Exploratores like this couldn't have possibly destroyed a dungeon they'd visited for the first time in the few days that had passed. So, she simply put on her business smile.

"I see. Do you have any evidence to support that?"

Ateia reached into her pocket and pulled out a scroll, handing it over. The receptionist opened it up. At first, she raised an eyebrow, then her eyes widened, then she frowned. She was holding a request completion form, given to the village elder when he'd asked the Exploratores to come check out the dungeon. It stated the dungeon had, in fact, been destroyed, confirmed with the village elder's seal. She turned and went to a back office, where they stored the original requests, and took out the elder's, bringing it close to the completion form before channeling a bit of mana through them. Both forms flashed green, indicating a match in the mana signature on the enchanted paper.

She stood there for a few minutes, blinking, then walked back to the counter in a daze.

"I see . . . Um, since a dungeon was involved, I'll have to send someone to verify it's truly gone. Once that's done, I'll log this as complete. Is that fine?"

Ateia just gave a wry smile. "Yes, that's fine."

The receptionist shook her head to clear her thoughts, then smiled. "Well, in any case, I've received a recording crystal. If you show me that illusion again, we can file a missing persons mission across the Exploratores. Would you like to do so now?"

NSLICE-00P stepped forward. "Affirmative."

The receptionist nodded. "Give me one moment to retrieve it, then."

She went to a back office again and came out with a metal box surrounding a magic core. She activated the device, and the core started to glow.

"Well then, could you please show me that illusion again?"

"Affirmative."

NSLICE-00P's robotic eye glowed and displayed the holographic screen of the persons of interest once more, along with their names translated into the local script as best as NSLICE-00P was able. The receptionist brought the device up to the illusion.

Nothing happened. The receptionist frowned.

"This is strange. Is this . . . not Illusion Magic? The device isn't reacting to the mana . . ."

Ateia and Taog jumped and stared at NSLICE-00P. Even Estrith's eyes widened, and her head tilted slightly.

"Not Illusion Magic? Um . . . Taog, what does that mean?"

"You think I know? You know more about magic than I do, Ateia."

Meanwhile, NSLICE-00P was calculating.

"Negative. Query: Is a mana-based image format required for storage and transmission?"

The receptionist tilted her head . . . but, well, NSLICE-00P's method of speaking was still more coherent than many a drunk Exploratore's might be.

"Um . . . if I understand this correctly, then yes. The recording crystal is tuned for Illusion Magic specifically, so we may need to order something custom if you're using something else."

"Acknowledged. Statement: This unit will attempt to convert image format."

NSLICE-00P filled her holographic projector with mana, like she had once done with her flamethrowers. She utilized Light mana, assuming it would function well with the display.

You have learned the skill Illusion Magic!
You have learned the spell Project Image!

She took the new mana and formed it around the holographic display, creating a second image overlaid right on top of the first, before letting the original image fade.

"Query: Is this image compatible?"

The receptionist blinked a few times but raised the device once more. It flashed once, and then began displaying the same image in the air above it. "Yes, it . . . seems so. Uh, thank you. We will submit a request on your behalf, Miss NSLICE-00P."

"Acknowledged. Expressing Gratitude: This unit thanks you for your assistance."

"Um, you're welcome? In any case, we didn't find any information on those names, but . . ." The receptionist frowned. "I have something to report on the Exploratore Aulus Caedicius Niraemius."

Ateia couldn't stop herself from stepping forward. Her heart pounded. "Yes? W-What is it?"

The receptionist furrowed her brow and took a deep breath.

"That Exploratore . . . doesn't exist."

Ateia froze.

". . . What?"

"I've looked through our records and couldn't find a single mention of an Exploratore by that name; not even in the official rosters. Admittedly, it's not like we have all the records out in a branch like this, but it's very odd he's not on the roster, unless he was a brand-new addition?"

Ateia shook her head and gritted her teeth. The receptionist took another breath.

"Well, it could be an alias? Exploratores must go undercover at times, so the name you were given might not be what we have on record. You may want to check with a larger branch, though; if they *are* undercover, it's likely classified, but the Magister Exploratore might be able to help for an Amicitia Populi Elteni."

Ateia just stood staring at the air. She started to sway before Taog grabbed her shoulder and turned to the receptionist. "Thank you. If that's all, we'd like to rest from the trip."

The receptionist smiled and nodded.

"Of course. That's all I had to report, in any case."

With that, the group made their way back to their rooms, Ateia completely silent.

Taog glanced at NSLICE-00P. "You go on ahead, I'll take care of Ateia for now."

"Affirmative."

He took Ateia to his room as NSLICE-00P and Estrith made their way to their own, sitting her down on a chair and getting her a glass of water.

"Ateia . . . you alright?"

Ateia slowly blinked.

"My dad . . . doesn't exist? That's not his real name? What . . . what does that mean?"

Taog frowned and crossed his arms.

"I mean, from what Magister Tiberius said, it's clear there's more going on than we realized. Your dad was someone people would recognize . . . and might have grudges against, apparently. And it seems he was trying to hide you? So it would make sense if he changed his name when you moved to Turannia."

Ateia frowned, clenching her hands into fists.

"But then, why wouldn't he tell me? Why wouldn't he let me know? What if I came looking for him? How would I find him if I didn't even know his real name?"

Taog rubbed his chin. "From what it sounds like, I don't think he wanted you to come looking for him. I think he was hoping you would stay back home."

Ateia's frown deepened. "But to not even tell me his real name . . ."

Why didn't he want them to find him, was Ateia's next question. A question she couldn't bring herself to ask, not even to herself. Because depending on the answer, the hope she'd clung to all this time might die, whether her father lived or not. Her eyes started to moisten.

Then she felt Taog's hand on her shoulder. She looked up and found Taog looking into her eyes with a frown on his face.

"Hey, I know what you're thinking, and it's *not* like that, okay? I've . . . Well, I've seen *plenty* of people just pretending to care when they don't actually want someone around. Your father was NOT like that. I'm sure he had a good reason to leave, and I'm sure he had a good reason not to tell us who he really was. We're going to find out, okay?" Taog smiled wryly. "After all, if there's anyone who can figure this out, it's Seero."

Ateia stared at him for a second before laughing. "Taog, you're supposed to say *me* there!"

Taog flushed. "That's not what I'm—I-I was just trying to cheer you up! And we both know Seero's the Amicitia Populi Elteni slash dungeon destroyer slash one-woman army here!"

"I mean, you're not wrong, but still!" Ateia just laughed some more at him while Taog groaned. And after she finally quieted down . . . "Thanks, Taog."

He paused for a moment before nodding quietly.

"Anytime."

Ateia nodded and stood up. She clenched her fist again. "That's right . . . we'll find him. Even if we have to travel to the end of the Empire, we'll find him."

She glanced at Taog once more.

"And then . . . our family will be whole again."

35

Like Cats and Dogs

"I've had this boy for five minutes, but if anything happens to him, I will kill everyone here and then myself."
—Exploratore Augustus Menenius Cerularius, after
taming a canus monster he didn't want.

That evening, Ateia and Taog stopped by NSLICE-00P's room.

"Seero, would you mind leaving this town sooner rather than later? Under the circumstances, I think we should move toward a place with a larger Exploratores branch; maybe make our way to Velusitum. Ah, that's the capital city of the Utrad Province. And now that the Exploratores are posting an actual mission on your behalf, you should be able to check its status from the closest branch office wherever we go."

"Acknowledged. Analyzing . . ."

NSLICE-00P connected to her subordinates and ran a facial recognition scan across their logs from the day. She detected no matches. Well, it wasn't like her subordinates had viewed every face in the city in the few days she had been gone, but they had gotten a decent chunk. And now that she had passed the names and faces of the persons of interest to the Exploratores, she could expect local authorities to continue the search in this area. As such, moving to a location with a larger Exploratores HQ that had more available resources could be beneficial.

"Analysis complete. This unit finds that suggested course of action acceptable."

Ateia nodded. "Thanks, Seero. Let's head out tomorrow, then?"

"Affirmative."

NSLICE-00P sent out a message to all her subordinates, requesting they converge on her location or else move toward one another.

The next morning, she managed to walk around while Ateia and Taog were restocking their supplies and Transferred the monsters back to the hangar, absorbing some mana along the way.

Level up! You are now at Dungeon Level 97!

As the group set out from the city, NSLICE-00P conducted an analysis. Aquilo Perfugium had been more densely populated than even Castra Turannia had been, and from conversational context, she'd determined Aquilo Perfugium was not necessarily a large city by Imperial standards. As such, her current subordinates were insufficient to cover the updated expected search areas in a timely manner.

However, additional subordinates would require additional room. The spiders and rats, being very small creatures who could share space, had been doubling and tripling up, but even so, the available rooms were all occupied at this point.

Well, at five points—eight if including the new implant slot cost—Monster Hangars weren't the most expensive thing in the world, but NSLICE-00P's Dungeon perk points weren't particularly high at the moment, so she took a second to evaluate alternatives.

Available Upgrades for Monster Hangar:		
Name	**Cost**	**Description**
Monster Hangar (Small) +1	**1 Perk Point**	**Adds five additional living spaces. Increases mana upkeep by 1.**

One point was not a problem, and one additional mana upkeep wasn't either, so NSLICE-00P went ahead and purchased the upgrade. Inside the Monster Hangar, five new doors formed on one of the two sidewalls.

First things first, she filled out the current rooms by summoning more cyber-rats and cyber-spiders. Whereas basic rats and spiders had different mana upkeeps, the cyber versions were the same at one mana a piece, so she summoned five rats and seven spiders to bring the total counts of each up to ten.

She then considered some new options.

Subordinates → Summon Subordinates			
[Holy - Minor]			
Name	Summoning Cost	Upkeep	Description
Sacred Otterkin	500 mana	25 mana	An otter monster with more humanoid features, patterned off of the Dobhar. Intelligent, resilient, and naturally wields Holy mana. It's also a very serious headache, you know?
Sace Luter	100 mana	10 mana	An otter monster transformed by Holy mana, granting it a significant edge against other aquatic monsters. Because, you know . . . monsters aren't supposed to have Holy mana . . .
[Water - Minor]			
Name	Summoning Cost	Upkeep	Description
Mare Luter	25 mana	5 mana	A fully aquatic otter monster. Its thick fur and natural agility make it surprisingly resilient . . . and ferocious.
[Beast - Minor]			
Name	Summoning Cost	Upkeep	Description
Canus Minor	15 mana	3 mana	A basic canine monster. Not the most imposing, but natural teamwork allows it to threaten more powerful opponents when in numbers. Strong sense of smell to track down prey.

Canus Aqua Minor	20 mana	4 mana	A canine monster adapted to the Water attribute. Will not lose your scent when crossing a river. Extra slobbery affection.
Canus Ignis Minor	20 mana	4 mana	A canine monster adapted to the Fire attribute. Breathes fire. Can burn you via licking.
Felix Minor	15 mana	3 mana	A basic feline monster. A natural-born predator who kills for fun. So, you know, a cat. The main difference from its mundane counterpart is the mana core.
Felix Aqua Minor	15 mana	3 mana	A feline monster adapted to the Water attribute so that it can ambush you from underwater. Just what it needed.
Felix Ignis Minor	15 mana	3 mana	A feline monster adapted to the Fire attribute so that its scratches also burn.

She considered only mammalian options for now, as her ultimate goal was to integrate her monsters into the NSLICE network, and the situation with Lilussees has demonstrated issues with other species. Next, she ruled out otter monsters. While the otters could provide aquatic search and combat options that her current monsters lacked, Estrith and the other Dobhar already had that area covered. The Sacred Otterkin's promise of superior performance was noteworthy, but its high cost meant she needed to identify a specific use case for it; otherwise, a cheaper option would be more efficient. At the moment, she was not conducting significant amounts of aquatic combat, so the extra performance was deemed unnecessary.

On the other hand, the Beast attribute provided some interesting options. Dogs were excellent search assets, though perhaps not in this case, as she had no data on her search targets' scents. But even so, their innate pack hunting would make them a prime candidate for NSLICE integration. Cats, on the other hand, were highly efficient predators, and well suited to independent operations. And equally importantly—both cats and dogs were domesticated species well-accepted by human societies. From what NSLICE-00P had seen, that was the same in the Empire as it was for any nation of Earth.

She conducted the analysis of her current NSLICE network and made her choice.

Several magic circles lit up the Monster Hangar . . .

Three dogs and a cat appeared. They were all roughly the same size, the dogs appearing like Jack Russell terriers, only with sharper ears and larger fangs. One of the dogs had white fur with brown spots; another had black fur with red spots, and the last dark-blue fur with light-blue spots. The cat . . . looked like any other cat, except for the gleam in its eyes, which occasionally appeared to glow.

NSLICE-00P had summoned one of each type of canus minor. She calculated the dog monsters' strong senses of smell would round out a sensor type for the NSLICE network should it ever be needed. Likewise, having a pack of dog monsters would provide for a mobile response team in the field. Finally, she wanted to conduct a test to see if the monsters summoned with innate attributes could still integrate into the NSLICE network upon evolution. She'd utilize the dog monsters for this purpose, as they needed numbers to make use of pack-hunting tactics in any case.

The cat, on the other hand, was to be an independently roaming scout and combat asset within human settlements. Cats would not provoke any sort of suspicion or response from the locals, which was also why she'd summoned a basic, nonattributed variant who would appear as mundane as possible, at least until it was integrated with the NSLICE network. A cat was innately more powerful than the rats, and did not require time to set up stationary traps like the spiders, so it would provide an emergency combat asset to the covert team.

All of this reduced her maximum mana, of course, currently by twenty-seven when taken all together. So, she spent another five points to add a new Mana Capacitor +2, bringing her total back up by an additional thirty-five, including the effect from the new implant slot. Her Dungeon Mana was now sitting at three-hundred twenty-five total, of which two hundred and fifty-eight was available for use, leading to a Personal Mana total of two-hundred seventy-one.

With that, she decided to hold off on summoning more monsters. Eleven rats, eleven spiders, and some dogs and cats wouldn't be enough to cover an entire city, but she did need some time to integrate the new units into the network and upgrade them to match the performance of their predecessors.

The new monsters were all glancing around when NSLICE-00P's voice rang out in the hangar.

"Unit Designation: 00F. Unit Designation: 00C. Unit Designation 01C . . ."

In the Utrad capital city of Velusitum, a man stood on the walls of the local Legion keep. He watched in the courtyard below as countless legionnaires conducted drills and training. He was a large, bearded man himself, with scars across his face speaking to a life in the field. He wore the lorica segmentata of the Legion, only adorned with a red cape and some gold and silver highlights.

This was Mettius Burrienus Caelinus, the Magister Militum per Utrad.

A Legion clerk walked up to him and saluted.

"At ease. What word from Corvanus?"

"Sir, the full report from Turannia has arrived! Apparently, a wandering mercenary defeated King Uscfrea, took control of the Dobhar, and was declared an Amicitia Populi Elteni! Rector Provinciae Aemilia then granted them land, where the Dobhar have settled peacefully."

Magister Caelinus shook his head.

"What is she thinking? No one will accept a story that outlandish. And even if it is true, it's still a desperate play. But I suppose she had little choice. It's impressive Turannia's still around at all; a shame no one in Corvanus will choose to see it that way. So, Turannia is still Imperial, and both the Dobhar and the Selkies are independent now, huh . . . That could complicate things, depending on how much or how little control the rector still has. Is there anything else?"

"Sir, the Exploratores HQ in Aquilo Perfugium reported an Amicitia Populi Elteni arrived recently. Magister Vibius suspects this is the wandering mercenary from Turannia, under the circumstances."

Magister Caelinus rubbed his beard and hummed.

"I suppose we'll have to take her measure, then, find out just how much Rector Aemilia stretched the truth. Go call Magister Vibius; I'll speak to him about it. After that, inform the troops to prepare for the march. We have an incursion to handle; it's about time we headed to the front."

The legionnaire saluted and left. Magister Caelinus turned back to observing the training soldiers below, rubbing his beard all the while.

36

OOP Phone Home

"The communication artifact is a distinctly Elteni advantage. The rival Empire of the Sun, for example, had no need to develop such a tool. With every Sun Elf spellblade having the magical prowess they do, teaching their warriors short-range communication spells was straightforward. Communications beyond the immediate battlefield were deemed unnecessary, for the Empire of the Sun was organized into separate realms ruled by Archons and High Archons as their own practically independent domains. What need would they have for timely messages from the other side of their empire? The plight of another Archon far away would be seen as a cause for celebration, not a call to action.

As such, no Archon in the Empire of the Sun would ever spend valuable enchanting resources to expand the range of their communication. On the other hand, the Elteni Empire, with its relative scarcity of mages, wide range of authority, and need to retain numerical superiority on the battlefield, considered it a major priority. And so, the Empire of the Sun would be greatly surprised when the Elteni brought in legions from half a continent away in response to tactical defeats."

—*The History of the Empire,* by Hostus Tettidius Clodian.

Taog finished setting up the tents as Ateia set up the camp ward, and the Dobhar . . . dug some sort of ditch in the ground. Ateia had asked the Dobhar if she wanted to share one of their tents, but she'd just hissed at Ateia.

Call him crazy, but Taog got the feeling the Dobhar didn't like them.

Well, that was fine with him. Ateia couldn't call him out for being suspicious of someone who acted openly hostile toward them, so he didn't feel at all bad for keeping an eye on her. Not that he could do anything if she was a threat, though. From what he had seen in the dungeon, she could give Miallói a decent fight. He and Ateia were no match for her, by far.

But, well, it was refreshing, in a way, despite the danger. There was no mystery to the Dobhar's presence here, and no mystery to her behavior. Now that NSLICE-00P was the queen of the Dobhar, they could not let her go unattended, so some kind of bodyguard was a given. Likewise, the Dobhar rarely had contact with any other races, and almost all of the contact they did have was violent, so it was only natural this Dobhar wouldn't be particularly friendly.

Taog frowned as he glanced at Ateia. After all, they had mysteries aplenty, these days. Ateia's father lying to them about his name . . . made sense, actually. If he was trying to hide Ateia from his enemies, then it only made sense he would have changed his name and avoided logging his new one in the publicly available Exploratores roster. He would have been an idiot to move Ateia far away while leaving her last name the same, after all. Ateia was hurt by the fact that he hadn't told her any of this, but from Taog's point of view, he could understand. Ateia was someone who ran toward danger, not away, and was curious about the unknown to boot. She would have wanted to get involved if she had known, which would have defeated the purpose.

Still, that left the pair with an unknown number of mysterious enemies they couldn't identify and knew nothing about. It would be hard to protect Ateia from them if he didn't know who to look out for.

And then there was another issue.

Ateia had used Holy mana.

Yes, she had learned it from NSLICE-00P, who was *apparently* a hero and would thus have access to such things. But Holy mana wasn't just something someone could pick up with study and practice. For the most part, Holy mana had to be gifted by the Aesdes, though a handful of people and species had an innate ability for it. The Sacred Dragons, for one. Rumor had it the Celestial Elves had access to it, as well. The Imperial family seemed to produce an abnormally high number of Holy users as well, though that could be because they had more opportunities to earn boons from the Aesdes in the first place. Likewise, some of the children of heroes were known to have a knack for it, though given the low number of heroes on record and the fantastical stories about their lives, no one knew if any of that was true.

But Ateia had not done anything the Aesdes might acknowledge. And while she was by no means irreverent, she was not a zealous devotee either, and had not committed herself to their service. So how was she able to use Holy mana?

The most likely explanation was that it had something to do with her parents. So . . . just who were they?

Taog shook his head. He had no answers. Didn't even have guesses. He was closer to figuring out NSLICE-00P's identity than Ateia's.

Or, well, he had been. He had been ninety percent certain she was some kind of demon or demon lord, a conclusion he had been desperately trying to avoid thinking about. And then she had gone and become a Holy-slinging Hero approved by the Aesdes themselves, so that idea was right out. Holy was often granted to heroes specifically to *defeat* exceptionally dangerous demon lords and their dungeon armies, so the Aesdes would never grant said power *to* a demon lord, as far as Taog knew. He didn't think she was a Celestial Elf either, given her mostly human appearance . . . though to be fair, most people in the Empire, himself included, had never actually seen one of those.

A dragon in humanoid form, maybe . . . Figuratively, yes, but literally, he had no idea. She seemed somewhat . . . reasonable for a dragon, from the tales he'd heard. They were supposed to be highly temperamental, and prone to fits of extreme violence.

Well, there was that time she'd wiped out a Wulver warpack for attacking her . . .

And what she'd done to the Dobhar for a mercenary contract . . .

And the times she'd annihilated bandits and criminals who'd tried to rob her . . .

And that moment she was going to destroy Lar and his goons just for beating him . . .

And the complete destruction of every dungeon she visited . . .

Taog froze. He shook his head and decided not to think about it. Because ultimately, at the end of the day, he was no longer concerned about NSLICE-00P's identity or her intentions. She had come back and fought a war on their side. More than that, she had made it a point to protect him and Ateia, even when she'd apparently had a relationship with Magister Tiberius and was going to be proclaimed an Amicitia Populi Elteni for her deeds. Either of those things made her Contract with Ateia and Taog largely redundant. And yet, she was still protecting them, and still traveling with them.

As far as Taog was concerned, NSLICE-00P had proven herself as a trustworthy ally and friend. And in any case, he had other business to attend to other than pondering her background.

So, he walked over to NSLICE-00P. "Hi, Seero, I have a question for you."

"Greeting: Hello, friendly Taog. Acknowledgement: What is the query?"

"Do you have some way to contact Turannia? Maybe the Dobhar or something?"

"Affirmative."

Taog nodded at that. "In that case, could you do us a favor? I'd like to get in contact with Magister Tiberius, if at all possible."

"Affirmative. Please state the intended message."

"You see . . ." Taog glanced at the Dobhar, who was apparently trying to curl up in the dirt? He shrugged and leaned in toward NSLICE-00P, whispering into her ear, "It's about Ateia's father . . ."

It *was* a risk, asking NSLICE-00P to do this, but Taog now trusted her, and, well, if they couldn't trust her with this, they were probably screwed either way. The Dobhar . . . not so much. However, given their general isolation, it was highly unlikely they'd have anything to do with the enemies Magister Tiberius had warned them of, so it should be safe to send a message through them.

And so, NSLICE-00P put her long-range communication system through its first test . . .

Uscfrea rushed through the sea, a harpoon in one hand and an axe in the other. A dread orca rushed straight toward him, its mouth opened wide, letting out a Dread Song once again, but Uscfrea just grinned at the monster. At the last moment, he shot up and breached the surface, launching himself into the sky as the orca swam past. He pulled his arm back.

His new eye flashed and locked on to the orca, showing him exactly where he should throw his spear. He grunted. To be honest, he didn't appreciate that. It felt as if he was being coddled, as if this armor was taking the challenge out of the fight.

But he still threw his spear where the circle of light in his vision indicated. He was not so proud as to forgo an advantage. He had not risen to the heights he had and achieved all that he had by cherishing his own ego.

The orca cried as the harpoon struck it dead-on. Uscfrea then pulled on the mana chain with all his might, yanking the orca right out of the sea and sending it hurtling toward him. He let go and gripped the axe with both arms, swinging it down.

He cleaved the dread orca in two.

You have slain Dread Orca (Level 67)!
Your core has gained 212 XP! 159 XP retained for subordinate core.
Level up! Your dungeon has leveled twice and is now Level 7!

He nodded at the notification and turned to swim back toward the shore.

He returned to his dungeon and opened the sacred records once again. Or infernal records? The standard belief among most peoples in Aelea was that the dungeons came from the Realms of Mana and were more demonic in nature, as the more hostile inhabitants of those Realms were usually called. On the other hand . . . the records from the dungeon appeared no different from the records from the Aesdes. The experience, the boons—it all seemed the same to Uscfrea. And, well, his queen could also wield Holy mana, so it could be that she was just different from the other dungeons.

No, she was *definitely* different from other dungeons, that much was obvious. He just wasn't sure how far those differences extended. But in the end, those details didn't matter at present. So, Uscfrea shrugged and selected the options he wanted.

"*Command: Please relay this communication to Magister Exploratore per Turannia Tiberius.*"

Uscfrea blinked. His queen had contacted him . . . and apparently, sent a message directly to his head. He shrugged. She *did* state she'd created the second dungeon for the purpose of communication, after all. And he had full access to the message, so he could tell it was just a question about some Imperial's name. He guessed it was related to her quest in some fashion, but in any case, it was not an issue that would impact the Dobhar, so he moved to pass it on.

Magister Tiberius heaved a sigh as he looked over the report. Another felix pluvia on the outskirts of a farm. A new dungeon near Castra Turannia. And the usual bandits and looters that followed any major disaster.

And now, he truly had no hands to deal with it.

NSLICE-00P had left him, and the Selkies were now independent, so Miallói had asked for a leave of absence to help her people adjust. He had a sinking feeling she wasn't coming back; the Council of Hunters would likely not continue lending their First Hunter to the Empire now that they could negotiate on even footing. Miallói *had* promised to send someone to help in her place, but that hadn't been arranged yet.

He was trying his best to recruit some more, but a handful of teenagers and young adults with more enthusiasm than self-preservation instincts could not be trusted with these sorts of issues. And the reported monster rats in Castra Turannia had mysteriously vanished, so he couldn't even give them an easy task to build some experience.

Just then, there was a knock at his door. Tiberius sighed again. Probably more bad news.

"Come in, I guess."

His assistant walked in. "Sir . . . there's a message from the border with the Dobhar."

Tiberius groaned. "Wonderful. Are they causing trouble already?"

But to his surprise, his assistant shook her head. "No, sir, it's . . . Apparently, there's a message for you."

Tiberius blinked. "For me?"

The assistant nodded. "From NSLICE-00P. The Dobhar just passed it on; the border guards are wondering what they should do."

Tiberius blinked again, then shrugged. So NSLICE-00P apparently had a way to contact the Dobhar from wherever she was at. His policy with

NSLICE-00P had always been to accept whatever she did without concerning himself with how. After she'd soloed a corrupted dungeon, then repeatedly cast Strategic Magic to defeat an entire Dobhar invasion by herself, that was about all he could do.

"Got it. Have them send it to me immediately. In fact . . . contact Dux Canus and Rector Aemilia for me. If she can contact the Dobhar, we should discuss setting up communications with Steward Uscfrea ourselves."

As the assistant nodded and left the room, Tiberius glanced at his special cabinet. He debated if this news justified it. He shrugged and opened it.

His other policy regarding NSLICE-00P was "drink freely," after all.

37

Terminate the Ursanus Natura!

"Everyone laughs at the Nature attribute's flowers and trees until an unkillable, regenerating monster covered in toxic spikes starts chasing them."
—Dungeon Diver Galerius Coiedius Docilus.

And so, the group traveled to the next town and made their way to the Exploratores HQ. This one was almost empty as well, with a board full of requests. They spoke with the receptionist, but since all the Exploratores in the province were occupied, no one had any updates regarding NSLICE-00P's request just yet.

It was at that moment that someone approached them. A woman, dressed in a simple tunic and cloak with a bow strung across her back, rose from her seat in the tavern area and walked over. She also had feline ears at the top of her head and sharp, predatory eyes.

"Excuse me, you bunch over there? Are you Exploratores?"

Ateia turned to face the newcomer. Eventually, she nodded. "Yes, can we help you?"

The woman grinned, showing off her larger-than-normal fangs.

"I certainly hope so. My name is Metilia, a local hunter. Been looking for someone to help me with a hunt, but seems the Exploratores are busy with the barbarians, or so they claim. Could you spare some time before you run off to the front?"

Taog crossed his arms. "That depends. What's the request?"

Metilia nodded.

"A monster decided to claim a piece of the forest for its own. Normally, I'd just avoid it, but the problem is this forest is right next to a village I frequent. Won't be long before it wanders into town."

Taog frowned and narrowed his eyes. "And what exactly is the monster?"

Metilia grinned again, narrowing her eyes back at him. "Oh, nothing much for an actual Exploratore, I imagine. Just a little beastie called an ursanus natura."

At the mention of the word *ursanus*, NSLICE-00P's robotic eye turned red, and she stepped forward. "High-priority target identified. Request: Please provide target location."

Metilia blinked at the sudden question while Taog jumped.

"Wait, Seero?! What are you doing?"

"Response: Hostiles designated 'Ursanus' have proven a threat to this unit, and severely increase the danger levels in the operational area. They are therefore designated as high-priority targets that must be terminated before any other operations may proceed."

Metilia slowly smiled and nodded.

"Uh, yes, that's right! Let me show you where the village is, then!"

The receptionist behind them raised an eyebrow but reached under the desk. "Miss Vedrix there does have an official request with us. May I assume you'll be taking it, then?"

Taog glanced at Ateia, frowning as he did. She just shrugged.

"I mean, Seero's not wrong. An ursanus is pretty dangerous; if there's one close to a village, then *someone* should deal with it, right? And seems Seero wants to handle it."

Taog opened his mouth to object, but then closed it. He had a bad feeling about this, but Ateia was right. An ursanus moving close to town . . . Images of monsters assaulting a town and people rushing to stop them briefly flashed through his mind.

He heaved a sigh. No, he couldn't object to this without a specific reason.

"Yes . . . I suppose we're taking the request, then."

Metilia grinned at them. "Excellent. I'll meet you at the west entrance, then."

Metilia led them to a nearby forest, then began stalking through the trees, the group following as silently as they could. Well, Ateia and Taog did. NSLICE-00P avoided extraneous noise but had not activated full stealth protocols, while Estrith . . . cursed as she tripped over a branch. A glowing Mana Barrier caught her just before she hit the ground.

NSLICE-00P moved the Barrier up, letting Estrith regain her footing.

"Query: Does friendly Estrith require assistance with mobility?"

Estrith scowled and shook her head with all her might.

"No, queen of the Dobhar. I would not be fit as your guard if I required such assistance."

That, and Estrith's stomach curdled at the memory of the last time NSLICE-00P had *assisted her mobility*. She accepted her king's strange opinion that the Dobhar should move onto land, despite the fact that the dirt was coarse and rough and irritating and got everywhere, not like the soft and smooth water of the ocean. But she *definitely* drew the line at moving into the sky, where she was surrounded by nothing at all and subject to a swift death should this foul demon lord decide to drop her.

In that moment, she happened to glance at Taog. For once, he viewed her with something other than suspicion and nodded as fast as he could in agreement. Which fouled Estrith's mood even further.

But NSLICE-00P simply accepted her words. In any case, she had locked on to the largest mana signature in the forest, which wasn't moving at the moment. Metilia seemed to be a highly efficient tracker, as she was leading them straight toward it.

Soon, Metilia stopped and held her hand up, motioning for the group to remain quiet. She pointed through the trees as Ateia and Taog stepped forward to get another look. Estrith nearly tripped again, but she caught herself by planting her spear on the ground. She decided she wouldn't bother trying to get a glimpse herself. NSLICE-00P, of course, had identified the target long before Metilia pointed it out.

Far ahead of them, in a small clearing, a huge bear rested on the ground. It had green fur that appeared more like moss, and its characteristic shell was made of bark. Its spikes were replaced with sharp branches, leaves growing off their sides.

Metilia motioned for everyone to take a few steps back. Ateia, Taog, and even Estrith huddled with her as Metilia spoke in a whisper.

"That's it; one ursanus natura. As you might have guessed, a Nature-element ursanus, because you know the one thing those dumb bears need is extra HP and stronger regeneration. Traps and arrows don't bother them; they simply lumber on and regenerate before you hit them again. Do you all have a plan?"

Taog frowned and turned to Estrith. "I don't think we ever got your name."

Estrith scoffed. "Royal Guard will do."

He raised an eyebrow but continued on. "Okay, then. Royal Guard, do you think you could pin it down? Ateia has some fire potions, but the last thing we need is for it to go on a rampage."

Estrith frowned.

"Of course I can. Its shell cannot be harder than that of the steel turtles."

"Then, you and I will need to suppress it while—"

At that moment Ateia shrugged. "Actually, I don't think we'll need to do any of that."

"Ateia?"

Ateia pointed in the direction of the monster.

"Seero's got it covered."

The group turned, and Metilia's eyes widened. NSLICE-00P had stepped out into the clearing, facing the ursanus directly.

Alone.

Metilia cursed and pulled out her bow. "What is she doing?!"

Meanwhile, NSLICE-00P's robotic eye was flickering. She analyzed the monster's mana signature against her records and found it similar to the Nature-attribute mana from the strangling salicum and other such monsters. And so, she could predict with relative confidence what attributes would likely work well against it.

"Engaging ursanus termination protocols."

The ursanus noticed her as she stepped into the clearing. It slowly began to rise to its feet, shaking its body as it did.

It paused. Dozens of red magic circles appeared in the air around NSLICE-00P as she lifted her hand and fired the Equalizer at the ursanus, who growled and concentrated its mana, trying to repair the damage rather than avoid it. As that occurred, the magic circles activated, and dozens of Fusion Fire Beams shot out, coalescing together at a spot slightly in front of the cyborg.

A massive red beam lit the clearing on fire . . . as well as pierced through the ursanus.

The spell modifier Fusion is now Level 16!
The skill Fire Magic is now Level 10!
You have slain Ursanus Natura (Level 75)!
Gained 37 Personal XP, 3 Dungeon XP!

"Status Report: High-priority target terminated. Operational area secure."

Metilia just blinked at the sight in front of her. She rubbed her eyes. She looked again. The ursanus's charred corpse was still lying in the field, burning both inside and out.

Ateia suddenly ran forward. "Seero! Put out the fire! Don't burn the forest down!"

"Acknowledged. Moving to prevent collateral damage."

NSLICE-00P formed dozens of magic circles along the line of the beam. Jets of water doused the burning plants from above, while trenches appeared on either side of the Fire Beam's path, with stone walls rising on the far sides.

The skill Water Magic has leveled twice and is now Level 5!

Metilia's jaw dropped.

"Just . . . what?"

Taog just stared forward with unfocused eyes.

"You get used to it."

After that, the group returned to town. Metilia verified the request as complete, then parted ways, making her way to a certain butcher's shop and knocking on the door in a particular fashion before being allowed inside. She walked to the back of the building without a word and opened a hatch in the floor that led to a cellar. Within the cellar, she found and pressed a specific rock, causing a hidden door to appear. Making her way inside, she sat down at a desk, with a communication artifact sitting next to it.

Grabbing a sheet of mana paper, she started to write with a mana-infused finger.

Subject is a mage of incredible power. Contrary to apparent equipment, was able to kill a level 70+ ursanus natura in a single blow via Fire Magic, with power to spare. Method was either spell combination or an advanced spell of some sort, but multiple disconnected magic circles imply the former.

Subject has been observed Multicasting and Farcasting as well. Clearly still had abundant mana after the feat.

Subject has a strange speaking pattern and an emotionless, metallic accent. Almost certainly a foreigner, is either not fully human or magic is involved. Personality observed as follows . . .

38

Some In-Tents Events

"There's no excuse not to be polite."
— Magister Militum Considia Cassiana, on the flowery
language in her ultimatum to the Dimindium Pendem tribes.

And so, the group continued their journey. They were caught between towns at the moment, so they began to set up camp for the night once more.

Estrith shivered as a cool wind blew through the campsite. The days were growing shorter, and the nights were growing colder. She looked down at the ditch she had dug. It turned out, when her king had ordered them to practice "camping," she had spent most of her time organizing the other warriors and beating down the rebellious ones who would defy her king. So . . . she hadn't actually gotten much practice herself.

She frowned as she imagined yet another night curled up in the dirt. She glanced over. The Imperials . . . didn't seemed bothered by the cold. They'd started a fire with practiced ease before taking out their tents.

Estrith furrowed her brow. And then she remembered her king's orders once more. Was she not here to uncover the secrets of the Empire? Was she not here to study their ways?

She strode over to the half Wulver. Wulver weren't much better than humans, but at least they weren't her king's sworn foe.

He turned to face her, raising an eyebrow. "What is it?"

"You there, Wulver boy. Teach me how to 'make camp.'"

He glanced over at the human girl, then back to Estrith. He narrowed his eyes. "I'm busy. Go ask Ateia if you want."

Estrith scowled at him. "You would defy me, *boy*? You are but a welp, barely fit for the hunt. Know your place."

He crossed his arms and met her gaze, scowling back. "Oh, I do. You have no power here, Dobhar, so I'm not going to take your crap. Try to make me, if *your queen* will allow you to do so."

Estrith gritted her teeth but turned from the boy. "I will not forget this."

She marched over to the human girl. She couldn't help but glare at her.

"You there, *human*. Teach me how to 'make camp.'"

The human ignored her.

"Human, I said teach me how to make camp!"

The girl continued her work. "I heard you the first time."

Estrith clenched her spear. "You dare ignore me?!"

The girl shrugged. "I have a name, you know. *Human* doesn't work; there's more than one human here, you know. So, I don't know who you're talking to when you say that."

Estrith scowled again. "Human girl."

The girl pointed toward the usurper.

"There's more than one human girl as well."

Estrith gritted her teeth again.

"Fine. *Ateia*, teach me how to make camp."

Ateia shrugged. "Generally, people ask nicely when they want a favor."

Estrith closed her eyes, gripping her spear hard. These brats, who would not last a single minute in combat with her, were seriously getting on her nerves. But her king had commanded her to learn. He'd told her she would have to be clever about it. So, her pride battled against her loyalty.

The cold wind that blew through at that moment also affected her judgment.

Estrith opened her eyes. She couldn't help but grit her teeth, spitting out the words from between them, "Please . . . teach me how to make camp . . . *Ateia*."

Ateia smiled at her, causing a vein to bulge on her forehead.

"Sure! I was just about to set up this tent. Why don't you help me? We don't have an extra right now, but you can borrow mine during my shift tonight."

Estrith remained silent, trembling with unspeakable rage. But this was still not as much humiliation as her king had endured. She would dishonor him if she could not do the same. So, she quietly followed Ateia, listening to her words and watching her actions.

Meanwhile, NSLICE-00P was off to the side. She formed a magic circle in front of her, her robotic eye flickering and recording every detail. And then . . . an image of the persons of interest appeared before her.

She was trying to study this Illusion Magic she'd acquired. The structure of this magic circle was different from the others, so she was having trouble determining exactly which portion of it was responsible for the Illusion attribute . . . if such a thing existed.

Eventually, she decided to use the brute-force method. She cut off portions of the magic circle and tried to slot them into the attribute section of a Bolt spell, forming dozens of magic circles at once to attempt different permutations. All of them failed, either fading as the mana drained out of them or sparking and fizzling and then vanishing immediately.

Until . . .

One circle managed to complete. It flashed once, and then vanished with no effect.

The skill Illusion Magic has leveled twice and is now Level 3!
Modular spell casting detected: Illusion aspects are now available!

Available Illusion Aspects:	
Calm	Dampen target's emotions, calming them down. Higher levels may dampen specific emotions selectively.
Charm	Give a target positive feelings toward the user. Higher levels may direct feelings toward a target other than the user or choose a specific positive feeling.
Courage	Improve target's emotional resilience, reducing feelings of fear. Higher levels may inspire targets to better performance, boosting attributes.
Fear	Fill the target with fear. Higher levels may specify object of target's fear.
Fury	Fill the target with rage. Higher levels may direct this rage toward specific targets.
Hunger	Simulate a biological need for food. Higher levels may target other biological or psychological needs.
Sadness	Fill the target with sedative negative emotions, reducing motivation. Higher levels may cause an immediate reduction in attributes.

NSLICE-00P had not expected this, but it appeared Illusion Magic had the ability to impact emotions directly, so firing a targeted spell like Bolt would only work if she specified a target emotion. Of which the foreign system was now giving her a choice.

She decided immediately.

You have learned the Illusion aspect: Calm!

Her efforts had borne unexpected fruit. She tested it immediately, slotting Calm-aspect Illusion mana into an Infusion shape. She then cast it on . . . herself, after disabling her own emotional controls.

The Illusion aspect Calm is now Level 2!

Well . . . she wasn't feeling any powerful emotions at the time, so the test was not conclusive, but she did log a reduction in her heart rate, so it appeared the test was at minimum a partial success. She had acquired a spell that could reinforce her emotional controls.

She had lacked any sort of lead on how to recalibrate them. She'd even stopped separating herself into organic and cybernetic threads to gain data, as from what she could tell, that had been exacerbating the problem. But now, for the first time, she had made progress. She might not be helpless before the whims of her organic components the next time their directives clashed with her primary mission.

Well . . . that would remain to be seen. Her emotional controls were currently active with no problem at the moment, so she wouldn't know for sure until the next moment her organic components tried to resist. And of course, she also didn't know if there would be any consequences to relying on such a spell. The emotional controls were finely tuned to avoid any sort of neurological damage, after all. There was no guarantee this spell would have the same safeguards in place. She would need to gather more data on its effects.

But the point was, for the first time since the problem started, she had made progress.

Her cybernetic components marked the Calm spell as a high-priority capability to upgrade. Her organic components, on the other hand, did not react, though it was unclear whether they didn't, or whether they *couldn't*.

It was at that moment that someone stepped toward her. Taog slowly shuffled over, his brow furrowed.

"Seero . . . I have a favor to ask."

"Response: Please specify details of the request."

He took a deep breath. "Seero, can you train me?"

"Affirmative."

"It's just . . . Ateia learned that Holy Magic ability, and now that you have that Dobhar, I feel like I'm not really keeping up. I know you normally need payment; I don't know how I can pay you, but I'll figure something—" Taog's eyes suddenly went wide. "Wait, did you say yes?!"

"Affirmative."

". . . What?"

"Explanation: Survival of friendlies Ateia and Taog is now a major directive for this unit. Upgrades for the friendlies are predicted as the most efficient way to fulfill this directive."

Taog froze for a moment, his jaw dropping. "Seero . . ."

There was a flash of light, and something appeared in NSLICE-00P's hand as she retrieved an item from her inventory. She held out a short sword with a pitch-black blade. The Dark Blade she had acquired from the latest dungeon termination.

"Query: Friendly Taog primarily uses bladed weapons, correct?"

He stared at it for a moment.

"Seero . . . I . . . I can't just take this from you."

"Statement: This unit has a sufficient close-combat arsenal, and this weapon provides no value in storage."

Taog stared at it for a moment longer before looking up into NSLICE-00P's eyes. Her expression was as unreadable as ever. She . . . was giving him an enchanted weapon from a dungeon? Because she was worried about them, and didn't want them to die? Just like that?

Taog's heart pounded. His mind raced, searching for an angle, a reason why she would do this, of what sort of debt he would owe her if he accepted something like this. He knew for a fact she cared about them and wanted to protect them. But protecting them in a fight with Barriers and handing him an enchanted weapon from a dungeon boss were two entirely separate matters.

He shook his head and put aside his suspicions. They were neither valid nor fair in this case. NSLICE-00P hadn't displayed any secret ulterior motives as of yet. She had always stated exactly what she intended to do—at least if asked and if one could parse her manner of speaking.

He recalled when she'd paid the indemnity out of her own pocket, literally. Apparently, money was no longer an issue for her, and it was absolutely true that she didn't need a weapon like this. And even if she wanted a close-quarters weapon, she had apparently taken an axe from *Uscfrea Spellbreaker* himself, which Taog could not imagine was any weaker than this blade. So . . . perhaps the blade with life-changing value to Taog truly wasn't a big deal to her.

And as far as debts went, he already owed his life to her several times over, so what was a little more?

He took the blade, nodding with a serious expression on his face.

"Thank you, Seero. I'll make good use of it, I promise. And I'll do whatever I can to repay this gift."

"Acknowledged."

And Taog began practicing with the enchanted blade. He also asked Seero to Infuse him with different attributes during the evening rest times, hoping to acquire a skill like Ateia had . . .

The next day, Estrith reluctantly emerged from the tent. The warm, comfortable tent with warm, comfortable blankets. The kind of comfort she hadn't felt since she was a pup, resting on her mother's fur. She found everyone else already up, cooking breakfast and packing up. Ateia noticed her and smiled.

"Hi there, how was your sleep?"

Estrith averted her gaze. She felt warmth of a different sort at Ateia's gaze. The girl had been flabbergasted when Estrith had just curled up on the ground, and then she'd had to show Estrith how to use a bedroll. The girl had been even more flabbergasted when she'd learned Estrith had done this even when they'd stayed at inns, ignoring the beds she had never seen before.

It wasn't *Estrith's* fault the previously fully marine Dobhar never used beds!

But Estrith's pride would not let her lie.

"It was . . . good."

Ateia grinned at her. Estrith felt her vein bulge. She gritted her teeth and spat out her next words.

"Thank . . . you . . . Ateia."

Ateia's grin grew. "Anytime, Miss Royal Guard."

Estrith took a deep breath. This girl was weak, cocky, and didn't understand her place. She was one of the hated Imperials. And she had helped Estrith, even after the Dobhar had showed her nothing but hostility. Estrith spoke in barely a whisper, "My name . . . is Estrith."

"Hm, did you say something? I didn't catch that."

Estrith scowled. And then she turned away, refusing to look at the Imperials for the rest of the morning.

Later in the day, the group arrived at their next stop: Grex Magna, a relatively small town yet a well-known location in Utrad, for it was one of the largest pastures in the province. NSLICE-00P identified herds of sheep, cows, and other livestock in the distance. Well, save for the fact that the sheep had red wool, and the cows were twice the size she expected, and there were other animals she didn't even have on record. But that was not what NSLICE-00P focused on.

She zoomed in on the animals on the edge of the herd. There were dogs. Dogs that looked familiar to her.

"Query: Does the Empire utilize canus-lineage monsters for shepherding?"

Taog nodded. "Yes, I've heard of that."

"Follow-Up: So, the presence of monsters is acceptable within population centers?"

Taog rubbed his chin. "Um, normally, they have to be approved and logged with the Monstrum Censor, but if you do that, then yes?"

NSLICE-00P's robotic eye flickered. A major issue she had observed was the inability to train her monster subordinates while her friendlies were close by, due to the need to keep dungeon information confidential. But, if the Empire had a way to utilize monster subordinates as well, then hypothetically, she could reveal her monster subordinates without revealing dungeon-related intel, and so upgrade the NSLICE combat assets at the same time as the friendlies.

"Additional Follow-Up: Where would be the closest Monstrum Censor location?"

Taog began to tremble. "Seero, w-why are you asking that? Um, well . . . Grex Magna definitely has one, since they also breed monsters, but . . ."

"Request: All friendlies, please wait in this location for a moment."

NSLICE-00P walked into the forest. A moment later, she walked out with the three canus minor–type monsters, a felix minor . . . and a bear. With familiar metal armor.

Taog's trembling grew.

"S-Seero . . . w-what is this? W-Where did they come from?"

"Response: These are this unit's subordinates. Point of origin is currently classified."

Ateia trembled as well as she stared at them. "Seero . . . THEY'RE SO CUTE!" She was about to rush over before remembering these were vicious monsters that needed to be treated with care even if tamed. "Seero, can I hold them?"

"Affirmative. Addendum: NSLICE-00B often requests physical contact."

00B looked at her and cried, stating he did not want contact in general, but it was too late. Ateia picked him up and hugged him tight, squealing as she did. 00B wanted to swat at her, but she was already designated as a friendly both to his cybernetic components and in the dungeon records, so all he could do was look at NSLICE-00P and cry in protest.

Meanwhile Taog was clutching his head.

"She . . . has a bunch of monsters that we've *never* seen before now. They must have been following us the whole time, but how did she hide them? How did she keep them under control? And how . . . how did she tame a bear monster of all things? This . . . I . . ."

Suddenly, Taog stood up straight, lowering his hands. His eyes unfocused and stared off into the distance.

"You know what? It's because she's Seero. As expected. She's Seero, after all."

Taog said not a word as the group set off into town, for a bit of a chaotic entrance and trip to the local Monstrum Censor branch.

39

The Wandering Knight's Deadly Monsters

"No thanks. I choose life."

—Traveling author and former Exploratore
Placus Paesentius Statius, when requested for an ursanus
taming attempt.

Monstrum Censor Proculus Vagionius Augustalis could not help but sigh at the sight ahead of him. Grex Magna's security surrounded the group that had walked into his office with unregistered, highly dangerous monster species in tow. His employees had ceased their work to balk at the armored warrior, the pair of young Exploratores, and the Otterkin that had marched into their workplace . . . and the monsters at their feet.

He stared at the armored warrior's expressionless—and in one case, glowing—eyes.

"Let me get this straight. You want to register these monsters as fully tamed and approved for interaction with the general public?"

"Affirmative."

"They weren't registered at birth?"

"Negative."

He raised an eyebrow. "Do you have a record of taming?"

"Negative."

He resisted the urge to hold his head. "Can you at least tell us where these monsters came from?"

"Negative Response: That information is classified."

He sucked in his breath. "Are you a registered trainer with the Monster Tamers' Guild?"

"Negative."

His eye was twitching at this point. "Do you at least have a letter of recommendation from a registered tamer or government authority?"

"Negative."

But Proculus was a professional and managed to resist sighing. This individual was likely a person of means, judging by the quality of their armor . . . and the fact that they had a *monster bear cub* in their possession. So, despite her complete failure to follow even a single one of the Empire's guidelines for tamed monsters, he chose not to make assumptions on her intelligence until he knew exactly who he was dealing with.

"On whose authority are you requesting this?"

"Answer: This unit's own. This unit is designated as an Amicitia Populi Elteni."

She held out a brooch. Proculus glanced at his main receptionist, who nodded his head. Well, if they hadn't even verified that before escalating to him, he would have been very cross indeed. Proculus took a deep breath.

"Okay, Miss . . ."

"Reminder: This unit is designated NSLICE-00P."

". . . Miss NSLICE-00P. I get that you're a friend of the Empire and all, and technically yes, we're supposed to help you with any *reasonable* request. But what you're asking here isn't as simple as skipping a border inspection or having some town guards clear traffic for you. Monster taming is a *highly* restricted and *highly* dangerous affair. There are steps to this, procedures that *must* be verified. We cannot cut corners, and we cannot allow negligence. If we get it wrong, people *will* die. Entire towns have disappeared because an insufficiently tamed monster was allowed inside.

"And what you have here is not some simple diaboli ovis or a domesticated pegasus. Felix-type monsters are *extremely* dangerous unless you know exactly what you're doing, and even then, most felix trainers lose limbs with frightening regularity. Even a canus monster is a vicious predator if it hasn't been rigorously trained since birth. And don't get me started on the bear. Only those idiots at the circus do that, and they *never* allow them to interact with the public without extraordinarily powerful safeguards in place. So no, I cannot verify these monsters as safe for public interaction unless you can prove without a shadow of a doubt that they are completely and utterly safe to be around."

"Query: What would suffice as proof?"

Proculus heaved another sigh.

"For the canus types? Birth certificate and a detailed record of training by a registered tamer, verified and confirmed by at least two senior tamers and one Monstrum Censor with no affiliation with either the breeder or the tamer in question. There are no procedures in place for felix- or . . . ursine-type monsters, since they are not to interact with the general public in the first place."

The two Exploratores behind the warrior frowned and glanced at each other. Suddenly, the human girl grinned. She walked right over to the bear monster . . . and picked it up in her arms.

The staff and security gasped, then gaped as the bear *didn't* maul the girl's face off, just cried weakly instead. Proculus exhaled once more.

"Impressive . . . but for all I know, she's the original breeder, and the beast is imprinted on her. It does not suffice as proof that the public will remain safe."

The human girl grinned and started walking toward the nearest guard, who jumped and raised his weapon. Proculus raised his hand to stop them both, then looked NSLICE-00P in the eyes once more.

"Okay, if you're going to go that far, then we do it right. Are you willing to accept all liability in the case of injury or death, including criminal consequences and financial indemnity as appropriate? Forfeiting all rights and immunity granted by your status in that case?"

"Affirmative."

Proculus turned and nodded at a clerk, who began preparing a written document to that effect. One signed waiver later, and Proculus turned toward one of the guards.

"Manius, go pet one of the canus types."

Manius jumped and looked at Proculus with wide eyes. "Me?! Why?!"

"Because you brag endlessly about how you have the highest defense amongst the guards, and frankly, we're all tired of it."

All the other guards chuckled and began egging Manius on. He groaned and gingerly stepped toward the nearest canus, who narrowed its eyes and growled lightly as he approached, but it remained seated. Manius slowly reached his hand out . . .

He touched the fur of the monster's head. The monster growled and whimpered, but otherwise did not react. Everyone's eyes widened. Proculus himself took a deep breath. He couldn't stop a Friend of the Empire if her monsters were *that* unnaturally docile. But he also refused to be responsible for someone's death, so he would still insist on anything he could.

"We will need to run a full range of tests, but if they can pass to *my* liking, then, and only then, will we verify them. Is that acceptable?"

"Affirmative."

He sighed once more. "Well, let's get this over with."

Several hours later, NSLICE-00P and company were resting in a living room. 00F, 00C, 01C, and 02C were all curled up around her, whimpering. Ateia had 00B in her lap and was gently stroking his fur.

"There, there, it's all over now. You did great, you know?"

00B whimpered in response . . . but moved toward Ateia's hand. The monsters had been subjected to a full range of stress tests, including painful provocations, to test the limits of NSLICE-00P's control.

But they had remained calm as per NSLICE-00P's instructions, and so the Monstrum Censor had had no choice but to verify them as NSLICE-00P requested. They each now wore a collar with an enchanted jewel at its center—at the cost of a great deal of stress for the monsters.

NSLICE-00P watched Ateia and logged 00B's stress levels diminishing.

"Query: This unit is observing friendly Ateia restore 00B to ideal condition but cannot determine the mechanism. What sort of protocol has friendly Ateia engaged?"

Ateia tilted her head and blinked. "Um, they're just kids, you know? And they've just been through something unpleasant. It's common sense to comfort them afterward, right?"

"Requesting Confirmation: So physical contact and verbal encouragement reduce organic stress levels?"

Ateia suddenly stared at NSLICE-00P. Her face twisted in confusion. "Um, yes?"

"Acknowledged."

NSLICE-00P looked down at her other monsters. They were all looking up at her. She raised her hand and began to copy Ateia's actions, slowly stroking their heads.

"Encouraging Statement: NSLICE units have successfully accomplished the designated task. Units are not predicted to receive any further damage in the short term."

The canus minors began wagging their tails. The felix minor didn't respond . . . but moved closer to NSLICE-00P's hand and began to purr. 00B's eyes shot open, and he leapt out of Ateia's lap, rushing over to NSLICE-00P, who began petting him as well.

Ateia frowned, then sighed.

Meanwhile, in the Monster Hangar, 01R was frozen solid. NSLICE-00P had not registered the covert units in order to keep them classified, so they were all on standby at the moment.

"They are . . . receiving affection . . . directly from the wise-mighty-gracious boss-queen? That is . . . This is . . ."

01R swore in his heart he would fulfill his next task as excellently as he could.

And so, the team left Grex Magna after a bit of commotion. Ateia and Taog were quite shocked when NSLICE-00P went around a corner and the monsters vanished without a trace, but after NSLICE-00P told them it was classified, they just shrugged and said, "It's Seero, after all." There *were* stories of high-ranking monster tamers and archmages being able to summon monsters on demand, after all.

The rest of the trip was uneventful, and the group safely arrived at the next town, Ferreis Colles, a town of miners and blacksmiths. And as they checked in with the Exploratores HQ, the receptionist's eyes suddenly lit up.

"Excuse me, I don't mean to pry, but are you by chance the group who dealt with that dungeon near Aquilo Perfugium?"

Ateia and Taog's eyes widened slightly. "Uh, yes, that was us. Word travels quickly, huh?"

The receptionist nodded. "Taking on a dungeon with a group as small as yours is quite impressive, after all. Would you be willing to entertain a similar request?"

Ateia glanced at NSLICE-00P.

"What do you think, Seero? Want to take on another dungeon?"

"Affirmative Response: Dungeon terminations are highly efficient in terms of upgrades."

Ateia turned back to the receptionist. "What's the job?"

The receptionist beamed at that.

"A dungeon popped up right on the outskirts of town. I know it's a lot to ask, but would you be willing to take a look at it?"

Taog raised an eyebrow. "Right on the outskirts? Shouldn't it have been dealt with already, then?"

The receptionist frowned.

"Normally, yes. The Legion and the Exploratores would prioritize something like that even with an ongoing incursion. But this dungeon happens to have a lot of monsters highly resistant to physical damage; a normal team won't cut it. We need a full complement of dungeon-ready battlemages, and those can't be spared under the current circumstances. So, we're in containment until the incursion is dealt with, but the dungeon is growing with each day, and the incursion continues. I'm worried the dungeon might be *exceptionally* difficult to deal with if we leave it until then."

She looked at the group.

"Normally, I wouldn't expect you to be able to handle it, but you already surprised us once. Think you can do it again?"

Ateia and Taog glanced at Seero, then at each other, then turned to the receptionist and spoke as one.

"Yes."

40

The Gift of Iron Soldiers

". . . Hah. The sheer ignorance of even our own staff would be comical if it were not so appalling. Iron is a bare fraction of the elements used in our proprietary armor alloys. To call it as mere iron would be to call the ocean a puddle."

—Dr. Ottosen, on the use of "iron men" as a nickname
for NSLICE units.

NSLICE-00P glanced around the town. Ferreis Colles had been built where a river cut through the hills. There were large, long structures with waterwheels on the side, and she could hear rhythmic pounding indicating waterwheel-powered hammers at work.

"Observation: Technology in this town seems to lack mana power sources compared to the port facility in location Aquilo Perfugium."

Ateia shrugged.

"The innkeeper in Grex Magna told me this place is a pretty small operation that forges more for the surrounding countryside than the Legion, so they probably couldn't afford enchantments."

A bit later, NSLICE-00P excused herself to an unoccupied side alley, causing Taog's eyes to lose focus once more. She deployed the covert monsters with orders to search the town for the persons of interest, while taking out the registered monsters to join the dungeon termination. The entire street froze as she emerged from the alley with monsters in tow . . . but the people got back to work once they saw the collars around their necks, albeit with a great deal of hushed and excited whispering. Taog just heaved a sigh, and then the group continued onward.

They made their way toward the side of a hill where one of the town's mines awaited. As they approached, they found a ring of fortifications surrounding the entrance. Stone walls with parapets and towers stood in a half circle, lined with guards and small, one-man ballistae with lightly glowing bolts. Trenches and simple palisades crossed the area between the walls and the mine. Trebuchets sat next to piles of stone behind the walls as well.

A Legion officer approached them, her red cloak held in place with a hammer insignia indicating a praefectus architecti, specialized in building (and breaking) fortifications. She was short and stocky, with her beard braided and adorned with simple stone jewelry. In other words, she was a Dwarf. She raised an eyebrow at the group in front of her.

"Praefectus Architecti Blandia Frontalis. I'm in charge of this defense. You lot Exploratores?"

Ateia saluted and nodded. "Yes. I'm Exploratore Ateia Niraemia; this is Exploratore Taog Sutharlan, and our two companions. We've been requested to explore and, if possible, destroy the dungeon here."

Praefectus Frontalis glanced over them and frowned, crossing her arms.

"I don't think so. Forgive me, but you lot seem woefully unprepared for this place."

Ateia just smirked.

"Well, I know we don't look that impressive at first, but we might surprise you. This isn't the first dungeon we've dealt with."

Praefectus Frontalis shook her head.

"That's not what I mean. I know the lass at the Exploratores HQ nearby; she wouldn't send you here if she thought you couldn't handle yourself. What I mean is you aren't prepared for *this* dungeon. See, this here is a Metal-attribute dungeon, one of the more annoying kinds to deal with. Living armors, huge golems, slimes made of liquid metal, the works. And that means each and every monster in there is armored from head to toe. Better equipped than half the troops I have here, if I'm honest."

She looked over the group again, glancing at their weapons.

"So that means normal weapons don't work here. Arrows just bounce off, and there're no vital points for spears or swords to target. Physical damage in general doesn't work unless you can destroy metal armor outright. Even your little monster pets aren't going to cut it; your wee bear isn't big enough to just smash the bloody things."

00B cried in protest, but the Dwarf ignored him. She waved around at the siege weapons.

"Thus, why they called me in. And I'm only here for containment. If you want to actually push into the dungeon, you're going to need battlemages. Maybe the shiny lass knows some magic, since I don't see a weapon, but one battlemage isn't enough. You can't just have one mage on support; they're going to need to do the heavy lifting this time. One mage's mana pool isn't enough; you'll need a group to cycle spells if you're going to make it even halfway through."

Just then, a bell started ringing from within the mine. Praefectus Frontalis swore.

"We'll finish this talk later, the dungeon's sending another wave. Make yourself useful and get ready to fight. GET READY, TROOPS! WE HAVE INCOMING!"

She made her way up to the battlements as soldiers rushed out of the nearby barracks, grabbing wands tipped with glowing gems and loading up the siege weapons. Ateia turned to NSLICE-00P.

"What do you say, Seero? Want to show her what you can do?"

"Statement: Spreading intel on this unit's capabilities is not a particularly desirable course of action. However, if there are hostiles between this location and the target, they will need to be terminated to proceed with the current mission, assuming said hostiles are unaffiliated and not subject to nonintervention protocols."

Ateia took out her bow and nodded.

"That shouldn't be a problem. I'm guessing these are monsters from the dungeon. Let's go!"

The group made their way to the battlement, taking up a position near Praefectus Frontalis. Soon, they heard the thudding of heavy metal boots on the ground. And then, it began. Suits of armor made of bronze, iron, and steel marched out of the tunnel, carrying shining metal weapons. NSLICE-00P focused in, but detected no heat signatures nor any signs of organic life within the armor suits. By all accounts, it appeared the suits were moving on their own power, save for the powerful mana signatures they were giving off. Still, they did appear humanoid, so NSLICE-00P held off on the first volley, waiting to confirm she was not firing at a new unaffiliated faction.

Praefectus Frontalis waited until the armors shuffled out of the entrance, approaching the first of the palisades.

"Attack!"

The trebuchets and ballistae opened fire. Huge pieces of stone crushed the armors outright. Heavy bolts pierced through them, pinning them to the ground. The soldiers on the wall aimed their wands, firing simple Magic Missiles down the field. The mass-produced wands didn't do much, but the armors still stumbled back when struck, a few even falling as several bolts struck them at once.

As this occurred, NSLICE-00P's robotic eye spun as she zoomed in on an armor struck by a ballista bolt, analyzing the wound. She could see inside the armor . . . and found nothing there. No blood, no body. Nothing but metal and mana. And as she zoomed in on it, the foreign system popped up as well.

Species	Description
Living Armor (Level 30)	**A suit of armor animated by a mana core. A tough monster to take down, but vulnerable to magic.**

And so, she confirmed these were, in fact, monsters, and so not subject to any nonintervention protocols.

"Target affiliations confirmed. Engaging mass-termination protocols."

The Aurora Barrage magic circle formed in the sky once again. Light Beams fused together and rained from the sky, striking the armors at key points, aiming for the strongest mana signatures NSLICE-00P detected on each target.

The beams pierced through the armors and shattered their cores, taking but a few minutes for NSLICE-00P to wipe out the group.

You have slain Living Armors x45!
The spell Aurora Barrage is now Level 7!
Gained 135 Personal XP, 135 Dungeon XP!
Level up! Personal Level is now 61! Dungeon Level has leveled twice and is now 99!

Praefectus Frontalis stared with her mouth wide opened for a moment before a string of very unprofessional curses began, ending with: "What in the name of the Aesdes was that?!"

Ateia shrugged. "It's Seero. So, Praefectus, how do you feel about our chances now?"

Praefectus Frontalis cursed once more and threw her hands up, turning to walk off the battlements. "Sure, go destroy the bloody dungeon! If you brought a bloody archmage with you, then I suppose you can do whatever you bloody want!"

Ateia grinned as she stomped off. Taog sighed and shook his head.

"You're having too much fun with this, Ateia."

"Oh, come on, Taog. Don't you get tired of being the only one surprised by Seero?"

Taog stared off into the distance. "Yes. Yes, I do."

Meanwhile, NSLICE-00P jumped off the battlements and walked over to the fallen armors. Her robotic eye flickered rapidly as she analyzed the broken metal. Living armors were not something she had ever encountered before, but they did resemble something she knew. Something she knew very well.

By her current observations, these monsters were very similar in appearance and function to autonomous warbots, just powered and programmed via mana instead of electricity.

And that meant this dungeon could hold incredibly useful data for NSLICE-00P. Learning how these monsters functioned had a wide range of applications. It could help her upgrade her own components, manually fabricate cybernetic implants, or construct her own autonomous warbots.

Unfortunately, all the armors on the field were in terrible condition. And since NSLICE-00P had targeted and destroyed their mana cores, the wreckage remaining had become little more than mundane scrap metal. She would need to observe subjects in working condition if she wanted actionable data.

"Statement: Current mission updated. Additional parameters set. Data gathering designated as a major mission objective. Updating dungeon termination protocols with new parameters."

41

00B's Bear-y First Dungeon Termination

"Run."

—Exploratore Menenia Sulla, upon encountering a
seemingly lone ursanus cub.

The group arranged themselves and entered. 00B and the other monsters took the lead this time, with Ateia and Taog right behind them. Estrith and NSLICE-00P brought up the rear.

Inside, the walls and roof were made of bronze, lit by occasional metal torches. Ateia and Taog nodded at each other, then proceeded inside. They knew NSLICE-00P could identify the correct path somehow, but they had decided that for as long as they could still fight effectively, they should also try to lead the exploration. Just in case one day they had to explore a dungeon without her.

"Trap."

00B halted as Ateia pointed out the pressure plate ahead of him. He stepped to the side, but Ateia was used to dirt or stone, and so didn't notice the small gap in the floor.

Suddenly, two doors swung open right underneath 00B, revealing the pit trap underneath. He let out a cry, but NSLICE-00P caught him with a Barrier.

"Recommendation: NSLICE-00B should conduct individual sensor scans as well."

00B growled and rolled over in embarrassment. Accidentally rolling on top of the pressure plate Ateia had pointed out, causing arrows to shoot from the walls. Barriers from NSLICE-00P put a stop to them before anyone was injured.

00B refused to look at anyone for the next few minutes.

It was not long until the team encountered their first monster. It had metal armor that covered it from head to toe that . . . didn't reflect the light due to the amount of dirt and scratches on it. It carried a wicked blade . . . that was chipped and rusting. It stood tall . . . at about three feet.

It was a goblin, armed with scrap metal armor and a rusting dagger. It let out a shout and rushed the group.

00B swatted it. The goblin slammed into the ground and faded away, leaving behind its core. 00B then turned to NSLICE-00P and cried.

"Acknowledgement: This unit has logged NSLICE-00B's successful termination of a hostile."

00B grunted and turned back to the front. Only to see a full squad of armored goblins now approaching them.

00B charged right into the center of them. The goblins slashed at him but couldn't penetrate his metal armor. 00C then jumped forward and grabbed the ankle of one of the goblins, pulling it to the ground and away from the group where the other cyber-hounds, 01C and 02C, were waiting. They jumped the fallen goblin with their Fire- and Water-attribute fangs. 00F stayed on the edge of the room, the cyber-cat adjusting his stance before he pounced upon the back of one of the goblins, biting its neck.

Ateia frowned as she watched the little monsters fight. "Um, should we help them?"

"Negative Response: These units require upgrades and combat experience to reach minimum acceptable combat efficiency. This unit calculates assistance is not required or desirable for this engagement."

"Right . . ."

Once the fight was over, 00B and the canus monsters all rushed over to NSLICE-00P. 00F followed them, trying not to look too excited.

"Acknowledgement: This unit has logged a successful engagement."

00B turned and glanced at Ateia. Her face cramped, but she managed to form a smile as the bear cub covered in goblin blood kept glancing at her.

"G-Good job. You did a great job . . . murdering those monsters."

She stroked 00B's fur. He tried to look away but couldn't help his body relaxing, crying softly.

Ateia tried not to grimace as she wiped the goblin blood off her hand.

The first four floors were mostly armored goblins. NSLICE-00P couldn't get much useful data from these, unfortunately, so she focused on combat support and upgrading her newest subordinates. But on the fifth floor, the situation changed.

Bronze Living Armor (Level 19)

A suit of bronze armor thrust a spear down at 00B. 00B was looking elsewhere, but his components received a warning from NSLICE-00P through the
NSLICE network, and so he rolled forward and out of the way, then swung his
paw at the living armor's leg.

He didn't manage to knock it to the ground, but he did dent the armor's shin.

NSLICE-00P's robotic eye flickered and spun as she analyzed the fight, gathering as much data on the living armors as possible. Her monsters were struggling
at this point, limited as they currently were to physical attacks. But NSLICE-00P
didn't consider this an issue, as it gave her more time to analyze her targets.

And the monsters were not alone.

Ateia drew an arrow, activating her new Radiant Shot skill. The arrow glowed
with golden-and-silver light as she let it fly, striking an armor right in the eye
hole of its helmet and releasing a flash of light. The armor fell onto its back and
lay still.

Taog swung the Dark Blade, utilizing the Mana Infusion skill. The Dark
Blade, having its own attribute, converted the basic infusion into a black aura
surrounding itself. This aura appeared to count as magical, and so could bypass
the living armors' defenses. While Taog's sword still couldn't pierce the metal,
each blow from his sword caused the monsters to stumble back, and a few
repeated hits would lay them low.

So NSLICE-00P was free to conduct her analysis, as Ateia and Taog would
clean up the field soon enough, and Estrith was on standby if they started to get
overwhelmed.

From what she could tell, the actual armor of the monsters was no different
from any other. There were no components that would enable motion like her
own powered armor. Rather, mana was responsible for every step of the process.
The monsters were animated by a mana core, much like slimes and elementals.
Mana issued the commands, and more mana physically moved the armor to
execute those commands. The mana was both hardware and software.

It seemed inefficient to NSLICE-00P. Compared to her own setup and that
of her cyborg monsters, the living armors were spending far more mana just to
achieve basic movement. Designing the armor to move on its own via mechanical methods and then utilizing the mana as a power source was significantly more
efficient. As a result, the living armors were slow, and their blows were weaker
than their mana signature implied. They also lacked any sort of spells or special
skills, as they had no mana to spare.

On the other hand, their setup did minimize the number of vulnerable components. The mana core inside of them was the only point of weakness. Besides
that, the only way to terminate them was to destroy the armor outright or to
disrupt the magical bindings holding them together.

It was a trade-off between overall efficiency and pure physical resilience.

And the data was still useful to NSLICE-00P. Knowledge of how to animate metal parts via mana provided additional options, particularly in a society that could not fabricate complex cybernetic components.

As the fight ended, 00B lay on the floor.

"Observation: No damage detected; no issues observed. Query: Is NSLICE-00B experiencing a malfunction?"

00B grunted softly and turned over, facing away from her. NSLICE-00P connected with his components . . . and found some sort of emotional response. Ateia walked up to her as she analyzed it.

"I think he's upset because he struggled in the fight. What do you think of his performance?"

"Analysis: NSLICE-00B struggled with armor penetration of these particular foes but was able to resist hostile attacks and create diversions for assets with antiarmor capabilities. Areas for improvement have been logged and upgrades will commence to address them."

00B cried in response.

"Objection: That statement is inaccurate. By this unit's calculations, units 06R through 10R are currently the least combat-capable units in the network. NSLICE-00B is currently predicted as the third most capable. He possesses the toughest defenses and the strongest close-combat attacks."

In fact, NSLICE-00B was calculated to defeat most of her other NSLICE units, save two. Uscfrea was a given. Lilussees, with superior vertical mobility and growing magical firepower, could likely keep her distance and bombard 00B from range. Other than that, the other units in the network would struggle against 00B's natural strength and resilience. Even 01R, despite his performance in friendly spars, was not predicted as favored in an actual fight to the death.

00B rolled over and looked up at her. He cried softly.

"Negative Response: NSLICE-00B has not failed any primary or major directives at this time."

Ateia walked over and picked the bear off the ground, giving him a gentle hug.

"See? You're doing great."

00B turned his head away to avoid looking at them . . . but also didn't resist Ateia's embrace.

NSLICE-00P soon gathered the monsters back to the hangar to rest, as the level difference with the dungeon monsters was growing too large. Taog had *many* questions when NSLICE-00P took her monsters around the corner and then came back alone, but he settled on the answer of "Because it's Seero" and moved on. It was his and Ateia's turn now to take the lead in combat, after all.

A few more floors and three more levels later, and the two Imperials handed it off to NSLICE-00P. She concluded she had enough data on living armors—or at least as much as she could gather from external scans of hostile targets—at this point, so she lowered the priority on the data-gathering objective and reallocated her effort to efficient termination.

She walked down the hallway, detecting a group of living armors approaching in the distance. Panels opened up on her armor, firing a volley of anti-tank missiles, each targeted toward a different living armor's core.

You have slain Steel Living Armors x12!
Gained 36 Personal XP, 36 Dungeon XP!
Level up! You are now Personal Level 62!

"Oh, she found some more."

"Looks like it."

Ateia and Taog shrugged as the missiles soared down the hall toward targets they couldn't even see. A few minutes later, they found broken armor scattered across the ground, each with a large hole in its center.

It turned out, living armors had no magical defenses, since their mana was used solely to animate their bodies. They were only as tough as the armor they were made from, and that armor interacted with the physical world the same as any other.

And that armor was ultimately designed to be worn by an organic soldier, a few millimeters thick at most. So said armor was not at all sufficient against high-explosive anti-tank missiles designed to defeat several *hundred* millimeters of steel and composite materials. Missiles that had subsequently been upgraded since NSLICE-00P arrived here.

NSLICE-00P didn't even need magic to take on these foes. The several-centuries gap in weapons development was too much for them to handle. They were no match for a true living armor.

42

Terminate the Metal Dungeon?

"Why have mines when there are metal dungeons? Because, boy, regular iron veins don't stand up and try to kill you."
—Dwarven Foreman Doukdratin Hornsunder.

And so, the group made it to the tenth floor. Thanks to her subordinates defeating monsters within her dungeon field, NSLICE-00P's Dungeon level had increased over the trip and was now sitting at a hundred. Her Personal level hadn't leveled again yet, but was on the verge of doing so now that she was terminating foes directly.

NSLICE-00P entered a large open area. Unlike the previous floors, the ground and walls were not made of metal but of dirt and stone, and it was littered with boulders, each of which had exposed veins of metal across their exterior that would be easy to mine. NSLICE-00P scanned the room, finding mostly iron.

And a large mana signature.

The ground shook as heavy footsteps approached. A giant humanoid stepped into view, a towering construct of iron and steel, standing at twelve feet tall. It was in the shape of plate armor, but solid metal the entire way through. It carried a massive halberd and a thick tower shield.

Species	Description
Steel Golem (Level 50)	A solid construct of steel animated by a mana core. This is a monster variant with greater autonomy and initiative.

NSLICE-00P raised her arm toward the metal monster. A panel opened on her forearm, and an anti-tank missile shot forward. It struck the golem's chest with a small explosion.

And then the golem slowly fell backward and crashed to the ground, lifeless.

You have slain Steel Golem (Level 50)!
Gained 3 Personal XP, 3 Dungeon XP!

It turned out, even a completely solid steel golem still had less overall armor than a modern tank . . . and didn't use any composite materials or active defenses which might aid against shaped charges. NSLICE-00P's anti-armor missiles had had no trouble penetrating to its core, which her sensors had easily located.

Ateia and Taog just stared at the fallen golem.

"Oh, she killed the boss again, Taog."

"Looks that way, Ateia."

"Was that some kind of spell? I couldn't really tell."

"Uh, maybe? I didn't see a magic circle, though."

"Answer: Anti-armor missiles are a standard component of this unit's conventional armament. Magical offensive measures were not required in this instance."

Taog nodded as he stared into the distance. "Oh, got it. Thanks, Seero. So no, it wasn't a spell. Not even magic, according to Seero. Of course. Of course, Seero can destroy a steel golem in a single hit without magic. As expected."

Ateia frowned and tilted her head. "What sort of weapon is a . . . missile?"

"Explanation: A guided rocket-propelled projectile. In this case, carrying a High-Explosive Anti-Tank warhead."

"Ah, got it. Thanks, Seero!" She then whispered to Taog, "Do you know what those words mean?"

"Not really, but 'high explosive' seems to be the important part."

Estrith just scoffed. *Imperials.* Her king could do as much with ease!

She glanced again at the golem and the size of its armor. She frowned. Her king could definitely do it . . . with ease . . .

A large chest appeared, and NSLICE-00P walked over to it after scanning it for traps. She opened it up.

Inside were three metal ingots which seemed like polished iron at first glance. But NSLICE-00P detected something nonstandard and so scanned the metal. As she did, the foreign system appeared in her vision.

Name	Description
Mana Iron Ingot	Iron that has soaked in a mana-rich environment for a long period of time. Its base performance is slightly superior to that of iron, and it is significantly easier to enchant or channel mana through. This ingot has been smelted and purified for further processing.

NSLICE-00P gathered the ingots into her inventory and scheduled a full investigation once the dungeon termination was completed. A mana-adapted material with superior performance to standard metals could have significant implications to her own upgrades . . . though as she still lacked maintenance infrastructure, she couldn't do much with the raw materials at this time. The foreign system might be able to make up for the lacking infrastructure, however, so the possibility remained.

She scanned the room for any additional nonstandard materials, but found none, and so moved on to the next floor.

The next three floors were filled with steel golems, which NSLICE-00P terminated in short order. Estrith tried to fight one herself . . . but her harpoon couldn't pierce deep enough to strike the core, and the mana chains of the Harpoon Shot skill didn't bother the tough, powerful, and already slow-moving golems. She did know some Water Magic, so she took it down eventually, but it took much longer than she'd expected despite her ten-level advantage on the monster. So much longer that she allowed the queen of the Dobhar to monopolize further experience. She also refused to make eye contact with the Imperials for the rest of the trip.

It was on the fourteenth floor that something finally changed.

The walls were gray like iron, but polished to such shine that it seemed almost silver, lighting up the halls as it reflected the light of the torches. NSLICE-00P could detect mana flowing through and emitting from the metal. By comparing the scans, she identified the material as the mana iron she'd received earlier.

Another squad of five living armors stepped into NSLICE-00P's range. She zoomed in on them; from her scans and their appearance, they seemed to be made of the same mana iron as the walls.

NSLICE-00P fired one anti-missile at the lead living armor.

You have slain Mana Iron Living Armor (Level 56!)
Gained 4 Personal XP, 3 Dungeon XP!

The mana flowing through the metal resisted the attack. Still, a few millimeters of the improved metal weren't sufficient to resist an anti-tank missile, though the performance boost was significant. An opponent with thicker armor, such as the golem from before, might even survive one of her attacks.

So, for the first time since arriving in this dungeon, NSLICE-00P formed magic circles in the air. One for each opponent on approach.

A Light Beam, Holy Beam, Water Beam, and Fire Beam shot at each of the remaining opponents, with no modifiers or Supercharging.

She wanted to test as many elements as she could, though she ruled out a few. Earth wasn't very compatible with the Beam shape in general, and it focused more on physical damage, in any case. Poison . . . was not predicted to be efficient against targets with no organic components.

Well, even with the nonstandard metal comprising their armor, the living armors were not particularly strong against magic. The mana flowing in their metal did give them improved magical resistance, but only compared to their mundane counterparts, so all four of them quickly fell.

> *You have slain four Mana Iron Living Armors!*
> *Gained 16 Personal XP, 12 Dungeon XP!*
> *Level up! You are now Dungeon Level 101!*
> *The skill Water Magic is now Level 6!*

It seemed the Light Beam had fared the worst, some of its power reflecting off the metal. Water and Fire were both effective, but it was the Holy Beam that performed the best. NSLICE-00P logged the data against this type of opponent and carried onward.

> *You have slain five Mana Iron Living Armors!*
> *Gained 20 Personal XP, 15 Dungeon XP!*
> *Level up! You are now Personal Level 63!*

There was only one other squad of mana iron living armors, so the group quickly cleared the fourteenth floor.

The fifteenth floor featured another boss room. In the center was another twelve-foot golem, only this one was made of mana iron. And unlike the previous golem, this one was sleek and curved, almost appearing more like a human-like sculpture than a suit of armor. It carried a large sword and a kite shield, and quickly stepped forward toward the group.

NSLICE-00P launched an anti-tank missile, but the golem raised its shield. The missile exploded on the shield, but its shaped charge pierced through. However, as the missile struck far from the golem's body and had to pierce through the shield, the explosively formed penetrator lost its power and couldn't pierce the golem itself.

The golem moved at surprising speeds, but NSLICE-00P was faster. Dozens of magic circles formed in the air and bombarded the golem with Fusion Holy Fire Beams, putting a stop to its charge. Meanwhile, a panel opened on NSLICE-00P's shoulder and fired an anti-tank missile into the air. The missile arced around up and over the golem, then curved down to approach it from behind. The golem spun around to block the missile with its shield, tanking the Holy Fire Beams, which tore through its HP barrier but weren't piercing through its skin.

That is, until NSLICE-00P fused them together.

As the golem exposed itself to defend the missile, NSLICE-00P struck its back with the Equalizer. It had no defense when the fused and Supercharged Holy Fire Beam blasted into it.

And melted its core.

You have slain Mana Iron Golem (Level 60)!
Gained 10 Personal XP, 3 Dungeon XP!
The spell modifier Fusion is now Level 17!
The skill Spell Modification is now Level 4!
The skill Holy Magic is now Level 11!

Ateia's face scrunched up. ". . . Taog."

Taog was staring blankly into space. "Yes, Ateia?"

"Is it weird that I'm starting to feel bad for the monsters?"

"What a coincidence, I was wondering that myself."

Estrith was just muttering to herself in the corner.

NSLICE-00P walked over and opened up the chest that appeared, a sword made of mana iron inside. NSLICE-00P gathered it to her inventory and continued to the door at the end of the room.

She pushed it open to reveal the core room. And the dungeon master waiting for them.

It had a humanoid form, only with smooth, metallic skin. Its figure was vague, and its features couldn't be seen clearly. Its body shifted and melted as it moved, as if made of liquid. It took a step forward . . .

And thrust its head on the ground. Its whole body flowed like water and condensed down into a small, shiny blob.

It was a slime . . . but made of metal somehow.

"My master . . . my god. Oh, master of all things metal, please accept this unworthy peon as your disciple—no, your servant!"

Rival Dungeon Master Melion has offered to surrender. Accept?

43

Mines and Metal Craft

"Look, at some point we have to accept that 'ultimate weapon' does not mean 'unbeatable weapon.' How was I supposed to know that Resistance base happened to have a guy who could control metal with his mind? Do you know how much time and effort it took to develop a metal alloy capable of stopping modern anti-tank weapons at the thinness suitable for armoring a human-size machine? Even I cannot hedge for every possible contingency before it occurs! I am a scientific genius, not a miracle worker!"
— Dr. Ottosen, after an unsuccessful NSLICE raid.

"Affirmative."

Surrender accepted! Melion has become your subordinate!
Subordinate dungeon core acquired!
Would you like to absorb the Metal Armory dungeon core, or manage it as a subcore?

You have accomplished the Personal Feat: Dungeon Conqueror (Metal Armory)!
You have learned the skill Metal Magic!

Previously, NSLICE-00P had always absorbed the dungeon cores, but that was a protocol based on records of her battling Non-Standards before arriving here and was largely out of date. She now had significantly more data on the dungeon system and the consequences of either choice, and so reran the analysis.

On the one hand, absorbing the core removed the dungeon as a factor and improved her own capabilities, immediately granting several levels worth of perk points. On the other hand, subordinate cores provided local bases of operation, additional Dungeon XP, and secure lines of communication.

In this case, she had accepted a mission to terminate this particular dungeon, and so needed to choose the absorb option. But she did modify her dungeon termination protocols for the future: rather than defaulting to absorb, she would now conduct a case-by-case analysis for each dungeon-termination mission.

The dungeon core melted into light and streamed into NSLICE-00P, then the group found themselves in a mining tunnel.

You have absorbed a dungeon core (Metal Armory)!
Gained 15 Personal Perk Points, 15 Dungeon Perk Points!
Gained Dungeon Affinity: Metal!
Affinity level boosted to (Minor) due to compatibility with Primary
Affinity: Cyborg!

The metal slime flattened itself on the ground.

"My master, thank you so much! Now, let me check this out!" The slime launched itself up and landed on NSLICE-00P's shoulder. "Oh, this is interesting. So your armor isn't iron . . . or mana iron. Mithril? No, smells like . . . titanium? But also aluminum and . . . something else. Wow, wow, interesting! And what's this on the inside? It smells like copper mostly, but there's gold and silver. Is that mana flowing through it? No, it's lightning? Interesting! I wonder what that's for! You have to tell me how this was forged! And definitely show me those weird arrows later! I *have* to know how you made molten metal arrows!"

NSLICE-00P froze, her robotic eye flickering.

On the one hand, details on her implants' construction and inner workings were classified. On the other, Melion was now designated as friendly, and not subject to counterespionage termination protocols.

"Negative Response: Engineering details regarding this unit's implants and weaponry are restricted to command and maintenance personnel only. Please refrain from attempts to reverse engineer classified technology."

"Then I'll become a 'command and maintenance personnel' or whatever I need to, Master! How do I do that, anyways?"

NSLICE-00P's robotic eye flickered. Command personnel were restricted to the persons of interest for the moment. Maintenance personnel normally had to be designated by a commander of sufficient authority . . . but NSLICE-00P had already conducted some maintenance and upgrades on herself, so had already compromised on that protocol. It *was* true that maintenance personnel would be needed in the long term, especially as she was building a new NSLICE network, and it may not be possible to wait for a commander to provide them. So, she attempted to analyze and break down the actual requirements for a maintenance personnel designation.

"Response: Command personnel designation is restricted. Maintenance personnel designation may be applied to friendlies with sufficient trustworthiness and technical knowledge."

"I'll be infinitely loyal to you then, Master! And teach me; I'll learn as much knowledge as I can!"

"Acknowledged. Determining required knowledge . . ."

Well, NSLICE-00P did not actually possess any but the most basic maintenance protocols. She would have to determine how a friendly could learn the requisite knowledge on her own.

She decided the first step would be to upgrade the new friendly and determine if they could be integrated into the NSLICE network. At that point, she could simply share any nonclassified technical data and maintenance protocols she possessed for the aspiring maintenance personnel to study.

And as this was happening, Taog was staring right at NSLICE-00P . . . and the metal slime on her shoulder.

"Seero tamed . . . the dungeon master? And then absorbed the core, or something? That's . . . um . . . It's because it's Seero. Yes. It's because it's Seero. No other reason."

Ateia crossed her arms. "Taog, you can't just go into denial every time Seero surprises you."

Taog spun around and glared at her. "Ateia, do you have *any* idea what Seero just did?! What that implies about her?!"

She shrugged. "You already said it. She tamed a dungeon master and absorbed a dungeon core."

Taog held his head. "And not just that! She came out of nowhere with no knowledge of her surroundings, has ridiculous amounts of mana, barely needs to eat or sleep, and can pull monsters out of nowhere! That—"

"Sounds like a demon lord."

Taog blinked as Ateia finished his sentence, then nodded grimly.

"Then you should understand why it's upsetting! I know at this point she's proven herself to *us*, but do you have any idea what the Empire will do if they discover a demon lord walking around?!"

Ateia shrugged. "It's fine, though?"

Taog groaned and clutched at his hair. "What's fine?!"

"We already know Seero's a hero. And demon lords can't be heroes or use Holy Magic. So, all the demon lord–like feats are probably just her hero skills. Heroes can do all sorts of things that normal people can't, right?"

"That's . . ." Taog opened his mouth and raised his hand . . . then frowned, closed his mouth, and lowered his hand. He blinked repeatedly. ". . . right?"

Ateia smiled and nodded. "So there's no reason to get all upset, right?"

He blinked a few times. "Uh . . . that's right?"

Taog stood there for a second, but the rest the group started to leave him behind, so he shrugged and followed along.

The group made their way back to the encirclement after NSLICE-00P had excused herself and sent Melion to the Monster Hangar. The gates opened up, and Praefectus Frontalis came to greet them. She was incredulous at first, but after her soldiers verified the dungeon was indeed gone, she offered to buy them a round at the tavern instead. NSLICE-00P declined, as her protocols forbade ingesting any substances that could affect her organic components' efficiency, and so returned to her room at the Exploratores HQ instead as Ateia and Taog went to join the soldiers for a celebration.

In any case, she had something else she wanted to explore. She formed a magic circle in her hand, and a metal sword appeared.

The skill Metal Magic has leveled three times and is now Level 4!

Melion popped up inside the Monster Hangar.

"Oh, Master, are you learning Metal Magic now?"

"Affirmative."

Melion began bouncing around. "Oh, oh! Let me help! I'm really good at it!"

"Acknowledgement: Any assistance would be appreciated."

"Anything for you, Master! Let's see . . . first thing, I'd recommend manipulating existing metal. It's pretty difficult to form metal out of magic power, you know?"

NSLICE-00P had indeed logged a significant mana expenditure for the Metal Blade spell compared to the other attributes' variants. So, she searched for a source of spare metal for experimentation. She did have the mana iron ingots from the dungeon, but those were a new and higher-performance material, and so not suitable for initial experiments. Besides, she had logged a possibility to explore.

"Query: Friendly Melion created raw metal materials, correct?"

"Yep! I got tired of having my monsters dig around the area outside, so I created some myself! Eventually, I was able to buy a mine room!"

NSLICE-00P dove back into her menus, evaluating the different options. She knew she wouldn't have the same options as Melion at this point, but there might be an alternative that provided a similar function. She found it on the upgrades for the Item Foundry.

Available Item Foundry Upgrades:			
Name	Cost	Additional Mana Upkeep	Description
Geo-Replicator	10	1	Enables Item Foundry to produce minerals, metal ores, and other geological raw materials.

It was a bit expensive . . . but this time, NSLICE-00P had identified the use case that this upgrade would fulfill. Even if it only gave her access to the most basic of metals, it would still be sufficient for her needs. Or at least, there was a decent predicted probability that it would be so.

She went ahead and purchased the upgrade.

Geo-Replicator upgrade now available!
Analyzing available materials . . . Due to materials used in Implants, the following materials are now available: iron ore, copper ore, silver ore, gold ore, titanium ore, aluminum ore, vanadinite, tin ore, manganese ore, chromium ore, nickel ore, zinc ore, molybdenum ore, tungsten ore, cobalt ore, niobium ore, platinum ore, lithium ore, indium ore, beryllium ore, lead ore, gallium ore, silicon ore.

Ugh, I have to figure this out, don't I? This weird and complicated material that's not supposed to exist? The others told me I have to stop cutting corners with you . . . You're probably going to make a new race if I don't flesh this out for you, huh?
Ugh, fine.

The following materials are unlocked but unavailable, as the Item Foundry is currently not powerful enough to create them: Iesnuorium.

At least, I think that's what you call the material in that weird thing that wipes out mana?

Additional materials may be unlocked by allowing the Item Foundry to absorb them.

There. I told you how you're supposed to do it. So don't go manually deconstructing some metal and accidentally creating a

new material, okay?! It was hard enough trying to figure out that Iesnuorium crap!

NSLICE-00P's robotic eye flickered rapidly. There was a great deal of new data, including the game-changing possibility of creating Iesnuorium. Iesnuorium had been the rarest material on Earth, a super adaptive material capable of absorbing, amplifying, and emitting practically any energy type. It was the key component powering the Equalizer.

As for how rare Iesnuorium was . . . while NSLICE-00P didn't possess a full inventory of her original organization's stockpiles, to her knowledge, the Equalizer contained the entire supply of it. And now, she might be able to create more of it on demand.

But she filed that data away for the time being. The Item Foundry wasn't powerful enough to create Iesnuorium at the moment, and NSLICE-00P didn't have the blueprints on the Equalizer's construction in any case. Even if she could make Iesnuorium, she lacked the engineering knowledge to make use of it at present. After all, the properties of Iesnuorium meant it required special handling via methods she was unaware of. So, it wasn't as simple as just copying her own Equalizer; she'd first have to figure out how to shape the material in the first place.

She set it aside for future investigation and returned to her original purpose. She went ahead and created some copper ore. A green-and-brown rock appeared in her hand.

"Oh! I can help with this!" Melion leaped out of the Monster Hangar, forming into a humanoid form with vague features once more and reaching out a hand. "May I?"

NSLICE-00P wasn't sure what Melion was going to do but handed the ore off to the monster. They knew more about Metal Magic than she did, after all.

The ore sank into Melion's body. A moment later, an ingot of pure copper emerged. Melion placed it into NSLICE-00P's hand.

"Metal Magic is easier if you're working with pure metal!"

"Gratitude: This unit thanks friendly Melion for their assistance. Requesting Clarification: So friendly Melion is capable of smelting metallic ores without infrastructure?"

Melion crossed their arms. "Yep! It's a metal slime specialty! Well . . . normal metal slimes just eat the entire thing, though."

NSLICE-00P glanced down and scanned the metal in her hand. It was pure copper, at a purity matching or exceeding what modern processing methods could achieve. Her processors raced. She now had the ability to create metal ores on demand. She now had a friendly who could process those ores without any infrastructure required.

And . . .

She formed a magic circle. The copper formed itself into a sword. She formed another magic circle. The sword shifted and turned into a chain.

The skill Metal Magic is now Level 5!

She had the ability to shape the metal via magic, again without any industrial infrastructure.

The implications of this turn of events were staggering. Depending on how finely she could control the shapes of the materials . . . she might be able to replicate an entire industrial supply chain, all on her own.

44

NSLICE the Science Cyborg!

"Oh yes, I absolutely could. If I managed to get a hold of more Iesnuorium, only the rarest material on Earth. I don't suppose you happen to have some in your pantry?"
—Dr. Ottosen, on rebuilding the Equalizer after the sudden loss of NSLICE-00P.

The skill Metal Magic is now Level 8!
The spell shape Chain is now Level 7!
The spell shape Barrier is now Level 13!
The skill Spell Shaping is now Level 16!

NSLICE-00P spent the night experimenting with Metal Magic on the copper. She was ultimately able to produce thin copper wires through application of the Chain shape, and thin plates via Barrier. Melion watched with interest.

"Interesting! Most people try to make armor or swords and stuff. I never thought of training my control by making string out of metal! I should have thought of that; traps use those, now that I think about it, huh?"

Having confirmed she could shape the metal as desired, NSLICE-00P moved to her next experiment. She sent her mana into her own implants, specifically into her shoulder-mounted autopistols. She reached her mana into one of the pistols' magazine, into the first bullet waiting to be fired.

Her mana moved into the bullet. The lead tip was slightly harder to infuse, given its higher density, but it was no trouble for NSLICE-00P and her mana density and control. She took control of the lead in the same way as the copper before.

Then, she reshaped it. She tried to hollow out the tip. Of course, since the bullet couldn't get any longer inside the magazine, she had to get rid of some material to achieve this. So, she separated the excess . . . and tried to apply a new capability the foreign system had informed her of, absorbing it into her Geo-Replicator.

Lead absorbed!
Lead ore is already available in the Item Foundry!

Soon, her work was complete, and the bullet was reshaped to her liking.

Um, let's see, this is a . . . hollow-point bullet?

Upgrade unlocked! Hollow-point bullets now available for
Autopistol Traps!
Hollow-point bullets upgrade now available for purchase for
Assault Rifle Traps!
Gained 5 Dungeon Perk Points for creating a new Trap option!

The skill Metal Magic is now Level 9!
You have achieved the Personal Feat: Magic Crafter!

You really need to go through her records and map this stuff out; at least the basics.
You're just paying her for doing your job now.

Personal Feats		
Name	Description	Effect
Magic Crafter	Both crafters and mages reshape reality to fit their needs. One just does it faster. Unlocked by crafting an item purely through mana (excepting default spell shapes such as Blade)!	+1 level in Mana Crafting skill

> . . . Shut up, I'm working on it. You try going through a
> millennium of technological developments all at once!

She would need to test the bullet's ballistic performance at a safe location later, but the foreign system implied her efforts had succeeded. NSLICE-00P had confirmed that she could use Metal Magic to upgrade her own components without needing to rely on the foreign system or Dungeon perk points.

And she already had a new material she could attempt to apply. She opened her inventory and viewed the mana iron ingots she had received. A new option appeared.

Absorb Mana Iron?

She selected the option. One of the ingots broke down into mana, information on it streaming into her core.

Mana Iron absorbed!
Gained 3 Dungeon Perk Points for absorbing a new material!
**The following materials are unlocked but unavailable, as the Item
Foundry is currently not powerful enough to create them: Mana
Iron ore.**

NSLICE-00P paused for a moment, but the message itself already contained the answer. The wording of the message implied that the Item Foundry was ultimately capable of summoning this material but required upgrades to do so.

Available Item Foundry Upgrades:			
Name	Cost	Additional Mana Upkeep	Description
Item Foundry +1	10	1	Boosts Item Foundry's power, allowing creation of more powerful and more complex items.

She was spending a lot on this, but she had confirmed the use case for this upgrade, so it was worth the cost . . . depending on how many upgrade levels she needed to acquire mana iron.

Item Foundry is now Item Foundry +1

Her heart rate increased as she checked the available items. She was about to apply the Calm spell on herself as she read the menu . . .

Item Creation - Geological Materials		
Name	Mana Cost	Description
Iron Ore	4 mana per ore chunk	A piece of iron ore from the ground. Contains impurities.
Iron Ingot	8 mana per ingot	Iron ore refined and purified for further processing.
(. . .)		
Mana Iron Ore	25 mana per ore chunk	Iron ore that has soaked in and been changed by mana, reinforcing its properties and increasing its mana conductivity.

. . . but fortunately, it wasn't necessary. Mana iron ore was now available, along with refined versions of the mundane ores she had access to. Iesnuorium was still unavailable, but the upgrade had achieved its purpose.

She could now apply mana iron to her weapons.

Well, she would need to run tests on the material and its properties, as well as determine if alloys could be formed with it before she could go and start replacing parts. But now that she could create more mana iron as needed, she could start running as many tests as required. And once those tests concluded, she would have additional options to improve the performance of her conventional weaponry . . . and her armor plating. And, of course, there was the possibility that more nonstandard materials were available.

NSLICE-00P added 'locate, absorb, and test novel materials' to her personal upgrade protocols. With this experiment now concluded, there was one other thing she needed to evaluate. The Metal Dungeon affinity, or more specifically, what new subordinates it might make available to her.

She opened the Monster Summoning screen, evaluating for new options.

And froze. She saw one immediately.

Subordinates → Summon Subordinates			
[Cyborg - Primary]			
Name	**Summoning Cost**	**Upkeep**	**Description**
Mini Drone Golem	5 mana	0.2 mana	Okay, I think this is something reasonable? I hope you're happy; it was a lot of work figuring out how to do this! A tiny quadcopter drone using a golem core as a power source and brain. Mainly for scouting, but can also carry and release small objects, including small potions, poisons, and bombs.

She could now summon a basic autonomous unit. In the past, cyborg NSLICE units like herself had ultimately proven too expensive to be cost-effective for every use case. The NSLICE network had subsequently been expanded by introducing cheaper, fully robotic units that would act as loyal wingmen to the more capable NSLICE units. That was the point of the Loyal Wingman protocols she was using to guide her subordinates.

So, the addition of expendable, fully autonomous units would boost the capabilities of her new NSLICE network back toward the level of her original network. NSLICE-00P immediately moved to expand the Monster Hangar . . . and found something new there as well.

Available Monster Hangar Upgrades:			
Name	**Cost**	**Additional Mana Upkeep**	**Description**
Drone Hangar (Small)	10 points to unlock and purchase. (Includes cost of new Implant Slot and one Hangar).	1	Unlocks a new Monster Hangar variant. A hangar specialized for nonorganic monsters of limited sentience. Trades amenities for boosted storage capacity.

She went ahead and made the purchase, then summoned one of the drones. It was a basic quadcopter drone, made mostly from aluminum, and with a glowing mana core in its center. It came equipped with a basic camera, and a small, four-pronged claw for grasping objects. NSLICE-00P quickly linked it to the NSLICE network, and its camera feed started streaming directly to her. Melion started bouncing as they observed it.

"Wow! What kind of golem is that? I've never seen—" Melion went completely silent as the drone's rotor blades started spinning and it rose into the air. The metal slime began to tremble. "*OHMYGOSH! THAT'S A METAL GOLEM THAT CAN FLY?! AND, LIKE, NOT BY USING MAGIC?! TELL ME HOW IT WORKS, PLEASE! PLEASEPLEASEPLEASE!*"

"Affirmative."

Since this drone had been summoned by the foreign system rather than built by an organization, NSLICE-00P had no data on its patenting or classification level. So, she determined no issue in explaining its function to Melion in as much detail as she had available. She spent the rest of the night answering questions on rotor blades and airframes . . .

The next morning, Ateia and Taog had trouble getting up, so NSLICE-00P was able to gather her covert subordinates in peace. There were still no hits on the facial recognition scans, but at least none of them had come under attack this time. And so, the rats and spiders returned to the Monster Hangar.

And froze as they found a metal slime waiting for them.

"Hi! I'm Melion, newest servant of the master of metal! Former dungeon master or something, but that's not important anymore! Wow, all of you got that armor? That's amazing! Master, can I get the armor later, if I earn it or something?"

"Affirmative Response: Integration into the NSLICE network will proceed at first opportunity, assuming friendly Melion has compatible upgrades available."

Melion bounced around. "You're the best, Master!"

Lilussees reacted first.

"Ah, I guess, like, another one surrendered? Hi, I'm, like, Lilussees, or something. Well, I'm, like, tired from the mission or something, so I'm going to go take a nap."

Rattingtale turned to look at the roof of the hangar.

"Boss-queen, what are you doing? You can't just accept-recruit more dungeon masters, no-no! They are not to be trusted-believed, yes-yes!"

Meanwhile, 01R narrowed his eyes.

"So, another outsider has joined-submitted to the wise-mighty-gracious boss-queen? Well, the boss-queen's power and grace are obvious-apparent, yes-yes, but I hope you will demonstrate-display appropriate loyalty."

Melion bounced again.

"Eternal loyalty! She's the master of metal, doing things with metal I never even dreamed were possible!"

01R nodded his head. He would have to keep an eye on the newcomer, but this one seemed preferable to the other two. Still, enthusiasm could very well be a cover for deceit, so 01R would not trust them just yet.

And so, Melion joined the monster subordinates, much to the Great-High King's consternation.

45

Wingmen for Everyone!

"The most important thing to remember is that all NSLICE bots are connected. One NSLICE drone is easy to kill. Killing the dozen bots that it signals before its death is something else. Killing the super cyborgs that show up if you handle those . . . Well, there's a reason the Atomic Cult never made it across the sea."
—A Resistance veteran training new recruits.

All of NSLICE-00P's monsters stood in the Monster Hangar. Before each one was a newly summoned mini drone golem.

Rattingtale shivered; the boss-queen forcing him to be in the same room as the wretched spider-thing was a grave insult. But the boss-queen's commands were clear this time, so he had no choice.

"Statement: Each NSLICE unit will be assigned an autonomous wingman to expand unit capabilities. Establishing Loyal Wingman connections now."

NSLICE-00P connected to each of her cyborg subordinates in turn, applying the protocol between them and their drone. Rattingtale gnashed his teeth as he felt her presence in his armor once more. He had not managed to take control of these enchantments, but he was making progress. Soon, he would be free from this torment. But for today, he would have to endure her humiliations.

Her words appeared in his visions once more.

"Status Report: Loyal Wingman connection established between NSLICE Excellion Formantus Rattingtale the Third and Unit Rattingtale-A 00. Please test connection and issue a command to the linked subordinate unit."

He felt a connection to the new monster. He could now see out of the creature's eyes, and it seemed to report its status to him. Rattingtale wanted to resist, wanted to cry out. How dare she grant his glorious and esteemed name to this . . . this . . . this hunk of metal! But commands from the boss-queen could not be ignored, not least of all with her peons present and watching.

He looked at the hunk of metal and frowned. It had no legs, and only a single arm at the bottom of its body. He had no idea what it was supposed to do in the first place.

"The Great-High King of all the land commands you. Rise and submit-prostrate yourself to your better!"

Rattingtale jumped as the drone began to move, four blades spinning on its top. He was about to flee the new monster's wrath when it began to rise into the air. Then it tilted forward and remained in place, as if lowering its front toward him.

Rattingtale paused and stared at the floating metal.

"Um . . . fly-move higher?"

The drone moved higher.

". . . Fly-move lower?"

The drone moved lower.

"Fly-move around me?"

The drone started spinning around Rattingtale.

Soon, he started to grin. And then to laugh. And then to cackle. The boss-queen had made a mistake! She had finally made a mistake! She had given him a loyal servant that obeyed his every command! The Great-High King would rise once again!

He swore he heard one of the wretched-spider things giggling, but as he looked around, the others were testing their drones as well, so that must have been his imagination. He did frown at the sight, though. It seemed everyone was getting a loyal subordinate, including that traitor 01R.

Rattingtale rubbed his paws together. He would have to be very clever with his use of the new subordinate.

Meanwhile, NSLICE-00P returned to the Exploratores HQ, where Ateia and Taog were just waking up and about to go restock their supplies. She approached them.

"Greeting: Hello, friendlies Ateia and Taog. This unit is pleased to see the friendlies are now functioning with only minor symptoms of alcohol poisoning."

Ateia groaned. Taog just shrugged. "Well, one of us had to stay moderately sober. Good morning, Seero."

"Query: Do the friendlies know local laws regarding autonomous units, specific classifications: drones or golems?"

Taog froze for a second, then heaved a sigh and shook his head.

"Um, never heard of drones, but as far as I know, golems are treated as equipment. No particular rules, but you're responsible for anything they do. I think there *are* some rules about bringing larger ones in town to make sure you're not blocking the streets or something, but I don't know for sure. Let me guess, Seero. You're asking because you magically have a huge golem made of magic metals or something? I'm right, aren't I, Seero?"

NSLICE-00P summoned one of her drone golems. Taog blinked a few times.

"Huh, not as bad as I expected. I mean, I've never seen anything like that before, but it's small. What's the catch? Is it made of mithril or something?"

"Negative Response: The primary material for this model is aluminum."

Taog frowned.

"Really? There's nothing . . . abnormal about it?" Just then, the drone activated and started to fly. Taog crossed his arms and nodded to himself. "Ah, it can fly. There it is."

Estrith approached the group at this time, looking like she was chewing on something extremely bitter. She turned to Ateia.

"You there, human . . . *Ateia.* I require your assistance."

Ateia groaned. "Ugh, can you keep it down today, Royal Guard lady? I'm not in the mood."

Estrith gritted her teeth but spoke more softly. "Show me where I may acquire one of those tents."

Ateia heaved a sigh. "Fine, yeah, sure. We have to go buy supplies, anyway. You have money, right?"

Estrith went silent for a moment. Ateia felt her head pound.

". . . You have money, right?"

Estrith finally whispered, "What is *money?*"

Ateia stared at her. ". . . Seriously?"

Taog stepped over and whispered into Ateia's ear, "The Dobhar don't really trade or use Idrint, from what I hear."

Ateia groaned. "Ugh, I am not in the mood to explain money or where to go get it. Just, go ask Seero to spot you, or something."

Estrith trembled, clenching her fists. She, proud warrior of the Dobhar, the one assigned by her king to guard the queen of the Dobhar, was now reduced to begging from her charge? A failure and a humiliation of the highest order.

But . . . the memories of the cold nights on the road flashed through her mind.

Estrith thought to herself. Well, it was only natural for a Dobhar leader to split the bounty of the hunt as appropriate. If anything, she deserved more from the queen of the Dobhar, who . . . could have finished all their recent hunts without Estrith's help whatsoever . . .

She decided that was beside the point! If she took this *money* from the queen of the Dobhar, she would be taking resources from the humans and using it for the sake of the Dobhar. She would be guiding the queen of the Dobhar for the sake of their species as her king commanded. She could even go as far as to say she was raiding the Empire and plundering their treasure!

Such were the thoughts Estrith repeated to herself as she approached NSLICE-00P with her eyes locked down on the ground.

". . . Queen of the Dobhar, please lend your warrior some of this . . . money?"

"Query: What is the purpose of the request, and how much money is required?"

". . . For a tent. And I need . . . um . . ."

Estrith trembled but was forced to glance over at Ateia and Taog. Taog shrugged.

"Probably one hundred to three hundred Idrint, if you want a decent one. Could go as low as twenty if you just want something to cover your head."

"Acknowledged. Follow-Up Query: Does friendly Estrith have a method to transport required currency?"

Estrith gritted her teeth and looked away. "No."

"Acknowledged."

Fortunately, the Item Foundry had basic sacks available, so NSLICE-00P created one filled with three hundred Idrint, and then handed it to Estrith. Estrith blinked as she stared at the sack in her hand. Eventually, she lowered her head.

". . . Thank you, queen of the Dobhar."

"Acknowledged."

Ateia sighed. "Ugh, you done, then? Let's go."

Taog shook his head. "I warned you to slow down last night, you know?"

"Shut up, Taog. Not helping."

The group left Ferreis Colles and made their way toward Velusitum. Along the way, though, something happened.

Level up! Dungeon Level is now 102!

At first, NSLICE-00P didn't respond. She was aware that Uscfrea was doing his best raising his dungeon's level, so she was occasionally receiving experience from him.

Until ten hours later, that is.

Level up! Dungeon Level is now 103!

NSLICE-00P had received no dungeon experience on her own in that time, bar a handful of moments where they'd passed someone by on the road. She decided to check on the Otter Burrow dungeon directly. She could still perceive everything occurring there if she paid attention, though she generally left that task to Uscfrea and focused her attention on her own surroundings instead.

She identified the cause fairly easily. Uscfrea had expanded the dungeon's territory into the world around it, which she could now perceive. It had just reached the bottom of the staircase she had built. A group of Dobhar warriors stood guard by the staircase at all times, and other Dobhar occasionally made their way through the room or up and down the staircase. Uscfrea's dungeon was now absorbing mana from these Dobhar at all moments. It would rapidly and passively receive experience and dungeon levels.

And by extension, so would NSLICE-00P.

It was at that moment that Uscfrea contacted her.

"Ah, my queen, I have a question for you."

"Acknowledgement: Please state the query."

"Well, you see . . ."

Uscfrea currently sat in the main hall of the Legion keep at the top of the cliff. The Imperials had a throne room set up for when a high-ranking official came to visit or a hostile force wanted to negotiate. Of course, said throne room had never been used in this particular fortress, as the Dobhar hadn't been interested in diplomacy, and no one important from the Empire ever visited. So, the roof was leaking, the stones were cracked, and moss grew along the walls.

But Uscfrea didn't mind. Or rather, he had no choice, since the Dobhar couldn't exactly repair the fortress on their own. So, he'd leaned into the image, putting up all the torn and broken Imperial regalia the Dobhar had taken over the years and topping it off with the Dobhar's own symbols. Banners and trophies made from the bones, scales, and hides of aquatic monsters now rested on top of the damaged Imperial constructions.

He imagined his guest would appreciate that. A small clan of Wulver stood before him. Uscfrea sent a message directly from his mind, remaining expressionless and silent in person.

"*Right, so a Wulver clan is requesting to settle here. Do you have any preferences on how I handle it?*"

Uscfrea had wanted to get to it, but he'd figured he should at least check in with NSLICE-00P, especially after his components had logged her attention on his dungeon. He decided it was best not to give her any inclination he might be acting without considering her wishes, after all.

Suddenly, he felt her presence directly in his mind, viewing the scene from his eye. And then . . . his new eye began to glow and shine. A transparent image of his queen appeared in the room, made from light. Uscfrea had to stop himself from swearing in surprise. He . . . did not know she could do that.

The lead Wulver gasped as well . . . then snarled. "You! You are the one who slayed our chief!"

"Affirmative. Query: Have the Wulver returned to resume hostilities?"

The Wulver growled at her, but then grew quiet. She turned to Uscfrea.

"King Uscfrea Spellbreaker, what is the meaning of this?"

Uscfrea shrugged. "I am not the king of the Dobhar. Not anymore. She is."

The Wulver's eyes widened. "And you . . . you agreed to this?"

Uscfrea nodded. "The Dobhar are ruled by the strongest. She defeated me and my army, and earned our respect. I rule this land on her behalf now." He grinned. "Plus, she does not belong to the Empire, so neither do we, as long as we belong to her."

The Wulver went silent. Eventually, she looked down to the ground, and then back up again.

"I suppose . . . this changes nothing, then. No . . . if she has earned your respect, then it is appropriate."

The Wulver turned to face NSLICE-00P's projection.

"Queen of the Dobhar, Slayer of Great Chief Solamh Greumach, Victor of the Trial of Claws, I, Ceitidh Greumach, offer you leadership of my clan."

46

An Enchanting Trip Through the Countryside

"I have no love for those who wanted to make me a mindless weapon."
—NSLICE-00P's new commander, when negotiating
with Resistance leaders.

"Acknowledged. Please confirm all existing affiliations and hostilities will cease, and Wulver units will integrate into existing command structure."

Ceitidh closed her mouth. She had been about to explain how her clan, as Solamh's original clan, had taken the heaviest casualties and was thus too weak to survive for much longer. That she had heard the Dobhar had claimed some land in Turannia and was hoping to come to an agreement.

But, well, NSLICE-00P had already calculated that additional subordinates were beneficial to her, so long as she was not expected to take over their affiliations and conflicts. Ceitidh blinked a couple of times, then looked to Uscfrea.

He spoke to NSLICE-00P through their components. "My queen, it appears Ceitidh has not fully understood your question. May I clarify on your behalf?"

"Affirmative."

Uscfrea then spoke aloud. "My queen wishes to know if you will bow and become her people, or if you are simply seeking an alliance."

Ceitidh frowned.

"Leadership of our clan is her right to claim, but we do not live as the Imperials do, and have no intention of doing so."

Uscfrea grinned.

"Neither do we . . . for now. My queen is generous regarding traditions and autonomy. But you must respect her allegiances. You will not be permitted to fight who you please."

Ceitidh nodded.

"That is a given, though the clan will grow restless if there are no opportunities for growth."

At that, a magical contract appeared before Ceitidh, much like the one Uscfrea had signed.

"Acknowledged. Recommendation: Please review the terms of the agreement and sign if acceptable."

Ceitidh frowned, as she did not know how to read Imperial, and the Wulver did not have a writing system of their own. But the mana of the dungeon contract adapted, and she heard the terms spoken in her ears. She gritted her teeth, but bowed her head and signed it.

Contract signed! Ceitidh Greumach (Wulver - Level 32) added as a subordinate. Restrictions applied per contract stipulations.

"Acknowledgement: Ceitidh Greumach and subordinate units now designated as friendly." The hologram shifted to show the persons of interest. "Command: Please transfer any intel friendlies may possess regarding the displayed persons of interest."

Ceitidh blinked for a moment.

"My queen is searching for these people and wants to know if you know anything about them."

"Um, I don't know any humans . . . Clan Chief . . ."

"Acknowledged. Command: Please report to NSLICE Uscfrea Ymmason, who will relay all existing and future commands."

With that, the hologram cut out, and Uscfrea's robotic eye dimmed. The Dobhar grinned. A pack of Wulver, Turannia's expert land hunters, were now under his command, and could teach the Dobhar how to move and fight in the forest. And best of all . . . he hadn't even needed to negotiate with his queen to gain authority over them. She had gone ahead and assigned them under him herself.

"Come, Ceitidh. We have much to discuss."

Meanwhile, NSLICE-00P and her companions continued on their way. And as they traveled, NSLICE-00P ran some tests on a capability she hadn't utilized yet.

Passive Skills		
Name	Level	Description
Enchanting	11 *Upgrade Available	The art of infusing objects and beings with mana.

The skill had grown immensely when she had taken Uscfrea's axe, courtesy of the corresponding feat:

Personal Feats		
Name	Description	Effect
Most Worthy	Whosoever wields this skill, who is clearly worthy, shall possess the power of their opponent's weapon. Unlocked by taking control of an artifact bound to someone else.	+10 levels in Enchanting skill

Previously, NSLICE-00P hadn't particularly had a use case for this skill. From what she could tell, it was intended to make permanent mana-based upgrades, primarily to weapons and armor. But she already had infusion spells to boost her weapons' capabilities in the short term, and if long-term upgrades were necessary, she could conduct them via the foreign system.

But now, thanks to her new experiments with Metal Magic and the Item Foundry, the skill had become relevant. If she was working with weapons and components not directly connected to her status in the foreign system, then she might require upgrade options outside of her Implant and Trap upgrade menus. And Dungeon perk points were a precious commodity, currently her least abundant resource. Though, the increased experience from the Otter Burrow may change that in the near future.

She held a copper ingot in her hand and channeled her mana into it as per the knowledge granted by the Enchanting skill. If she were holding a weapon or a piece of armor, even this basic infusion could act as an enchantment, reinforcing the properties of the item itself. But since this was just a piece of metal, the item had no specific purpose for the mana to reinforce. So, she moved on to the next stage.

She started using her mana to engrave a magic circle directly onto the ingot, utilizing Metal Magic and Mana Crafting to support the process. The circle formed without issue. She channeled her mana into it . . . and the ingot began to glow slightly.

It was a simple magic circle, the most basic Enchanting formation. It simply took mana in and infused it into the ingot, with no particular effect.

NSLICE-00P then tried to change it. She compared the enchantment circle to her spell circles and tried to slot in a basic attribute. She finished her adjustments and channeled her mana once more . . .

This time, the ingot began to glow bright as the enchantment converted the mana to the Light attribute.

Glowing Copper Bar enchanted!
Enchanting circle manually adjusted! Modular spell casting detected! Compiling . . .
The skill Enchanting is now Level 12!
Modular Enchanting is now available! Upgrade replaced with Enchantment Conditions!

The foreign system's information shifted, seeming to apply her gathered data on spell casting to enchantment. NSLICE-00P formed another copper ingot to test the new information.

Enchantment circles were, after all, very similar to normal magic circles. They had slightly different inputs and outputs, since they accepted external mana rather than internal and then had to channel it through an object instead of forming a circle midair. They likewise might apply extra conditions onto the spell's activation, for example requiring a specific mana signature in the case of a bound artifact. But the parts regarding their actual effect were largely the same, depending on the spell in question. A Bolt spell, for example, would be noticeably different, since firing a bolt from a wand needed to avoid the bolt forming within the wand directly. But an Infusion spell, on the other hand, was almost identical, since both the spell and enchantment were just trying to apply attributed mana onto either the person or object channeling the mana.

And since NSLICE-00P had already learned how to identify and swap out the parts of the magic circle related to attributes, modifiers, and spell shapes, it was not hard to then slot these things into the enchantment circles.

So, she added in an attribute and spell shape without changing the enchantment-specific input and output portions, channeling her mana through the new ingot.

The ingot vanished from her optical sensors.

Vanishing Copper Bar enchanted!
The skill Enchanting is now Level 13!

It turned out the Invisibility spell was just a Light-attribute spell with an Armor shape, and so available in modular spellcasting . . . and therefore modular enchantment. The Armor enchantment, likewise, could be applied as is to an enchanted object. Now, applying an Armor spell to an object without any adjustments was not a common method, since it would cause the enchantment to apply solely to the object and not its wielder. An Invisibility enchantment on a piece of armor would only cause the armor to vanish without its wearer, and this was one of the least problematic cases. A Fire Armor enchantment conducted in that manner would cook its user alive.

But for NSLICE-00P, this use case was perfect.

She pulled out one of her drone golems and began to engrave an enchantment circle on its hull. NSLICE-00P didn't have much data on golem creation, her only relevant information being her sensor readings of the golems she had fought. So she wasn't aware that golems could not be enchanted. Or more specifically, golems were already enchanted in the process of becoming golems, so additional enchantments would interfere with their function. Any enchantments for a golem needed to be built in when the golem was first crafted.

But her drone golems were a bit special. Patterned off of her own situation, they did not use mana to animate their rotor blades and other moving parts but rather used a mana core to generate electricity for their mechanical components, as well as to accept verbal commands, since magical golems were slightly more flexible than programmed drones in that area. As such, the "enchanted" part of the drone golem was purely its core. The hull itself was not enchanted and did not have mana flowing through it.

And so, as long as the enchantment wasn't engraved directly onto the core . . .

NSLICE-00P ordered the drone golem to channel mana into the engraved magic circle. It subsequently vanished from view. She ordered it to fly around and test all of its functions; everything was still working, though its available power had been reduced.

The skill Enchanting is now Level 14!

Mini Drone Golem manually upgraded! Stealth Mini Drone Golem now available for summoning!
Gained 5 Dungeon Perk Points for creating a new monster summon!

Can you like . . . wait a bit? I'm a bit busy analyzing the millennium of technology developed in fundamentally different conditions that you brought with you, so I haven't exactly gotten to the every possible permutation of that technology with all available attributes and enchantments stage yet.

Taog frowned and shook as he watched NSLICE-00P make an invisible fly-ing golem, but then took a deep breath and decided to look at the scenery. All that farmland was incredibly interesting; Taog just couldn't notice anything else going on around him.

Meanwhile, in the Monster Hangar, Melion was convulsing.

"Enchanted . . . golems . . . ehehehe . . . AHAHAHAHAHA! Master, you're the best!"

The group came to a small town, the last before they would arrive at Velusitum. After arranging for a room at the Exploratores HQ, Ateia left, with Taog follow-ing along. He raised an eyebrow as Ateia walked into a local tavern but kept quiet as he tagged along.

He took sips out of a light drink as Ateia gulped down the contents of her mug. She was cheerfully making small talk with the barkeeper and the other patrons, and Taog furrowed his brow as he stared down at his cup.

Had Ateia really come here just to drink?

But then, she waved to the barkeeper. He glanced over her as he refilled her mug.

"What brings a lass like you around these parts, if you don't mind me asking?"

She leaned over the countertop.

"Actually, I'm looking for some people. Maybe you could help me?"

The barkeeper shrugged. "Lots of folks come and go on the way to Velu-situm. What's the name?"

Ateia smiled. "Have you heard of a guy named Bob? Or a girl named Londyn?"

The barkeeper blinked and shook his head.

"Can't say that I have. What kind of names are those?"

Ateia shrugged. "My client is foreign. How about this one: Sir Wonder Knight, I think?"

He smirked at that. "What kind of knight order is that guy from? Can't say I've heard of any using names like that."

Ateia sighed and shook her head. "No idea. Hoped it would make him easy to find, at least."

The barkeeper chuckled. "Indeed. I definitely wouldn't have forgotten a name like that."

Ateia nodded then tilted her head, taking a sip of her mug.

"Maybe this one? Xiong Huang. It sort of sounds like a Celestial Elf name, right?"

He shrugged. "As far as I know; don't know much about folks like that."

Taog's eyes widened as Ateia talked with the barkeeper, then with the other patrons. A short while later, they left together. She sighed and stared at her feet.

"Taog, are we helping Seero?"

Taog furrowed his brow. "What do you mean?"

She frowned. "Look, we were supposed to help Seero with her quest, right? That's the whole reason she helped us become Exploratores. But now, she's an Amicitia Populi Elteni. She's protected us every step of the way; she's even looking for my father to protect me from my family's enemies. I feel like we aren't helping her at all. If anything . . . I feel like we're holding Seero back."

Taog took a deep breath and rubbed his chin.

"Well, there *was* that time we stopped her from attacking the Necrotorum and starting a war with the Empire."

Ateia blinked. "Oh. Right. That could have been bad."

Taog chuckled before his face turned serious.

"Honestly . . . I don't know. Seero is *much* stronger than us, and outranks us to boot. It is true that there is very little we can do that she can't. But on the other hand, Seero is new to the Empire, and there's a lot of things she doesn't seem to know. Some of which are even common sense. So I think it's too early to just assume Seero can do anything."

Ateia went silent, so he continued.

"Look, we're about to reach Velusitum. Magister Tiberius's friends live there, right? We can speak with them, and maybe they can help with the search. But until then, we should stick by Seero and continue helping her get used to the Empire."

He smiled.

"Though . . . I guess we could put in some more effort. We should do our best to become as strong as we can while Seero is helping us so that when the time comes, we can help her in return. As for right now, why don't we check the marketplace for traveling merchants? They're more likely to know about some foreigners than a barkeeper, right?"

Ateia looked at him for a moment before she smiled slightly and nodded.

"Okay. Let's do that."

And then she tripped over her own feet. Taog caught her and helped her stand again, raising an eyebrow.

"And *maybe* try to stay sober?"

Ateia flushed and looked away.

The Illusion aspect Calm is now Level 5!
The skill Illusion Magic is now Level 4!

NSLICE-00P's robotic eye flickered. Her latest experiment had been a success. She could now view the recorded memories of the period before the Battle of Castra Turannia with no emotional fluctuation from her organic components. With the reinforcement of Illusion Magic, her emotional controls were once again working efficiently.

Still, while those memories produced an emotional reaction among her organic components, the strength of that reaction was weaker than it had been during the actual event. She wouldn't know for sure if the emotional controls were completely effective until a similar event occurred . . . and now that protecting Ateia and Taog was a major directive, NSLICE-00P did not intend to allow such a situation to come about if at all possible.

She had a brief thought of if that directive would be necessary now that she had reversed the degradation of her emotional controls. It had, after all, been put in place solely on behalf of her organic components and their emotional reactions. But that thought passed quickly. Directives were not mere protocols that could be adjusted if they proved inefficient. Directives were an NSLICE unit's fundamental objectives. They were the standard against which protocols were analyzed. They determined what efficiency meant in the first place.

It was a significant compromise for NSLICE-00P to add a new directive on her own. It was completely unthinkable for her to unilaterally delete one. Now, a major directive *was* inferior to a critical or primary directive, and so might be deprioritized or even deleted should it prove permanently mutually exclusive with one of those. But in any other case, she would not consider touching a directive, even one she had declared herself.

But still, even with that directive, there was no reason to allow her organic components to do as they pleased and modify her behavior at will. And with her latest success, she wouldn't have to.

So, her emotional controls had been reimplemented with magical support. She had discovered a way to produce new NSLICE units, both cyborg and autonomous, and a new NSLICE network was growing. She had begun establishing a new supply chain with the ability to produce and process metal ores. Her magical firepower had grown in leaps and bounds, proving effective both at mass-scale termination and terminating individually powerful foes, including those with innate resistance to magic.

By all accounts, her upgrade routines were producing notable results.

The same could not be said of her attempts to pursue her primary directive. The added search capabilities of the NSLICE network had not been enough to find a person of interest, or even any relevant data that would lead to one. Her attempts to mobilize Imperial resources had likewise not produced any results, as apparently the Exploratores of this province had been mobilized for an emergency situation. The Dobhar had not had contact with any humans outside of Turannia, and had produced no actionable data thus far.

Ateia was even attempting intel gathering among the local populace . . . and determining that the names of the persons of interest were entirely unheard of among Imperial citizens.

She was still no closer to achieving her primary directive than when she'd first arrived in this place. The probability had actually dropped since then, given the mounting evidence that she was not on Earth.

Her heartbeat began to accelerate before she applied another Calm spell.

At present . . . she had no alternative means. But at the very least, the group was approaching Velusitum, the capital of the Utrad Province. It was rumored to be significantly larger and more advanced than any Imperial settlement NSLICE-00P had observed thus far.

She could only hope that it would provide the resources and intel she needed to determine what her future course of action should be.

And that the unknown hostiles targeting friendly Ateia would not be present there. The last thing she needed was to be drawn into yet another third-party conflict.

NSLICE-00P's emotional controls wavered once again, and again she applied another Calm spell. And her primary directive success probability dropped by a tiny amount.

In the end, neither Ateia and Taog nor NSLICE-00P's subordinates found any relevant information in the town. And so, they quickly departed, making their way toward Velusitum, hoping that one way or another, their futures might be decided there . . .

NSLICE-00P's Dungeon Management

Overview	
Name	The Walking Dungeon
Level	106
XP	24/100
Available Perk Points	21
Mana	241/241 (330/330)
Exterior	Human/Automata Hybrid (LOCKED)

Dungeon Affinities	
Type	Strength
Cyborg	Primary
Fire	Minor
Holy	Minor
Water	Minor
Beast	Minor
Metal	Minor
Rodent	Minimum

Earth	Minimum
Arachnid	Minimum
Slime	Minimum
Light	Minimum
Nature	Minimum
Dark	Minimum

Implants		
Type	Mana Upkeep	Description
Bionic Prosthetics +3	0	Overwrites STR and SPD, Values: 130 STR, 65 SPD
Armor Plating +5	0	Overwrites DEF and RES, Values: 150 DEF, 75 RES
Bonded AI	0	Enables direct contact with the System. Overwrites DEX, Value: 1000 DEX
Techno-Organic Interface	0	Enables conscious control over organic and emotional functions. Resists mind-influencing effects.
Advanced Sensors +2	0	Vastly expands scope and effectiveness of senses.
Internal Weapon Bays	0	Enables use of dungeon traps as weapons.
Repulsors +1	0	Enables flight and tactical boosts.
Energy Channels +2	0	Enables user to channel internal energy into external attacks.
Dungeon Field Generator +1	5	Surrounding area counts as dungeon territory. Enables mana absorption within area of effect.
Monster Hangar (Small) +1	2	Provides 10 living spaces for small monsters. Unlocks subordinate summoning.

Item Foundry +1	3	Unlocks Item Creation.
Mana Capacitor +2 (x6)	0	Boosts maximum mana by 30 each.
Drone Hangar (Small)	1	A Monster Hangar specialized for nonorganic monsters of limited sentience. Trades amenities for boosted storage capacity. Provides 5 storage spaces.

Inventory	
Name	Description
??? dagger	A dagger, likely enchanted given the amount of mana held within. Further information could not be determined.
Ursanus pelt	The pelt of an ursanus alpha. Tough, well-insulated, and full of mana.
Ursanus bones	The bones of an ursanus alpha. Extremely durable, and full of mana.
Idrint	Quantity: 5,000. Basic solidified mana, now a standard medium of exchange.
Mana Iron Sword	A sword made of mana iron. Sharper than normal and well suited to further enchantment.

Subordinates				
Name	Species	Level	Mana Upkeep	
Rattingtale	Cyber-Rat	15	1	Check Status
Lilussees	Cyber-Spider	15	1	Check Status
(TEMPORARY) Ateia Niraemia	Human	27	--	(Status locked)

(TEMPORARY) Taog Sutharlan	Human/ Wulver	26	--	(Status locked)
01R	Cyber-Rat	14	1	Check Status
02R	Cyber-Rat	12	1	Check Status
03R	Cyber-Rat	13	1	Check Status
04R	Cyber-Rat	13	1	Check Status
05R	Cyber-Rat	12	1	Check Status
(Cyber-Rats Continued . . .)				
01S	Cyber-Spider	13	1	Check Status
02S	Cyber-Spider	12	1	Check Status
03S	Cyber-Spider	13	1	Check Status
(Cyber-Spiders Continued . . .)				
00B	Cyber-Bear Cub	12	5	Check Status
Uscfrea Ymmason	Dobhar	95	--	Check Status
Estrith Edilddaughter	Dobhar	61	--	Check Status
Aldreda Aetheludaughter	Sacred Otterkin	1	--	Check Status
00C	Canus Minor	8	3	Check Status
01C	Canus Ignis Minor	7	4	Check Status
02C	Canus Aqua Minor	8	4	Check Status
00F	Felix Minor	8	3	Check Status
Melion	Metal Slime	65	15	Check Status
Ceitidh Greumach	Wulver	32	--	Check Status

Non-Sentient Units		
Name	Quantity	Upkeep
Stealth Mini Drone Golem	25	0.2 each (5 total)

Traps			
Name	Number Active / Deployed	Mana Upkeep	Description
Assault Rifle +3	2/2	2	Rapid-fire projectile weapon with high penetration.
Autopistol	2/2	2	Rapid-fire projectile weapon with medium penetration.
Anti-Armor Missile Launcher +2	2/2	2	Homing explosive designed to penetrate armor. Very high penetration.
Anti-Personnel Missile Launcher +2	6/6	6	Homing explosive designed for area damage. Medium penetration.
Stun Ray	1/1	1	Nonlethal electric weapon. Can inflict stun and paralysis statuses.
Wrist Blade +2	2/2	0	Wrist-mounted blades that can be deployed at high speed.
Flamethrower	2/2	2	Deals fire damage and applies burn status in a large cone.

The Equalizer +1	1/1	0	Huh? What the heck is this? Some kind of weird metal that doesn't even exist here? Um . . . well . . . best I can tell it's some sort of antimagic field generator? Eh . . . well, it's yours, not mine, so you don't need me to tell you, right? Like, you already upgraded this thing yourself, so you're good, right?

Dungeon Skills		
Name	Level	Description
Analyze	N/A	Check the status of a target. More detail for targets within the dungeon. Details depend on level difference.
Contract	N/A	Bind a consenting target to the dungeon, per terms agreed upon by both parties.
Transfer	N/A	Move yourself, a subordinate, or a consenting target within your dungeon.

Dungeon Perks	
Name	Description
Human-Dungeon Hybrid	Enables Implants tab. Enables unique Dungeon Combat skill. Enables direct manipulation of dungeon mana. +100 HP Rooms tab locked. Exterior locked.
Affinity Sharing	Can share Primary and Major affinities between subordinates' cores and master core.

Dungeon Feats		
Name	Description	Effect
Dungeon Victor	To the victor go the spoils. Unlocked by destroying or subordinating another dungeon.	+1 Perk Point Unlocks Dungeon Warfare category perks.
Dungeon Overlord	A master of masters. Unlocked by subordinating another dungeon master.	+2 Perk Points Unlocks Subordinate Core category perks.
Raid Boss	Fine, I'll do it myself. Unlocked by destroying or subordinating another dungeon with no assistance.	+2 Perk Points +1 level in HP Regen skill +1 level in MP Regen skill +50 HP Unlocks Raid Boss category perks.
System Upgrade	Unlocked by manually performing a system upgrade. Which is not supposed to be possible. Ugh, this is going to get complicated, isn't it?	Um, I don't know. Just have +20 Dungeon Perk Points or something. Whatever. You're figuring this out yourself anyway, so close enough.
Purifier Dungeon	Dungeons are supposed to protect the world; you took that duty more literally. Unlocked by destroying a corrupted dungeon core.	+20 Perk Points Unlocks Purifier category perks.
Monster Creator	Granted to a dungeon master who has created a new, never-before-seen monster species.	+20 Perk Points Unlocks Monster Customization.

Matron of the Sacred Otterkin	Thanks to your efforts, a new intelligent species has been born.	+40 Perk Points Additional Perk Points may be granted based on the development and contributions of your client species.

NSLICE-00P's Personal Status

Personal Status			
General Information		Physical Attributes	
Name	NSLICE-00P	STR	130* (Overwritten)
Species	Human/Dungeon Core/Automata Hybrid	DEX	1000* (Overwritten)
Level	63	SPD	65* (Overwritten)
XP	59/100	DEF	150* (Overwritten)
Perk Points	102	RES	75* (Overwritten)
HP	220/220	Magical Attributes	
MP	254/254	Mana Density	102
		Mana Control	175

Active Skills		
Name	Level	Description
Infused Mana Beam	15	Focus mana into a channeled energy attack. Infused: May infuse Mana Beam with attributed mana.
Sneak	1	Move quietly to avoid notice. Makes it harder for others to notice the user. Effectiveness highly dependent on environment.

Multicasting	13	Can cast several spells at once. Number of simultaneous spells increases with level.
Anti-Mana Beam	3	My best guess is that this projects a kind of inverse mana that reacts destructively with normal mana, including HP. While it can fully deplete HP, it does not harm matter itself. Requires The Equalizer.
Power Strike	1	Infuse mana into a weapon for heavier damage. Power and range increase with level.
Farcasting	7	Allows the user to manipulate mana and create magic circles at far distances.
Strategic Magic	5	Governs the use of Strategic Magic spells.
Supercharge	9	Fill a spell with additional mana to boost its effects. May cause the spell to misfire. Effect boost depends on the amount and density of mana added. Misfire chance depends on Mana Control and amount of mana added.
Continuous Casting	3	May use additional mana to retain a spell form, allowing the spell to be instantly recast.
Spell Fusion	8	Allows the user to combine compatible spells.
Purifier Flame	1	Imbue a weapon or Flame-attribute attack with purifying Holy-attribute fire, dealing extra damage to corruption, monsters, dungeons, and beings from the Realms of Mana.
Heroic Power	2	To handle great responsibility, a hero needs great power. Doubles Mana Density for a short time. May damage user if reused too quickly due to strain from excess mana.
Holy Strike	1	Infuse Holy mana into a weapon strike for heavier damage. Power and range increase with level.

| Spell Shaping | 16 | Enables user to understand and modify the portion of spell circles related to shapes. User may utilize known spell shapes with any available and compatible school of magic. |
| Spell Modification | 4 | Enables user to understand and modify the portion of spell circles related to spell modifiers. User may utilize known spell modifiers with any available and compatible spell. |

Passive Skills		
General		
Name	Level	Description
Dungeon Combat	--	Dungeon traps and skills count as personal weapons and skills.
HP Regen	7	Automatically recover HP pool. Increased regeneration speed for damaged body parts.
MP Regen	7	Automatically recover MP pool.
Presence Detection	4	Detect living entities around the user. Range and scope of detection increases with level.
Trap Detection	4	Detect traps. Range and scope of detection increases with level.
Challenger	--	Damage dealt x1.5 against targets of higher level. Damage received x0.75 against attacks from targets of higher level.
Hero Dungeon	--	Unique Hero Skill for NSLICE-00P. PLEASE don't do anything bad with this! Removes dungeon vulnerability to Holy attribute. Grants Dungeon Affinity: Holy (Minor).

Magic		
Name	Level	Description
Spell Penetration	3	Enable spells to bypass a portion of RES. May spend more mana to boost the effect.
Geomancy	2	Elemental spells reduce the target's resistance to that particular element. May spend more mana to boost the effect.
Mana Shield	1	When active, may convert HP damage received into Mana damage. Mana Density will be used instead of DEF/RES in that case. HP damage will resume if Mana is fully drained.
Utility		
Name	Level	Description
Enchanting	14	The art of infusing objects and beings with mana.
Mana Crafting	1	Crafting items through mana rather than physical processes.
Resistances		
Name	Level	Description
Poison Resistance	2	Resist and recovery from poison status. Resist Poison-attributed damage.
Schools of Magic		
Name	Level	Description
Arcane Magic	11	The school of magic governing the manipulation of unattributed mana. A solid foundation for students of the mystic arts, though somewhat less mana efficient than the more specialized schools.

Earth Magic	9	The school of magic governing the manipulation of Earth-attribute mana. One of the basic elemental magics, strong at defensive spells and spells that deal physical damage.
Fire Magic	10	The school of magic governing the manipulation of Fire-attribute mana. One of the basic elemental magics, strong at offensive spells and spells that inflict the burn status.
Water Magic	6	The school of magic governing the manipulation of Water-attribute mana. One of the basic elemental magics, fluid and flexible with many applications.
Light Magic	13	The school of magic governing the manipulation of Light-attribute mana. One of the basic elemental magics, quick and precise spells that are excellent against Dark-aligned foes.
Dark Magic	1	The school of magic governing the manipulation of Dark-attribute mana. One of the basic elemental magics, powerful and obscure, though dangerous if not treated with appropriate caution.
Nature Magic	5	The school of magic governing the manipulation of Nature-attribute mana. Focuses on growth and living things.
Poison Magic	6	The school of magic governing magical poisons. Excels at spreading poison status and dealing damage over time.
Metal Magic	9	The school of magic governing the manipulation of metal. Generally focuses on manipulating existing metal, though may create metal directly at great cost.
Recovery Magic	7	The school of magic governing healing through magic.

Illusion Magic	4	The school of magic governing the manipulation of senses and emotions.
Holy Magic	11	The school of magic governing the manipulation of Holy-attribute mana, the attribute of the Aesdes that protects the world.

Hero		
Name	Level	Description
Heroic Challenger	1	A hero never gives up, no matter the odds. Attacks ignore a small percent of target's DEF/RES/Immunities and always deal a minimum amount of damage. Gives a small chance to survive a fatal hit with 1 HP.

Spells		
Spell Shapes		
Name	Level	Description
Armor	1	Coat a target in mana, generally for defensive purposes.
Bomb	5	Pack mana into a dense package that explodes.
Barrier	13	Form mana in a defensive surface or wall.
Beam	15	Concentrate mana into a precise, fast-moving beam.
Blade	6	Form mana in a sharp sword that may be held.
Blast	7	Condense mana, then release it in an explosive blast.
Bolt	18	Form mana into a package that can be launched.
Chain	7	Form mana into a binding that wraps around a target.

Infusion	13	Fill a target with mana.
Spell Modifiers		
Name	Level	Description
Dense	18	Condense mana even further, increasing the mana density and effect of the spell.
Fusion	17	Spell can combine with itself or other compatible spells.
Hardened	1	Improves spell defense against piercing/disruption effects.
Unique Holy Spells		
Name	Level	Description
Holy Ward	1	Protect an area with Holy mana, warding off monsters and evil. Also boosts HP and Mana recovery. Does not protect from attacks.
Banishment	1	Attempts to return a target creature to its origin realm. No effect on inhabitants of the world.
Divination	1	Attempt to read the state of the world. May reveal things that were, things that are, or things that yet may be. What, exactly, none can predict, only that what is revealed should not be dismissed.
Illusion Aspects		
Name	Level	Description
Calm	5	Dampen target's emotions, calming them down. Higher levels may dampen specific emotions.

Strategic Spells			
School	Name	Level	Description
Light	Aurora Barrage	7	Continuously rains Light Beams on the target area. If Fusion Light Beam is available, beams may be combined at will.
Fire	Rain of Fire	3	Bombards a wide area with large Fireballs.

Personal Feats		
Name	Description	Effect
Against the Odds	Do not ask how many there are, but where they are. Unlocked by winning a fight when outnumbered by equal or higher-leveled opponents.	+1 Perk Point
Solo Conquest	I am the dungeon master now. Unlocked by conquering a dungeon alone.	+1 level in HP Regen skill +1 level in MP Regen skill +1 level in Presence Detection skill +1 level in Trap Detection skill
Arcane Prodigy	The career of a supreme sorcerer does not start on the beaten path. Unlocked by learning a high-tier magic skill under level twenty without spending Perk Points.	+3 Perk Points Unlocks more advanced magic perks.

Enchanter	The first step on the path of the magic craftsman. Unlocked by manually accomplishing a Mana Infusion.	+1 level in Enchanting skill
Skill Creator	You don't just master the path. You define it. Unlocked by creating a brand-new skill.	To be honest, this normally happens when you're a MUCH higher level, so I'm a bit worried about passing you this much this early, but, um, okay. +20 Perk Points
Healer	Anyone can deal in death. It takes an expert to deal in life. Unlocked by using mana to heal a wound.	+1 level in Recovery Magic skill
Challenger	Levels and odds are just numbers. Unlocked by defeating an who is the greater of level 10 twice your level while alone.	+3 Perk Points + Challenger skill
Strategic Mage	A strategic mage is king of the battlefield. Unlocked by affecting a hundred or more equal-size opponents (or equivalent mass of other-size opponents) at the same time with magic.	+1 level in Strategic Magic skill Unlocks Strategic Spells.
World Defender	You have protected the world itself, at great risk to yourself.	+20 Perk Points +1 level in Holy Magic skill

Hero	You faced terrible odds for the sake of the world and proved victorious. You are truly a champion of the world. Please, please, please keep it that way!	+20 Perk Points Grants Unique Hero Skill: Hero Dungeon
Most Worthy	Whosoever wields this skill, who is clearly worthy, shall possess the power of their opponent's weapon. Unlocked by taking control of an artifact bound to someone else.	+10 levels in Enchanting skill
Hero of the Sacred Otterkin	So . . . we normally give this when someone has done something that protected the existence of an entire species. And like, you just *created* a new species, so . . . I guess that means you are, in fact, responsible for their continued existence. You know what? Whatever.	+20 Perk Points +1 level in Holy Water Ball spell +1 level in Holy Strike skill
Spell Shaper	Mana may take many forms, but the true mage knows that the mana remains the same. Unlocked by manually adjusting a magic circle into a new spell.	Grants Spell Shaping skill.

Spell Adjuster	Magic is the art of changing reality. So why would a spell be static and immutable? Unlocked by manually applying a spell modifier to a magic circle.	Grants Spell Modification skill.
Magic Crafter	Both crafters and mages reshape reality to fit their needs. One just does it faster. Unlocked by crafting an item purely through mana (excepting default spell shapes such as Blade)!	+1 level in Mana Crafting skill

Dungeon Conqueror Feats		
Name	Description	Effect
Dungeon Conqueror (Rat Cave)	Unlocked by conquering the Rat Cave Dungeon.	+1 Perk Point +1 level in Sneak skill
Dungeon Conqueror (Earth Tunnels)	Unlocked by conquering the Earth Tunnels Dungeon.	+1 Perk Point +1 level in Earth Magic skill
Dungeon Conqueror (Spider Tree)	Unlocked by conquering the Spider Tree Dungeon.	+1 Perk Point +1 level in Poison Resistance skill
Dungeon Conqueror (Slimy Pit)	Unlocked by conquering the Slimy Pit Dungeon.	+1 Perk Point +1 level in Poison Bolt spell
Dungeon Conqueror (Glimmering Grove)	Unlocked by conquering the Glimmering Grove Dungeon.	+1 Perk Point +1 level in Light Magic skill
Dungeon Conqueror (Nature's Wrath)	Unlocked by conquering the Nature's Wrath Dungeon.	+1 Perk Point +1 level in Nature Magic skill

Dungeon Conqueror (Beast Lair)	Unlocked by conquering the Beast Lair Dungeon.	+1 Perk Point +1 level in Power Strike skill
Dungeon Conqueror (Darkest Dungeon)	Unlocked by conquering the Darkest Dungeon Dungeon.	+1 Perk Point +1 level in Dark Magic skill
Dungeon Conqueror (Metal Armory)	Unlocked by conquering the Metal Armory Dungeon.	+1 Perk Point +1 level in Metal Magic skill
Dungeon Purifier Feats		
Dungeon Purifier (Inferno)	A dungeon is dangerous to everyone in the world. A corrupted dungeon is dangerous to the world itself. And you conquered it all the same. Unlocked by purifiying the Corrupted Dungeon (Inferno Realm).	+5 Perk Points +1 level in Purifier Flame skill

About the Author

Icalos is a lifelong fan of sci-fi, fantasy, and video games, and the author of the Terminate the Other World! series, which was originally released on Royal Road. To learn more, visit his website at icalosbooks.com.

DISCOVER
STORIES UNBOUND

PodiumAudio.com

9 781039 454895